MEANT TO BE BROKEN

BOOK ONE IN THE CAROLINA CLAY SERIES

BRANDY WOODS SNOW

Sugah Publishing

Sugah Publishing

Fountain Inn, SC and Kansas City, MO

www.sugahpublishing.com

Cover Design © 2020 by JRC Designs/Jena R Collins

www.jenarcollins.com

Meant to be Broken/ Brandy Woods Snow

ISBN 978-1-7363019-0-6

ISBN e-book 978-1-7363019-1-3

Praise for *Meant To Be Broken*

"A well-written and intriguing story that will leave your mind spinning and your heart aching. Definitely a can't miss."
—Michelle Lynn, Assistant Indie Manager, YA Books Central

"Brimming with romantic tension...this intensely emotional debut kept me reading late into the night. Romance lovers, you're in for a treat!"
—Katy Upperman, author of *Kissing Max Holden*, *The Impossibility of Us*, and *How the Light Gets In*

Praise for *As Much As I Ever Could*

"Well-drawn characters, expressive language, and a slow reveal of the details of the accident will hook readers...A swoonworthy summer read with a hopeful lesson about how to move forward without fear."
—*Kirkus Reviews*

"Readers looking for a gentle read about recovering from grief, buoyed by a community of welcoming new friends and new love, will find Snow's (Meant To Be Broken) latest fits the bill."
—*Library Journal*

*To Gene
who saw me even when I couldn't*

1

RAYNE

At 9:30 Saturday morning, I find out Preston Howard wants to date me. At 11:30, my mama hears it from old lady McAlister and has a "spell" in aisle three of the Piggly Wiggly. It's taken seventeen years, but I finally understand the two things my social life and Mama have in common. They're both erratic and one usually suffers because of the other.

The store manager calls me on my cell and asks me to come get her. He has my number because he's Daddy's best friend's brother and used me to babysit his kids a few times last year. I answer, expecting another job offer.

"Rayne? This is Dave Sullivan, you know, the manager down at the Piggly Wiggly? There's been an incident with your mama."

Apparently, it'd happened in front of the Luzianne tea bags. She was comparing the family size to smaller ones when Mrs. McAlister offered her a coupon... and a piece of news.

The details get a little sketchy from there—something about her sinking to the floor and gasping for air. That's when the manager came over with one of those small brown paper sacks they use to bag up ice cream and had her breathe in it. A nurse and a vet, both in the crowd assembled around her, agreed from their varied medical expertise it didn't appear to be life-threatening. When the paper bag seemed to work, he decided to call me instead of the ambulance.

I pull into the parking lot ten minutes later. She's sitting on the front bench beside the automatic doors where the employees go to smoke, under the "I'm Big on the Pig!" sign. Mrs. McAlister sits beside her, a little too close, waving a folded-up circular in her face. I wonder what the store employees and shoppers think of me, casually parking the car, walking-not-running, and looking both ways before crossing the main traffic flow. It doesn't take a genius to figure out they're all watching from between the weekly specials scribbled on the plate-glass windows.

I don't feel the need to rush. It isn't a heart attack or stroke. I call it her bipolar though Daddy gets mad when I refer to it like that. The diagnosis is anxiety, better known as my evil little sister—always around, always a pain, and always ruining my life.

This sort of episode has happened before, just not too often in public. In most societies that's considered good news—but not in the South. They say we don't hide our crazy, we dress it up and parade it on the front porch. And even if we don't, someone else will do the parading for us—telegraph, telephone, tell-a-Southern woman. We know how to reach out and touch some people.

Mrs. McAlister jumps up from the bench and grabs my arm as I step up on the curb. "I suwannee, child. She liked to turned over her buggy and spilt them groceries everywhere."

Talking to some of the older ladies in town always feels like walking out of real life and into some part of *Steel Magnolias*. She gives me her version of the sordid details. Mama created quite a scene, not just with her episode but also by her scandalous choice of groceries. The mayonnaise was the only casualty, rolling out the leg hole of the kiddie seat portion of the cart when Mama accidentally gave it a rough shove while collapsing on the linoleum.

Mrs. McAlister hadn't bothered to pick that up and put it back in the buggy, which was now waiting by the customer service desk. *It wasn't Dukes Mayonnaise.* She leans in close to whisper because how embarrassing would that be for Mama. To her, it's further proof Mama hadn't been feeling well long before their conversation. What Southern woman in her right mind buys off-brand mayonnaise?

I nod my way through the conversation and thank her again for being there. She pats me on the hand, telling me that's what good neighbors do, but by the time she's halfway to her Cadillac, the cell phone is already glued to her pink-tinted bottle-blond head.

Good neighbors, my butt. She just scored the juiciest scoop of the summer, and best believe she's capitalizing on it. Good gossip's better than credit in this town.

I squat down in front of Mama, patting her knee. "You okay now, Mama?" She doesn't speak, just stares past me with pupils dilated into miniature tar pits. I grab her purse from the bench and give it a shake. "I'm getting your card and going to pay for the groceries. You hang on to this." I slip the debit card from her wallet then plop the purse in her lap. "I'll be right back."

Inside it's uncomfortable, everyone pretending to go about their business but sneaking peeks at me when they think I'm not looking. *There's that crazy woman's girl. I bet she has a hard time at home.* Part of me can't blame them. Part of me wants to punch them.

She's still sitting on the bench, staring out across the asphalt, when I get back.

"Come on, Mama." I take her elbow, helping her stand. A slight tremble still courses through her sporadically. "Let's go home."

"My car." She points to her old brown sedan as we walk to my Civic. "I have to…"

"Daddy'll come get it when he's back from fishing. You don't need to drive right now, Mama," I say, opening the passenger door and pulling the seatbelt around her.

"I can get it myself," she snaps, yanking the clip from my hand and clicking it in place. "I'm not a baby." The inevitable next phase in her anxiety cycle. *Yay!* Bat-shit crazy is always followed by undue anger, guilt, and then some sort of weird, forced happiness where she tries to convince us she's fine, it was just a freak episode.

"I'll be right there." I slam the door before she can utter another word she'll regret later.

My phone rings just as I pop the trunk. "Hello?"

"What's going on at The Pig? My mom talked to Ainsley's mom who heard from Mrs. Pressley that your mama had some kind of meltdown in Aisle Four." It's my best friend, Jaycee Tucker.

"Aisle Three," I correct her, loading in groceries. "It's nothing. She's fine."

"Ri-ight." She takes a deep breath and moves on. "Anyway, you did read the text I forwarded you after we talked earlier? The one Trevor sent Ainsley about Preston?"

Sure, I'd read it—a million times, the words playing on repeat in my head. *Preston thinks Rayne Davidson's pretty, smart and he wouldn't mind going out with her.*

Of course I've fantasized about dating him, kissing him, just talking to him, but so does every other girl at Hillcrest High. That's why I don't get it. Preston dates the hot girls—tall, leggy ones with ginormous chests and barely-there skirts; the whole "big boobs, no brains" syndrome. So how on God's green Earth does my 5'3" slim build, b-cups, and mop of curly brown hair catch his eye?

"And you're sure he told Trevor 'Rayne Davidson'? He didn't mean someone else and Trevor got it mixed up?"

The Howard family was Fountain Inn royalty, far outside my own realm. I'd never even talked to Preston… at least, not really. He nodded at me once, just slightly, with a grin. And then there was this one time he actually said, "here you go," and handed me the pen I'd dropped in the school hallway. But other than that, nada.

"Do you know another Rayne at our school?"

"Well, no, but you know the town is gossiping about this already."

"Of course they are. They have nothing better to do."

She proceeds to fill me in. Apparently, I'm not the only one questioning his sanity. It seems people all around town have me on their lips, using phrases like "unbelievable," "never saw that coming," and "she's so lucky." And the occasional "Who? Never heard of her." It's a shot in the arm of ol' self-confidence when you find out the entire town considers you sub-par for their favorite son.

"So everyone thinks he's gone loco?"

"No, everyone thinks you're damn lucky to land someone like Preston. They think you should take advantage of the situation. And so do I, so quit it with the 'Doubty-McDoubterson' crap. We'll figure it all out later."

"I don't know…"

"Well, here are two things you need to know. One, we're going to the bonfire tonight, so you better prepare your mama. And two—are you still at The Pig? Cause I talked to Ainsley a minute ago. She'd talked to Trevor who was with the Howard boys—as in PRESTON HOWARD—and they're on the way there to get hot dogs and drinks or something for later."

While she's talking, a familiar black Mustang GT peels into the lot. Oh dear Lord. Fate yet again conspires to give me the proverbial finger. The guy who wants to date me is pulling into the space directly in front of my car— the hot guy... the unattainable guy. And here I am loading in a bag of hemorrhoid cream and Tampax with my crazy-ass mama waiting in the front seat post-meltdown.

Kill. Me. Now.

"Rayne? Rayne!" Jaycee yells through the phone.

"Shhh!" I slink behind the still-opened trunk lid, my hand cupped around the speaker just in case Preston has super-sonic hearing. "Call you later." I shove it in my pocket.

Meanwhile, the boys get out of the car, Preston from the driver's seat, his younger brother Gage from the passenger seat, and Trevor from the back. Gage and Trevor are seniors like me. Preston graduated in June.

The sun glints off Preston's sunglasses, and my eyes travel from there down his body. Dirty blond hair with lemony streaks in a crew cut, bronzed skin, and abs you can bounce a quarter on. Pair that with the fact he's Mr. Sports All-American, football MVP, voted Best All Around, and the boy's a godhead in the high school hierarchy.

Honk! Hooooooooonk!

Suddenly, my car's horn is blaring, and the boys jerk their heads around, sweeping their eyes over the parking lot. My stomach knots in on itself, and I drop to my knees, crouching down behind the buggy on the opposite side of the car to peer around the side. Once the three of them disappear behind the large Mountain Dew display at the side entrance, I get up, slam the trunk lid and shove the buggy into the rack.

When I slide in behind the steering wheel, Mama looks at me, her brown eyes hard and angry. "Took you long enough. What's the matter? You're all sweaty."

I push my sunglasses onto my nose and flip the visor down. "It's August in South Carolina, Mama. Even Hell isn't this hot." I stick the key in the ignition and turn it. My '80s hair band rock blasts through the speakers, and she winces like I've poured acid in her ear canals. Now "the devil's music" is playing in her daughter's car on top of everything else. I throw the car in reverse, shift to drive and speed away from The Pig and my hot new admirer, who'll surely reconsider this whole thing once he gets to know me.

By the time we get home, Mama enters the third phase of her attack—crying uncontrollably and begging me to forgive her for the embarrassing display. I put away the groceries, give her a glass of room-temperature water with passionflower, and walk her upstairs to bed. Sleep's always best after such an episode. I fluff her pillow and when her eyelids begin to droop, I tell her I'm going with Jaycee to a bonfire.

Suddenly she's wide awake and eager to discuss my need to stay away from boys, get my education and get out of this town for the nine millionth time. I don't know whether to be honored or insulted. She obviously either feels I have more potential than this place, or she wants me to go away.

"Will there be boys at this bonfire tonight?" She sits up against her pillow, eyes wide.

"Of course, Mama, but considering most of the junior and senior classes are going, that's kind of unavoidable. Besides, Jaycee and I are looking forward to some girl time." I make sure to nod. I read an article in Cosmo that our body language never lies so every time I talk to Mama about boys, I keep reminding my head to bob up and down to affirm that, yes indeed, I'm being truthful. And technically, I don't outright lie to Mama. It's more avoidance.

"What about those Howards? Mrs. McAlister said..." Her breathing quickens and gets harder. She has to take a break.

"That rumor? I heard it. It's whatever." Indifference is the key to communicating with Mama. Not too hot, not too cold. "Besides, he's a respectable guy. If someone asked me out on a date, I'm thinking you'd approve of him before anyone else, right?" Making it sound like her preference is usually a solid approach.

"I don't know," she mutters, scooting back down under the covers, eyes wide as if the boogeyman's dancing on my head. "Be home at eleven."

"Eleven? But Mama all the other kids…"

"Eleven. Sharp."

Check and mate. She's won the battle, but I, Rayne Davidson, am going to the bonfire and talking to Preston Howard tonight.

So long as he hasn't already changed his mind.

2

———

GAGE

*T*his is the best ending to summer a guy could ask for.
A hot grill ready for some charbroiled beef, a long stretch of red Carolina clay, and my big brother riding shotgun in my 4x4 without any parental hassles—and later, a bonfire.

"Gage! Watch this!" Preston sprints down the slatted dock, grabs the rope hanging from the massive oak and swings out above the pond. At the uppermost part, he lets go, hitting the water with a splash that shoots ripples out in every direction. After a few seconds, he resurfaces, head and shoulders bobbing above the water, blond hair wet and spiked out in every direction. He throws his head back laughing, for once, not caring about how much hair gel will be needed to correct it.

At least he's having fun.

It's a foreign concept for him, though he'll never admit it. And no one else would believe me either. But they don't know him like I do. They don't see how pent up he is living inside the box everyone puts him in.

Preston's a pleaser. Always has been, but I hope that won't always be true. He never totally lets go. The way he could when we were little kids. Before all that other junk mattered. The older he gets, the worse it gets.

Everyone at school flocks to him. Girls salivate over him. Grown-ups worship him. *There goes Preston. Look how he commands the room. Athletic, smart, and capable—that boy's going places.*

Yeah, he's going places, all right—straight to the family accounting firm for the rest of his life. I hate how Mom and Dad cookie-cut him into some new age version of themselves.

Trevor jumps next followed by a few guys from the football team. I roll up my jeans and kick off my boots on the bank, then walk out to the edge of the dock where I sit, dangling my feet in the water.

"What ya waitin' for?" One of the guys yells out, slicing his hand over the surface and spraying my face with water. "You still pissed about the turtle from last summer that bit your ass?"

I roll my eyes. One little mud turtle—on the thigh, not the ass. And they'll never let me live it down.

"It's not about the turtle." I laugh, grabbing the hem of my muscle shirt and pulling it over my head. The guys fix their eyes on my new tattoo. "Can't go swimming until after all the scabbin's done."

A garbled chorus of voices rings out as they all swim closer for a better look—my brief moment of celebrity.

NO RULES APPLY.

I like everything about it. The way the needle pricked my skin, shooting little slivers of fire and ice underneath. The ways the block letters make my abs look extra firm. How it captures my attitude on life.

And yeah, the fact it's lying there in wait to piss off my parents is just the cherry on top. I'm the resident Howard screw-up, so might as well take it to the next level.

"I had nothing to do with that." Preston holds his hands up in the air like he's being arrested. He refused to go with me, saying Mom would flip her lid when she found out. He's probably right.

She caught me looking at tattoo designs on the internet a couple months ago and completely lost it, wrenching my phone from my hand and slamming it on the table so hard I was sure she'd cracked the screen. That's the day she subjected me to an hour-long bitch-fest about how tattoos are "outward expressions of internal chaos."

Whatever the hell that means.

Everything that comes out of her mouth is expertly designed to make her appear as some highly intellectual, pretentious Southern queen.

Preston says I should cut her slack if for no other reason than she's our mom. But he doesn't get it. He got bedtime stories, snuggles, and "Mother of the Year."

I got screwed. Nothing. Nada.

Dad tried to explain it once by saying Mom was shocked when I came along so soon after Preston. She clung to him, trying to preserve his right to be the baby, but then bam! Gage came along, and all hell broke loose.

How that's my fault, I have no idea.

After the tattoo tantrum, Mom kept harping on the fact she should've "expected as much from me, all things considered." No doubt I'm a big fat failure in my parents' eyes.

Unplanned pregnancy. Unplanned problem. Unplanned future.

But I'm not a "woe is me" kinda guy. If Preston's chains are any indication of their attentions, I consider myself happily skipped over. But what I want to see, more than anything, is Preston rebel. Cut that short leash Mom keeps him on.

Join me on the dark side.

"That tattoo's badass." Trevor hangs on the side of the dock, nodding with approval. "Now you just need an awesome car like Preston's instead of that old rattletrap you drive."

Rattletrap, my ass. My old Scout might have some age on him but he's tougher than all these other pretty-boy cars and flimsy excuses for 4x4s. He's a 1979 rugged beast. They're just jealous.

"Yeah, you sure that old thing can make it out of the mud in one piece?" Preston laughs. I knew it wouldn't take him long to chime in. He loves ragging on my Scout because it irks me. It's what we do.

I relax back on my elbows, the hot sun warming my chest as I shake my head. "That old thing can whip your prissy car's ass any day."

"Please." Preston swims to the dock and hoists himself up. Trevor follows.

I arch my right eyebrow in a challenge. "This from the one who's car is parked up on the nice concrete driveway by the petunias because that big, bad, scary mud pit is too much to handle."

"Leave her out of this." Preston wags his finger in my face with a grin.

"Her? Preston's having a love affair with his car." Trevor wraps his arms around his own body, rubbing them up and down while making kissy-face.

I laugh and nudge Trevor in the ribs. "That explains all those late nights out in the garage."

"Does poor Rayne know she has competition?" Trevor asks, and then adds under his breath, "Speaking of which... good luck trying to crack that nut."

Preston's expression sours. "There's nothing wrong with Rayne."

"Her, not so much. That mom, though..."

Woah. That's hitting below the belt and dangerously close to home for me. "Hey. Don't judge people by their parents. If everyone did that, y'all would expect my nose stuck ten feet in the air and a cobb up my ass." Preston side-eyes me while the others dissolve into laughter, but the corner of his lip edges up slightly. He wants to laugh, even if he swallows it down.

"So what's the deal? I mean, she's so not your type."

"I don't have a type."

"Uh... yeah. Big boobs, small brain." Trevor holds his two hands in front of his chest making a squeezing motion.

A deep scowl shades Preston's face. "Maybe I'm looking for something different. Who cares?"

He is looking for something different. Preston first mentioned Rayne after prom this past year. Something about how sweet she was, how mature. When he said it, I had to look twice at the yearbook picture just to make sure I was positive who he was talking about. The guy who could have any girl at school wanted the nice, conservative one? He's dated consistently since sophomore year, his experience the stuff of legend. He's the guy never without a girl.

I'm the guy never with one.

But he hasn't dated since May when he first noticed her. I'm sure Mom's constant badgering to find a mature, level-headed girl weighed in on the growing interest, though I'm thinking that wasn't Mom's intention. To her, mature and level-headed translated to "approved" and "easily controlled." That's why she's pushing her pick—Ashlyn—harder and harder every day.

Trevor deadpans. "Who cares? Apparently the whole town. That's all they were talking about at the Pig earlier."

I blow out a loud breath and glare at Trevor. Why bring that up? Preston never had a clue about that when we were there earlier.

But he continues as the other guys in the water swim closer. "Dude... everybody was whispering about it. Rayne's mama heard about you asking her daughter out and totally flipped. Panic attack right in the middle of the tea bags."

Trevor's spilling his guts like it's some sort of sideshow, the guys on stand-by with bated breath. Preston shifts on the dock's edge, kicking his legs back into the water. Enough is enough. There's no use picking on this girl who can't help how her mama acts. Besides, Preston really wants to get to know her. I applaud it. He needs someone out of his norm—someone who can challenge him.

I stand up, waving my hands in the air between Trevor and his audience. "Enough guys. When is this town not talking? We have better stuff to do."

I don't mind being the kill-joy, especially if it takes the heat off Preston. He shoots me a sideways smile as he gets to his feet beside me. "Thanks," he mumbles.

"Anytime," I say, slapping him on the back. "What are brothers for?"

The words barely come off my tongue when a female voice, high-pitched and familiar, shouts across the pond, "Preston!"

On the opposite bank, across from the dock, three girls, all in tank tops and miniskirts that leave little to the imagination, wave at him. Two of them I don't know. One of them I do— Ashlyn, daughter of Mom and Dad's business associate friends. The girl Mom believes Preston's destined to be with.

But she's no different than the others. Bonnie, Tiffany, Anna Kate, and the countless others that have shamelessly thrown themselves at Preston over the years. None of them actually cared about him. They just wanted to leech on to his status and boost their popularity.

I shove my hands in my pockets and lean toward Preston. "What's she doing here?"

"Mom asked me to invite her."

Fire scorches my insides. Here I am protecting him and he's doing stupid crap like inviting this trash to the bonfire?

"Asked or told?" I fold my arms over my chest, waiting. He doesn't respond. "Let me get this straight. Mom asked you to invite the girl who's hot for you to a bonfire where you're planning to ask another girl out? And you did it? Are you insane?"

Preston waves me off with a laugh. "Ashlyn's not hot for me. We're just friends. Have been since we were kids. You know that."

My mouth falls open. At this point, I might have to scrape it off my feet. "Well, then you better tell her and Mom that cause they're already looking at engagement rings for your Old Southern arranged marriage."

He doesn't react, just waves back to her as she and her entourage saunter off toward the main house. I grab his shoulders and spin him to face me. "God, Preston. Open your eyes! I'm your brother. I've got your back over anybody else in this world, but... it's okay not to be perfect sometimes. It's okay to do what you want. You don't always have to play by the rules. It's your life, live it."

"I'm living my life." So matter of fact. So straightforward. So oblivious.

"You're living their life."

He closes his eyes, takes a deep breath, and then pats me on the arm. "Let's not talk about this right now. Let's just have fun."

He turns and jumps feet-first back into the water, leaving me alone on the dock.

Sure. Blow me off. Ignorance is definitely bliss.

3

RAYNE

I twist the radio knob, blaring Aerosmith through the car speakers. Jaycee glares at me from the passenger seat and reaches over with a quick jab to the on/off switch, leaving us in silence.

"Oh, no you don't. You owe me details." She kicks her feet up on the dashboard, wiggling her fresh-painted toes, and then leans forward to swipe Perfectly Pink polish over a few nicks.

"And *you* owe me some information from Google maps. I don't have a clue where we're going." Open fields sporadically dotted with grazing cows and flanked by endless lines of barbed-wire mirror each other on both sides of the road. The e-mail said to look for a cow pasture and a fence. Yeah, that's specific. I grab her phone from the cup holder and toss it in her lap. "Look up the address again, and for the love of God, quit it with that nail polish. It's stinking up the whole car." I press the button on my armrest and her window slides down two inches.

A humid breeze floats in and Jaycee bristles, pawing at me like a rabid cat. "What the hell are you doing? God, Rayne! I told you A/C only. My hair!" She leans across the console, nearly in my lap while using the pinky of her right hand to press the button, sliding her window closed. "I spent a lot of time on my hair. I didn't just wash-and-go like you."

Jaycee has one personality setting—blunt. She never means to hurt my feelings; she just has no brain-to-mouth filter. Other people hate it, but I respect it. She never makes me guess.

"Bitch, please." I wrench the nail polish from her grip, tighten the lid while I steer with my forearms, and toss it over my shoulder into the backseat.

"Hey!" She throws her hand back trying to intercept it but misses, turning to me, mouth molded into an upside-down "u." "You can't say that to your best friend."

"I'll say it *because* you're my best friend. Now get those directions or no one'll even see your hair, because we'll never find the freaking farm."

She yanks hard on the seatbelt, readjusting to a 45-degree angle in the seat, looking out the window and flipping her long, blond locks over her shoulder hard enough to graze my face, the spikey-ends clawing at my nose. In a few taps and finger slides over the phone screen, she pulls up directions. "Left at the next four-way stop, then two rights." She pivots in her seat, eyes boring into me. "Well?"

I glare at her sideways. "Well what?"

"I gave you directions. Now give me the goods." She crosses her arms and cocks her head to the side. It's as if she believes once Preston's declared his intentions to date me some mysterious data file uploaded to my brain, but I don't know anything more than I did before 9:30 this morning.

"You know as much as I do."

Her eyes nearly bug out of her head when I tell her I haven't taken the initiative to cyber-stalk him on Facebook or Twitter. She flips to her app and within seconds gives me a rundown of his most irrelevant stats—Killer Abs in 10 Minutes. Late nights at the Waffle House with the boys. Playing football with Gage. Cheeseburgers.

"After tonight, your name will be all over his page—check-ins, selfies, sweet tagged posts about how much he's in-love with you." She clasps her phone to her chest, sighs, and leans back into the seat, closing her eyes. A grin creeping across her face.

"Why are you so giddy?"

Her eyes open and she glowers at me. "Everyone knows we're besties, a package deal. If he gets you, he gets me too." She crinkles her nose and bites her lip. "I honestly figured he would've chosen me, but it's you."

"What's that supposed to mean?"

"Preston has a yen for big boobs and long legs. Hello." She waves her hand down the length of her leg. "And hello." She twitches her index finger back and forth in front of her chest.

She has a point. By late middle school, Jaycee towered a whole head taller than me, her chest swollen three times the size of mine. I was shopping with her and her mom when Mrs. Tucker picked up a blue lace bra with cups as big as my head and plastered it to Jaycee's chest. The small white tag hanging off the side, marked 36-D, was like a badge of honor. When Mrs. Tucker glanced up at my doe eyes, she side-hugged me and promised I'd hit my growth spurt soon. Four years later, I'm still waiting.

"And what's wrong with these?" I point to my own meager girls, barely making cleavage with the help of a good push-up bra.

Jaycee sweeps her eyes over my face and chest, a smirk inching up the corner of her mouth. "Bitch, please."

"Hey! You can't say that to your best friend."

She shrugs one shoulder up to her ear. "All I'm saying is you break his pattern. What's his angle?"

"Does there have to be one?"

"Isn't there always?"

"He said I was pretty and smart."

She frowns. "Qualifiers. Every guy'll say that to get in a girl's pants."

There's no way I'm a booty conquest, unless Preston's playing a game of "conquer the virgin." I swat her shoulder. "I know! He's gone blind. Got brain damage? Needs a tutor for all those college classes coming up?"

She snaps her fingers. "Good one. You are a nerd. I hadn't even thought of that."

"Shut up." I stomp the gas, the car lurching forward on the curvy two-lane.

After I make two three-point turns and play a game of chicken with an F250 passing a slow-moving John Deere, Jaycee spots the wooden-planked fence and long gravel drive winding across knee-high pasture grass. A couple guys are perched on the top rail, and one of them jumps down and swings open the large steel gate for us to drive through.

Jaycee unbuckles, rolls down the window and leans halfway out, waving at the guy in skin-tight Wranglers. "Keeping the uninvited out?" She giggles and pinches her elbows to her side, popping her chest up and out even further.

Hot Gate Guy tips his cowboy hat and smiles back. That's when I recognize him as Barrett Sanderson, one of Preston's friends, the party host and grandson of the farmer who owns the place.

"Just keeping the cows in, ma'am," he says with a Southern drawl thicker than usual. Jaycee slinks back into the seat, mouth wide open as she follows his every movement in the side mirrors of the car.

"Did you see his ass in those jeans?" she asks as we continue down the gravel road and pull into a grassy patch alongside the other cars. "He could put his cows in my pasture any day."

"Tell him that. Great ice breaker."

Jaycee flattens her lips into a line, and then shoots me the bird when I crack up. She flips down her visor, slicking on one last coat of pink gloss in the tiny mirror, then kisses the air in front of her reflection. "We both may have an interesting night ahead." She winks, swings open the door and slams it behind her. Only Jaycee can make a wink look both sinister and inviting.

I lock the car and shove the keys in my pocket. "Unless I screw it up. Kinda my thing."

"Quit being such a doubter. What the hell could be worse than your mama going spastic at The Pig today?"

"Really? You're gonna jinx me like—" Suddenly the ground doesn't feel even. It's firm under my left foot, soft under my right—and warm.

My gold Jack Rogers squish deep in cow pie, the manure oozing up around the edges of my sandals and onto the tips of my toes. "Shi-it." I pull my foot from the half-baked, grass-laced brown clod with a *pffwt* as I break the suction and shake my foot aggressively, throwing poop bombs into the surrounding grass. So much for throwing down $180 of my hard-earned cash for the expensive French pedicure and the new designer sandals. Right now, they look no better than skanky chipped toes in dollar store flip-flops.

I yank a fistful of dried-up cornstalks from a large mound of debris heaped in the grass and swipe them down the sides of my ankle and foot, peeling brown ribbons from my skin and stopping every so often to gag. If this keeps up, I'll have crap and puke on my sandals.

"Ugh, that's nasty. Hurry up and wipe it off!" Jaycee clamps one hand over her mouth and waves the other one quickly in front of her face. *Yeah, that's helping.*

"Looks like you got into some serious shit."

I'm mid-gag, bent over with my butt in the air when he says it. We didn't see him coming up the gravel road. Oh God, please no. Just no.

I shuffle my foot as far away as possible so he won't see and peer over my shoulder, but it's not Preston. Gage Howard stands there, thumbs hinged in his belt loops, rocking back on his heels and smiling like he's just won the jackpot.

I blow out a breath and squat down to scrape even harder. "No shit, Sherlock. I guess this puts me on your shit list. Poor little Rayne is up shit creek without a paddle."

His smile fades, eyes searching me like a crossword puzzle.

"What's wrong?" I ask. "Did I scare the shit outta you?"

"Actually, that's impressive." He nods, the apples of his cheeks rounding. "I guess you're a girl who has her shit together. That gets you brownie points in my book. Get it? Brown-ie points?"

I toss the poopy-stalks into the grass and extend my hand, wiggling my fingers. "Gonna stand there with that shit-eating grin on your face or help me up?"

He extends his hand partway then yanks it back, smiling. "Nah, I think you might be shit outta luck." He nods back over his shoulder, at what I don't know, until Jaycee kneels down beside me, so close it's as if she's climbing on my lap. Her nails dig three inches in my skin.

"Get up," she hisses. "We've got company."

"Uh...yeah," I tick my head back toward Gage and pry her nails from my arm.

"Not him." She stabs her finger to the side of Gage, further down the gravel road. "Him." Of course it'd be him. Of course it'd be now. Preston saunters toward us, teenage perfection in his khaki shorts and green polo with just a peek of white tee-shirt through the unfastened buttons, emerging like a phoenix from the gravel dust still hanging in the air from the last truck that pulled in.

Kill. Me. Now. How many times am I going to say that today?

He slows once he gets to my side, his feet no more than a few inches to my right—large, thin feet with long toes and freshly-trimmed nails and no callouses. Could feet be this perfect? And then there's mine... covered in crap. Please God, just send an earthquake now and suck me under.

He squats down. "Rayne? You okay?" His first real words to me. Sweet. Caring. Totally embarrassing.

"I... uh... stepped in... uh... it's on my foot..." The words lump together in meaningless brain piles, none matching the others. I keep my head down but peep up at him. His prismatic brown eyes almost make me forget I'm covered in crap—except they're just about the same shade.

He pushes a wild curl behind my ear, his fingertips feather-soft across my cheek. "You are on a farm... in a pasture... with cows."

"Hey, Rayne," Gage interrupts. I twist sideways to where he's still standing in the same spot with the same grin. He scuffs the toe of his well-worn boot in the dirt, sending a spiral of dust up around the ankles of his ripped jeans. Two or three inches shorter than Preston, he's brickhouse-stocky with more hair everywhere, thick, coarse, and dark as night. Everything about him is grittier, except his sky-blue eyes.

I blink up at him, the sun glinting across the lenses of the sunglasses propped on his head. "What now?"

His grin expands, stretching out his lips. "You shouldn't booze tonight. We wouldn't want you to get... shit-faced."

I narrow my eyes, but my lips betray me, curling up despite my struggle to stitch them down. I laugh, losing my balance, then teeter backwards and drop spread eagle onto the dirt at the feet of the hot guy who wants to date me.

"I've got this." Preston slides his arms behind my knees and back, scooping me into his chest, the strength in his muscles rippling under the cotton polo. I want to nestle my head into him, but that'd be weird, so I circle my arms around his neck and squeeze, maybe a little tighter than necessary.

He smells of cologne and bug repellent, an odd concoction,

but it masks the stink coming from my foot. The curve of where his neck reaches down to his shoulders is taut, his skin the color of cinnamon toast, probably from the Howards' recent Caribbean vacation.

He stops at the pond's edge where the murky water melts seamlessly into the grass bank, sets me on my feet and kneels beside. He pinches the clean strip of leather on the top of my sandal between his fingers and delicately slides if off my foot, careful to not drag his own hand through the filth. A few semi-hardened chunks fall off in the grass in front of us. He grimaces. I cringe and look up at the sky. I don't know what I'm looking for, maybe an asteroid hurtling in my direction or the four horsemen of the apocalypse. Could there be anything left to suck as bad as this?

As he scrapes the edges and bottoms of my sandal across a large rock at the water's edge, the majority of the poop, now nearly dried and starting to crack across the top, flakes off, leaving a thin muddy smear across the leather and bottom treads. He sweeps it back and forth in the pond, and then commences rubbing it in a tuft of grass. Over and over again, he goes from grass to water and back again, each time, more of the poop dispersing.

I follow his lead, walking through the grass, dragging my foot behind me like a maimed animal, letting the friction rip away some of the larger dried clods. Then I thrust my naked foot in the water and slosh it around, turning the poop remnants into sticky brown swirls over my toes. With each foot drag and subsequent pond-water bath, my skin's natural color finally returns—even if the stench remains.

Jaycee and Gage stand by, watching the whole thing with ridiculous smiles. It's like being on one of those old-fashioned courtship affairs complete with awkward chaperones. Except I'm pretty sure those don't include cow shit. I'm also pretty sure

Preston didn't bargain on his first act of seduction to include cleaning said crap off my sandal.

Preston walks over to me, squats down and grabs my calf, tapping his fingertips against my skin as a way of telling me to pick up my foot. When I do, he slides the newly-cleaned sandal back over my toes, but when he's done, he leaves his fingers there, pressing into my skin. The lingering dampness causes my leg hairs to bristle, morphing them into tiny razors beneath his touch as he rubs up and down my leg. Surely I should say something flirty or giggle or do some other girly thing, but my mind goes all stupid, and I mumble out the one thing I can't screw up. "Thanks, Preston." I glance down and lock eyes with him.

"Welcome." His gaze sinks to the edge of my cut-off shorts and pauses there, and instinctively I drop my hands down in front of my thighs. Preston jumps to his feet, standing so close his elbow grazes mine. "Barrett's Grandma probably has some soap up at the main house." He points to a white porch-wrapped farmhouse on a hill in the distance. "That'll probably help with... the smell." He looks down quickly and grins, stifling a laugh.

Gage snort-laughs, and Jaycee clamps her eyes shut, shaking her head back and forth. The flame of embarrassment in my throat shoots heated spirals across my cheeks. "Yeah... thanks," I mumble.

Preston bites his lower lip and nods, and then does just what I'm praying for. He changes the subject. "Y'all coming over to see the main event?"

"Main event?" I shift back and forth between legs, more self-conscious than ever and unsure of exactly where to put my hands. On my hips? No, too bossy. Hanging by my side? No, too boring. Certainly not crossed in front of me—that's classic body language for "stay away."

"Mudslinging. There's a pit on the other side of that hill."

He points beyond the grassy pasture where a line of jacked up 4x4s slowly creeps out to an expanse of red Carolina clay. "Ever been?"

Yeah, right. Mama would probably get some sort of ESP and come down here herself to jerk me out of the truck. If she didn't kill me, the embarrassment would. "No, I've never been."

"Probably a good thing," says Gage, walking closer. "You might not be able to handle it." Everyone stops in their tracks and turns toward him. He's chewing on a thick reed of grass, eyes locked on me. When I narrow mine, he wriggles his eyebrows twice.

Preston shakes his head and skims his fingertips along my arm, scattering chill bumps over my skin. "He's a bad influence. You'll learn that if you hang around with him long enough."

Before I can speak, Jaycee pushes in the middle, shooting glares all around. "Where's Barrett? Is he slinging?"

Preston and Gage exchange grins. "I told him those tight Wranglers would get him some play," Gage snorts. Jaycee's face tints different shades of red and pink. Like a bouquet... of evil.

"I did not say..." she starts as Preston steps between them.

"Barrett's over there waiting." He points across the field to the top of the hill where Barrett's sitting on the roof of an old blue Bronco, his legs hanging down in front of the windshield.

"You're driving, too?" I ask. Preston in a 4x4? No freaking way.

Gage grabs Preston from behind and smooches him on the cheek. "No, his pretty boy car can't cut it out here. He's riding bitch with me. Right, big brother?"

Preston wrenches from his grip, ducks low, and turns around, plowing right into Gage's stomach. He stumbles backwards laughing and Gage bends, hands on his knees, struggling for breath.

I gasp and jump to the side.

"Relax." Preston laughs and nudges my shoulder. "It's all in fun."

"Oh..." A heat circulates in my cheeks, partly from embarrassment and partly from the friendly pressure of his palm on my bare shoulder.

Gage horse-collars Preston from behind and begins dragging him toward the pit. "Yeah, Preston, don't get bent out of shape. You know you'll be the best bitch out there."

Jaycee darts to my side, glowering after them. "Gage is an ass."

"He's a smartass. There's a difference, and you're just mad because he interfered with the whole 'meet Preston' scenario in your head. And he picked on you for crushing on Barrett."

I try to link arms with her, but she nearly trips over her own feet, dodging my contact and flailing her arms in my face.

"Whatever it is, I hate it... and him." She un-puckers her pout-lips into a wide grin, rubbing her hands together. "But I do like Preston. He's awesome for your image." She grabs my arms and holds them out to the sides, nose wrinkled, smile faded. "Now for God sakes, go clean yourself up. You still smell like crap."

4

GAGE

"Thanks for making me look like a total idiot," Preston grumbles.

Here comes the drama, and all because I called him my bitch in front of Rayne. If I roll my eyes any harder, they're sure to stick that way. The fact he's even worrying about it is ridiculous. Mr. Popularity himself deemed an idiot? An impossible feat in this town where his proper place is on a big golden pedestal. Preston sets the standards around here with his All-American boy-next-door charm that he graciously hands out like candy. He could come out wearing his boxers on his head, and there'd be a rush on Fruit of the Loom at the local department store.

And then there's his newest love interest in Rayne. The girl who stepped in a steaming pile of crap and forced Preston to get his hands dirty for once. I smile. I thought so before, but I'm even more positive now. She's going to bring big changes his way.

It's about time.

"I was just leveling the playing field. She was the one with cow patty stuck all between her toes."

Preston laughs under his breath and side-eyes me. "That was pretty gross, right?"

He still reeks of it, and I'm pretty sure a couple specks of it splattered his cheek while he helped Rayne clean up. Three brown dots freckle the area under his right eye, but I'm not saying anything about it. It's almost gratifying to see the non-perfect Preston.

"Yep, but terrific ammo you can use to tease her later." This is the kind of leverage to hang over someone's head for a long time.

Preston stares at me like I have worms crawling out my nose, his head and hands waving in rhythm. "No way! You never intentionally embarrass a girl. We're going to forget that incident and never mention it again."

"What? That's a golden opportunity!" I give him a rough shove, and he stumbles forward a few steps. "Besides, Rayne seems tough. I think she can take it."

"This," Preston says, wagging his finger in my face, "is why you don't date."

He might be partially correct. My personality isn't exactly in high demand with the female crowd, though I can't discount the obvious disinterest parading around on my face 24/7 factors in as well. That's probably a major deterrent to anyone crazy enough to give me a second look. Not that I care. My brain operates on two wavelengths—the Scout and football. There haven't been many girls who'd even get close to making me think otherwise.

My mouth drops open as I slap both palms to my face. "You must be right. I'm just a jackass. Mystery solved."

He taps his index finger on his temple as we walk toward the Scout, which is waiting on the hilltop, the first in a long line of 4x4s on the fringe of where the pasture grass meets the ruddy clay. A mix of country music and classic rock blares from their respective radios, punctuating the monotonous current of rumbling engines.

I sit on the hood, boots resting on the bumper, while Preston leans against the fender. The late afternoon sun casts golden arms out over the grass, the orange tint broken up by the long, thin shadows from the trucks.

I lay back, arms folded behind my head, and take a deep inhale, the cloud of exhaust and gasoline expanding in my lungs. I love that smell. Powerful. Strong. Mechanical. A warm breeze floats over me, sneaking in the armhole of my muscle T-shirt. Absolutely nothing could ruin—

"Hey, Preston. I finally found you."

Except that.

I slit one eye, watching Ashlyn and her two cohorts saunter over to Preston. She flicks her fake blond hair over her shoulder and licks her lips. I hate how she stares at him with an open mouth, like she's ready to take a bite or something else equally nasty.

What I hate more is how Preston stands up to greet her, like he's actually happy to see her.

Idiot.

I sit up on the hood and shoot a quick glance over my shoulder. Rayne's no longer on the sideline but heading off toward the main house, no doubt in search of that soap Preston alluded to. Good. Her seeing Ashlyn fawn over Preston would throw a monkey wrench in things from the very beginning. She doesn't strike me as the type of girl eager to engage in petty drama, and it's not like Preston will actually tell Ashlyn to scram. He thinks she's harmless, innocent.

A small laugh escapes as I think of it. She rolls her eyes at me then reaches out, fingering the collar of his polo. "Where've you been? I was looking for you everywhere."

I bet she was, like a bloodhound sniffing his trail. Before he can speak, I butt in. "He was talking to the new girl he's dating. You should meet her. She's sweet and smart and funny."

The other two girls exchange glances, but Ashlyn smirks. "If you like her so much, why don't you date her?" Her voice is sugar-coated foulness. Kind of like when people offer you sweet tea and you take a sip, only realizing it's unsweetened with a spoonful of saccharin stirred in.

Her reaction is fake-covered-bitterness and pure validation of my suspicions. "I have to defer to my brother. He's completely smitten already." I squeeze Preston's chin in my fingers, giving it a small shake.

Preston grabs either side of my kneecap, sinking his fingers into the pressure points. A searing pain slingshots up my leg as he stares at me with a maniacal grin. "I can speak for myself, Gage."

Oh, Preston. Always the diplomat.

He releases his fingers, and the tingling begins to subside. That's when I notice again the three brown dots on his cheek. "You have something on your face," I say, tapping my skin in the coordinating area.

"Where?" He starts toward the side mirror, but Ashlyn reaches out and grabs his sleeve.

"Here. Let me," she says in her honey tone and runs her finger through the muck, scooping it up into one pile.

"What is this? Chocolate?" She giggles and sweeps her finger up to her nose for a sniff. A grimace seizes her face, nose wrinkled and lips pinched.

"Um... that's, um..." Preston stammers, blushing.

I jump off the hood and stand behind Preston, my hands on his shoulders. "What he's trying to say is that's cow crap."

She screams and flails her arm in the air, the clump sailing sideways in the pasture grass. "Gross!" She turns and beelines for the main house, nearly tripping several times on her sandals, with the other two in tow.

Preston shakes his head. "You did that on purpose."

"What? I got rid of the problem, didn't I?" I shrug and point to the Scout. "Now get your butt in the passenger seat. Let's show 'em how it's done!"

The last rays of sun sink below the horizon as I pull my mud-caked Scout by the bonfire, backing in to a slot near where Rayne stands, arms folded, searching the shoulder-to-shoulder crowd. I can only guess what she's looking for. Or who. But he's MIA at the moment. One minute we'd been cleaning the mud spatters from our clothes, the next minute he vanished without a word.

And I can only imagine with who. To be so smart, he's completely oblivious.

I walk around, drop the tailgate and pull a couple camp chairs from the back, opening them up. Footsteps crunch the grass all around, but a snapping stick, close behind me, catches my attention.

I glance over just as Rayne taps me on the shoulder, one eyebrow cocked into her forehead. "Nice driving out there, but I could've done better."

"You just love to argue with me, don't you?" I turn around, hands on my hips. "Lucky for you, I love a challenge, and I might just give you an opportunity to prove it sometime."

"You're on." She smirks and nods toward one of the chairs, silently asking me for a seat. I pick it up and set it in front of her, panning my hand in an open invitation and she sits down, propping her hands behind her head.

Smug. Confident. Naïve.

I grab another chair and pull it beside hers, but before I can sit down, Jaycee barrels toward us and yanks Rayne up by the arm, dragging her toward the fireside. She leans into her ear,

mouth moving feverishly while she stabs her finger at something on the other side of the flames. It doesn't take a body
language expert to deduce something's wrong.

I stand up and ease closer to them, Jaycee's shrill jabbering
becoming actual words within earshot.

She furrows her brows and hisses, "You better handle that.
Fake nails, hair extensions, and legs longer than your entire
body? She's everything you're not. Everything he usually
wants."

The orange flames spiral against the dark sky, and I stoop
lower for a better look, focusing in on exactly what's causing
the stir. Preston, standing in a mixed group with a tall, leggy
blonde who's leaned into his shoulder and rubbing circles on
his back.

Ashlyn.

Rayne's face falls, her smile replaced by thin, drawn lips.
"How can I compete with that Legs-a-lot chick?" She steps sideways, reaching for her chair, and sinks into it. Jaycee whirls
around, her eyes flaming as they land on mine for the briefest
moment, before she shoves past me, barking orders at Rayne.

"Get up! Get over there and do something."

Rayne doesn't make a move to get up, only shakes her head
then rests it on the back of her chair, clamping her eyes shut. "I
want to go home," she mumbles.

Fuming, Jaycee retreats to her own chair halfway around
the circle and flounces into it, pouting with lips rolled out a
mile. I slip my phone from my pocket.

<Gage> *What are you doing with A?*
<Preston> *Talking. Why?*
<Gage> *Rayne saw. She's leaving*
<Gage> *Idiot. I told you*
<Preston> *Be right there*

I walk to my Scout and sit on the tailgate, waiting—watching. On the opposite side, Preston grabs Barrett's arm and pulls

him away from the crowd. Ashlyn protests, but he ignores her. When they pass Jaycee's chair, a huge grin spreads across her face—one that grows even wider when Barrett breaks away and slides into the seat next to hers.

Oh well. At least Preston's getting his act together. Barrett will have to deal with his own bad decisions.

Preston pats me on the shoulder then kneels down by Rayne's chair.

I shake my head. He might be the ladies' man but even he has to admit I saved his butt on this one.

5

RAYNE

*H*ay bales. Two big, round hay bales pushed together in the pasture on the fringe of the bonfire crowd. And he wants me to climb them. Me. Climb them. This boy has a lot to learn about my shortcomings.

"Here?" This has to be a joke, but he's not laughing.

"Here." He unfurls the blanket across the top of both, and then nudges my elbow. "Don't worry. I'll help you up." Grabbing one of the baling wires, he plants his foot on the side and hoists himself up in one seamless motion. *Oh dear Lord.* He's already seen me half-covered in crap today, and now he'll see me sprawled out at the bottom of a hay bale when I fall. Possibly bloody... and broken. On his knees, he reaches over the edge and grabs my hands. As he pulls me up, my feet scramble for traction like a cat being pulled from a flea dip bucket.

Finally making it to the top, I crawl beside him and sink into the crevice between the bales, legs thrown up on one side and back resting on the other. Like one of those adjustable beds, only scratchier. An unseasonably cool wind tousles my curls, and the bonfire flames pirouette in the distance, orange fingers spiraling against the blackened horizon that spice the air with aromas of charred wood.

Preston tugs me to his side, so close my hand smooshes into his thigh where his smooth skin edges out the bottom of his shorts—silky smooth. Preston's clean-shaven from face to foot, and the peaks and valleys of the muscles hidden below his khakis tease my fingertips. He slides his right arm across his body and runs his fingertips up and down my arm. The sensation's so gentle I glance down to make sure his fingers are, in fact, touching me. They are, and not on accident.

But why's he not talking? I sweep my tongue around my cottony-dry mouth, ensuring the barbecue from earlier is gone and focus my eyes on everything except him. People talking around the fire. A few clouds swirling by the moon. A wily piece of hay sticking out from the others. Put me out of my misery already...

"So..." He drums his fingers on my arm. "Have fun today?"

Finally! "Yeah, I did." I prop up on my elbow. The moonlight gilds the top of his hair, illuminating a brown clump lodged above his right ear. "Looks like you missed a spot cleaning up that mud." I pinch out the dried clod and flick it to the ground.

"Thanks." He relaxes into the bale, elbows behind his head and a slight grin settling into the corners of his mouth. "Tell me something about yourself."

"Okay... I'm seventeen. Closet nerd with a slight coffee addiction. A cheerleader, but only because Jaycee forced me, and to relax, I enjoy long runs through downtown." I stop and pinch my lips together. Desperate much? "Wow. That kinda sounds like a personal ad."

"Yeah. Kinda does." He smiles, both rows of teeth perfectly straight and bright white against the darkness, and traces meandering circles with his finger over the top of my knuckles. "So, Miss Personal Ad, what kind of guys do you like?"

I twist my mouth sideways, tapping my finger to my chin. "Hadn't given it much thought." Lies. All lies.

"Don't. Thinking about anything too much ruins it. You have to let things happen. Ignore the rules—a famous Gage-ism."

I squint my eyes. Rule-breaker is not a word I'd use to describe Preston. "And you're okay with that?"

"Absolutely not. I don't like surprises." He reaches up and strokes my hair, singles out one ringlet and curls it around his finger. "So, tell me more. Favorite food, favorite color, college plans?"

So, he does want to know more than the shape of my tonsils or the feel of my ass.

"Sure. You first."

He smiles. "All right. Lasagna. Red. Tech starting this fall, then transfer to a four-year school—probably Clemson." He ticks each off on his fingers.

"Why Tech first? Weren't you recruited for football?"

He presses his lips together. "I was. Got a lot of offers, too, but mostly up North and out West, and I want to stay here. My parents have this dream of me one day working in my dad's accounting firm. That's why I'll be working there when the fall semester starts. Shadowing, going to meetings, that sort of thing."

"Wow. Sounds grown-up."

"That's Mom's philosophy. A nineteen-year-old high school graduate should act like a man and put away 'childish diver-sions.'" He says *childish diversions* like he's imitating her, but he's not snide, just matter-of-fact.

"What are your *childish diversions*?" I wiggle my fingers in air quotes.

"Anything not directly related to school or the firm, according to mom. For me, it's football. I miss playing, but..." He shrugs. "You do what you're supposed to, right?"

"I guess." A nasty grimace takes my face hostage, and I drop my head so Preston won't see. My whole life's been about *doing what you're supposed to*, but sometimes I want to do what I want for a change.

"Anything else you want to know about me?"

I glance up at him. Something's been bothering me since the news broke this morning, and if I don't ask, I'll wonder. And if I wonder, I'll doubt. And if I doubt, I might as well forget this whole thing right now. "Why me?"

"What?" He rises back up on his arm and narrows his eyes.

"I'm not like any of the girls you've dated before. So... why me?"

He shifts his legs along the hay and blows out a loud breath. "The town's gotten to you, I guess?"

I fiddle with some hay sticking out from underneath the baling wire, refusing to look at him. What's the appropriate way to ask why he's suddenly decided to go slumming? "I mean, yeah, I heard it around town, but that's not why I'm asking. I just need to know."

He tips my chin up with his fingers. The shadows haunt his face, the only light an orangey glow warming his chocolate eyes, which deadlock on mine. "You're not like other girls I've dated. I'm tired of that."

Who does he think he's fooling? "The perfect guy is tired of perfect girls?"

He sighs and shakes his head. "You think I'm perfect? You think they were?"

Uh, yeah. My shoulders shrug to my ears.

"Rayne, people believe what they see, but what you see isn't necessarily true. The other girls I've dated... oh, they had some issues, but I'm not perfect either."

"Sure you are..."

He grabs my shoulders and squares me in front of him. "Okay, let me tell you a story. I'm the championship quarterback. Led the team to victory, right?" I nod. "My junior year, there was one game I got my ass kicked all over the field. I could throw it deep but not scramble, and once they figured that out, it was over. The coach was in my face, and I really just wanted to say screw it. When we got home, my dad took me in his study, sat me in the leather chair, propped his feet up on his desk and stared at me over his glass of scotch."

"Was he mad?"

"No. He said he was glad it happened. It exposed my flaw, got it out there in the open so I had to deal with it. I still remember his words, 'Son, address it, face it, beat it. The weak points are where you grow. Failures bring success.'" He snorts and shakes his head. "I thought he was drunk at first. Now I know he's right."

I study his face for a minute. He nods, eyes wide and smiling as if he's just revealed some great truth. "So much good advice to be had from you Howard men. And that's a convenient answer, but..."

"It's truthful." He pauses, swallows, and starts again. "You want to know why I'm interested? At prom I saw you with that geeky dude... Thad, right?"

Oh God. I bury my face in my hands. No good deed goes unpunished yet again. I'd gone with Thaddeus McKelvey, grade-A class nerd, because I could relate to him. We both had that square-peg-in-a-round-hole-thing going on. Besides, Mama wouldn't agree to my going with anyone else. Jaycee swore it'd come back to bite my ass, and here it is.

"Anyway, everyone was making fun of him, but you stayed on his arm all night. That dude had a smile on his face the whole time, while I was stuck with a date that complained about everything, hated her food, hated her hair, and hated all my friends. I wish I could've smiled like Thad."

No freaking way. My going with Thad won Preston over? So much for Jaycee's theories.

I drop my hands to my lap, grab his fingers, and squeeze. A new connection, a better understanding of each other, smolders in the touch. "Now I guess I owe you some answers. Chicken-fried steak, blue, and I have absolutely no idea, but Mama's got a whole crop of college applications waiting on me at home."

He reclines into the bale, running his fingertips up my backbone, and then pulls me into the niche between his neck and shoulder. In between our school discussions and quiet moments of gazing up at the multitude of stars freckling the inky blackness, Preston meanders his fingers to mine and interlaces them, the length almost double mine, folding nearly all the way back to the meaty part of my palm. The warmth radiates up my arm. With his other hand, he scours the bale and plucks out single strands of hay he twirls between his fingertips before letting them drop into a little pile beside him. Maybe he wants to ask me about Mama and the Pig fiasco? If so, what do I say? I can tell the truth, but I don't want him thinking Mama's crazy because if Mama's crazy then her daughter can't be far behind, right?

He loosens his grip and props up on his elbow, hovering above me. He cups my chin and lines me up for a direct impact, my nose brushing against his. "I really like you, Rayne..." His words faintly stand out against the high-pitch humming of crickets and cicadas in the surrounding pasture.

His lips come at me like a shark in the ocean. Searching. Seeking. Intimidating. I've kissed a few boys over the years, but no one special. A peck here or there. A spin-the-bottle game. Never a hot guy like Preston. Never a make-out session. Oh my gosh—is this about to be a make-out session?

His lips greet mine in a flurry of kisses. I can't catch up. By the time I acclimate my lips to one type of smooch, he moves on to another. Full-on contact to bottom lip nibbling to some sort of licking motion along my teeth. I'm glad I checked for leftover barbecue. His lips are more soft and supple than I expected, and they glide over mine with a faint heat.

I slit one eye open. His are closed. Stop it, Rayne. Enjoy this. Quit getting in your own way.

His lips still and linger close but not touching, our foreheads leaned together. I lift my eyes. He's looking back. "It is okay if I kiss you, right?"

Not trusting my voice to actually work, I nod. He smiles and kisses me again, harder and faster, this time letting his hands roam over my body, down my shoulders, arms, side, and to my butt, where he digs in his fingers a little and tugs me closer. Mama would kill him. She'd crawl up on this bale and beat his... Mama. My curfew. I forgot all about it, so while he's kissing me, I sneak a peek at my phone. All hell breaks loose when the digital numbers flash on the screen.

I rip my lips from his. "Oh shit! It's almost eleven. I gotta get back before curfew." I stand up, brushing hay from my clothes. I sure don't need Mama wondering how I got straw stuck all over me tonight. "Talk to you later." I jump off the edge of the hay bale, my ankle screaming in a jolt of pain as I hit the hard dirt.

"Wait," Preston yells and jumps off right behind me. "I want to see you again." He presses me into the hay bale and leans in close, past my lips to my neck. When Jaycee runs up, he jolts backwards.

"I hate to interrupt whatever this is," she says, waving her hand around, "but it's ten 'til eleven. If we're not back by curfew, your mama'll send up the search helicopters."

"I gotta go." I grab his phone and hand him mine. We quickly enter our numbers in the other's contacts. "Call me." I run to Jaycee, who grabs my hand and pulls me to the car.

6

———————

GAGE

The flames are head-high now, big wisps of smoke curling up into the night sky. I sniff the air. Charred wood with a hint of pine from the broken branches they threw on for kindling. The base of it's so wide I can't see the people on the other side. Not that I care. From the swell of loud laughs and shrieks coming from the abyss, I'm content to be over here on the quiet side. Just me and my trusty pair of camp chairs, one for my butt and one for my feet. Other than my Coke and a few bags of chips I snagged from the food table, I'm alone, and have been since Preston dragged Rayne off to the hay bales and Barrett made his move on Jaycee and they disappeared somewhere toward the barn. The way she was gawking at him, I'm surprised his Wranglers didn't peel up and fall off right there on the grass. God help him.

I pop another chip in my mouth. The crunching echoes so loud in my head, it blocks out all the other noises around me. Without warning, the chair underneath my feet disappears to the right and sends my legs flopping to the ground like heavy weights, the momentum nearly flipping me forward out of my chair.

Preston plops it down beside me and sits back, arms folded behind his head. Barrett walks behind him, chewing on a long blade of field grass.

"You two back already?" I glance at my watch. "Damn. That must be some sort of record to get dumped by 11 PM."

Barrett slaps me on the shoulder and spits the straw to the ground. "This from the boy who got no play, all day."

I shoot him a nasty smirk over my shoulder. He's obviously qualified to make the "no play" statement. From the looks of it, plenty came his way tonight. Barrett's button-down is no longer tucked in, and deep creases cut across the front, like it's been pushed up or crumpled underneath something—or someone.

Ugh. The mere thought of Jaycee mauling my friend punches my gag reflex, inducing a burning in my stomach that inches its way up my esophagus.

Preston laughs. "Gage would rather sit here alone all night than worry about impressing a girl." He turns and fixes his eyes on me. "But one day, brother, someone will change your mind."

"I wouldn't count on that." I stand up, fold one camp chair and toss it in the back of my Scout while Preston folds the other. "Since you two losers are officially girl-free now, are you ready to go?"

Preston loads in the second chair and slams the tailgate. "Barrett rode with me earlier, so I'll probably stick around for a while. Help him clean up after everyone leaves. Would you take us up to the main house to get my car before you go, though?"

"Sure. Get in." I nod toward the passenger side.

Barrett gets in the backseat and leans forward over the front bench. "Go out the gated entrance and up to the third drive on the right. It'll be easier at night instead of trying to drive across the fields."

I turn the key and the engine rumbles to life. I love the sound of it. Heavy, tough, and gritty. Kinda like me.

We peel down the gravel path to rocks clinking against the

underside of the Scout and yank our seatbelts around us. "Y'all never did tell me. Why'd your night end so early?"

"Preston's girl has a curfew." Barrett sulks in the backseat, arms folded across his chest. "Sucks, too, cause things were just getting good between me and Jaycee."

Good and Jaycee—isn't that a contradiction in terms? I didn't know her on any sort of personal level, but there'd been a few rumors over the years that'd run their course through the school. Some speculation on her being a little bit wild and a lot clingy, usually with guys considered the "uppercrust." Apparently, she has a thing for latching on and bleeding them dry—of money and patience—and then discarding them like filthy rags. Why Barrett's even bothering with her confounds me. The allure of wild fun must trump certain drama.

"Yeah, it's all good until she gets what she wants then chews your head off." I laugh, glancing up at Barrett in the rearview mirror, imagining him as a doomed praying mantis.

He scowls. "You salty?"

"About you hooking up with Jaycee?" I laugh, circling my finger in front of my face. "This is not salty. This is pity."

"Come on, Gage, she's not that bad." Preston presses his head into the front seat where Barrett can't see and makes a face then thumbs over his shoulder into the backseat. "Besides, if anyone can handle her wild streak, it's him."

Barrett leans forward, head and arms creeping over the back of the bench seat. "I can confirm that part of the rumor is true. Jaycee's... not shy." He pulls down the collar of his shirt, displaying two big purplish welts marking the slope of his neck like a badge of honor. Preston takes one look, closes his eyes, and shakes his head as Barrett slugs him in the arm. "What about Rayne? She hidin' a little tiger inside her goody-two-shoes self?"

Definitely. Her shit-talk comebacks this afternoon were on point, with just enough sarcasm to undercut that honey voice.

"Nah. She's level, man. Smart, mature, kind."

"Yeah. Kind of boring." He flicks down the collar of Preston's polo. Tanned skin with no splotches whatsoever. "Obviously."

A wave of relief floods over me. I don't know why. Maybe it's because I'd formed my opinion of Rayne already, seeing her ankle-deep in cow patty and still slaying the sarcasm. A fire danced in her eyes—not of bitchiness but of competition. A fire I know well. Preston's lack of hickeys only proves she is, in fact, nothing like Jaycee.

Good. That's the last thing my brother needs.

"Did anything happen between y'all?" I ask, not sure if I really want to hear all the details.

He shrugs. "We kissed."

"And?" Barrett asks, rolling his hand, beckoning for more.

"And talked."

"That's it?" I joke. "Did you invite Ashlyn up there with you, too?"

The corners of my mouth inch up, and as we pull out onto the main road, Barrett meets my smile with one of his own and nudges my ribs with a snort. "Sounds like a perfect PG evening. Afterwards, did you hold hands and skip?"

Preston unbuckles and reaches over the seat, taking a swipe at Barrett, who slumps backwards. Both are laughing and trash-talking when up ahead, on the shoulder of the road, a small car sits halfway hidden in the tall grass, the flashers blinking.

"Hey," I snap my fingers, calling their attention. "Isn't that Rayne's car?"

Silence falls around us as I pull off the road behind them, the headlights reflecting off the back glass, silhouetting two figures in the car's front seats. I get out first and sprint to the window, giving it three sturdy wallops.

"Rayne. It's Gage Howard. Y'all okay?"

The driver door swings open so fast I have to two-step out of the way as Rayne bolts out, face-to-face with me. She leans forward and wraps her arms around my middle.

"Thank goodness it's you. We couldn't see anything except your headlights, and Jaycee had me convinced you were a mass murderer who'd leave us for dead beside this country road." She says it between laughs, but her hands are still trembling. Go figure. Jaycee stirring up drama. "We tried to call Jaycee's mom but she's not answering. And my 11 PM curfew... I'm in big trouble."

Big trouble for less than 10 minutes late and a valid explanation? Damn, I thought my mom was hard. But then again, Mrs. Davidson's reputation is well known in town. Super over-protective. And now with Rayne missing curfew after that episode at the Pig earlier, Preston's chances may have just swirled down the drain.

Jaycee's door squeaks open and she stumbles from the car through the grass clods. "You do realize you better come up with a good excuse now?" She pauses then snaps her fingers. "Ooh, I know. Tell her you stepped in shit and had to clean up and then—" She stops short at the back fender where two more people join our roadside party, her sneer morphing into a fake, toothy grin. "Barrett? I didn't realize you were here, too." Her voice fills with honey as she reaches out to stroke his arm.

Preston steps around them and in between me and Rayne, taking her by the shoulders. "What happened?"

She shrugs. "We just pulled out when the car shook and this *womp-womp-womp* sound started. We were trying to call someone when y'all drove up."

The diagnosis is immediately clear. She has a flat tire. I check the first two. Everything's okay, but the back right tire is flat, the black rubber puddling onto the ground. I squat down and run my fingers over the tread's peaks and valleys. Near the bottom, they snag on a hard, metallic lump. A screw, diagonally protruding from the tire. "Can't fix this. The sidewall's punctured. I'll have to change it."

"You know how to do that?" Jaycee taunts me from her position under Barrett's arm, snug and smug all at the same time. I stare at them for a minute, wondering what in the hell he's thinking and when she's going to take that fatal bite.

"Please. I practically rebuilt my Scout. This is just a tire. Tires are easy." I pop the trunk and lift the carpet cover. Nothing.

"Apparently, it's gonna be pretty hard if you don't have a spare tire," Jaycee says with a smirk.

Rayne runs over to the trunk and peers in, eyes fixed as if she's willing a tire into existence. As if she could make one magically appear through her concentrated thoughts. Still nothing.

"Ooo-oh no-oo." She holds it out for like, five syllables and slams the lid, slumping against the side.

Jaycee hops up on the trunk, her feet resting on the bumper, arm still linked in Barrett's. In one of those up-down preschool sing-song tunes she says, "You know what this means."

"Mama. That's what this means. I have to call home." Rayne pulls her phone from her pocket as if it weighs a million pounds.

Everyone exchanges glances. Rayne tries to play it cool, fashioning her finger into a gun, which she holds to her temple, rolling her eyes for exaggeration. But I can see what's really there.

Fear.

Uncertainty.

And total embarrassment.

"Tell your mama we'll give you a ride," I offer.

"In this?" Jaycee pipes up, taking a minute from sucking face with Barrett to point at the Scout. She wrinkles her nose and sticks out her tongue.

Not like I want her riding in my Scout anyway. She needs to thank Rayne and Barrett for that privilege. If it was just her out here, she'd still be waiting come morning.

"I can tie you to the back bumper. That's usually where I put roadkill." I shoot back as Jaycee rolls her eyes then smooshes back into Barrett's face.

Rayne darts her gaze between the phone and everyone else as she punches in each digit then holds it to her ear like a loaded weapon. It's obvious when Mrs. Davidson picks up because Rayne's eyes widen to the point they look like they'll pop out of her head at any moment. A few beads of sweat trickle down her forehead.

"Yes, Mama. I know I'm late. I'm okay. It's just a flat tire..."

Shrill sobs bleed through the phone and spill out into the night air. Even Jaycee and Barrett stop long enough to gawk at Rayne, who turns sideways, trying to use her hand to block out the sounds from the other side.

"No, Mama. Don't put Daddy on the phone. There's no reason... hey Daddy." She side-eyes me, her cheeks flushed, shoulders slumped. Something about it resonates with me. My mom freaks out on me the exact same way, but I guess I'm lucky. She only does it in private, never in front of a crowd. I turn my back, blocking Rayne from the rest of the group and corral everyone toward the Scout. Jaycee and Barrett scramble into the backseat, still attached at the face, while Preston and I wait at the front fender.

"No, it's just a flat tire. I'm fine." It has to be the hundredth time she's repeated it, and I contemplate recording it on my phone so she can play it over and over on a loop.

Rayne exhales and pushes the red button, staring down at her phone for a minute. Preston pats me on the arm and walks to her, leaning down to whisper something in her ear. She nods, grabs her purse from the car and locks it with the key fob. I slide behind my steering wheel to wait. In the back, Jaycee and Barrett are still lip-locked, half sprawled out over the seat. My poor Scout. He's going to need a good disinfecting after tonight.

Preston holds the door open for Rayne. "Why don't you ride up here between me and Gage?"

Her eyes rove over the bench seat like she has a mental yard stick and is doing the math. Yes, it'll be a tight fit, but anything's better than riding in the backseat with... *that*. The rearview glimpse sends shudders down my spine.

Rayne slides in across the bench seat to the center, having to straddle her legs around the stick shift.

And my hand.

Preston slides in beside her and slams the door. Her left thigh squishes into me, her right into Preston, and I'm shifting gears between them. In the back, the serenade of lip smacking and quiet moans continues. Awkward. Made even worse by the fact Preston keeps prodding around Rayne's fingers like he's trying to hold them, but she's not biting. Her palm is pressed flat into the edge of where her shorts meet skin. He squints and chews his bottom lip, the way he does when working on homework. Trying to figure out what's going on. Most girls would've grabbed his hand without hesitation. Hell, most of them would've been like that one in the backseat.

Maybe she's not into PDA. Maybe she's worried about her mama. Whatever it is has Preston rattled. He finally pulls his hand away and rubs it along his jawline instead.

I'm in the middle of a freaking soap opera—and I hate drama.

First gear.

Clutch. Pull the stick back to second. My forearm grazes her thigh. She shivers. Just a small one but enough for me to sense the vibration as it runs down her body.

Clutch. Push up to third gear.

Clutch. Pull back to fourth. My skin once again makes contact. This time hers is freckled in chill bumps.

She fidgets, readjusting herself—crossing her arms, uncrossing her arms, one knee up, one leg stretched out. "I'm a Howard sandwich," she finally laughs, pointing between the two of us.

Preston smiles but says nothing, like he's trying hard to think of a snappy comeback but isn't getting anywhere. The words are on my tongue, however, before she even quits speaking. "We're the white bread to your bologna."

"Bologna? Honey please. I'm grade-A, thin-sliced roasted turkey."

Battle of wits? Bring it on.

"My bad," I shoot back immediately. "Bologna's made of crap. You just stepped in it." I stop and sniff the air close to her. "At least you don't smell like it anymore."

She sniffs back, a wicked grimace painting her smile. "More than I can say for you."

"A challenge, huh?" I counter, leaning in toward her.

She straightens her spine and mirrors me. "Absolutely. And I don't back down."

Preston watches us like a sideshow, then wraps his arm around her shoulders with a little tug so slight most people wouldn't notice, but I do. Her thigh's no longer pressed into mine, her elbow no longer grazing my side when she fidgets in her seat. This smells distinctly of territory-staking. I hope he doesn't pee on her to prove a point, but I have to wonder why he even feels the need.

He's never been good with the roll-off-your-tongue banter with anyone except me, and that's only because he's had 18 years to practice. Preston's not spontaneous. He follows a strict set of rules and procedures, either set up by mom or himself. She's challenging him—the way he said earlier he wanted to be challenged. Now he doesn't have a clue how to deal with it.

Still, Rayne's a girl. A smart girl but a girl no less, and they always want Preston.

Not me.

He's safe.

I push myself against the door, and we ride the rest of the way in silence, the three of us in the front keeping our eyes straight out the windshield to the tune of slurping and smacking in the backseat. Consequently, the only talking comes from Rayne shouting over her shoulder for Jaycee to button her blouse and reapply gloss. Red blotches and swollen lips parading in the front door of the Davidson house is a no-go —especially with her mama already on the warpath.

When we pull into the drive, a silhouette darkens the front triple windows and the curtains push back slightly. Rayne immediately stiffens against the seat.

"Maybe if we go in and explain..." Preston starts.

"No!" Rayne almost yells it, stop-signing her hand in his face. "We'll take it from here. Thanks for the ride."

Preston leans in, eyes closed, lips puckered. It's about damn time he makes a move. But the closer he gets, Rayne's eyes turn to saucers, and she begins backpedaling, jerking backwards and inadvertently into my lap. Her feet nail Preston in the side, knocking him halfway out the open door. In the dim glow of the streetlight, her cheeks fire up. The flames dance in mine as well.

"Sorry," she mumbles, struggling to get herself out of an almost full-on sprawl she's doing in the front seat. She uses her elbows to scoot her butt to the end of the bench, sliding out the passenger door onto the grass where Preston stands, eyes downcast.

She reaches out and grabs the tips of his fingers. "I can't," she whispers, darting her eyes toward the house. "Not where Mama can see."

He smiles and nods, finally making eye contact once again though he chokes on a reply. "I'll... call you."

That's all he can eke out? *I'll call you?* My brother the stud has transformed into my brother the dud.

Preston slams the door and watches as Rayne struggles to pull Jaycee across the yard, all the while finger-combing her hair and de-smudging her make-up. I stare at Preston, the idling bass of the engine vibrating around us.

"What?"

"You croaked. If your conversation on the hay bales was anything like that, you're through."

"It wasn't, okay? The hay bales were nice, relaxed. We talked plenty. But..."

"But what?"

"It's when she gets around you... it's like you bring out this whole other side to her. Y'all have this witty back-and-forth and I'm totally out of the loop."

"You go back-and-forth with me all the time."

"Yeah, but you're my brother. She's... a girl."

"Then when you're with her, just pretend you're having a conversation with me."

"Perfect. Just what I always wanted. To date my brother."

Barrett pops his head over from the backseat, traces of pink lipstick smudged all over his face. "You guys are jacked up. Know that?"

The guy who makes out with Jaycee thinks we're jacked up. Damn. I believe that's an insult.

RAYNE

She stands by the staircase, holding onto the banister like a crutch, a wad of mascara-streaked tissues in the other hand. The oscillating fan sweeps by and billows out her blue cotton nightgown like a tent over her terry socks and slippers. A few graying tendrils, loosened from her ponytail by the breeze, circle her head like a wiry crown.

No one would believe Mama was once the local beauty queen. Not that many of the kids my age know. I'm sure the older people in town remember, but seeing her now, they probably wonder what sort of tragedy befell her. Best I can guess is she had me and lost her ever-lovin' mind, because she didn't always look so haggard and nervous before—back then she was beautiful, warm, and lighthearted. I have evidence—teenaged versions of my parents hugged together in 3x5 glossies that now lay tucked away in a memory box in her cedar chest. Those pictures don't look anything like the scrapbooks on the hallway shelf cataloguing my childhood.

It was somewhere around the time she got pregnant with me that the real smile, the genuine one, left her face. In all the pictures after that, it's forced, as if she put up barriers between us before I was even born. She never told me why, and I don't think she ever will.

Daddy steps out from behind her, completing the united front, but his eyes are downturned. Mama's clearly strong-armed his participation in the intervention of their delinquent daughter. I take out my phone and hand Jaycee my purse. "Take this upstairs. I'll be up in a minute." She darts up the stairs, eager to get away from the impending third degree.

Daddy sweeps his eyes between me and Mama. She's staring at me as if running some sort of internal lie detector, waiting on me to screw up so she can nail me. She sighs loudly and shakes her head. "No good comes from late-night galli-vanting with boys. I've told you this." She locks her jaw, unwilling to budge. The fictional scenarios she's crafted in her own mind are the only truths she'll accept because in Mama's world, everyone's a suspect. We can't all be as righteous as she is. "Where were you all night? Were you even at the bonfire or was that a lie? And why did your tire just suddenly go flat? It was perfectly fine earlier!"

"I don't know, Mama. Why does any tire go flat? Preston and Gage said something about the sidewall being messed up..."

"See? Suddenly Preston's there. Why was he even there? What were you doing when you discovered this flat tire?"

"I was sitting on the side of the road with Jaycee when the boys stopped to help us, Mama."

"And suddenly it's *boys*. Plural," she says with air quotes. "Where did all these *boys* come from?"

"They were all riding together and saw us on the side of the road! Excuse them for being gentlemen and stopping to help us. I guess you'd rather they just drove off?" My eyes blaze, and I throw my hands in the air.

Mama has this habit of sucking her tongue across her teeth when she's pissed off. She's doing it now. I hate the squeaky, squishy sound of it. "I think you should have called us."

"I did call y'all. You freaked out on me!"

"Only because we didn't know where you were or what you'd been up to..." she starts.

"Check it." I shove my phone in her face. "There are selfies of me and Jaycee from the party with timestamps. Call logs and texts. I have nothing to hide!"

Daddy steps forward and pats my shoulder. "No one thinks you're lying."

"She does!" I stab an accusatory finger at Mama. "She always thinks I'm lying or sinning or something because I can't possibly live up to her holier-than-thou standards. What are the church ladies gonna say? Who might be talking about you? Really? Talking about me? They're talking about you, Mama!"

I stagger backwards as the words come out of my mouth. Everything that's been building inside is splattered in front of me via word-vomit. Preston's words ring in my ear. *Do what you have to do?* I love my Mama. Really. But I can't keep doing this.

She huffs and fingers a piece of peeling paint on the railing, refusing to look at me, but fresh tears streak her cheeks. Daddy immediately steps back to loop his arms around her shoulders, drawing her in, protecting her from me, her own evil spawn of Satan. "That's enough, Rayne," Daddy says.

"No, Daddy. It's not gonna be enough until something changes." I lower my voice. "I've never given y'all a reason to doubt me, but you treat me more like a suspect than a daughter."

"That's not true," Mama whimpers. "We're protecting you."

"I'm seventeen. You're smothering me." I walk toward her and grab her hand, tears stinging my eyelids. "Quit putting walls between us." She tilts her head further away from me, peeling a strip of the white paint from the wood rail. "Good night, Mama. I do love you." I kiss her on the cheek, salty from the tears I caused, and trudge up the stairs.

Jaycee's already changed and lying across my bed, posting

bonfire pictures on social media. She rises off the pillow, leaning forward on her elbow. "What happened?"

The only thing I want now is silence, so I can slip back into my head and drag out all the happy moments from earlier to ease me into sleep. I kick my sandals off, unzip my shorts, and peel off my blouse, leaving them in a pile on the floor, and slip my old t-shirt over my head. "We'll talk tomorrow," I say, ignoring her gaping mouth, and turn off the lamp.

Daddy wakes me up at the butt-crack of dawn, chipper and smiling as if last night wasn't some huge Mama-drama-fiasco. Of course, she isn't standing right beside him either, so he's no longer being coerced into "suspicious Daddy" behavior.

You'd never guess from his weekend attire that for five of seven days Daddy wears a suit and tie and works in a corporate office. Weekends always mean seeing the true Daddy I know and love. Relaxed Daddy. Hang out and chill Daddy. Scruffy-faced, t-shirts-and-Adidas-track-pants Daddy. He gets me up early to go with him to change my tire and bring my car home, and I sneak out, leaving Jaycee still face-down sound asleep in her pillow.

Daddy and I grab a to-go coffee on the way and chat about nothing in particular. I ask him about work and business trips. He asks me about my upcoming school schedule and if I've considered colleges. He even braves the waters to chat about the bonfire, but only in general terms like *did you have a good time* and *what did you eat.*

He even asks if there was mudding because apparently that was a big thing during his teen years, too. He winks and talks about how he and Mama used to go all the time and how much she loved it. How the life had once danced in her eyes as they spun through the mud. How she screamed so loud when it'd splattered her shirt and face. Mama loved life before. Before what I don't know. Before me?

Daddy stops, gazes out the windshield, his mouth and eyes pinching together to create three little lines above his nose. Then he clams up.

My car's still on the roadside in a patch of tall grass. Daddy makes quick work of changing out my tire, and just before I slide into the driver seat, he hugs me, awkwardly holding out one black-stained hand so as not to smear dirt and grease all over.

"You did the right thing last night... calling us and letting us know what happened. And please tell the Howards when you see them that I appreciate what they did."

It's Daddy's way of smoothing the wrinkles from last night. I smile and squeeze him tighter around the waist. "Thanks, Daddy."

He pulls back and swallows hard, his Adam's apple bobbing up and down. "Don't thank me yet. When we get home, take your shower and get dressed for church. Last night when you were gone, your mama signed you up to sing a solo in service today."

"Awwwww, Daaaa-ddy," I whine, stringing it out like Christmas lights.

"Consider it a peace offering?" He grins in that please-just-do-this-for-me way.

I sigh and nod before sliding into my seat. As the engine roars to life I have an unsettling theory roaming my brain. This is Mama's ultimate lie detector test, like an exorcism where the possessed person can't say Jesus' name. If I'm hiding a guilty conscience from last night and then have the audacity to stand in the pulpit and sing today, surely my head will burst into flames or something, then she'd know the truth.

A couple hours later, my head un-burnt and still firmly on my shoulders, Jaycee and I sneak up to my room after Sunday lunch. I sit on the bed, legs crossed with a clipboard on my lap, a black pen, and a stack of about 20 college applications Mama gave me at lunch with a firm deadline of completion by week's end. Jaycee sits at my vanity, brushing her long blond hair into a bun, and when finished, arranges all of my lipsticks in a neat row across the marble top.

She slicks on a hot pink hue and angles her head a variety of ways to get the full effect. "That was some solo. Thought you might fly right off the stage and through the roof. Did that purge all your sins from last night?" Frowning, she blots her lips with a square of toilet paper.

"Shut up. You sound like Mama." I flip through the first application. The first five pages are general questions like name and address, technical questions about my GPA and extracurricular activities, forward-looking stuff on majors and minors, and the dreaded essay. One form gives a snapshot of your first eighteen years of life for a school to decide if you're worth their time.

But I'm not thinking about college. I'm thinking about Preston. What if he had a form like this to determine whether I'm dateable or not? Name, age, and address?—no problem there. Past experience?—negligible. Future prospects?—undecided. I'm hardly a prime candidate. I throw the clipboard and papers on the bedspread.

Jaycee looks back over her shoulder and smiles. "I've been waiting since last night. Exactly what kind of sinning *did* you do?"

I didn't have to ask her that question about Barrett. It'd taken nearly twenty minutes this morning with concealer and powder to cover the several reddish-purple blotches on her neck. I laugh and fill her in on our general conversation and kiss, remembering to tell her Preston noticed me because of the very prom date she'd nicknamed my "social suicide."

She sticks out her tongue, balloons her cheeks, and makes a fart sound. "Thad? You're telling me going out with Mr. National-Merit-Scholar-I'm-smarter-than-you-pocket-protecting-nerd landed Preston?" She turns back to the mirror and swipes black liquid eyeliner across the rim of her eyelid. "Unreal."

"Maybe some guys are interested in more than boobs and ass. Maybe they like a mind." *Yeah, because Preston always liked a mind before.*

"At least that's what they tell you until they get the boobs and ass," Jaycee laughs. "You're so naïve. It's cute."

"You always think—"

"Fine, let me guess. He took you off to be alone? He asked you dorky questions like your favorite color? Your sign? Did he kiss you hard then suddenly back up and ask if that was okay or if you liked it, then launched right back in and felt you up since you were just so agreeable by that point? At the end, did he make an actual date or just say something like 'I'll text you'?"

The heat bubbles up in my cheeks and floods down my neck.

"I—"

"That—," she points her finger at me in the mirror reflection, "Is game. All rehearsed, practiced, and polished game."

Her words drive the doubt back in, curling up like a snake in my head and poisoning all the positives from last night. Was Preston playing me? Why? Sure, everyone thinks it's pretty far-fetched he actually likes me, but why torment me? It's not like I've made myself a target. Still there's another voice of reason chiming in through the fogginess reminding me of Preston's gentleness, his eagerness to know more about me, the way he stepped in to save the day when the tire blew. A booty call wouldn't do that.

Jaycee's looking at me in the mirror as if I've grown two heads. "Quit. I can see all the little wheels turning in your head. I didn't say Preston doesn't like you. I said he has game. But he's dated—a lot—so you shouldn't be surprised." She flings my compact on the vanity and whirls sideways in the seat. "You're my bestie. I'm keeping it real since you're new at this. I can't have you screwing it all up." She sighs, smoothing away frizzies from her hairline. "We'll know more when he calls."

I grab my pillow and wrench it over my face. "If... if he calls," I mumble through the fluffy down. No sooner are the words out than my phone rings. I pull the pillow down across my nose and mouth, leaving my eyes free to follow Jaycee as she leans over and snatches the phone from the dresser.

She looks up with a smile. "I'll be damned. Speak of the devil."

"Give it here!" I squeal, dropping the pillow and wriggling my fingers.

She holds up one finger in wait mode. "Hello?" Her accent's suddenly thick and syrupy. "Hi Preston. Rayne's right here. Hold on a minute." She half-ass covers the mouthpiece so he can hear her. "Oh Ray-ayne. It's Pres-ston."

I scramble across the top of the covers and wrench my phone from her hand. "Hello?" I consciously try steadying my own voice when I hear his. It's him. It's really him. It's kinda unbelievable because I'd almost convinced myself last night was nowhere near what I had in my memory. *You can do this, Rayne.* I coach my brain to hunker down and come up with some good convo. Except I don't get a chance because he's inundating me with questions, one after the other, before I can even answer the first.

"Did you have fun last night?" he asks.

"Sure, I thought it was—" I start before he interrupts.

"Did you get your tire fixed?"

"Yeah, actually Daddy took me this—"

"Your parents—how did they react when you got home?"

"It was okay, I guess, I mean I figured—"

"You and Jaycee are hanging out again?"

What I really want to tell him is that between Mama and Jaycee, I have enough third-degree questioners in my life. I don't need another one.

"Yeah, she spent the night, and—"

"So what are y'all doing today?"

"Shut up!" I slam my balled-up fist wrist-deep into the pillow. My jaw drops and Jaycee cuts her eyes at me from across the room, mouth gaped open as well. It's radio silence on the other end.

Until I hear laughter. And if I'm not mistaken, it sounds like Gage. "She told you to shut up," he says in the background.

Me and my big mouth, always screwing up. "Preston? You there?"

"I'm here." His voice is sullen, deep, and drawn out like grandma's molasses. "My brother thinks it's hilarious you just told me to shut up. Really rethinking this speakerphone thing..."

"Sorry. I don't really want you to shut up. I just want to talk about now, not fifty questions about before." His tone mellows as he agrees and tells me about his day and plans for the upcoming week.

It's about five minutes later when he requests my permission to ask me one last question, not about last night but next weekend—a date next Saturday. In an actual restaurant where actual people will see us together, and afterwards a private swim at his house. I accept and by the time he hangs up, I know my little faux pas from earlier is already forgotten.

Jaycee pounces on the bed beside me and grabs my arm, shaking it. "A go-out-in-public date?" She crooks her eyebrow and nods her head in my direction. "Everyone will be talking. If that's not a 'back the hell up' to every girl around, I don't know what is. Props, girl."

She's right. Maybe my being seen with him will finally shut the town up, quiet all their doubts about me. There's just one little problem. I have to tell Mama the rumors are true. "What about Mama?" I whisper, my hands cupped on either side of my mouth as if my room's bugged. A low rumble interrupts us. I get up and flick my blinds apart with two fingers to see heavy purple-bottomed clouds building. "A storm's brewing," I say as another wave of thunder rattles the glass pane.

Summertime storms remind me of being a little girl when Daddy scooped me up in his arms and told me thunder was nothing more than the sound of potatoes rolling down a hill. It always made me smile though I secretly wondered just how big those potatoes would have to be to make a sound like that. And from the rumbles outside, there's about a thousand potatoes rolling right now.

Immediately, Mama's footsteps echo in the hallway. Mama hates thunderstorms. While Daddy sits on the back screened porch with coffee cup in hand, Mama paces the hardwood floors, opens up the hallway coat closet and insists I sit inside just in case, eyes wide and misty as she repeats the words I've heard her say a million times. "Hush! It's dangerous. You never know what could happen in a storm."

The door squeaks open, and she pokes her head around the edge. "What are you two chatting about?"

"Boys." Jaycee smiles wickedly as the words leave her tongue. Bitch. She throws me right under the bus.

"What boys?" Mama's eyes narrow.

"Not boys in general, Mrs. D. Really just one particular boy —Preston Howard." Dear Lord, does she ever shut up? "He finally called Rayne. I think he's a smitten kitten!" If my eyes were laser beams, Jaycee would burn hotter than a thousand Hells.

"He called you?" Her tone's more turbulent than the gusts outside.

"He asked me for a date on Saturday, Mama. Nothing big, just dinner out in town."

"I don't like this. I warned you about..." she starts, her chest rising harder, a faint wheezing mixing in with her words.

"Just a date, Mama," I interrupt, shaking my head. "Simple. Casual."

"I don't like it." Her eyebrows scrunch together as if she's trying to think of some punishment to keep me in next weekend. The thunder rolls again, and Mama jumps. "Get downstairs before the worst gets here."

"Looks more like rain than anything."

"Hush! It's dangerous. Never know what could happen in a storm." There it is—million-and-one times. We line up and follow Mama downstairs. Maybe Daddy still has some coffee in the pot

8

GAGE

hack!

The first victim of our medium-sized "bucket of balls" sails past the 150-yd marker. Preston stands back, hand-visor over his eyes as he watches it fall on the green. He nods, lips pinched together before he turns to me. "My driving game is on point. Just goes to show you, practice makes perfect."

Surely, he's not standing here on brothers' morning out, clipping and throwing out verbatim lines of parental rhetoric. "Oh, hello Mom and Dad. Didn't realize I came to the driving range with you. I thought I came with my brother. If you see him, please tell him I wanted to spend this morning with him. Not y'all. Sorry."

"Haha," Preston says, brandishing his club like a sword and jabbing it into my thigh. "This morning is all about fun, but it doesn't hurt to get a little practice time in, too."

Who the hell needs to practice the most boring sport known to man? The only thing I'm practicing is football—a real sport. The get-face-to-face-and-put-hands-on-them sport. "I don't need practice time. I hate golf. I don't play it." I rifle through the bag and pull out a 5-iron. "I come to the driving range to hang out with you. That's it."

He stalls, his lips wavering between a gentle smile and a downturned scowl like he's deciding whether to let it go and have fun or take up the righteous cause. "But anything worth doing is worth doing right."

Righteous cause it is.

"Keep talking like that and I'm gonna give you a colonoscopy with this 5-iron." I point the club in his direction, giving it a few quick upward thrusts. "Believe me. I'll do that one right."

He shakes his head, the same exasperated look I've seen from Mom one too many times. "You should really think about getting more into it, Gage. Dad says it's a great way to network and meet new people. The company is even co-hosting that spring tourney next year."

I grab a ball from the bucket and place it on the tee. "They aren't priming me for business networking and country clubs, Preston. That ain't me and it's never gonna be." I step to the side, line up the club with the ball, pull back, and then wallop the hell out of it. It sails through the air, becoming a tiny white speck against the blue sky and lands farther out than Preston's, though it's off to the side, where a few other balls are lying.

"If you'd straighten up your stance, you could take that power and aim it toward your target better." Preston steps up behind me, putting his hands on my hips as he presses behind me, attempting to physically manipulate my posture. It's all too romantic-movie-wannabe, so I jump forward out of his hold.

"Personal space, dude," I say, waving him back to his own tee. "I'll give you better aim, if you don't touch my butt again." I glance at him, waggling my eyebrows. "Save that for your date."

He laughs, lines up a shot, and sends his next ball floating in a perfectly straight arc out to the 200-yd marker. With him, it looks effortless.

Everything does.

"Speaking of date, where are you taking her?" I pull another ball from the bucket and align it on the tee, stepping up, squatting in my hips a little the way Preston said.

"The steakhouse. Then back home for a swim."

Whack!

My ball takes off on a fiery path until *Blam!* It connects with the metal cage around the golf cart that's picking up all the balls off the green. The driver turns in his seat with a glare.

Preston stands with club in hand, his mouth open.

"Improved my aim," I laugh. "And what the hell are you thinking—taking her to dinner there?" Obviously, he's the one who needs to improve his aim.

He frowns. "The steakhouse is the nicest place in town."

"That's the problem. In town. Don't you want to take her somewhere... else? Where you can hang out without everyone knowing you?"

"That doesn't bother me like it does you. Besides, it's only for dinner and then we'll be back at the pool."

"But have you prepared for this date?"

"It's a date. I've gone out on a hundred." That's not an exaggeration. It's probably more of an understatement. And while I don't have the experience, I do see something in Rayne that's been lacking with all Preston's previous girlfriends. I'm just not sure he totally gets it.

"Yeah, but Rayne's in AP classes, and she's got a little fire in that personality, too. She's gonna want to talk about actual stuff. Smart stuff." Preston stares at me, unfazed, so I drive the point home again. "And she can string two sentences together, which is more than I can say for your last girlfriend."

His lips crinkle on the edges as the laughter breaks free. "You're probably right about that one, but leave the details to me, little brother. I got this." He winks, grabs another ball, tosses it in the air and catches it in his palm. "Now let's finish up this bucket."

I glance at my watch. A little after 2 PM. Dad's out of town on business, Mom's at home, probably still reaming the maid for fading her blue blouse, and Preston's hogging up the bathroom and primping for his date. Across the street from the gas station, a worker at Cups and Cones, a kitschy little hole-in-the-wall ice cream parlor in a converted fast-food restaurant, is sliding plastic letters on the sign out front.

Saturday Special: 2-For-1 Scoop-tacular

Ninety-eight degrees in the middle of August. Home with the family or ice cream alone?

Ice cream. Definitely.

I pull across the road and park out back behind the dumpsters. Everyone else comes here to socialize. I come here to eat run-of-the-mill ice cream and sit incognito in the back booth that's hidden behind a stand of artificial ficus trees and some green viney-thing that creates a makeshift privacy curtain.

The guy at the counter in the rainbow striped shirt was in my chemistry class last year. His name escapes me. Ricky? Randy? Something with an R. All I really remember about him is that he was quiet and sat in the second row. As I walk up and order my two scoops of chocolate peanut butter, he takes the order, gives me my change and nods. I nod back—the standard greeting for those looking to avoid long-winded discussion.

The dining area is empty except for the few people in line behind me who're getting their cones to go. I slip into the booth and thumb through my phone, searching the best sites to order parts for my Scout. The door chimes over and over as people come and go, but when one chime is followed by a barrage of loud talking and giggling, I shift forward, peering through the leafy camouflage.

Rayne, Jaycee, and Ainsley stand at the counter with a junior—I think her name is Mallory—from their cheer squad, eyeing the selection of tubs in the freezer case. Non-fat, no-sugar-added vanilla frozen yogurt. Times three. Then Rayne steps up and orders a double scoop of rocky road with chocolate sprinkles.

Hell yeah.

The others stare at her as if she's an alien who's revealed herself to the human population, but she just shrugs and plows a spoonful in her mouth.

I told Preston this girl had some fire in her.

They sit down in the adjacent row, two booths up from me, and I slump further down against the hard plastic bench. No need to take a chance that anyone sees me. No sooner do they slide into their seats does Jaycee's shrill voice kick into its usual mile-a-minute jaunt.

She grabs Rayne's hand, holding it up in front of her nose. "Why'd you pick out that color?"

"Because I'm wearing a pink blouse tonight. This matches," Rayne says, slurping another bite off her spoon as she wrenches her hand from Jaycee.

Jaycee narrows her eyes, shaking her head. "It looks little-girlish. Preston should feel like he's dating a woman, not some high school kid."

"I am some high school kid."

"Obviously." Jaycee packages her smugness into a few side-eye glances at the other two girls across the table. A phone vibrates against the laminate top, but as Rayne reaches for it, Jaycee snatches it first and waves it around. "It's your mama."

Everyone giggles, except for Rayne, who frowns and drops her head. "Shit. I gotta take this. Be right back." She gets up and walks out the front door, the chime echoing behind her. In the plate-glass windows, she paces back and forth as she talks.

I'm staring at her when Mallory's voice catches my attention. "Are we living in an alternate universe? Since when does Preston Howard date Rayne?" She takes a bite, continuing through the lip smacks. "Y'all. I can't even. I mean, I heard the rumors. I saw them together at the bonfire. But I never thought it'd go this far."

"I know, right?" Ainsley pipes up, tossing her spoon into the empty cup in front of her. "When Trevor told me, I asked him like five times—Rayne Davidson? Are you for real?" She pauses to drag a napkin over her mouth. "She's a sweet girl. That's why we keep her around, but she's just socially... inept. Then you add her Mama into that equation, and..." She whistles the cuckoo sound.

Jaycee leans back in the booth, waving both hands out in front of her. "Don't even get me started on her mama." She shakes her head, clicking her tongue. "I pity her, really. Rayne's basic and doesn't see what an opportunity this is."

"What do you mean?" They ask almost in unison.

Jaycee rolls her eyes. "Come on. A girl doesn't date Preston Howard for intellectually-stimulating conversation. She dates him for that hot body and the fact his popularity can open doors for her."

"So you're saying she should totally use him?" Ainsley asks.

"Why not? I'm sure he plans on using her if he lives up to his reputation. She should get it while the getting's good." She giggles through the snide grin on her face. I want to slap her. How dare she talk about my brother that way? My calf muscles twitch, responding to my brain that's screaming for me to get up and confront her. But I force it down and keep listening.

Jaycee continues. "This whole thing is a positive for me as her best friend, because all that newfound popularity will trickle right on down to me."

Best friend. Yeah, right.

Ainsley gathers their trash and pitches it into the receptacle at the end of the row and walks back standing beside the table. "If dating Preston can open so many doors, Jaycee, then why didn't you go after him?"

Because he wouldn't want her. Preston might've dated dumb girls, but not bitchy ones.

"You can't go after Preston. You can put yourself out there, make sure he sees you, but he picks you." She looks down and bites her lip. "And for some reason he picked Rayne. Must be some sort of a moral cleanse. Least we can do is take advantage of it."

Mallory reaches over for a high-five. "Damn Jaycee, you have this all figured out."

"Yeah," inserts Ainsley, "but do you think it'll last?"

Jaycee glances out the window to where Rayne is still pacing back and forth, talking. "Unlikely. She'll find a way to screw it up. I give it two weeks max. Unless..."

"Unless what?"

She leans in close across the table. "We all ensure they have the best possible shot at making it work. Then we all benefit."

The door chimes as Rayne walks back in, and they clam up, reverting the conversation back to hair styles and fashion. She takes Mallory and Ainsley's place who slip out, saying they have errands to do. One can only hope they're in such a hurry because of guilty consciences eating their insides. But I'm not sure these girls have consciences.

Rayne drops her phone on the table and turns her cup up to her mouth, draining out the remnants of melted ice cream. Jaycee grimaces. "Your mama forget to strap that GPS tracker on you before we left?" When she doesn't respond, she continues. "About tonight..."

"Why do you care?"

Yes! Exactly! Thank you, Rayne, for asking the question of the day.

"Duh, you're my bestie." She pauses as if gauging Rayne's response. "And... this could be big. The Howards—they know people."

"So?" Rayne shrugs. "I know people."

"You know the cashiers at the Pig. I mean people. Big people. Influential people. With money."

"So?"

"So! They have connections that can open doors. College scholarships. Internships. You name it."

"I'm not dating Preston for his money. I'm going out with him because he's sweet and seems interested in really getting to know me." She stares off into space for a minute, and then refocuses on Jaycee. "Besides, Mama's had my college fund put together for years..."

"Do you have to be so selfish? I'm talking about for me!" Jaycee plunges her finger into her chest before continuing. "I don't have the two-parent household with a college fund. I have a single mom who's barely making ends meet." She blows out a loud breath and jumps up, slinging her purse on her arm. "Don't screw this up. After all these years of saving your ass from loser-dom, you owe me." She motions Rayne to get up and follow her then glances back over her shoulder. "Oh, don't look so hurt. You know I'm just kidding... kinda."

My stomach churns as they walk out the door and disappear around the corner. Those girls had laid my brother on that table like a juicy T-bone, ripping at every part of him. To them, he's nothing more than a hot body and a paycheck. And Rayne is just a device to get them in the door. They're supposed to be her best friends, but as soon as she's away, they're butchering her like some sacrificial lamb. Girls like Jaycee and her cronies —opportunists and connivers—affirm my decision to be single. Drama-free.

I should tell Barrett and Trevor all about the girls they're dating, but it's useless. They're so wrapped at this point, they'll refuse to see the truth. It'll just be a joke that poor, dateless Gage is a big ol' bunch of sour grapes. I hope they don't find out the hard way.

Rayne's genuine, though. A little too trusting, maybe—okay, completely naïve—but at least she's in this for the right reasons. Preston's a lucky guy.

9

RAYNE

The dog-day humidity kinks my curls into a frenzy. My Mama-approved knee-length black skirt is covered in pink fuzzies from my cotton blouse, and my stomach's knotted-up tight. I skulk behind the curtains in the upstairs rec-room, waiting for the first glimpse of Preston's Mustang in the driveway. He called earlier to tell me he'd be here at six, but I couldn't drum up the courage to warn him against Mama. No need scaring the crap out of him. Besides, if I time it just right, maybe I can intercept.

I step in front of the mirror to check my mascara and slick on another coat of lip gloss. The doorbell rings, and I dart back to the window. His Mustang's in the drive. He's not in it. Of course. I step away for two minutes and he shows up. Downstairs, the front door creaks open, and muffled voices float upstairs. I peek around the wall at the landing. Preston stands at the bottom of the stairs, Mama in front of him, looking him up and down, rubbing her fingers across her throat. Short and slightly pudgy, Mama only comes up to Preston's chest, but she's staring him down like a bulldog.

I barrel down the stairs and insert myself between the two

of them. Preston isn't black-eyed or bleeding, so maybe it's not as bad as I think. "Ready to go?" I grab his hand and usher him to the door, looking back over my shoulder at Mama. "I'll be home by curfew."

When we're safely in the car and down the road, I sink into the soft leather seat, the muscles across my back unwinding. "Sorry about Mama. She's... special."

"She's protective of her only daughter. She only asked about our plans."

"You didn't tell her..." I begin, my heart leaping into my throat.

He looks over and smiles. "I told her we'd be local. I didn't think she'd appreciate us going back to my house if my parents weren't home."

I blow out the breath I'm holding. Of course she'd try to confirm my story on the sly. Good thing Preston's smarter than that. My bikini's tucked safely in my oversized purse. I'd left that part of the plan out of the conversation with Mama. Mr. and Mrs. Howard are away for the night, and Mama'd have a coronary if she knew we went there without adult supervision.

Preston pulls into the parking space in front of the local steakhouse and all the people in the window seats crane their necks for a better view. A man walking a Doberman on a leash passes us on the sidewalk then looks back over his shoulder, crashing into a metal trashcan. It topples over with a bang, papers and crushed-up foam cups spilling out onto the concrete.

I sigh and thread my arms over my chest. Being on display when coming to Mama's rescue is bad enough, but being judged on my worthiness of Preston? Torture.

The hostess greets us with a smile directed only at him. "Table for two?"

"Against the wall toward the back?" I volunteer. She flicks her eyes at me and frowns, then turns to survey the room.

"All full, but I have a table right up here." It's more like a table in the very center of the room. She lays down our menus and trots back to the hostess station while I slide into my seat. Everyone turns in their chairs to see. Not sure I can get used to this. Preston reaches out to grab my hand across the table. I clench his fingers as their eyes bore harder.

"Ignore them," he leans forward and whispers.

The waitress makes goo-goo eyes at Preston while she scribbles down his order. She never glances in my direction, just says, "And you?"

"Steak, medium-well. Baked potato." *And a side of kiss my ass while you're at it.*

She nods and plucks the menu from my hand. Preston reclines in his chair and swigs his sweet tea. "Got your class schedule yet?"

"Yep. Three AP classes and Honors French fourth period. It's my only class with Jaycee."

"Gage's in that class, too."

"Really?" We've never had a class together before.

"Pres-dawg! What you been up to?" A gruff voice interrupts our conversation as a group of six guys and four girls flocks to our table. I recognize them from the football crowd that graduated the year before Preston. The girls—I can't remember their names—are the type that smile to your face but would just as soon step on you. I'd been around them before, but they'd never spoken to me. Not because there wasn't an opportunity to do so, but more because they were those kinds of girls—self-absorbed, unless it came to popping up their boobs and flipping their hair in front of Preston.

They stare at me briefly, eyes narrowed, before Preston starts talking and becomes their sole focus. I guess some things never change.

"Diesel! Tank! Guys! What are y'all doing here?" He shoots to his feet in a fist-bumping, bro-hugging flurry. Diesel and

Tank? And these giggly girls are Dopey, Sleepy, Snotty and Trampy? This date is turning into a major eye roll.

The boys' talk of football glory days hovers about two levels higher than the other hushed voices in the restaurant, but no one's pissed. No one even complains. They all stare, slight smiles on their lips, like we're a group of peacocks with our butt feathers stretched wide.

"Rayne?" I snap my eyes back to Preston, who's standing in front of me, his entourage curved around him, all eyes on me. "Say hello to my friends."

As he introduces them, a few of them pull their cell phones from their pockets and purses, giving them a quick tap-tap before smiling in my direction.

My phone buzzes against the tabletop, and I swipe my finger across the screen. New Facebook requests. Are these people for real?

It's that precise moment Elizabeth Anne, better known as Snotty, flips her long auburn hair over her shoulder, declaring her lips are impossibly chapped then plops her brown hobo bag on the table and goes fishing for her gloss. She plunges her fingers to the bottom, the leather sliding across the table and into my tea glass, which topples over. Golden brown rivers of tea rush off the table, flooding my lap, and the barrel-shaped ice nuggets pelt my thighs, running down my legs into my shoes. A shiver races down my spine.

I jump up, my chair sliding against the tiles with a screech, heat coloring my cheeks. Preston rushes around the table, fisting a wad of napkins, which he presses into my wet crotch as his entourage giggles behind him. The waitress walks out with a tray perched on her shoulder, eyeballs me, and quickly slides the tray onto our table. She yanks the white bar towel from her apron and joins the assault on my ruined skirt.

"It's fine!" I insist, pulling away and blocking their hands with mine. "Can we just get it to go?"

The waitress thumbs over her shoulder toward the kitchen. "I'll just go put this in some boxes and get your check."

Our empty take-out boxes lay on the dining-sized wrought-iron table by the Howard's Olympic-sized pool. My clothes decorate the backs of the other dining chairs, air drying in the waning slivers of daylight.

I lay back on one of eight teak loungers in my black bikini, modest by any stretch of the imagination with its high-waist bottoms and halter-style top, one arm draped across my stomach, knees arched upwards. *God I hate my body.*

The door to the pool house bangs closed as Preston struts out, the lines of his torso rigid and angled to perfection and the blue palm tree shorts slim-fitting just enough to show the bulge of his thigh muscles. My arm cinches tighter into my abs.

He stops beside the chair, tapping his toes on the blue-green mosaic fleur-de-lis accents lining the stone pool tiles. "I'm really sorry about—"

"Quit worrying. It's okay." I've repeated it a million times, but Preston won't stop apologizing. It wasn't him that doused me in tea. Although it was him that let all those people invade our date. Still, I'm letting it go.

"I know, but I'm sorry our dinner was ruined."

"It wasn't." I point to the pile of foam boxes. "It just got us back here quicker."

Before I can say another word, he leans in and presses his lips to mine, using his tongue to part them slightly. His hands rub up and down my arms then move to my back as he pulls me in closer, our skin glued together from lips to toes.

My heart and mind race. I can't enjoy the moment for wondering what I'm probably doing wrong. Clamping my eyes shut doesn't block out the thoughts, it just makes me hyperaware of every sound going on around us—a bird chirping, some cars out on Main Street, a kid yelling from a few houses over... the gate clinking shut.

The gate? Oh my God, the gate. Someone's here. Watching us. Mama. It has to be her. She's figured out my lie-by-omission and now she's here to drag my butt back home.

I slam backward, arms flailing, and accidently elbow Preston in the nose, propelling myself halfway out of the chair and onto the stone edging. I glance up. It's not Mama. It's Jaycee and Barrett, swimsuits and towels on, hands clamped over their mouths like they've just witnessed a train wreck, which they kinda did.

"What are y'all doing here?" I jump to my feet. Preston's still seated, his hand pinching his nose even though there's no blood.

"We came to hang out." Jaycee throws her bag on the folding chair, walks up to me, and whispers, "Don't screw this up. Looks like we got here just in time."

"Everything was fine until you showed up." Okay, so that isn't entirely truthful.

Preston, wriggling his nose up and down a few times, walks to Barrett and bro-hugs him. Jaycee whips off her towel, the oh-so-tiny triangles of her bikini barely covering what looks like two large cantaloupes on her chest. As if it wasn't already hard enough to keep Preston's attention on me.

Preston and Barrett take turns flipping off the diving board while Jaycee wades in from the tiled steps, her boobs bobbing along the top of the water like floaties. *This sucks.* I sit on the edge and dip my feet in the water, bathtub warm from the August heat.

"I'm hot," Jaycee complains. "Is there anything to drink?"

When Preston says there's water in the fridge, I offer to run in and get—might as well make myself useful for someone tonight.

I open the backdoor and peer into the short hallway, which looks a little too regal for a mudroom entrance. Preston said it's the second entrance on the right, a butter-yellow swinging door. Something about the Howard house makes me feel as if I'm walking in a museum, where running and speaking above a whisper is frowned upon. I push open the door, slip inside, and close it without a sound. It's dark, except for the glow from two pendant lights over the island and an open refrigerator door.

Behind the stainless-steel block, Gage bends over, rifling inside, only his butt and legs visible. The keys to his Scout hang on one of four hooks underneath the family's calendar on the wall to my immediate left. I grab them and tiptoe closer. On the opposite side of the fridge door I wait in silence, undetected. At least until he slams it closed.

When his eyes fix on me, he jumps backwards, narrowly missing the granite-topped island. "What the—" he says, running his hand through wet hair. As a matter of fact, he's wet all over. Not sopping, just dewy. He's wearing only black boxers and there's a towel slung over the barstool. He's shower-fresh and hotter than I remember from the bonfire.

I dangle the keys in front of me. "Went muddin' in your Scout. Third gear sticks a little."

The corner of his lip turns up. He lunges forward to grab the keys, but I pull them back just in time. "Like you could handle a stick," he says, stepping back to assess my position. He fakes left, goes right, wraps my arms tight to my sides and plucks the keys from my fingers. I give in quickly, not just because of the strength in his arms. His touch is different on my skin, like electricity's running through it. It zaps the breath from me. He feels it, too, because he leans back and rubs his fingertips together. "Sorry. Static electricity, I guess..."

"Yeah," I mutter. With his arm up, the dim lighting washes over his abs, and my eyes fixate on the black lettering that runs over the ripples of his obliques, straight down his side. "You have ink?" I'm unable to fight off the urge to run my fingers across the words. I stroke the top of them, smooth on his skin.

"My eighteenth birthday present to myself." He pulls his arm back so we can both admire the view.

"You're eighteen already?"

"For about three weeks now. My birthday's July 26." He looks up at me and smiles. "I know what you're thinking. How can Preston and I be so close in age?" He laughs and drops his arm down, smooshing my fingers, which linger on the tattoo, even closer to his skin. For a minute I contemplate leaving them there. But the shivers running up my spine excite me in places they shouldn't.

That and I probably shouldn't be touching Preston's brother. I curl my fingers into my palm and pull them away.

"Everyone asks. Let's just say my parents should be poster-children for the unfortunate side-effects of unprotected sex so soon after having a baby. Turns out people can end up with unwanted children."

"Don't say that. I'm sure you weren't unwanted."

"Yeah, sure," he scoffs. "So what're you doing in here? Shouldn't you be out there on your date?" He thumbs toward the backyard.

"Oh yeah... them."

"Them?" Gage walks over to the window overlooking the pool. "Barrett and Jaycee are here? Y'all couldn't handle your first date solo?"

"Apparently not."

He smirks and walks back to my side. "Date crashers. That sucks."

"Story of our night." He arches one eyebrow and pinches his lips. I wave my hand. "Long story. Don't ask." I open the fridge and bend down to grab four bottles, my butt sticking out behind me like his was earlier. "I'm supposed to get waters. Not that rump roast I saw when I first came in."

I look at him over my shoulder, his grin so big I can fully see both rows of teeth. "Funny thing," he says, "I was looking for some cherry pie, but it looks like Preston might've nabbed it first."

I snap upright, bobbling the water bottles, and lose grip on one, which falls to the floor and rolls by Gage's foot.

Still smiling, he picks up the runaway bottle and drops it onto the others in my hands. "Didn't mean to embarrass you…"

"You didn't. I… I just need to get these out there…" I rush to the swinging door and pop it open with my hip. "See ya later."

Outside, the three of them are in the shallow end, hitting a volleyball back and forth. "Waters," I say, plopping them down on the poolside table. I sit on the edge and dangle my legs over the side, unscrew my bottle cap, and take a swig.

Jaycee looks over with a scowl. "Took you long enough."

I shrug. She sure as hell wouldn't approve of my being in the kitchen chatting with Gage. "Sorry."

A light flicks on in an upstairs room where the window is cracked open. I can't see him, but I can hear him singing something to himself before the first bars of a song filter through. Oh no he didn't. Warrant's song "Cherry Pie" blares through the screen. I sing along in my head, my lips curling involuntarily into a smile. A heat explodes in my chest, springing to life like someone's struck a match against my ribcage.

Preston swims over to the side and grabs my legs. "Whatcha smilin' about?"

"Nothing." I shake my head, put down the water bottle and slide over the edge into the pool.

10

The overhead sun is scorching, too hot for what's supposed to be late summer. I peel off my black T-shirt, which absorbs the heat like a sponge, and tuck it under my arm as I walk out on the dock. Barrett's grandparents' pond is the perfect place to spend such a day, diving in and out of the cool water and laying on one of the long plastic floats soaking up the rays.

A flash of red catches my attention. Rayne sits on the farthest edge, kicking her feet in the water. Clouds of tiny droplets spray the air with each foot lift. Her brown hair hangs loose, barely past her shoulders and curlier than I remember, meeting the back of her red tank top, which is open lengthwise down the middle, laced together in a crisscross pattern with a black fabric strip. Peeks of skin, sun-kissed and coppery brown, show through.

She must be expecting Preston. I glance around, but he's nowhere to be seen, so I walk toward her and take a seat. She looks over and smiles, her lips a perfect match to her shirt.

"Hey, Gage. I've been waiting on you." Her voice is mellow, almost musical.

I narrow my eyes. "Waiting on me? Why?"

"Because, silly, I brought you something." She pulls a large picnic basket onto her lap and rifles inside until she locates a round pie tin. It's covered in foil. She sets the basket to the side and folds the top partway back. The crust is a golden brown, and when she digs the fork in, crimson fruit and filling pours out. She rakes on a large bite and extends it in my direction. "Cherry pie. I knew how much you wanted some."

Shouldn't she be waiting on Preston? Having a picnic with him? Still, my mouth waters at the sight of that pie. It looks so good, I can't resist, so I lean forward, mouth open.

One taste won't hurt.

The sweet cherries are almost on my tongue when the wooden board I'm sitting on unexpectedly gives way and cracks down the middle, the jarring movement sending me into the pond headfirst. I flail my arms against the water, bursting back through the surface.

My breath escapes me, my heart beating 90 miles a minute. The red digits of the alarm clock say 7:32 AM as I sit straight up in my bed, the covers tousled and half hanging off the side, my pillow on the carpet.

A small sliver of sunlight peeks through the six-inch gap of the open window, and I squint as my eyes adjust to the brightness while the memories of last night filter in. Preston and Rayne's first date. Our chance meeting in the kitchen. That cherry pie reference.

So that's where the crazy dream came from.

I fumble off the mattress and slip on the pair of gray basketball shorts and navy T-shirt that are slung over the desk chair. The hallway is empty, the entire house quiet. Preston's door is still shut. No doubt he's asleep after that late night they all had by the pool. When his Mustang pulled out a few minutes before 11, I'd mistakenly thought that'd be the end of it. But Jaycee and Barrett stayed, moving back and forth between the shallow end and the attached hot tub, and within ten minutes, were joined again by a solo Preston. That's where they all stayed until about 1 AM, when Mom and Dad came home and interrupted their private party. After that, it was finally quiet enough to fall asleep.

I trudge downstairs and look into the garage. Dad's car is gone. Usually one Sunday a month they get up early and head to the country club to have brunch with friends. Sometimes Mom enjoys a few spa services while Dad takes in a round of golf. And if that's where they are then...

I walk through the back hallway to the kitchen. It's dark. Abandoned.

Exactly what I thought. No breakfast.

My stomach growls in protest so I grab my wallet and head out the front door. The weekend farmers' market runs until noon, and lots of people talk about how much good food's available. Here's hoping they didn't exaggerate and that the quick half-mile walk will be worth it.

People crowd the pavilion, the monotonous hum of their voices creating an electrified static. Like bees buzzing in a hive. Occasionally, one of the old men gathered around the produce crates laughs out loud as a sort of punctuation mark to the whole back-and-forth. Vendors line the edges with coolers of free-range eggs and gallon jugs of fresh milk from the dairy. Bushel baskets of red tomatoes, strawberries, blueberries, and blackberries seamlessly merge with truck beds brimming with shucked ears of corn and green okra pods. On the outskirts of the crowd, food trucks serve a variety of hot foods and coffee.

For a minute I almost feel as if I'm part of something good. Decent. Wholesome.

Almost.

Mrs. Knight, loving grandmother of four by declaration and gossiping old biddy by reputation, hunches over a tub of fresh-cut flowers, chatting with the lady by the cash register. "Why Preston Howard decided to date her is a mystery to most of us. I mean, she's a sweet girl, bless her heart, but she ain't..."

The hairs bristle on my neck as I push through the crowd, heading for the briny sweetness of maple bacon floating in the air. I finally make it to the large chalkboard menu standing out front of the food truck when I see her.

Rayne sits on the decorative fountain's stone wall, cross-legged, eating a pile of biscuits and gravy. I walk over and take a seat beside her, ignoring the persistent protests gurgling from my belly.

"You might want to feed that." She smiles and points to my stomach. "He sounds angry."

"Very angry. Irate even." The smile drops from my face. "Okay, I'm starving. There was no breakfast at home."

She pouts and traces her finger down her cheek like a tear. "Aw, poor baby. These biscuits and gravy sure are good, though." She shoves another mouthful in, and then licks the fork up and down.

"You dirty, dirty tease."

Her shoulders collapse as she blows out a loud breath, pretending to send up the white flag. "I guess I can share." Without warning, she plunges a forkful of biscuits dripping with gravy in my mouth, and I have to slap my hand over my lips to keep it all in.

She forks another bite, this time putting it in her mouth, and smiles as she chews. The morning sun glints off the strawberry blonde highlights that mix with her brown hair, which is pulled up in a messy bun. Unlike last night, she doesn't have on a stitch of make-up and for the first time, the smattering of freckles across the bridge of her nose is visible.

This is a wild and wonderful girl. Most of the ones I've ever met would've licked the pavement before sharing a utensil with me, but then there's Rayne, completely unfazed, scarfing down her breakfast like she's perfectly comfortable sitting here with me.

I swallow and clear my throat. "So, what's the verdict on last night? Good first date?"

She nods and presses her lips together in a firm line, the response a little more lackluster than I anticipated. "Yeah. It was... fine." Most of Preston's first dates ended with the girl all high-pitched and giddy, fawning all over him and asking about "next time." But Rayne's staring at me as if there's a lemon lodged under her tongue saying the mother of all qualifying words. *Fine.*

Before I can ask, Mrs. McAlister interrupts us, sprinting toward Rayne, waving one hand in the air while clutching a plastic clamshell container of blueberries in the other.

"Rayne?" She screeches. "Bless your heart, hun, I saw you over here with..." She pauses a beat and stares at me with dead eyes. "Preston's brother... and I just had to tell you to tell your Mama to buy some of that stain cleaner in the purple bottle. It's on the top shelf at the Piggly Wiggly. It'll get that tea stain right outta the crotch of those—"

"Thanks. I'll tell her," Rayne says, her eyes expanding to three times their normal size as she flits them between me and Mrs. McAlister. Pink swirls appear in her cheeks and reach down her neck.

"Hey, isn't that Mrs. Knight over there at the vegetable truck?" I butt in, pointing to the 1950-something black Ford that's backed in on the pavilion's far edge. "There's a good deal on zucchini today—four for a dollar—and I heard her saying earlier she was going to buy him out."

She whirls around, grinding her fists into her hip bones, then blows out a loud breath to match her foot tapping. "That greedy hussy thinks the world revolves around her. She's not gonna get all my zucchini." With a quick glance over her shoulder to remind Rayne about the stain treatment, she stomps off in a quest for reasonably-priced veggies.

"So..." I nudge Rayne's knee with mine. "Fine, huh?"

"It's a long story."

"I have the time, if you have the biscuits."

Five minutes later, she's re-enacted the entire tea-in-the-lap incident, demonstrating with frenzied hand gestures how everyone basically assaulted her crotch in an attempt to get it all cleaned up. In her words, a freaking fiasco.

By the time she finishes the story, every biscuit crumb has vanished and my sides ache from doubling over in laughter.

The entire time, I keep thinking how damn lucky my brother is.

11

RAYNE

$\mathcal{F}$eet to the pavement—my sweet escape. I plug my iPod into my ears, crank the music, and stare ahead of me, physically putting distance between myself and everyone else. It's great for perspective. And after two weeks of classes, a quick Sunday afternoon run might do some good.

It's not that classes are hard. They're so-so, about what I expected, though it's different not having Jaycee with me most of the day. She's my safety net, my conversation starter, my social conduit. Without her, the M.O. has become slinking in my desk and burying my nose in a book until the teacher starts. Funny thing—most of the kids in my classes are now my virtual friends even if they walk by me without a word in public. Only when Preston's around am I suddenly a hot commodity.

I live for fourth period French. Jaycee's beside me, Gage's behind me, and for one sixty-minute segment, all is right in my high school world. Not that it's particularly drama-free, especially with Jaycee's vow to hate Gage eternally and his smart-ass responses to just about everything she says. I pretend it's all a joke, but I think they really do hate each other.

If Jaycee's my best friend, Gage has become next in

command, not only because of our French class but because nearly every date with Preston has somehow made our paths cross. Our personalities are similar, more than mine and Preston's, and our friendly relationship has evolved around healthy competition. He's one-upping me or I'm taking him down—and neither of us likes to lose. He's easy on the eyes, too, but I'd never tell Preston that. No guy in the world wants to hear his girlfriend say his brother's hot.

By the time I round the corner onto Main Street, the sun is low in the sky and the September air swirls with a definite chill. I tuck my fingers under the sleeve hem to warm them. Up ahead on the opposite side of the road is the Howard house. I never run on the sidewalk right in front of their place because hello? Stalker. Preston's hardly there anyway.

Our first couple weeks of dating were awesome, seeing each other most every night even for ten minutes, but since his classes started, his schedule's sketchy. Study groups and the internship take up a lot of time—time he'd been spending with me before. At least he calls and texts religiously. It just sucks I sometimes feel like I don't know him as well as I should. Like we're stuck in some sort of time warp where everything's paused, and when we do get a moment, someone's always crashing it.

The corner gas station is my turnaround point where the sidewalk runs out. I jog in place, finger to my jugular to check the thump-thump-thump beneath it, then head back up the hill toward town. Usually I'm in a zone, but today something's different. My peripheral vision homes in on something or someone paralleling me on the opposite side of the street.

Gage runs alongside. He waves and smiles, then explodes forward, arms chopping through the air. I speed up and pass him, my knees aching with each stride, then smile back over my shoulder with a thumbs-up. In two-seconds flat, he's in my sights, pulling ahead once again with a "what's up" head bob.

Like moths to the flame.

The see-saw of first place bragging rights continues all the way into town. I pass him again, and this time, he fades from sight. My lungs rage like volcanoes, burning with the chilled air I'm sucking in as I jog to a stop. But when I turn around, hands in the air, Gage is sprawled out on the sidewalk, flat on his back, not moving.

"Gage!" I dart across the four-lane road, nearly getting smashed by a Jeep whose driver honks at me. I kneel down, hovering over him. His eyes are open and fixed on mine, chest moving up and down, arms and legs stretched out in four different directions. My hands wash over him, searching for blood or bumps, and somewhere beneath the worry, that swoony-crackly feeling pulses under my skin, and images of his tattoo flood my brain, the black block lettering smooth to the touch. The way it rolled across the rippled muscles. I shake my head. *Stop and focus. He could be dying.* "What happened? Did you trip on something?"

He blinks rapidly and bites his lower lip. "My pride? I think it's back there somewhere," he laughs and points behind him.

"In that case, I won't point out that I won... beat you. Killed it. Owned it..."

"Okay, I get the picture," he interrupts. I help him to his feet and we sit together on the grassy bank bordering the cement. "Just wait 'til next time..."

"Bring it." I square off with him, eye-to-eye, nose-to-nose.

"You and your competitive streak..."

"You have no room to talk, mister." I wag my finger in his face.

"I'm a dude. We're supposed to be testosterone-y. You're a chick. You're supposed to be catty and whiny, not hardcore."

"Do you not remember the cow patty incident?"

"Who the hell could forget you with your foot in crap?" he snorts.

"Shut up. What I meant is I'm not catty and whiny. You'll have to see Jaycee for that."

"Hell yeah." His face winds into a nasty grimace. "That's one friendship I don't understand."

"Hush. We've been friends since she moved here in first grade. Some kid stole my paste, and when I cried, she blacked his eye."

"So your friendship is based on violence?" Gage arches his right eyebrow with a grin.

"No," I shake my head, leaning in to shoulder nudge him. "Jaycee and I are total opposites, but it works. She forced me into cheerleading, I make her take French class. She's up on the latest fashions, I'm up on the latest books."

"You're honest. She's a backstabbing opportunist..."

I roll my eyes. "I keep her grounded. She looks out for me."

"You got me now." He plunges his finger to his chest. "I'll protect you." Something about the glint in his eyes lets me know he means it. We sit so close, arms mashed together, that our long-sleeve cotton shirts suddenly feel invisible, like the tender skin of my arm and the hard ripples of his burn together, melting, smoldering.

Just then, my phone buzzes against my leg. I pull it from my pocket and swipe my finger across the screen.

<Jaycee> *What's going on with you and Gage?*

Before I finish reading, her second text comes through.

<Jaycee> *I'm at coffeehouse. 2 kids in front of me talking about you and Gage laying on the sidewalk together? IDK what the hell you're doing but STOP.*

I lock the phone, slide it back in my pocket then bury my face in my hands. "Dear Lord..."

Gage tugs my hands down. "Let me guess. Someone in town saw us talking, and now everyone thinks something's up?"

I drop my jaw in feigned surprise. "Wow. It's like freakin' ESP with you."

"Also known as 'growing up here.'" He grins and shakes his head, but when he turns to me, his eyes are hard, his lips flat-lined. "Why the hell do you care so much what this town thinks? Don't you ever just wanna break the rules?"

"Like you?" I point to the tattoo hidden by his t-shirt.

He smirks and looks down at his feet. "Good in theory, right?"

"Yeah. Until you have to live with the consequences." He looks up and we stare at each other for the longest minute. I'm not sure what we're sidestepping in this conversation, but my insides feel like a rubber band stretched to the limit.

"Aren't some consequences worth it?" His words are barely audible over the traffic.

"Maybe?" I offer.

Gage stands up and extends his hand. I take it, and he pulls me to my feet. "Don't worry. When the news gets to Preston, I'll tell him how gracious his girlfriend was in scraping my ass off the pavement." He smiles. "Need any help getting home?"

I do a 360-degree glance, half-expecting Jaycee or someone else to spring from the bushes and take our picture. "Better not push the town's limits. See you at school." I plug in my earbuds and take off toward home. I don't look back because I know he's watching me—and so is everyone else.

12

GAGE

She runs down the sidewalk and disappears around the corner. Not once does she look back to see if I'm still here, and my stomach drops a little. I kinda wanted her to, even though I shouldn't.

This girl has been in my classes for years, quiet and content to skip the limelight, and now I'm kicking my own ass for dismissing her without a second thought. It's not that I did or didn't think she was pretty. I just put all my focus into football. Why worry with impressing girls? The girls don't flock to me, never talk about me in the hallways or whisper when I walk in class. No one breaks down my door for a date.

If anyone in our school has bypassed these years with more stealth than Rayne, it might just be me. But then again, with Preston as a big brother, I'm easy to overlook.

I sigh and brush the dirt off my shorts. My shoelace puddles out onto the sidewalk, and as I bend over to tie it back, someone walks up behind me, shoving me hard. I stagger forward, regain my balance and turn around. Jaycee stands there, crossed arms and blazing eyes, her lips so pinched they nearly disappear into her face.

"What's your problem?"

"I could ask you the same thing."

"I'm not the random idiot pushing people on sidewalks." The words echo off the buildings and a few people on the other side of the road look in our direction.

Jaycee steps closer, her voice a low hiss. "And I'm not the dumb jock lying around on sidewalks in public with my brother's girlfriend."

I roll my eyes. Cue the small-town gossip queen herself. "I tripped. She helped me. Not that I owe you or anyone else in this town an explanation."

"I don't know what kind of underhanded shit you're trying to pull, but—" She plunges her finger in my face before I swipe it away.

"Underhanded shit? You want to talk to me about being underhanded?"

"I'm interested in one thing," she growls. "Making sure Rayne doesn't screw up with Preston. He's good for her. They could really make it."

That's laughable, considering it was only a few weeks ago Jaycee and her gang were criticizing Preston's choice, taking bets on how long it'd be before their "bestie" Rayne screwed things up royally. "Really? Cause I thought you only gave it two weeks max?"

Her face goes blank, and she steps back, mouth open. "What are you talking about?"

"Maybe you should check the other booths at Cups and Cones before you talk shit about people."

She clenches her fists and slams them into her thighs. "If you really care about Rayne at all, you'd see that dating Preston is the best thing for her. He can open up doors for her social life."

So that's it. Rayne's just a pawn in Jaycee's self-serving plan. "Is it really Rayne you're concerned about, Jaycee, or is it yourself? After all—how did you put it—you don't have a clue why he'd want her basic self, but you were damn sure gonna capitalize on it?"

She screams and stomps her foot on the concrete, scaring away a few birds from the nearby bushes. "You stalker asshole! How dare you—"

"Stalker? I was in Cups and Cones before y'all even came in, and I'm not the one sending wacked-out texts threatening my friends not to talk to someone." I turn my back, shaking my head, before glancing back at her over my shoulder. "You need help. Maybe if Rayne really knew what you were like, she'd—"

"Don't you threaten me, Gage Howard!" Jaycee runs around in front of me, pushing herself way too far into my personal space. I step back to inject some air between us as she wags her finger in my face. "You're the one who's gonna need help when this goes public!"

"When what goes public? I talked to my brother's girlfriend? That happens a lot, you know... since she's dating my brother!"

"You know what I mean." Her eyes narrow to slits.

"Don't think I do." I shrug, the simple gesture appearing to conjure up the devil in Jaycee. Her eyes turn to fire.

"You've been warned. Stay away from Rayne."

"No, I won't, Jaycee. I'm Rayne's friend, which is more than I can say for you. So take your drama and this town's gossip and shove it." I side-step her and jog down the sidewalk toward my house, imagining the air waves around me brimming with a gazillion texts and calls.

Idiots. All of them.

I kick off my shoes in the mud room, not taking the time to pick them up and put them away in Mom's specially-marked storage basket. When she comes in and sees them, fireworks will probably explode in the house, but that's the least of my worries.

With the way this town talks, it'll be better for me to go ahead and inform Preston of this afternoon's events before he hears it from other people and gets the wrong idea. Not that there'd be any reason to believe their speculations. I mean, she's dating Preston. So what if my hands get clammy, my mouth goes dry, and these electric shocks run down my arm each time she touches me? No one knows that but me, and no one's going to. And in the scheme of things, none of it matters, because she already has Preston. My liking her or not is a moot point, and I'm man enough to realize that.

But getting to know her—having her around—is something I don't want to lose, and if things go South between Preston and Rayne, where would that leave us? Would there have to be side-taking and ignoring the other one? That's the way these things have always gone before.

Preston's sitting at his desk, slumped over the top, pencil squeaking along the paper. When I knock on the door, he leans back and smiles. "What's up?"

I swallow hard. "Thought I'd tell you that I ran into Rayne and—"

"Y'all were lying on the sidewalk?" He laughs and tosses his pencil onto the desk. "Yeah, I already know."

I deadpan. Gossip at light speed—Know the latest in ten minutes or less—that should be town's new slogan. "How'd you know already?" Preston picks up his cell phone and shakes it around as I continue. "The town's getting it all wrong. I tripped. She happened to be there to help—"

Preston waves off my explanations. "Gage, relax. Ignore it. One of the charms of living in a small town."

Charms? For the golden child, maybe, where everyone's gossip is either about how great you are or is some vigilante-filled search for justice on your behalf. For us common people, it's anything but charming. It's a curse.

"Rayne's concerned about people talking. Last I saw her, she was on her way home. Maybe you should go over there and make sure she's okay."

He scrunches his lips and shakes his head, looking back at his papers. "Can't. Too busy. Gotta finish this project."

"Too busy for your girlfriend?" The words slip out before I can stop them, the tone filling in the gaps of what I'm not saying out loud.

Preston blows out a breath, picks up his pencil and begins tapping it on the wooden top. "Look, I'm not in high school anymore. This stuff is important. It has to be my priority."

His lips are moving but Mom's voice is coming out. Like she's some evil ventriloquist, and he's her puppet. "Hello, Mom. Thought I was talking to Preston." I grimace. "Dude, her hand's so far up your butt, you don't even know she's there anymore."

He side-eyes me and flips me off. "I'm not a puppet. I'm working toward my future here. In a few years, I'll be out of school completely, and Mom's already said there'll be a management position waiting on me."

"Terrific, but what about Rayne?"

He shrugs. "What about her? She understands. I love spending time with her, but right now it's hard with Mom, Dad, and school on my back. Things will eventually calm down."

"And you're so sure she'll be waiting on you? Rayne's not like the other girls you've dated."

"My point exactly. She's not clingy and needy. She gets it." He walks over and pats my shoulder. Diplomatic and dismissive all at once. He's truly our parents' son. "Thanks Gage, but Rayne and I are fine."

13

———

RAYNE

The Howard's double front doors are impeccable, painted black with elegant gold-metal script that spells out their address. *One hundred forty-three.* It's more regal than the big block numbers we have on ours. Each door has its own square boxwood wreath, the right one adorned with a red painted "H," and the doorbell with its own curly frame. I'll bet it plays a cutesy song.

"Ready?" Preston squeezes my hand and swallows hard. If it's possible, he's more nervous than I am. Meeting his parents is as close to royalty as I'll ever get, but, then again, I live with Mama. If I can handle her, I can handle anything.

We walk through the doors and Preston yells, "Mom. Dad. We're here." The foyer is open with a view of the large staircase that separates the living room from the dining room on either side. The walls are painted a soft vanilla with large oil paintings on canvas, vases with dried flowers, expensive looking knick-knacks, and leather-bound books set just-so on built-in shelves.

Everything in its rightful place—except me, conspicuous as a two-dollar-hooker in the front pew of church.

Almost immediately, the thump-thump of someone

approaching echoes in the space, and Gage joins us, his spiked-up hair, jeans, and boots an obvious snub to the formal dining requirement.

"Hey Rayne, nice cardigan." He fingers the embroidered hem. "Been running lately?"

"Every day. You're never gonna beat me."

He grins. "We'll see."

When we hear two more sets of footsteps heading our way, one much harder and click-clacky than the other, both boys straighten up, replacing slumped shoulders with tall, strong ones, hands down at their sides. *What is this, boot camp?* Instead of questioning, I push back my own shoulders and smooth out any tiny wrinkles on my sundress.

Charlotte enters first, followed by Jackson. Seeing them in person and mentally comparing them to my parents leaves me awkwardly conscious of the fact my pedigree may not be up to snuff.

"Hello, Rayne. Welcome to our home." Charlotte fingers a peaches-and-cream cameo choker—probably an antique. An expensive one passed down through the generations no doubt. It perfectly matches her cream-colored silk blouse and peachy linen trousers, tailored to hug the curves of her body. Her blond hair is pulled into a loose bun.

Next to my mama, a tad frumpy from the years in her "mom suit" of jeans and long-sleeve t-shirts, Charlotte embodies the royalty thing to a T, and she wears it well, her backbone stiff and straight, shoulders pushed back, neck elongated. Her picture-perfect posture, straight from Southern charm school, adds a good inch to her stature, making her near eye-level with Preston.

Jackson leans around her and shakes my hand. He shares Gage's thick eyebrows and hair but with a sprinkle of salt-and-pepper at the temples. His white oxford, chocolate brown sweater vest, and khaki dress slacks with military-precision creases skim his thick frame, well-toned, though the beginnings of middle-age spread squeeze out just over his belt.

"Rayne, you're as pretty as Preston said." Jackson's voice pours over me like warm caramel, his drawl slow but more nasal than mine, reminiscent of the Lowcountry.

I thank him as Charlotte waves us into the dining room and taps her nails on the back of a Queen Anne dining chair. "Rayne, you'll sit here." Preston slides the chair underneath me as I smooth my dress and sink onto the beige microfiber. Charlotte rings a small porcelain bell, the tinkle-tinkle beckoning the maid with a tray of garden salads. The silence roars in my ears, cut only by the faint slurping of Jackson's lips pulling in maroon sips of his Cabernet from his position at the head of the table. I'm beside Preston, across from Gage and catty-cornered from Charlotte, who eyes me sideways, never fully turning her head in my direction.

I fumble with the fifty-million forks lying beside my plate, pick one up and just as I'm ready to spear a lettuce leaf, Charlotte finally looks at me. "Wrong fork, dear. It's this one." She holds up a three-pronged silver piece.

I nod and switch forks. "Thank you, ma'am." Called down over a silverware violation within the first five minutes? I glance up at Gage, grinning ear-to-ear and rolling his eyes in circles, and have to bite my lip to keep from laughing. Other than small talk about how I'm enjoying school, the salad course passes with little problem, and the main course of roast beef, potatoes, and green beans is brought in.

We eat for another five minutes before it becomes apparent Charlotte's waited on the "meat and potatoes" of the conversation as well.

"Preston, have you told Rayne you're not only taking college courses but also shadowing your father at the company?"

"I've mentioned it," he says, continuing to chew slowly without looking up.

"That's an honor," I say, nodding at her.

Charlotte narrows her eyes. "It's his birthright. Preston's been groomed to take over the business since his youth, and now he's finally coming of age. It's imperative he maintain focus on the goal and not be sidetracked by trivial dalliances." Maybe she could use big words around his previous girlfriends, and they'd be none the wiser. Not me. I understand what she's saying—our romance is insignificant, a distraction more than anything. Charlotte didn't want to meet and welcome me to her family. She wants to enforce the boundaries.

She continues as if she hasn't just insulted me to the nth degree. "Speaking of which, Preston, I hear Ashlyn's doing very well at USC. She plans to join the firm after graduation, though she hasn't decided which location just yet. I suspect that will depend on you."

When he doesn't respond, she turns her eyes on me. "Has he told you about Ashlyn? Her father is a dear business associate of Jackson's. She and Preston are just the same age. Her mother and I have always said our children were destined to be together. It'd happen to... if Preston would quit being resistant."

She cuts through her beef and forks a miniscule piece in her mouth, chewing it delicately and slowly before swallowing it down. I'm hoping she swallows her tongue along with it. Preston's face is red, and he looks only at the halved red potatoes he's pushing around with his fork. Gage's mouth is gaped open as he whips his head back and forth between Preston and his mom, probably looking for some sort of reaction. But Preston's not giving one.

Crawling under the table sounds like a plan at this point. Maybe if I can get under there, the tablecloth will block me until I can crawl right out the front door, back home, and beneath my covers where I can pretend none of this ever happened. I lay my fork across my plate and sip tea from my goblet. My churning stomach can't handle any more.

Until someone comes to my rescue. "Maybe Preston's not interested in Ashlyn because she's a bitch? Maybe he wants a girl he can actually talk to, like Rayne?" Gage says. I flick my eyes up at him. He's staring at Charlotte with so much venom I don't see how she doesn't drop dead in her seat.

"Maybe Preston needs to understand that good breeding and family—"

"Maybe everyone should shut up and let my oldest son live his own life. He's a man capable of making decisions. Good ones. Forcing him into some old-South arranged relationship is out of the question. You and I both know those never work, my dear. Preston's quite capable of deciding who is and who is not a match for him. End of discussion." Jackson tosses his fork down on the plate, and it clangs against the china. He pushes away his chair and stands up. "I'll have dessert in my study."

As he walks away, Charlotte's face turns fifteen shades of red and she flounces back in her chair, refusing to eat another bite of dinner. Preston still hasn't said a word, Gage is smiling like the Cheshire Cat, and I'm doing my best not to lose my temper or my tears. So this is how the rich do dinner? And I thought the dramatics were all made-for-TV. Turns out life does imitate art.

We suffer through the dessert course—angel food cake with strawberries and whipped cream—with little to no conversation. Charlotte looks at her plate. Preston looks at his. And every time I look up, Gage is staring at me from across the table. He winks and smiles, and I force a grin in return. I use my fork to swirl cream around the plate but never actually put anything in my mouth because I'm too busy silently praying this nightmare will end.

When Mrs. Howard rings the bell for the dessert course to be removed from the table and dismisses us, she's careful not to let us sneak away before one last warning. "Not too late, Preston. You have an exam this week. That takes priority."

"Yes ma'am. We're going to watch a movie, and then I'll drive Rayne home."

"Good," says Charlotte simply as Gage rolls his eyes and stomps around us, up the stairs and out of sight. "It's been a pleasure, Rayne," she continues, though something tells me it's been anything but. She looks at me as if I'm trash, some project her son brought home instead of an actual person.

Charlotte Howard could certainly be the poster child for such arrogance, and what concerns me most is I see a little of that reflecting back in Preston. Not to the same degree, of course, and with none of the callousness, but he does have that air of importance. At least it's tempered by Mr. Howard's cool, laid-back genes, which Gage has inherited, though both demonstrate a short fuse when dealing with Charlotte.

My nana used to say "appearances are deceiving"—the Howard family mantra, no doubt. The front porch painted a picture of the Howards that the dinner table threw right out the window.

Preston grabs my hand and tugs me toward the stairs. "Let's go."

I nod at Charlotte as Jackson pops out from the study. She nods back with a curt smile, but Jackson walks over and pats my shoulder. "Pleasure meeting you, Rayne. Preston's found himself a fine girl." At least one of them isn't a flaming asshole hell-bent on getting rid of me.

"Thank you, sir," I say as Preston pulls me to the stairs.

The media room is all dark wood with a large projection screen at the far end and two rows of black leather reclining sofas. I sit in the middle of the first one. Preston grabs the remote and slides beside me, pulling a blanket over our legs. Here together, close, comfortable and away from the microscope, I snuggle in, hoping to recapture some momentum, but twenty minutes into the movie, the intercom interrupts.

"Preston..." It's Charlotte. *Of course.* She's a monkey wrench with stilettos and big hair. "You have visitors from your western civ class. Something about the term paper you're working on. Please come down and discuss with them." Before he can respond, she's gone. And then, so is he. And I'm alone watching a movie in the Howard house, in their media room, which is the size of our den, kitchen and dining room combined.

I pause the movie and venture into the hallway. The perfect paint, the perfect furniture, and the perfectly-aligned photo frames of perfect family pictures paint an image I've discovered is pretty fractured below the surface. It's all fake-outs and lies, and now something about this whole thing is beginning to feel off—like my feelings for Preston. I like him. Who wouldn't? But he's not giving me butterflies. He's not getting in my thoughts and messing them all up, and I can't lie. That's what I want.

Down the hall on the left, rock music spills out of a partially open door. And not just any rock. 80's hair band rock, which is my favorite. It's what Daddy listens to in his car since Mama doesn't allow it in the house. It's what I cut my teeth on. I creep toward the music, cowering against the wall as if at any moment, Charlotte will spring out from another door and accuse me of prowling around her house... which I kinda am.

I lean on the door jamb and peek in. Gage stands in front of his dresser mirror, counting off reps of bicep curls. His clothes from earlier are tossed on the bed, and he's wearing only navy athletic shorts that sit low on his hips, just enough to expose a good inch of his boxers' waistband. The sweat glistens on his chest, and my heart speeds up at the sight. He switches arms and turns his body slightly in the mirror to where his tattoo is visible in the reflection. I want to touch it. Touch him. I shouldn't be thinking this. I should be concentrating on Preston, but once again, here I am, all torn up by looking at

Gage, being near him. *Turn and leave, Rayne. Go back to the media room and wait on—*

"You coming in or you gonna stand out there all night?"

Shit. Shit. Double Shit. The door swings open, and Gage leans against it, still breathing hard from his workout. He's smiling like let's-see-you-get-yourself-out-of-this-one. Except I have no words. At least nothing I can say aloud. Nada. "Uh... how, uh... did you... see...?"

"Mirrors are good like that." His grin widens as he nods back toward where he'd been standing. *Smartass.*

"Who'd have thought you'd see me when you're so busy looking at yourself?" I shrug then reach out to stroke his bicep. Icicles. My veins just turned to icicles.

He laughs and stands back, waving me in. "I was looking at lots of things, I'll have you know. My form. My room. You spying on me."

I walk in, edging past him through the sweetly pungent aroma of boy sweat. "Not spying. Observing."

"Observing? Like a science experiment?" He folds his arms in front of him and cocks his head to the side.

"Exactly. For research purposes. The standoffish jock in his natural habitat." I sweep my hand around. "Cool music by the way. Cool room, too."

It is cool. Very industrial and gritty. Like him. The bed and desk are both galvanized metal-framed and the dresser and desk shelves both use the same distressed dark wood. There's a metal wall lamp hanging over the head of the bed, and I can't help imagining Gage sitting against the headboard and pillows late at night, studying under its light. A massive weight bench sits in the corner, a rack of dumbbells beside it, and on his walls are a collection of Guns N' Roses posters and Clemson football memorabilia.

"Wait." He grabs my shoulder. "Standoffish? Me?"

I pull away and bend down to get a closer look at a row of

football trophies on his shelf. "Aren't you? That elusive guy no one really knows?"

He snorts, walks over and sits down on the side of his bed. "Nah, nothing elusive about me. I'm pretty face-value. Just selective on who I let in."

He pats the spot beside him and I walk over to take it. "But you let me in."

His smile grows with my words. "I know." The hairs prickle on my arms as if someone's blowing down my neck, covering my entire body, which is suddenly on high alert—until he douses it with cold water. "So... where's Preston?"

"Downstairs with some college friends who dropped by. Something about a term paper."

"And he left you alone?" He angles his head toward me and narrows his eyes as if I'm telling him some colossal riddle.

"Well yeah, but this is important... for school." It's sad how quickly I make excuses for Preston based on my own irrelevance. Like that's actually an okay thing.

"You do realize you sound just like mom?" Gage exhales loudly and shakes his head. "Don't give anyone permission to treat you less-than, Rayne."

"No one's treated me less-than." Lie. Everyone's treated me *less-than* my whole life. Except Gage.

"Please. Don't tell me you're okay with Mom's snarky comments. Don't pretend with me. She drove over you then backed up and hit you again. I'd tell you she regrets it now, but she doesn't. And she won't. Preston's her pride and joy."

"Does she treat other girls like this?" Surely the attitude can't all be about me.

"No. Preston's dating you threw them for a loop. They never saw it coming."

The words sting. Another snub by this town and the Howards. "Yeah? Well, they can join the entire town in speculating why Preston's lost his freakin' mind by being with me."

"Why do you do that?" Gage's mouth drops open as he shakes his head. "Assume you're not good enough? What I meant is you're different. Preston dates dumb girls. You're not."

"Thanks," I mumble. What's wrong with me? I can handle insults in stride but not a compliment?

He grabs my hand, and instead of pulling away, I grasp his just as tight. "Don't listen to mom. She doesn't sweat the dumb ones, but you scare her. She can't control you, so she's lashing out. With you," he lifts up his arm and points to his tattoo, "no rules apply."

Oh my God, I need to touch it. Touch him. My fingers twitch at the thought so I stand up and wrap my arms around Gage, hugging him to my chest. "Thanks for the pep talk."

He whispers, "Anytime. I mean it."

I squeeze him hard once more then let go and walk towards the door. "I'm gonna use the restroom then go back and wait some more." I slip out of his room and into the one across the hall. I shut the door and lean against the counter, my heart thumping in my chest, head spinning from the conversation. I splash my face with water, cold like icy thorns, in a ploy to knock some sense into myself because all I want to do is run across the hall, wrap my arms around Gage and kiss him, which makes no sense at all. Especially when Preston's right downstairs.

There's a muffled knocking in the hallway. Gage's door squeaks open, and I press my ear to the door, eavesdropping on the conversation.

"Where's Rayne?" asks Preston.

"Bathroom." Gage's voice is flat, heavy.

"Okay. She wasn't in the media room when I came back."

"Probably because you were gone for like, 20 minutes and left her by herself. I'm surprised she's still here. I would've left your ass." Gage's definitely picking a fight, but as much as I don't want them to argue, I do want to hear Preston's rebuttal.

"For talking to a couple kids from my class? What's wrong with that?"

"It's called a phone, dude. Or texting. Or email. Take your pick. You don't leave your girl alone in the middle of a date."

"Let me take your advice. You have so much experience. How many girls you been out with again? I must've missed a few." Preston's tone is cutting, arrogant.

"Don't be a jackass, dude. I'm trying to help you. You sat there like a lump at dinner when Mom was being a bitch and—"

Preston cuts him off. "Mom's not being a bitch." *Yes, she was most definitely a bitch.* I push my ear closer into the woodgrain to hear his explanation. "She's concerned. Yeah, she could've been nicer but it's nothing personal against Rayne. Just mom being mom."

Gage makes a half-spitting, half-snorting sound. "Are you shitting me? Mom's a bitch. I took up for your girlfriend more than you did. I'm telling you straight up, keep acting like this and you're gonna lose her."

"To who?" He sounds confident, untouchable—like he doesn't have a care in the world.

"To someone who realizes what you have when you obviously don't." Gage's voice has no inflection. It's a quiet and direct warning, and I can't help wondering to whom he's referring, and in the back of my mind, I'm hoping it's him.

"That's wrong. I care about her... a lot."

"Then act like it. You leave her alone all the time, don't stand up for her. She's not one of those idiot sub-humans you're used to. She's got brains, goals, and interests. Do you ever ask her about those or just make her bask in your greatness?"

"What's your problem tonight?" The anger seeps through Preston's words.

Bam! The wall shakes at what sounds like Gage slapping the sheetrock. "You know what? Never mind. You're right. You know best, so do your thing." Gage's door slams, and I quickly turn on the faucet just in case Preston can hear me in the bathroom.

After washing and drying my hands over and over again until the skin is red and shriveled, I open the door and flick off the lights. Preston's waiting in the hallway, leaned into the wall, flipping through his phone like nothing's wrong. But the closed door beside him and the rock music now thundering behind it tells a different story.

"Hey there."

Preston looks up and smiles, eyes calm, jaw relaxed. "Hey. Ready to go watch that movie now?"

"Yeah, let's go." I choose not to perpetuate the drama because truth be told, Gage is right. Preston's genuinely a nice guy, but I'm beginning to wonder if maybe dating me is just a novelty—something different for a while. He isn't as attentive as I'd hoped, and I'm not responding how I expected. Love is supposed to create a spark, a chemical connection that roots around in your gut and drives you just a little crazy but in a really good way.

Preston's not quite doing that, but I know someone who is.

14

GAGE

The earthy scent of fresh-cut grass wafts around us, a little sweet, a little musky, as we all huddle in the end zone behind the big banner with its painted-on slogan "rip the rebels" or something like that. I suck in a deep breath, the chilled air burning the inside of my nose, the first hints of fall surging in. I take another long inhale, filling my lungs.

Ah. The smell of a crisp night ahead—stadium lights blaring, the band in their stupid hats playing *Louie, Louie* and *Crazy Train* nonstop... and football.

I love Friday night home games.

And Rayne in that cheerleading skirt.

Give it a rest, you idiot. She's so off limits.

She's standing at the front of the group, holding onto the banner, head cocked, and eyes sweeping the stands from side to side. I scoot forward, sneaking around guys on the outside edge, clanking shoulder pads with them as I squeeze into the very front, directly behind her.

"Boo," I whisper in her ear.

She jumps, losing one hand's grip on the banner momentarily as she whips around, sticking her tongue out at me over her shoulder. At least she's smiling now.

"You 'bout scared me half to death!" Her giggle rings out against the drumline in the background but fades when she darts her eyes back to the quickly filling stands.

"Looking for Preston?"

"He said he'd try to make it to the game tonight, but I didn't put much stock in it." She shrugs. "Hasn't made it to one yet. I did see your dad finally made one, though."

The words register at a snail's pace. Either I misunderstood her, or the world quit spinning on its axis for a minute. She must be mistaken. "My dad? Here?"

She nods and points to a spot in front of the stands. "Yeah, right over there." I maneuver myself around the crowd for a better look. Dad leans on the fence line, alone, without his cell phone in hand for once. Just watching us on the field. When he sees Rayne pointing and connects with my gaze, he waves nonchalantly, like it's perfectly normal for him to be standing there. Like it's something he actually does on a regular basis.

I relax on my heels, pushing back into the midst of the other jerseys. "I can't believe it."

She turns around and grabs my arm, her fingers pressing into the skin above my elbow, and I instinctively flex my bicep under her palm. "Why not?" she asks with a smile. "He should come see his son play. You look terrific out there."

I don't respond. What words could top what she just said? But my lips spread wide, my teeth all out there goofy-like in a smile I can't wipe off my face.

Another chill roves over my skin, heightening my senses, pumping my blood even harder. It's one of those sensations where you don't know how it's all going to turn out, but you don't really care because the possibility's there. The opportunity. The connection.

Invincible. That's the word. This has to be what people are

talking about when they describe themselves as "ten feet tall and bulletproof."

Dad's finally here for me. Not Preston. Not Preston and me. Just me.

And Rayne said I look terrific on the field.

The crowd's cheers fade to background noise as the whistle's shrill ring hits my eardrum. Damn, I love Friday night home games—tonight's, especially.

A few droplets of water race down the back of my neck from my still damp hair, the wind blowing across it and shooting ice down my shoulders. Maybe I should've toweled off a bit more after the shower. Everyone else was heading to the diner out by the highway, but the thought of loud people crammed four-deep in booths and greasy food in my face made my head ache, so I splurged on an extra-long shower until the locker room became a ghost town.

The parking lot is empty as I walk out, duffle bag in hand, and football tucked under my arm, except for a Honda parked on the far edge near the tree line. Rayne. The glow from her cell phone lights up the window.

What's she still doing here?

I jog up to her car. She's sitting there in a t-shirt and gym shorts, hunched over the blaring phone screen when I tap three times on the window. The glass sucks down into the door as she smiles up at me.

"Everything okay?" I ask. "You have a dead battery or something?"

"Oh... uh, no... I was just... texting Preston," she stammers, looking down at the phone in her lap. "He said if he didn't make it to the game, maybe we'd hang out afterwards, but he's not answering."

"Sorry." Really, I am. It's not fair for her to be sitting alone in this parking lot, waiting on him to call. The way her lips curve down at the edges and her shoulders slump is proof enough this is weighing on her. Exactly what I've warned him about, and he's too far over his head in this business of Mom and Dad's he can't see he's losing her. Little by little, each time he disappears or breaks a promise.

She forces a small smile and shrugs, but her tone is deflated. "He's probably just busy with work and school stuff."

"Probably." My stomach drops. Why isn't Preston listening to me? I'm only trying to help him. Rayne deserves someone to be there for her, not keep stringing her along. I clear my throat. "So, you headed home?"

She sighs and pretends to smash her forehead into the steering wheel. "I don't really want to until I have to."

"Yeah, I know that feeling."

She scoots close to the door, leaning out the window, hands clasped on the edges and puppy dog eyes. "You want to hang out a bit?"

Hell. Yeah.

"You and me?" I flick my finger between us, my eyes widening at the suggestion. Preston's loss could totally become my gain.

"I'm sorry... I'm an idiot." She pushes back inside, cheeks on fire, and reaches for her keys. "You're probably headed to the diner..."

"No, I'm not, actually." I spit the words out before she can crank her car and leave. Before this chance passes me by. She stops, keys in mid-air, and looks up at me with a grin. "What'd you want to do?" I ask.

The car door creaks open and she steps out, shoving her phone in the pocket of her black gym shorts, which, even though she's short, make her legs go on for miles and her—

"You do have a football." She slams the door, yanks the ball from my arms then throws it in the air and catches it again. "We could go throw a few."

"You know how to play?"

"Please. I might be a girl, but I'm my dad's only child. He taught me everything."

"Is that so?" I drop my bag beside the rear tire and snatch the ball, running down the hill toward the field, yelling back over my shoulder. "Let's see what you got."

Before I make it halfway down, she bolts past me, arms stretched out in front of her like an NFL receiver.

She's kidding me, right? No way she can field a ball on the fly.

But that same old competitive streak between us ignites, and I'm compelled to prove her wrong. I launch the ball in the air as she glances over her shoulder, turning at the last minute to scoop it into her arms, cradling it against her as she makes it to the end zone.

She nods toward the field, and I run past her as she launches a bullet straight toward me. I pick up the pace, turning and running backwards with my arms out, ready for the ball. For a moment it disappears in the lights then reappears. My eyes fix on the brown leather hurtling toward me, ready to snatch it from the air.

Damn, she's got a rocket for an arm. Impressive... and hot.

Suddenly, the buzzing of the stadium lights silences, the darkness tumbling down on us like a heavy blanket. Temporarily blind, I reach for the ball when...

Wham!

The leather makes angry contact with my lip, the skin underneath ripping against my teeth. The metallic taste of blood infiltrates my tongue as I drop to my knees, hand covering my mouth.

The grass crunches beneath her shoes as she sprints to my side, kneels beside me and washes her hands over my face. The way her fingertips graze my skin only speeds up my heart a little more, which in turn keeps pumping blood out the cut.

"You're bleeding!" Her voice wobbles as she stands up, using the edge of her t-shirt to clamp over the wound. Standing this close, hints of her perfume pepper the air, inviting me to press my face into her and breathe it all in.

Stop it, Gage.

I pull backwards, sitting on the 50-yard line, and press my finger into the gash. She sits down beside me, pressed so close the heat from her body warms the side of my leg, a barrier from the chilly night air.

"I'm okay," I assure her. "No big deal."

She nods, and after a few minutes of silence and a fully clotted lip, finally speaks, her voice soft but steady. "You know... I never did tell you, but... thanks for standing up for me at dinner last week. You didn't have to do that."

"Yeah, I did. You didn't deserve that." I pause, picking at the turf, pulling up individual sprigs of grass and letting them fall into a mound. "Preston... he should've shut Mom up once and for all. It's hard for him, though. He basically worships her, but I told him—"

She reaches out and grabs my shoulder, her palm hot through the cotton shirt. "I know what you told him. I overheard."

"Oh."

"I get it. He's busy and trying so hard to impress your parents. I just think... he's got so much on his plate... and then trying to please everyone... maybe it's all just too much for him..."

Hell yeah it's too much for him, but then again he's always had that pressure to be the best. In elementary school, he was the top seller for every fundraiser. In middle school, he beat out everyone for student body president. In high school, he was a sort of Renaissance Man with a 3.85 GPA, chairman of the honor society, and championship quarterback. I'm pretty sure he would've swept every senior year superlative, too, but since that was against the rules, Best All Around had to do.

Now he's going to be an accountant in a suit and tie. A manager in the family business because Mom and Dad say so. Preston will always do what's expected of him, even if it means sacrificing his own happiness. It's exactly what he's doing now with Rayne.

"Maybe." I blow out a loud breath and lay back on the grass, arms folded behind my head. "Much easier to be like me and not give a damn."

Rayne follows my cue, laying back with her head beside mine, body in the opposite direction. Her hair splays out all around, the wispy ends tickling my ear. "You're not foolin' me. You care. More than you'll ever say. You just keep it all inside."

"Oh yeah? And how do you think you know me so well?" I roll my head toward hers, locking eyes. The truth hovers in the air between us. She does know me. Like no one else.

She licks her lips, never taking her eyes of mine. "Cause it's like looking in a mirror. We're too much alike. We say we don't care. Deep down we want to fly in the face of everything in this town, prove everybody wrong, it's just..."

"What?" I whisper.

"There's always something holding us back. Fear? Expectations? Loyalty?"

All of those. Tying my hands. Keeping me from the thing I want most.

Her.

I laugh, easing the tension building between us, the force threatening to explode at any moment. "I know what you mean. Maybe we should rebel in small ways? Work up to the big-time?"

Her phone buzzes with an incoming text. She slips it from her pocket, reads it, and then tosses it to the ground with a sigh.

"Preston?" I ask.

"Yeah." She lays still, staring up at the rashes of stars spread out over us. The phone buzzes again, but this time she makes no move to pick it up.

"Aren't you gonna text him back?"

She bites her bottom lip and shakes her head back and forth on the grass. "Nah. Think I'll let him sweat it out a while."

My heart flutters against my ribs and icy pellets coat my spine as we lay there motionless, her looking at the stars and me looking at her, with one thought circulating in my brain.

She could've left, but she didn't.

She stayed here.

She chose me.

15

RAYNE

"Jaycee, are you in love with Barrett?" I drop the question on her out of the blue as we're walking down the sidewalk toward the coffeehouse where we're meeting the other girls for our monthly girls' outing. One weekend each month they have karaoke night, and the whole town shows up. It's one of the few times Mama doesn't create a huge scene, partly because I'm with the girls and partly because the whole town's eyes are on me. Sharon Ables, one of Mama's oldest, dearest friends, owns the place. If I screw up, she'll know about it before I get home.

Jaycee looks at me as if I've asked her to explain differential math and twists her bracelet on her wrist. "You're mad at me, aren't you?"

I squinch my eyes together wondering what her being in love would have to do with me being mad. "No. Why?"

"You found out I invited the boys tonight, didn't you?" Before I can answer, she defends herself. "I know it's supposed to be girls' night, but the boys are downtown anyway watching football, so I told them to stop by if they had time. Nothing big. Just low-key."

I laugh at her doe-eyed explanations. "Jaycee, I'm not mad. I'm just wondering how close you've gotten with Barrett?"

She presses her lips together in a line and makes a smacking sound as she separates them. "I told him I love him. And before you say anything, I know what you're thinking. 'Jaycee's said that before.' This time it's different. I mean it."

For once, I actually believe her. She's nervous, and she's never nervous about boys. "I'm happy for you."

Her shoulders relax, and a smile floods her face as she grabs my arm. "What about you and Preston? Any love talk yet?"

"No. I don't... we're not..." I shake my head and look down.

"Wait. Barrett's told me how into you Preston is. I've seen it. You're sabotaging this." She wags her finger in my face as she continues, "Your mama's in your head. You always do this—get excited about something, Mama gives you flak and then you're standing in your own way. You better figure it out before you ruin a good thing."

I shrug my shoulders then let them slump. "I'm open... really. I'm just not... feeling it..."

I might as well have hit Jaycee square in the face with a pie. She pulls back like I just took a swing at her. "How do you not feel it with Preston? I mean, look at him."

"I didn't say he's not hot. It's not clicking, sparking, something..."

She stops in the middle of the sidewalk, grabs both my arms and turns me toward her. "How far have y'all gone?"

"Kissing." The heat rushes to my cheeks even telling her.

"Kissing?" She juts her head towards mine, eyes bulging. "Mama been chaperoning your dates?"

"No. I don't... want to..." I stammer, staring at the sidewalk.

"Preston's had lots of girlfriends before, so he's expecting..." Now she sounds like Mama.

I glower at her. "I don't care what he expects. I'm not doing something major trying to feel something for a guy."

"I'm not suggesting you do, but you need to put yourself out there. Get out of your own head for a change." She pushes her index finger into the middle of my forehead and continues, "Do this. It's a little psychological test I read about in my magazine. Close your eyes. Imagine you're curled up on a couch, snuggled up to your man. The movie on TV is boring, and so you look up at him, ready to spice things up." She snaps her fingers in my face. "Quick! Who're you with? Who's the guy? Preston, right?"

Wrong. So wrong. But I know the face. The scruffy man-hair. The smile. The eyes. "Uh... sure. Preston."

"See? Everything's telling you to chill out and enjoy. Be patient. The fireworks you want will come. Quit thinking about it so much and get in there and seal the deal." She laces her arm through mine and pulls me to the coffeehouse entrance.

Maybe she's right. We walk through the glass door, the bell on the handle jingling with the movement. A wake-up bell. Am I scared and sabotaging my own happiness? Am I using Gage as a buffer between me and Preston? It's a possibility. But it's also probable I'm falling for Gage instead. And if the latter is true, I've just eclipsed Mama as the most screwed-up person in this town.

It's after eight o'clock before the boys get there. Barrett comes in first, scans the crowd, then waves like crazy when he spots us. Preston's next, his smile as big and gorgeous as always. Trevor follows with a few guys from the football team, and at the tail-end is Gage with clenched jaw and hooded eyes. I know what he's thinking—too many people, too much noise, too much chaos.

Every chair in the place is occupied so the boys grab their drinks and join us, taking our seats then pulling us down into their laps. On my left, Jaycee wiggles around on Barrett, leaning back over and over to shower him with kisses. On my right, Ainsley snuggles into Trevor as they drink coffee. Preston's beneath me, but we're not as lovey-dovey as everyone else. I lean back into him, pressing my back into his chest, my cheek smooshed to his. He nuzzles my neck and plants a kiss there, soft and gentle. I smile at him then glance over my shoulder.

Gage is right behind us, his Styrofoam to-go cup still untouched. He sits on the edge of a wooden table, leaned forward with his elbows on his knees so no one can use him as a seat cushion. I'm glad, too, because seeing some girl sitting atop him would crush me. At least this way, I can keep him all to myself. He looks up at me and mouths "hi."

I mouth back, "hi" and smile just as I hear my name over the speaker. I jerk my head forward to the announcer who's definitely saying my name. "Rayne Davidson. Where are you? You're next!"

Jaycee giggles loudly and claps her hands together. "Your mama knew what she was doing with all those church solos." She leans in close to my ear. "You can thank me later. Go seal the deal." She winks and nudges me forward, but I move as if my legs are made of lead. I so don't want to do this. Church solos are one thing. Karaoke solos in front of my friends and tons of other people are something else.

I must look squeamish because Preston runs over to give me a hug. "Just relax. You got this. Focus on something that calms you." His encouragement might go on hiatus after I puke on his shoes.

I mumble "thanks" and head towards the guy running the machine to select my music. He shakes his head. The selection's already been made and is ready to go. Jaycee's choice. From the corner of my eye, I see her smiling. This can't be good. All I can imagine is singing some crude song full of sexual innuendo. She'd so pick that for me.

I sit down on the wooden stool, hard and unforgiving, although I'm not doing much to make it more comfortable. My legs are tense, my arms rigid, and my stomach in knots—a sea of faces, both familiar and new, stare back at me. What did Preston say? Pick a focus point? My heart bumps hard against my ribs as their eyes scrutinize my every move. The first notes play, slow and easy, so unlike the booty-grinding music I expect.

When the song title flashes on screen, I get it. "Can't Help Falling in Love." Jaycee loves Elvis, but this is more than that. She's pushing, manipulating the situation. I should've never told her earlier I wasn't feeling all the sparks with Preston. She's on a mission to light the fire, starting with me singing this song to him. "Seal the deal"—her words exactly.

As the bouncy ball on screen ticks off the last instrumental notes, it's go-time. With the first words, I scan for a friendly face to help me focus on the words and the feelings I need to invest in this. And just like that, he's there. Handsome Preston, with his dazzling grin and chocolate brown eyes, leans forward and awaits my song. And over his left shoulder, Gage sits upright on the tabletop, arms folded over his chest. And he's staring at me. Right at me. And I stare back. And with every word that pours out, I invest in the connection. Locked in tight.

I sing to him, and I can't stop myself. And the screwed-up thing is everyone thinks I'm zeroed in on Preston—except Gage.

What scares me is I'm on autopilot, the song coming from my subconscious because as the words flow, I'm not looking at the screen or thinking about the song. I remember our competitive run. I recall hanging out in his room. I picture his tattoo. I daydream about the way he looked in those boxers. It's all Gage, no Preston.

Exactly how would any of that work anyway? I can't date one brother and have feelings for another.

The song ends to thunderous applause. Preston's waiting at our table when I get back, and he jumps up, bends me backwards and plants a huge kiss on my lips to the crowd's cheers.

His arms crush into my waist, and I squeeze back, but when I open my eyes, Gage is watching. He smiles and nods, so formal-like, and when I get upright on my feet and smile back, Gage stands up, throws some money on the table and walks out.

16

———————

GAGE

*W*hoever came up with how to pronounce "R" in the French language should be tortured and obliterated. Madame kept yelling in class that our "Lazy Southern Drawl" originated the sound against the rooves of our mouths instead of in the throat, the way native French speakers did it. I think we "lazy Southerners" do it best. Who the hell wants to sound like they're hocking up a loogie while they're talking?

The other patrons in this coffeehouse obviously agree because every time I practice this list of "R" words and get some good throatiness going, they turn and stare, eyes squinted and lips snarled. Like they're waiting to see a big loogie come flying out onto the table. That'll spoil their cappuccino break.

The chimes on the door ring out, and I look up from my notebook. Rayne walks in with her backpack on both shoulders, wearing a strappy red tank top that dips just low enough to leave me wanting more. The French "R" and the monster test coming up next week slip from my mind as I watch her absent-mindedly playing with her earring. She considers the menu, and then smiles at the girl taking her order—a lopsided grin that shows just a flash of white between her pink lips.

These are not things I should be noticing about my brother's girlfriend. I mean, it's a free country, and I can think she's hot. My mind's fair game. I just can't ever do anything about it. That'd be breaking the bro-code, complicated by the fact Preston's my actual brother and not just some random guy, so the thoughts alone are bad enough.

Latte in hand, she pauses by the counter, scanning the room. She must be looking for Preston. He left home before I did, saying he was going to see someone, and I'd automatically figured he meant Rayne. Maybe they're meeting here instead.

When her eyes land on me, she waves and smiles. My heart skips a few beats, like a butterfly flapping around in my chest, as she heads in my direction. It isn't the only thing affected. A deep stirring—in a place where there should be no stirring when thinking of my brother's girlfriend—forces me to readjust in my seat.

"Studying for the French exam next week?"

"Trying. You?" I nod toward her backpack.

She shrugs off the straps and plops it on the table. "Yep. Mind if I join you for a minute?"

I choke back the words because anything at this point would sound too exuberant. *Yes! Please! Now!* I nod and use my foot to slide the chair out towards her. She takes another quick scan around the room then sits down across from me.

"Looking for Preston?"

She takes a sip of her latte, leaving a smidge of coffee on her upper lip that disappears under a tongue swipe. *Dear God.* "Jaycee, actually. We're supposed to study together. Why?"

"Just wondering. I thought when he left this morning, he was going to see you."

She shakes her head and shrugs. "He's texted me a few times, but I haven't seen him in days. He said he might have some time this weekend but... I guess not. He's always so busy with school and work stuff. Guess I'll have to get used to that, right?"

No, she shouldn't have to get used to it. Preston's a fool. Just because those other shallow girls he's dated were willing to wait at his beck and call, doesn't mean this one will.

"What part are you studying?" She takes another sip and reaches for my notebook, angling it towards her as she reads the page. "The dreaded 'R,' huh?"

"It's useless. I'm gonna fail the speech portion of this thing."

"No, you're not. I'll help you." She scoots her chair closer, pushing up on her elbows to scour the notebook.

She's not wearing much make-up. Her freckles spread out over her cheeks and nose then spill down across her shoulders and chest, a few disappearing into the neckline of her tank that gapes open a bit as she leans in toward me. My eyes follow the freckles down the rabbit hole, my body reacting in more ways than one when the thought of her...

Snap!

I glance up. She snaps her fingers again, dodging around and trying to catch my gaze. "Did you hear me?"

Fire rushes to my cheeks. "Uh... no... missed it."

"Say this phrase," she says, tapping her nail beside raison d'etre.

Making the loogie sound is not the impression I want to leave her, but she's staring at me so I have to. "Hhrrray-zon"

She grimaces. Please don't say I've spit all over her.

"Too hard. R's are supposed to be throaty, not snotty." She reaches over and grasps my throat, just under the jaw bone, the gentle pressure of her fingertips spiraling out into euphoric waves down my body. Once again, I have to shift in my chair, the visceral reaction so strong and immediate it's a bit painful. "Push the word from here." She pinches in as I say the word again, this time creating the perfect pronunciation.

I squirm as both her fingers and her eyes fix on me as she nods, a huge grin spreading across her lips. I want to tell her how awesome I think she is. How she makes me actually want to try to master this damn "R." But I can't. The words would be treason to the one person I admire most.

"What the hell is going on?"

Rayne jerks her hand away. We didn't see Jaycee walk up, but she's standing beside us, hands on her hips, scuffing the toe of her shoe against the tile floor.

"Just helping Gage with his French," Rayne stammers, jumping to her feet, backpack in hand. "Exciting stuff."

Jaycee steps up to the table, darting her eyes between me and Rayne. I shift in my chair. Apparently the wrong move, because she glances down, her eyes fixing on the exact thing I'm trying to keep hidden. She smirks, licking her tongue across her teeth and motions to a table on the opposite side of the room. "Come on, Rayne. Let's go study. I think Gage has had enough excitement for one day."

———

When I get home, a white work truck is parked in front of my garage door. Mom's on some sort of kick. Last month it was all new curtains for the living room; the month before that, a new chandelier in the dining room, big and showy with lots of crystals hanging everywhere. What now?

I open the front door. The workman is standing back beside his ladder as my mom stands at the wall with her tape measure, verifying the new shelf is level and that each Chinese vase on top is equidistant from the others. Controlling much? The hefty paycheck is probably the only thing keeping him from stabbing her through the ear with his screwdriver.

She turns around, only momentarily, to glare in my direction. "Where've you been?"

"At the coffeehouse, studying."

"In that?" She runs her eyes up and down my clothes. Jeans and a t-shirt, totally fine except for the smallish rip near my knee. Big deal.

She heaves out a hard breath and turns back to her measuring, dismissing me without a word. I used to care that everything I did seemed to irritate her. That inclination stopped a long time ago.

I'm heading to my room when voices from the dining room catch my attention. Preston and Ashlyn sit side by side at the table, a massive pile of paperwork spread out in front of them. He's pointing to some multi-colored graph talking about sales figures and projections while she's propped on one arm, leaning into his side, giggling from time to time.

Yeah, because accounting is so hilarious.

"Pres? I didn't know you were working on internship stuff today."

They both dart their eyes toward me standing in the doorway. Ashlyn flounces back in her chair, crossing her arms over her chest with a sigh.

"I wasn't planning on it. Mom said Dad needed help on this project and thought it'd be a great way to get some experience."

"Of course she did," I mumble. Preston seems unaware of my sarcasm, but Ashlyn glares at me under her fake eyelashes. This is so typical of mom, manipulating this "work date" between them and all under her watchful eye. Preston's not interested in Ashlyn, so mom's forcing the issue. Her way or no way. But what Preston should be doing is praising the universe for a girlfriend like Rayne and spending his free time convincing her he's worth all the waiting.

"Is there a problem?" She jacks one eyebrow up into her forehead, the corner of her lip curling into a sneer.

"I can think of at least one."

Her chair scrapes across the hardwood as she jolts to her feet, hands on her hips. "What's that supposed to mean?"

I wave her off with an eye roll. "Pencils down, Ashlyn. Better luck next time."

Her jaw drops open as she flips her fake hair extensions over her shoulder in disgust. Like I care her shallow, self-absorbed feelings are hurt.

Preston stands up, inserting himself as a barrier between us. "Calm down, y'all." He turns to Ashlyn and points toward the kitchen. "Let's take a quick break. Why don't you get us some cokes from the fridge?"

She deadpans a minute, then finally nods and stomps out of the room.

Preston nudges my shoulder and pans his hand across the table. "Why are you so mad at Ashlyn? We're working."

"You're working. She's shoving her boobs onto your arm."

"That's ridiculous. I don't like her like that. Besides, I have Rayne."

He has Rayne? It's becoming painfully obvious he has no idea what kind of person she actually is. She won't be happy Preston simply chooses to talk to her. She'll want to be a priority. Why can't he see what he really has? Or what he stands to lose if this keeps on?

"Oh yeah?" I counter. "Then why aren't you with her? Y'all were supposed to hang out this weekend."

Preston shrugs, palms up. "I know, but this came up. What could I do?" He sits back down at the table, shuffling papers into neat rows, and then glances over at me. "How do you know that anyway?"

"Because I was just at the coffeehouse. With your girl."

17

RAYNE

The following Tuesday, Gage slides into the desk behind mine. "Has Madame said what the big project is yet?"

"Not yet, but I hope it doesn't involve a lot of—"

Madame Martine taps her ruler on the podium. "Vous attirez l'attention!" She looks more like a French storybook character than a teacher, her orthopedic shoes, long chambray skirt, and oversized cardigan channeling Mother Goose.

"Class, it's mid-term project time, accounting for forty percent of your semester grade. You'll need to work in pairs, of my choosing, to select a location in Paris, present a short history, create a backdrop, and lastly, my favorite part, prepare an authentic French dish. Transport me to Paris—the city of lights and love!"

She places a glass jar on the podium, pulls out strips of paper in pairs, and begins announcing partners. Jaycee matches early on with a girl she hardly knows. I hold my breath, hoping I get someone semi-decent. "Mademoiselle Davidson et..." Please let it be good. "...Monsieur Howard." Yes!

He taps my shoulder, face lit up when I look back at him,

and whispers in my ear, "I'm thinking this is the most action Madame sees all year. So... what are we cookin' good-lookin'?"

I strum my fingers on my cheek, but it's all for show. There's no doubt in my mind what we're making. "Tartes aux cerises." He wrinkles his forehead as if leafing through his mental French dictionary in a desperate translation attempt. "Cherry pie," I finally say.

"My favorite." He wiggles his eyebrows up and down as he says it.

"Of course it is." God, he's sexy. Though technically, I shouldn't think it.

The rain freckles my windshield as I turn in the Howards' drive the following Sunday afternoon. I've spent the better part of the drive feeling guilty about my less-than-honest conversation with Mama before I walked out the door, purposefully vague with a dash of accuracy and a dollop of evasion. She asked if I'd be working in approved "public spaces" such as dens, dining rooms, kitchens, and garages with absolutely no bedrooms—ever. Check.

She asked if the Howards would be there. Kinda check. They were away for the weekend but messaged their kids religiously each day at four o'clock. That counted, right? She asked if Preston and I would ever be there alone together. Nope. Preston's at a study session at the campus library so it'd only be me and Gage. I'm honest on a technicality. She asked about the wrong brother.

If I'd told her the whole truth, she'd have railroaded it, and working on this project with Gage can't be jeopardized. The grade is important. Time with him is more important.

Too often lately my wandering thoughts start off with something perfectly innocent, like a conversation with

Preston, and then somehow meander into the forbidden fraternal territory. Images of Gage—his lips, his eyes, barrel into my mind like little wrecking balls that pulverize my flimsy pretenses. I picture him in my daydreams, never us, because that'd be what the preacher calls "lusting in my heart." Mama always says if you're thinking about it, it's the same as doing it already. The Bible says so. The people in town think that, too. The last thing I need is to tick off the town and Jesus.

Gage stands in the driveway before the car is in park. He opens my door and grabs bags of groceries and craft supplies from the back floorboard.

"Quit! You can't carry all that." I get out and slam the door. He twists toward me and switches the plastic sacks into his left hand, a smirk on his lips.

"You doubt my strength?" He plunges his finger into his chest. "I got all this... and you." I squeal as he hoists me up, circling my arms around his shoulders and burying my face into his hair as he walks up the sidewalk, through the front door, not stopping until we reach the kitchen.

His grip is different from Preston's. Sturdier. Tighter. Every nerve ending lights up, fiery hot and frenzied, like a thousand lighters at a rock concert. I've been trying to avoid this mental situation and now here I am on some sort of physical tight rope. Forget lusting in my heart. Now my whole body's yearning to break the rules.

"We can work in here. Want something to drink?" He drops the craft supplies onto the table and swings open the refrigerator door, sliding in the groceries and surveying inside. "Pepsi, Dr. Pepper, Cheerwine?"

Mama never buys soda at the store. Besides the morning coffee, we have three options on any given day—milk, water, and sweet tea. She says soda rots your teeth. "Pepsi, thanks."

He grabs two, pops the top on both and hands one to me.

The fizz tickles my nose as I take a drink, the hot sweetness burning a trail down my throat, causing me to cough.

"You all right? Need mouth-to-mouth or something?"

Oh God, do I ever. "Went down the wrong way." I pray he doesn't see the redness burning in my cheeks.

"Just checking. I kinda need you alive to do this project with me." He lays belly-down on the kitchen floor, now littered with paints and brushes, and pats the tiles beside him. "We can spread out down here."

I join him on the floor, side-by-side, our shoulders lightly grazing and an unseen force sucking us together like attracted magnetic poles. If I stop fighting it at any point, I'm sure to go flying right into him. *Dammit, Rayne, stop this.* My relationship with Preston is a good thing, and he's a good guy. So why can't I quit thinking about his brother?

"So, for the project, I'm thinking..." Gage starts. My intense focus on his lips lulls me into a quiet trance. Pucker, pinch, straighten, and part. As they move with each syllable, I drift backwards into myself. He's saying something about the project, and I should be listening but all I can focus on is the heat from his shoulder touching me and how much I want to run my fingers along the stubble on his chin and brush my cheek against the lettering down his abs. "What d'ya think?"

"About what?"

He shifts his eyes to me and frowns. "The project..."

Oh yeah, the project. "I'm thinking Montmartre. Not too touristy. More artsy. Cool lights and love, not that movie junk."

He nods. "Yeah, that's what I just said."

Really? "Yeah, I know," I stammer, looking down to spin a marker in circles on the floor. "Just agreeing with you." Two days ago, Preston said I'd be a fool to do anything but the Eiffel Tower if Madame wanted lights and love. What girl could resist the fantasy surrounding it?

Me, apparently. I'm more Midnight in Paris—quirky, whimsical, nostalgic. Now Gage sits here regurgitating that exact logic.

"Awesome," he says, holding up his hand for a high-five. "Let's do this."

Over the next couple hours, we paint our version of Paris's original artist village across a series of three foam boards, complete with narrow streets, sidewalk cafes, and a string of Christmas lights stapled along the border to play up the eclectic vibe. But the best part is when Gage narrates a string of childhood memories from secret handshakes in the backyard tree house to frog-catching conquests. I love imagining him as a kid, how cute he'd be running around in overalls, dark hair scruffed up with skinned knees. But something about it hurts, too. It's how he talks about his brother. The whole town loves Preston, but Gage idolizes him, and listening to his memories only makes me cringe.

When we finish, Gage props the boards in the corner of the breakfast nook and plugs in the light string. "Shut that." He nods toward the yellow swinging door leading to the hallway, while he snaps the blinds closed. When he flips the wall switch, the lights spark life in our faux Paris scene.

We stand side-by-side in silence, except for the faint slurping of Gage gnawing his lower lip. "I don't know, Rayne..."

There's no way he isn't satisfied with this. "What? I think it looks—"

"I don't know how we won't get an A," he interrupts, grinning.

"I know, right?" He slides his arm around my shoulder, awkwardly side-hugging me as someone would a little sister. Maybe I've been reading him wrong. Maybe that's how he sees me—his brother's girl and, consequently, his pseudo-sister. Torture. My secret pining reciprocated with good ol' sibling affection.

Maybe it can never be more. Saying it's easy. Accepting it's something else. There are moments I wish I'd met Gage first. This is one of those. My throat stiffens, difficult to swallow, and my abs knit together tightly. I hate that vomit sensation.

"Rayne?" Gage pulls my chin up, his blue eyes lit up with the happy golden flecks ringing the pupils. "We rocked this project."

Is spontaneous combustion an actual thing? My spirit bounces around with untamed energy and threatens to burst out of my skin and blow my body to smithereens. I imagine dissolving into a pile of sooty residue at his feet in an instant.

I circle my arm around his waist, relaxing my head on his shoulder. His body is warm and inviting like the favorite pillow from my bed. "I could fall in love here," I whisper to myself. He doesn't need to hear it. I just need to say it. Let it out and expel the energy.

"What?" He leans down, his ear close to my face, his cheek closer, his lips closest. Two inches of air separate us, but it might as well be two miles.

"Nothing." I slow my breathing, redirect, and drop my arm from his body. "We need to make those tarts."

He frowns, then turns and walks to the fridge, holding the door open with his hip as he piles the ingredients in his arms. He kicks the door shut and shovels everything on the island's granite top.

"All you." Gage waves his hand in a circle over the food. "Just tell me what to do."

"I think I can handle that." I tweak his nose and pick up one of the canvas bags I'd brought.

With a wink, he laughs, "I bet you can."

"Oh, I have my plans for you." I wag my finger in the air then pull out an apron from the bag. He clamps his eyes shut, scrunches his nose, and throws back his head, but I ignore him, looping the strap around his neck before stepping behind to tie the strings into a bow. My knuckles graze the ripples of muscles crisscrossing his back under the lightweight tee-shirt, and my fingers tremble, wanting to explore further, following the valleys down, until—

"I can pit the cherries. Can't mess that up, right?" His words snatch me back to the present.

I grab the plastic clamshell carton and toss it to him. "I don't know. How good are you at working with cherries?"

He turns the container over in his hands and checks out the red fruit. "Let's just say I'm an eager student." He glances up at me as he says it, and suddenly my mind is going places it shouldn't, and my cheeks flame up again. This toeing-the-line, sarcastic back-and-forth we're so good at is making it hard to concentrate on this baking project when all I want to do is have him demonstrate his skills.

"Good to know." I smile like a fool because I literally cannot help it. I can't force my cheeks down. He does that to me, and it's getting harder to hide, so I do what I do best—change the subject. "I'll work on the custard and the crusts, and then we'll put it all together."

Gage sits at the dinette table, reclined back on the legs of his chair and pits each cherry before tossing it in a bowl. I finish the rest, and once the tarts are perfectly prepared and packaged in the large clear-topped pastry box, we only have to clean up the mess.

I load the dishes into the sink, swirl soap across the top, and turn on the water until foamy bubbles peek over the basin's edge. The mixing bowl, still sitting on the counter, has small clumps of custard around the bottom. I dredge my finger through the remnants and hold it out to Gage. "Taste test?"

"Heck yeah." He walks over, leans down, and takes my finger into his mouth. His tongue slides against my fingertip, shooting an icy blast down to my toes. While his lips are still wrapped around my finger, he lifts his eyes and wiggles his brows in approval. "Ummy," he says, garbled.

I giggle. "I think that translates to 'yummy'?"

Gage grabs my hand then pulls back to say, "Finger-lickin'." He sticks out his tongue and runs it down the length of my finger again just as Preston arrives.

"What's this?" Oh dear God. His voice catches me off-guard, and I retract quickly from Gage, stumble backward and nearly fall over the kitchen barstool. Preston stands in the threshold, hand pinning the swinging door to the wall, eyes darting back and forth between me and Gage.

If I were a cartoon character, you'd have seen my heart imprinting through my shirt. It pounds in my ears. "We finished our project." My voice registers two octaves higher under the influence of guilt. "Come see."

"I didn't realize you'd still be here." Preston walks over and kisses my temple. I'm surprised he can find it because he's looking at me as if I have three heads. Suspicion? Jealousy? Maybe my conscience kicking my own butt?

He looks over the boards. "Buildings? I thought you were doing the Eiffel Tower? Kinda misses the 'lights and love' mark, doesn't it?"

I wince. It's personal.

"It's Montmartre," Gage inserts, his voice low and tense. "Home of Degas? Artist headquarters?"

"Obscure. Maybe that'll get you extra credit. What's in here?" Preston takes the stainless-steel bowl from my hands and peers in.

"Vanilla custard for the pies. Try some." I absentmindedly scoop up a taste onto my finger—the same finger Gage has just been licking clean.

Preston studies the sample, licks his lips and shakes his head. "No thanks."

I jerk my finger back and wipe the remnants onto the bowl's edge. Gage stands behind Preston, arms folded across his chest, looking as if the custard has soured in his stomach. Preston leans over the table and peeks in the pastry box.

"Looks good, guys. Y'all are done now, right?" Preston loops his arm through mine. "Let's go hang out before you have to leave."

I pull away and point to the sink. "I have to finish cleaning up and load this stuff into my car first."

Gage steps forward and waves me off. "I got it. Go ahead with Preston."

"You sure?" I search his gaze for any sign he wants me to stay. Nothing.

"Yeah." He takes the bowl from my hands, drops his head and walks to the sink. I want him to intervene, insist I stay with him. He doesn't. He lets me go to Preston without batting an eye. I guess this means it really has been innocent flirtation on his part, and if so, Gage and I didn't enter any kind of forbidden territory, so that lusting in my heart thing is null and void.

I should be relieved. Only I'm not. I'm disappointed.

18

———

GAGE

o ahead with Preston.

That's what I told her.

Why does it taste like swallowing a whole jar of pickle juice? Each time I remember the words, that same reaction tears through me—clamped eyes with a grimace and being rocked by bristles that tear up and down my spine.

The worst part is that piece of me thinks she didn't really want to go. Her eyes begged me to insist she stay and help clean up.

Didn't they?

I don't know.

I don't know a damn thing anymore.

And maybe that isn't the worst part. Maybe the worst part is I'm questioning any of this when he is my brother.

And she is my brother's girlfriend.

"Idiot," I grumble under my breath, grabbing the backpack off my bed and throwing it onto the floor when a knock sounds at the door.

Who is it? Mom and Dad are gone, and Preston left with Rayne a while ago. I walk to the door and sliver it open. Preston sticks his nose in the crack, using his hand to push the door open as wide as he can. It stops short when it hits the toe of my boot. I don't move it.

"When did you get home?"

"Just now. Rayne had to be home early, so I called the guys." He tries to open the door further to no avail. Again, I don't offer to move my boot. Preston narrows his eyes then shrugs it off. "What are you doing?"

"I was going to study," I lie, pointing at the backpack on the floor.

"That can wait. Tonight, we paintball." He holds up the black bag that holds his gun, CO2 canisters, and tub of paint-balls. "Come on, Trevor and Barrett are meeting us there."

Ten minutes later, we're in Preston's Mustang heading toward the course. I bring up football, but he quickly dismisses it. Apparently "real life" has no time and patience for such high school activities. He says high school like he didn't just grad-uate like half a year ago.

What he can talk about, however, is Mom's wonderful advice. Mom says this, and Mom says that. Mom has such great insight. Mom thinks Preston's a god walking on Planet Earth. Mom is weirdly obsessed. Mom, Mom, Mom.

When we pull into the parking lot, Barrett's Bronco is already there. He and Trevor are propped against the back bumper, waiting, and Preston barely shifts to park before I'm unbuckled and jumping out of the car.

We walk inside and pay the fees, gear up, and load our weapons.

"How are we doing this?" Trevor asks. He asks the same thing every time we play. It's rhetorical. Usually. It's always been the same—me and Preston versus Trevor and Barrett. Everyone always assumes it'll stay that way. The question is a mere formality, a polite gesture that holds no value.

Until today.

Frankly, I need a break. When I say so, their eyes saucer like I've just committed some felony.

"But we always play two-on-two."

"Well, today I feel like playing every man for himself. What's wrong with that?"

"Nothing... I guess."

"Good." I rub my hands together, gun slung over my shoulder. "Four corners, capture the flag?"

They all nod in agreement... or confusion. I can't be sure, but at least they're all moving to their respective starting points with no more resistance. It feels good to make the rules for once.

"Oh yeah," I holler and each of them turns around. "A shot to the upper torso, front or back, is the kill shot. No head shots and everything else is just a flesh wound. Got it?"

Everyone moves to position. I crouch behind the stack of pallets in my corner, peering out the side. In the center of the playing field, a red banner flaps at the top of a tall metal pole.

The prize—and it's mine.

The air horn breaks through the silence, signaling the start of the contest. Almost immediately, the trash-talking begins, everyone yelling back and forth. For what seems like hours, we circle each other in some testosterone-fueled dance of guerilla warfare. But while the others keep yelling, I fall silent. And wait.

Barrett's in my vicinity. His voice has gotten closer, and the shuffle of his feet is discernible. If I'm patient, he'll deliver himself on a shiny, silver platter, and he'll be the first casualty. Fitting for anyone willing to date Jaycee. His sacrifice is a necessary evil.

To my left, a collection of four fifty-gallon drums stands alone, and I make a beeline for them, slinking down to my knees. In a small gap between two of the drums, I watch the field. From the corner of my eye, a shape emerges from the tree line and darts towards a large wooden structure, shaped like a building.

Barrett. And he's not even looking in my direction.

I line up the shot as he pauses at the structure, carefully making sure it's unoccupied before he climbs in. It's all the opportunity I need.

Pull.

Bam! My shot lands on his back, off to the right where the ribs wrap around.

Man down.

"I'm out!" Barrett yells almost at the same time a loud yelp echoes from the opposite side of the field.

"I'm out, too!" Trevor this time, which means one thing.

It's down to me and Preston. And only one of us can win.

The next ten minutes happen in a blur. Preston holds nothing back when he continuously charges me, firing off several paint bullets that graze my arms and legs, and one that flies seriously close to my face. It's almost as if he doesn't think I have it in me.

To shoot him.

To dare to beat him.

Bam! Electric blue paint splatters across my T-shirt sleeve.

"I hit you!"

"On the arm. Flesh wound."

"Still... you know it's just a matter of time. Might as well give up now. I always win."

Not today, Preston. Not today.

"Sure about that?"

"Yep. I don't know how to lose."

The dry grass crunches under Preston's feet, and then silence. Surely, this fool isn't standing out in the open, challenging me. Of course, it could all be a ploy to lure me out so he can take a shot. I squat lower and creep around the side of the bale.

It's clear.

But when I turn back, the barrel of his gun is pointed square at my chest.

Dammit.

"Told you I always win," he laughs and pulls the trigger.

Nothing.

He pulls again.

Nothing.

"What the —?" he starts, slamming his hand against the side of the canister. The paintballs are stuck, lodged in tight. Jammed. We realize it at the same time, and he dashes for cover before I can aim and shoot.

A generous competitor might've waited until the playing fields were leveled again and the gun was working properly. But I'm not in a generous mood.

I sneak around the hay bale, tiptoe running to Preston's location, finger poised on the trigger. He's kneeling behind the cover, feverishly readjusting the canister. I raise my gun, planting the sight on him and shoot.

Bam! Neon green paint sprays out between his shoulder blades, the impact, both sudden and unexpected, throws him forward on his hands and knees.

That felt good.

Preston jumps to his feet and turns to face me with a sneer. I want to knock that look off his face. I want him to understand for once that I—kid brother, less handsome, less wonderful Gage—am a competitor.

Bam! My finger seems to react on some express link from my thoughts, completely bypassing all things sane and logical. Another burst of neon green blasts into his shirt, right above the front pocket.

A direct shot to the heart.

"What the hell?" Preston throws his gun down then folds his arm over his chest. Like he's waiting on an explanation. But he wouldn't like what I have to say, so I tell him the simplest truth.

"You said you didn't know how to lose. Just thought I'd show you how it feels."

I leave him standing there open-mouthed and fuming as I strut to the pole to retrieve my flag. And when my back's completely turned, I smile.

—

I walk into the kitchen. Preston follows.

The ride home was quiet, only the radio filling the dead space between us. Shooting him felt good. Too good at the time, though a slight measure of regret creeps in. He didn't do anything to provoke it. He was just being his usual self. It never used to bother me, but lately, this wave of angst has been rising inside me like a tsunami, ready to break the walls and blow all his "look at me" shit apart.

Maybe I'm being too hard on him. Underestimating all the pressure Mom and Dad put on his shoulders. Maybe I should practice some sympathy instead of getting pissed and maybe a tad... jealous?

No. I'm not jealous. I just want Preston to wake up and realize what he has.

Yeah. That's it.

I open the fridge door and stoop for a better look. "You hungry?" I ask him over my shoulder.

"Eh, I guess." His tone isn't friendly, but monotone. Flat. "What is there?"

"There's some leftover cherries and custard from the tarts."

Preston lets out an unhappy laugh and reaches for the bowl I'm holding, dredging his finger deep in the vanilla cream. "Want to lick it off my finger?"

Oh. That. Of course. "What's that supposed to mean?"

He flicks the custard back into the bowl and wipes his finger on a napkin. "Why don't you tell me? I've been pretty confused by it myself."

Wow. So that episode really did get under his skin. The way he whisked Rayne away upstairs, it was hard to tell. Suddenly, my mind's reeling. Did he confront her with what he saw, and if so, what did she say? It's not like anything happened... technically... but there were some definite iffy moments that toed the line.

"What the hell's your deal?" I spit out at him.

"What's your deal?" His voice increases an octave and echoes against the glass panes in the cabinetry. "You're the one with the chip on your shoulder."

I blow out a loud breath, crossing my arms over my chest. "I'm not doing this. Why don't you say whatever it is you need to say?"

"Okay, fine. What's going on between you and Rayne?"

I'm not expecting his bluntness. My heart may have stopped beating a time or two, just hanging out in my chest like a dead lump. I swallow hard. How can I give him an answer to a question I've asked myself a million times?

A question I'm still asking myself.

"Me and Rayne? What are you talking about?" I stammer.

"You've never even spoken to the other girls I've dated, yet I find you in here licking cream off her fingers?"

Okay, so that was extremely suspicious... and completely hot. But, of course, I can't tell him that. So I say the next best thing. "Dude, we were doing a project. She gave me a taste. That's it."

"That's it? I've seen you two... laughing, talking, hanging out. Now you have your tongue on her? And you say that's it?"

"Yeah, because it's just that, Preston. Rayne and I have become friends. Yeah, we laugh and talk and hang out. We're comfortable with each other. And, just so you know, we both care about you."

That last part is definitely true. His arrogance makes me want to smash my head into a wall, but I love him. And Rayne cares about him, too. And it's for that reason, I must assure him that nothing's going on between us.

Because nothing can.

Because we can't let it.

"Maybe you should check yourself," I continue. "Would you be questioning me if you weren't feeling guilty? Are you spending enough time with her? You blow her off a lot because Mom tells you to. Because school gets in the way. Or the internship. Or your study buddies. It's always something. I've told you before. Don't lose her because you don't appreciate her."

Preston looks down at his shoes. "I'm sorry. Maybe you're right."

I pat him on the shoulder, and when he looks up, I meet his stare with a grin. "Of course I am."

19

RAYNE

The French presentation in class ends when Madame claps her hands and says, "Magnifique!" When our presentation boards are already folded and leaned against the wall, Gage grabs the food box and carries it to the back table. He picks up the lone leftover cherry, resting it on a tripod of his thumb and first two fingers and smiles. Devilishly.

"Don't start," I laugh and point my finger in his face, knowing full-well what's running through his mind.

"Moi?" He milks the innocent act so well, then leans in, his face so close to mine I can smell the faint sweetness of cherries and cream on his breath. "A present. From me to you." He places the cherry to my lips, parting them slightly and then slips it onto my tongue. How does he make fruit so hot?

I chew it slowly, my eyes fixed on his. They spring open wider when I wipe a trickle of cherry juice from my chin and say, "What am I going to do with you?"

"I have some ideas." He smirks and walks back toward his desk as the bell rings.

I watch him go, shaking my head laughing. In my periphery, I see Jaycee staring.

She's pissed.

"So... your French project... interesting..." Jaycee says, chewing her thumb nail. It took all day, but she's finally caught up with me at the end of cheer practice. "Maybe it's just me, but you and Gage look pretty chummy. Better be careful. Boys aren't so understanding about divided loyalties."

I throw my pompoms on the ground by the bench. "I have no idea what you're talking about."

"I'm talking about the chemistry between you and Gage, you talking about lights and love and him looking all goofy at you. Then he fed you?" She, too, throws down her pompoms and folds her arms in front of her, head tilted waiting on an explanation or a confession.

"Everything's innocent. You're imagining stuff, Jaycee." I hope my face isn't giving me away, because she's right. There's a ton of chemistry there, and I don't have a clue how to deal with it.

Ainsley collapses onto the bench near us. She hasn't opened her mouth, but I know what's coming. I'm starting to hate this time of day because it always presents the same scenario—me surrounded by the girls, fielding questions on my love life. This newfound celebrity status is more like a vice grip, squeezing me to the point I'm sure my head will explode at any second. They don't even call me Rayne half the time anymore. I'm "Preston's girlfriend."

"What's it like kissing him?" asks Ainsley, all dreamy-eyed, looking off into some undetermined spot in the sky, while she traces her fingertips along her collarbone. "Is he always that hot?"

I prop my foot up on the bench and pretend to tie my shoe, ignoring her. I gaze past my laces to the opposite field where the football team is practicing. Gage is at the water cooler. He gulps down the majority of a cup then pours the rest over his head.

My breath hitches when he glances over and waves.

I discreetly lift my hand and wiggle my fingers but jerk them down when Jaycee returns her attention to me. "Chill guys. Rayne's my BFF, and I barely get info. She hoards Preston to herself..." she says, then giggles under her breath. "...and apparently his brother, too."

"His brother? You mean Gage?" pipes up Mallory. "He's no Preston, but he's getting there. A little scruffy but not bad."

Talking about Preston is irritating, but something breaks when they start in on Gage. He's freaking off-limits. I don't know why, and I can't explain it. He just is.

Fury burns up my insides and spills out like a lava flow. "Shut up, y'all! I'm sick of hearing it!"

They circle me like sharks to bloody chum. No one even knows I'm struggling with the Preston thing except Jaycee, and all she's doing is using it as ammo. My phone buzzes with an incoming text, and his name pops up on the screen.

"Ooooooooh," they sing-song in unison like I didn't just have a meltdown. "It's Preston!"

I block the sun from my screen to read.

<Preston> *Tonight's free. Let's hang out.*

Surprising. It's been nearly a week and a half since our last pseudo-date.

<Rayne> *Ok. Rode with Jaycee to school. Have to get car first.*

The phone buzzes almost immediately.

<Preston> *Wait. I'll handle it.*

Within seconds, across the field, Gage pulls his phone from the duffel bag he's packing up on the sidelines then looks over at me.

I grab my pompoms and shove them into my duffel, cramming the red and black streamers deep inside, when the girls begin snickering and whispering. I look up and see him headed my way, hair wet and splayed across his forehead, short jersey barely covering his abs. When our eyes connect, we both smile. He walks in front of me and stoops to my eye-level, leaning in where his lips brush my ear. "Why's everyone staring at us?"

I look over my shoulder at their faces, eyes wide and mouths wider. "They're stupid."

He smirks. "Preston says you need a ride."

"You offering?" I ask, zipping the duffel closed.

"Yep." He throws my bag on his back with his own, and then grabs my hand. "Let's give them something to look at as we go." Laughing, we head to the parking lot.

I'm climbing into the Scout when a text comes through.

<Jaycee> *Now I get it. Two for the price of one.*

I don't respond, just click it off and toss it in the cup holder. Gage slides into the driver's seat and looks over. "Let me guess. You're in trouble with Jaycee?"

"When am I not?" I roll my eyes and buckle the seatbelt across my lap.

Gage cranks up, the deep rumble of the engine muffling his voice. "Want me to put the top up?" he yells over the noise.

"Don't you dare!" I yell back, sweeping my hair into a low ponytail. As he pulls onto the main road and accelerates, the wind rushes through a few loose tendrils and sends them flailing. It's freeing, liberating—something that's escaped me always living under a microscope either by Mama, the town, Jaycee, or sometimes even Preston. Gage doesn't do that. He lets me be me—crazy, messy, non-perfect me.

He nudges my arm with his iPod. "Pick us out some music." I slip the iPod on the dock of his stereo system, the Scout's only hi-tech gadget, which sticks out compared to every other manual-operated device, and rifle through the playlists. They each have a name. Running. Weight Lifting. Chill. Country.

Rock. Rayne. For a minute, I stare at the last one, thinking my mind's playing tricks. Wait... Rayne?

"You have a playlist named after me?" I point to the screen and the digital letters spelling out my name.

Gage's eyes follow my finger to the screen and his smile fades. For a minute, his face goes blank. He'd forgotten it was on there, and now I've found it. But what does it mean?

"Oh... uh... yeah... that." He swallows hard a couple times and glances over at me. "You mentioned liking my 80's rock, so I'm putting files in a playlist for you. To burn you a disc sometime."

"No way! That's freakin' awesome." I clap my hands and bounce around in my seat, so cheerleader-y of me. "Thank you!"

He nods and smiles. "Now pick a song."

I play one from my playlist, and we sing-along, oblivious to the stares from other drivers beside us when I use the hairbrush from my backpack as a microphone. We're still laughing and singing when we pull in the Howard drive and Preston rushes out to meet us, his eyes scrunched together, a frown curving his lips.

"Rayne, I'm so sorry" are the first words I hear as Gage shuts off the engine. I lean back into the seat and cover my eyes as he looks in through the rolled-down window. Too bad doing that doesn't magically shut out the world or his bullshit. "Mom called. Dad's attending a seminar this evening and wants me to go along. I can get class credit. I'll drive you home on the way."

I pull my hands from my face and purse my lips. I can't look Preston in the face, so I turn to his brother. He's staring at us, mouth hanging open. "Thanks for the ride, Gage." I kiss my fingertips and hold them to his check, then grab my bags and hop down on the driveway. When Preston reaches for me, I snap, "I've got it."

He sighs and drops his hand. "Don't be mad, Rayne."

"Why would I be mad, Preston? I'm so over it already," I say with a smile. If he trusts that smile, he's stupid. You never, ever trust a woman who smiles and says she's not mad because she's probably plotting your death at that very moment. With a candlestick. To the head. In the driveway. Ugh.

I slide in the passenger seat of his Mustang and slam the door. Preston gets in and cranks up, while Gage stands by the Scout, hand clamped over his brow. He waves bye with the other hand and I mouth it back to him as we drive away. Immediately Preston begins making excuses, and I'm looking out the opposite window, giving one-word responses. *Fine. Okay. Whatever. Sure.*

I hop out before his Mustang even comes to a full stop in my driveway. He apologizes once more and says he'll text me afterwards. I won't hold my breath unless I have a death wish, so I nod and walk inside to find Mama waiting on me in the foyer, wringing her hands. As if this afternoon wasn't on a shit spiral already.

"What's wrong?" Her eyes are like puddles. "What're you doing back here so soon? You texted and said you'd be at Preston's a while. Did something happen?"

"Yeah, his oh-so-busy college man life." I ease past her, heading for the stairs and the silence of my room.

"It's just as well. You spend too much time with those boys lately, that Gage as much as Preston. And he's a bit rough around the edges." She shakes her head, her mouth pinched into a deep frown.

Funny how judgments come easily to her when she loathes people in town for extending her that same courtesy. "Isn't he the one who drove you to the Howards?"

"Yes, Mama. And he's a gentleman. Always has been." This third degree never ends.

"It's odd. What brother 'fills in' for the other? I don't like it."

I slap my hand against the banister. "I needed a ride. What's wrong with that?"

"If you have to ask me, you already know the answer to that question," she concludes, hands planted firmly on her hips and lines creased deep in her forehead.

I pinch my lips so hard between my front teeth, I'm sure they'll go right through. No point arguing and honestly, I don't have the patience or give-a-crap right now.

It's ten o'clock and I'm lying across my bed studying when my phone buzzes. It's about time. His seminar should've been over at least an hour ago, but Preston hasn't called. I pick up the phone. It's not him. It's Gage.

<Gage> *Check your front porch swing for a surprise.*

I toss the phone on my blanket and run downstairs to the porch. A piece of me wants him to be there. He's not, but a square envelope is. It's a CD with my name scrawled across the front in Gage's handwriting. My playlist.

Back upstairs, I text him back.

<Rayne> *Thank you! So excited. Listening to it now.*

As I'm loading the disc into my stereo, the phone buzzes again.

<Gage> *#8 makes me think of you. Goodnight. See you tomorrow.*

I fast-forward tracks to the song and recognize it immediately. November Rain by Guns N' Roses. One of my favorites. One of the greatest power ballads of all time.

And it makes him think of me.

20

GAGE

Rock music blares from the speakers, the beat pumping through me like blood. Trevor adds a couple plates on the bar, and I adjust my grip. My fingers wrap around the cool metal as I brace myself, abs digging into my spine, and lift the 325 lbs. with a loud exhale.

Heavy weight, low reps—the formula for building mass and gaining definition.

As I bring the bar toward my chest, the muscles constrict like a vice grip. A trickle of sweat rolls off my nose and into my eye. Damn, that stings, but I muster the strength, gritting my teeth, and push through to fully extend my arms once again.

One down.

Only four more to go.

They rattle off easily enough. After Trevor helps me cradle the bar back in place, I sit up on the bench's edge, arms trembling, and rub my terry cloth towel over my face as my breath and pulse ease back to a normal level. When I pull the towel down, the smell of the room assaults me—musky BO and sweat cut with an undercurrent of bleach wipes. Nowhere is this smell appreciated or accepted but in the weight room—the afternoon hangout for the football team and the bullpen for ridiculous amounts of male testosterone.

"Hey." Barrett steps forward, spinning his towel, then thwacks it against my side. The loud pop connects with my bare skin and shoots knives up my back. "What's the deal with Preston and Rayne?"

Terrific. Locker room talk, usually centered around topics on which I have no opinions, experience, or interest. Especially now, when it involves my brother.

"What about 'em?"

He deadpans like I should know exactly what he's talking about. And I do. But I don't let on in the hopes he'll take it elsewhere.

"You know." He waggles his eyebrows up and down. "What's going on with them?"

I shrug. "They're dating."

He tries to pop me again with the towel, but I duck sideways, missing it.

"No shit. I mean, to what extent are they a couple? Rayne's a bit of a prude, but Preston... man, he has his ways." He laughs and looks around for support, which he gets from all the other guys who laugh and nod like a background chorus. "Amiright?"

The last thing I want to discuss are my brother's ways or how he might be using them on Rayne. The thought of it churns my stomach.

"How am I supposed to know?" Venom laces the response, a blinking highway sign for Barrett to tread lightly. His spine stiffens.

"He's your brother. He has to tell you the deets." He narrows his eyes and twists his mouth sideways, all smug-like, as if he just finished a thousand-piece jigsaw puzzle. "Unless..."

"Unless what?"

"Unless there's some competition there? I mean, you're with her all the time."

I jump to my feet, kneading the towel in my clenched fist. "Cause she's dating my brother, and we're friends. That's it."

"But you've thought about it, right?" He smiles—a sleazy one—and cocks his head to one side.

"Thought about what?"

"Tagging in? A little brother-to-brother relay event? Some fraternal timeshare?"

The embers burning inside rush to an all-out inferno. Black spots float in my vision, stars fizzle in the periphery. I lunge forward, pressing my nose to his.

He may be taller, but I'm bigger. And stronger.

"Y'all are sick. Get me and my brother out of your mouths." I have to pause and regroup as the anger boiling inside vibrates into my voice. "And Rayne—don't you ever talk about her like that again. You want to talk skank, Barrett? Then go get your girl because that's Jaycee. All. Day. Long. Not Rayne."

"You stupid son of a—" Barrett rears back as Trevor bolts across the mat and shoves himself between us.

"All right! Break it up, guys."

Barrett jabs his finger in my face with a sneer as I launch my towel toward the bin and stomp to the locker room. Damn him and his stupid insinuations. And I wondered how he could like Jaycee, but time's proving one thing. He deserves a girl like her.

I slip a muscle tee over my head and throw my regular clothes in the duffel. If I don't get out of this school right now, I'm going to explode. The rage burrows inside all my crevices like a parasitic worm. Eating me alive on the inside until I want to turn around and rearrange his face.

Dammit. I slam the metal handle with my fist, and the gym door flies open, knocking into the concrete block walls. I stomp through into the small hallway leading to the parking lot. That's when I see her.

Rayne's standing along the wall with Jaycee and Ainsley, their pom-poms at their feet. She looks up with a frown that quickly dissolves into a smile once her eyes land on me.

Those damn eyes. They're getting me into trouble.

She's getting me into trouble.

"Hey, Gage!"

This is not the time or the place. Especially with all the talk going on in the locker room. Especially with the evil-eye Jaycee's burning into my chest, probably using her witchy x-ray vision to pluck out all my deepest secrets so she can run them straight to Barrett.

I don't smile back at her. I don't even walk closer. I just throw my duffle on my arm and yell back over my shoulder as I head to the door. "I can't talk right now. I have stuff to do."

Nothing settles a pissed off mood like pounding out a few repairs on my Scout. There's just something about the metallic ding of the tools when I drop them on the pavement. The sweet scent of gasoline that hovers. The nervous energy expelled when I have to grit my teeth and really lay into some wrench work.

I'm on the creeper underneath the jacked-up front end when something kicks my boot. I roll out on my back, the sudden burst of sunlight from overhead temporarily blinding me. I squint as the haze dissolves.

Preston stands by the front bumper. Rayne's with him.

He's smiling. She's not.

As a matter of fact, the eat-dirt lip pout and her eyes, locked on something in the distance, tell me everything I need to know.

I messed up earlier. Big time.

"We're going upstairs to watch a movie or something."

I don't care about a movie. It's the *or something* that scratches at my throat. I cough, trying to dislodge the heavy lump.

"Well, Mom and Dad are gone until late, so the coast is clear."

"Sounds good!" Preston says. He pats Rayne on the arm, signaling he needs to get something from the car before they head upstairs. She nods, still without words or her usual smile, shifting from foot to foot.

I venture a peace offering. "Can I talk to you for a minute?"

But no matter what I do, she won't look at me.

Until finally she does, and I wish she hadn't. Her eyes are shaded, grayed out. Almost sad. Or mad. Maybe a mixture of the two. I can't be sure.

She blows out a loud breath and clenches her jaw, an intense glower suddenly piercing me like a dagger. "Can't right now. I have stuff to do."

Her words sting. She turns and joins Preston at the car. He grabs her hand, pulling her along behind him, up the sidewalk, and through the front door. It slams shut, a barrier between them and me.

I stare at his window, the lump in my throat back and bigger than before, my heart somersaulting against my ribs.

The light flicks on. She walks by the window. He's right behind her.

The bile burns in my chest as I lie back on the creeper and slide under the Scout.

I can't look anymore.

Two hours. That's how long they've been in his room together. And they're still in there. Preston's voice seeps through the walls.

About an hour ago, I worked up the nerve to dash up the stairs to my room, without stopping once. I know they're in there. I just don't want to know anything else. Or imagine. Or see. Or hear.

Now, my stomach's grumbling, yelling out for food, and going downstairs means going past his room. I press my ear to the door, listening. For what I don't know. Some cosmic sign I'm supposed to maintain my distance, but nothing comes. The rumble happens again, louder this time, the insatiable beast demanding to be fed.

I ease open the door and step halfway out in the hallway. Preston's door is cracked, and his voice comes out in long stands, freckled with words like *spreadsheet* and *audit report* and *inventory*. Is he really talking accounting to Rayne?

That's when he picks up a new line of discussion. "Yes, Mom. Yes, Dad. I can put together a..."

Everything coming out of his mouth fades to white noise. I don't give a crap about accounting, but I do care about Rayne. And once again, Preston's pushing her to the background so he can answer a call from Mom and Dad. I sneak past the door, catching a quick glimpse. Preston stands by his desk, cell phone glued to his ear, as he shuffles through papers. Rayne's not in there with him.

Where is she?

I creep to the stairs and shuffle down two at a time, coming up on the balls of my feet so I don't make much noise.

Rayne stands in the foyer, staring at those stupid Chinese vases Mom had installed with the new wall shelf. She's about to touch one—her fingertip a whisper away—when I clear my throat. She jumps and clasps her hand over her chest, eyes shut.

"You trying to give me a heart attack?" she gripes, her voice hard between the ragged breaths.

"You know Mom measures those things, right?" I tip my head toward the vases. "Like down to the millimeter."

She studies them a minute and shrugs. One of those I-don't-give-a-crap ones, complete with eye roll.

I sigh and trudge across the room to stand beside her. She refuses to look at me, but her hair is only inches from my nose and smells of lavender and vanilla. I reach out and touch her arm, just above the elbow. She shivers but doesn't pull away.

"I'm sorry. I had a bad day in the weight room. I was just… stressing out."

She side-eyes me, her lips stretched so thin they disappear into a flat pink line. "You could've talked to me, you know. I would've listened."

"Not to this. It was stupid guy stuff, but I… I shouldn't have taken it out on you."

Though she's still staring at the vases, a smile spreads across her face, her cheeks appling. "So, she freaks out if they're out of place?"

"It drives her nuts. She'll have a tape measure in here if they look remotely off."

She bites her bottom lip, nodding, then reaches up, and with a quick motion, pushes one vase backwards and over to the left. A noticeable difference. One that'd drive Mom crazy.

"Naughty, naughty," I chide, clicking my tongue.

"I know. You like that about me." She turns her eyes on me at that moment, and chill bumps scatter down my entire body. I do like her grit, her edge.

It's a side I doubt most people have seen. Probably not even Preston.

"So, I'm forgiven?"

"Yeah," she nudges me with her hip. "Just don't be a jerk again."

"Never." I laugh but a loud creaking followed by heavy footsteps from upstairs captures our attention. Preston's coming, so I back towards the door, grabbing for the wooden molding behind me. Not running away. More like avoiding suspicion. "I'm gonna grab a bite from the kitchen. See you tomorrow."

21

RAYNE

*P*reston revs the Mustang in the driveway. There's something about the low, gravely rumbling that irks Mama. Like it has too much testosterone in it. Like it's Preston's own primal beat-your-chest thing. *Mrs. Davidson, me here, take your daughter. Have my way with her.* Something along those lines with a lot of grunts.

She flicks the blinds apart with her fingers, peering out at him from the safety of the den, eyes wide as if at any moment he might hit the gas and barrel into the room with us. "And y'all won't be alone?"

Last night, the Howards left for a long weekend in a Tennessee mountain resort. They stocked the fridge, told their sons good-bye, and when their car was out of sight, the boys planned a party.

"No ma'am. Just a small group hanging out tonight." Yeah, if small is somewhere in the three digits. I'm not worried she'll find out the truth. Mama doesn't go out at night and she most certainly won't be out driving. If she sends Daddy, he won't trail me. He'll just drive around a bit, go home and tell her everything's as it should be. I'm not worried about town gossip either. They'll never rat out Preston.

Mama walks out on the porch as I run to his car. Preston waves out the rolled down window. "Hi, Mrs. Davidson." She deepens the glare but reluctantly waves back.

We're quiet until my house is no longer in sight, like somehow Mama will be able to hear us if she can still see us. "Nice outfit," he says, eyeing my jeans and Chucks.

"I'm assuming from that comment you know..."

"Yep. Jaycee dropped off your outfit change this morning." He winks. "Sneaky, sneaky."

Maybe. I call it conscientious. I'm proactively helping Mama not have a heart attack. Better to let her think I'm a dress-down-jeans-and-chucks girl than a little-black-dress-and-heels harlot. "It's in my room. You can change when we get there."

Three hours later, the Howard house is slammed, the music is ear-throbbing, and I'm seriously considering ditching the stilettos. I've seen Jaycee about one minute all night, but she's been MIA a good two hours, and I can pretty much guess where she is considering Barrett's also missing. Preston's made his rounds with me on his arm, and now my feet are killing me. That's partly why I'm hiding out here on the couch. And I really just need a break from smiling and pretending to like all these people.

I go undetected for a split-second until the cushion beside me moves, and Gage nudges my arm. "You hiding out?" he leans in and whispers in my ear. "Where's Preston?"

"He's supposed to be getting me a drink."

"I hope you're not too thirsty. You know how it is when you turn him loose alone."

"Hell yeah," I say and turn on the cushion to face him. "Just the other day—"

A shrill voice, belonging to a girl with long blond hair and six feet of legs, interrupts me. "So, you're dating Preston?" She arches her eyebrows and stares down at me. That *you're* is loaded. *You're* as in no way am I good enough. *You're* as in we're mortal enemies.

"Yeah, I am." What's with this chick? Then I remember where I've seen her before. The bonfire. The one I called Legs-a-lot. The one who'd been pissed Preston ignored her for me. Her face is still twisted up just like that night.

"Unlikely." She steps back and sweeps her eyes over me from top to bottom. "I heard he's been slumming. Didn't realize he's this committed to the cause."

No words. I push myself back into the couch cushions, stunned by her use of guerilla tactics on the social level. And where's Jaycee? She lives for this drama. Never do I worry about anyone going toe-to-toe with me. Jaycee will annihilate them, but now she's nowhere to be found. I'm alone.

Until I'm not.

Gage physically inserts himself between us, fists clenched tight. "Shut up, Ashlyn." Ashlyn? This is the chick Charlotte wants with Preston? He's in her face, yelling so loudly other people hear it above the music and gather around the commotion.

For a moment, he bucks up, but I know he'll never hit her. Gage would never hit a girl. Not even a skanky one. And where's Preston in all this? I crane my neck around and finally spot him in the kitchen, talking and drinking a beer. The red solo cup he's picked up for me stands beside him on the table, still full and covered in condensation.

"Don't get pissy with me because your brother's looking for a charity case." Ashlyn slams her hand in Gage's face, so close her palm bumps the tip of his nose.

Gage erupts. "You," he says, the vile pouring freely from him as he jams his finger toward her, "are jealous. Preston chose a smart girl, a classy girl, and you losers can't compete with her. None of you can." Gage's eyes are wild, brimming with hatred, as he spews out the words, but even his last declaration makes him stagger backwards.

Talk about double takes. I have to look back at him twice to make sure he really said it. Everyone in the immediate crowd gasps. I check over my shoulder—Preston's still chatting in the kitchen, ignorant of the fact his brother and I are about to cut a bitch.

"Whatever. She's as crazy as that weirdo Mama of hers." She cups her hands around her mouth. "Clean up on aisle three."

Something snaps. I used to wonder why people called it that, but once it happens, you know. It's like my sanity's held in place by a little rubberized string, then *bam!* The whole thing rolls up like a window shade and leaves behind nothing but a blinding darkness and a mish-mash of sounds blaring in my brain all at once. In an out-of-body rush, I charge forward off the couch, slam into her and throw her back against the wall, during which she jerks her hands toward me, spraying my right arm and shoulder with her beer.

Gage grabs me from behind, pins my arms to my side, and then throws me over his shoulder like a sack of oats. I use up the rest of my energy on him, pummeling his chest with knee jabs as he carries me to the mudroom.

He kicks the door shut behind us and plops me on the countertop next to the utility sink and a large bottle of stain remover. He grabs a cloth from the drawer and wets it with the cleaner then rubs it into the stains with their sour-sweet smell hovering around us. For a moment, it's silent except for our heavy panting.

"This is the stuff the maid uses on our uniforms." Gage wedges himself between my knees as close as the countertop allows. He pulls my arm straight alongside his, and I wrap my fingers around the bulge of his bicep underneath the black button-down, his muscles flexing and relaxing with each stroke. "Want me to get Preston?"

"No." *Too quick.* My lightning speed response causes him to look up. If the silver lining to this whole mess is stealing a few extra moments, then I'm taking it.

He swallows hard. "I'm really sorry about Ashlyn. Mom always favored her, so she thinks she and Preston are meant to be."

"Not your fault." I put my free hand on top of his, momentarily stopping his vigorous scrubbing. That's when he notices the large cut on my hand with little droplets of blood leaching to the surface like a connect-the-dots game.

"Bad ass. A battle bruise," he laughs, snarling his upper lip.

"It's because of her God-awful claws," I mumble as he rubs his thumb over the mark. "Ow. That kinda stings."

"Poor baby. We'll fix it." He pulls my hand to his lips, hot and damp against my skin. He might as well have kicked me in the chest. My heart butterflies against my ribs, stealing my breath, and making me lightheaded. And tingly. All over tingly.

My boyfriend should inspire this. Not a boo-boo kiss from his brother. Preston's touch is nice, but not hot. Like this.

"Gage..." I whisper. "About what you said... to Ashlyn..."

"Forget about it."

"I can't. Why'd you say it?"

"Cause I meant it. None of those girls..." he trails off.

I reach out and cup his chin in my hand, his five o'clock shadow scratchy against my palm. Guiding him in for a kiss would seem natural. Easy. But he pulls away and turns his head, looking at the beige tiled floor. "Don't."

I retract my hand as if burned by a hot stove. "Sorry. I didn't mean..." He still won't look at me, but his Adam's apple bobs up and down as he swallows back whatever it is he won't put into words. "Gage… please talk to me."

Finally, he looks back up, his blue eyes no longer vibrant but cloudy. Tempered. "Rayne, I…"

The door bursts open in a frenzy of arms and legs with Jaycee and Barrett tangled up in each other, back-pedaling through the opening and straight into Gage, who's knocked forward into me. Our faces slam together, his lips a teeny-tiny fraction from mine. I want to kiss him. We're so close. The musk of his cologne tickles my nose. The heat from his breath radiates down my neck. But what surprises me most is the look in Gage's eyes. Hungry. Eager.

And for one split second, he tilts his head to the left like he's going to initiate it. Please God, oh please…

"What the hell is this?" Jaycee screeches in slurred words, staggering sideways into the cabinetry, glassy-eyed and hanging on to the door handle like a crutch. "Wait… are you two… messing around? Did he try something with you? I mean, I know you two are friends," she frames her words in air quotes, "but come on… this is weird."

The vein in his neck throbs as his hand, which has landed on my thigh, presses deeper into my flesh. Spinning on his heels, he pushes past both Jaycee and Barrett, shoving them out of his way. Barrett falls backwards onto the floor, his beer bottle still stuck between his lips as he laughs. Jaycee wobbles on her heels.

I've only seen her this way once before, last year at a party of Ainsley's we'd gone to after I told Mama I was spending the night with Jaycee. She drank until her face turned bright red, her eyes puffed up, and her attitude turned to crap. Happy drunk she was not. More like belligerent. Vile. She looks that same way tonight.

Jaycee pushes herself off the cabinetry and runs to the door, leans out and yells after Gage, "Like she'd want you! She's got Preston. Not even close, Gage!"

She turns around, a flimsy grin on her face, and saunters over to me. "I just took out the trash. You can thank me later." She drops her nearly empty beer bottle on the countertop, turning it over and spilling out the last remnants in a sticky, golden trail.

Inside, the anger boils in me like an unchecked pot on the stovetop and the lid's about to fly off.

"Shut up!" I scream, scrunching my hair to the scalp. Why that helps, I have no idea. Maybe it's a subconscious effort to the keep the anger from shooting my head right off my shoulders. Maybe it's my way of binding my hands so I don't put them around her throat. "Shut up! Where were you earlier when that Legs-a-lot heifer was assaulting me? Oh, that's right —drinking and hooking up. Gage is the only one who stood up for me. Not Preston. Not Ainsley. Not you. Him. And then you bust in here starting drama? I'm done, Jaycee! D.O.N.E."

I jump off the counter and shove past her, digging my shoulder into her arm as I pass. Halfway up the hallway, I pause and close my eyes, taking a deep breath and leaning against the vanilla-colored walls. I need to find Gage and finish our conversation. I open my eyes and immediately wish I hadn't.

In the den, Gage is backed up in the corner beside the fireplace. Mallory presses closely in front of him, closer than any two people not flirting should be, and swirls her red hair around her finger. She laughs and touches his arm, a high-pitched squeal somewhere between a dying pig and braying donkey. And the way she smiles at him? Definitely donkey. But he's no better, touching her shoulder, laughing at her stupid conversation like a fool.

Anger, hurt, and jealousy churn my insides like a washing machine on a spin cycle. I'm messed up. In the kitchen, Preston's back talking to a few girls I recognize from his biology study group, but I couldn't care less. Gage has the audacity to even look at the red-headed she-devil, and I'm out for blood. For clumps of red stringy hair on the floor. For fake nails ripped off and shoved down her stupid junior throat.

Blind rage comes on like heated fingers grappling with my skin from the feet up. He smiles at her, and my knees burn. She lays her hand on his bicep, and my hips burn. She leans in close, whispering, and my stomach burns. He runs his fingers through his hair, and she wiggles her spirit fingers, and I want to slap them both. Rap music is blasting in the background, the bass turning into a pseudo-second heartbeat, bumping deep in my chest. It lulls me into a dangerous tunnel vision. One should never listen to rap music when murder feels imminent.

Maybe I'm more like Mama than I want to admit. She's a victim, now I am, too.

No. Not tonight. I'm going to kick my own butt into shape. I run over, grab his arm, and pull his chiseled torso into mine. "Where've you been all night?"

Preston smiles and wraps his arms around me. "I could ask you the same thing. I missed you."

"I missed you, too. Why don't we go upstairs and let me show you how much?" I grab his hand and pull him toward the stairs.

"Upstairs?" he asks, both eyebrows arch as far as they'll go.

I swallow the last of my reluctance along with the promise I made myself years ago about not having sex until I was eighteen. At this point, being with Preston is the only thing that'll dump Gage from my mind once and for all. After tonight, no one can say I got in my own way ever again.

"Upstairs." I point above us, then tug him into me and pull his head down close, unleashing a firestorm of hard, heavy kisses. Through slitted eyes, I see Gage across the room, staring in our direction. I grab a handful of Preston's shirt and pull him up the stairs behind me but keep turning around to look at Gage.

He's ignoring Mallory, eyes fixed on us puppy-dog like. No. I'm not changing my mind. Preston's my boyfriend. Gage... he isn't. And he has no excuse to guilt me while he's standing there with her.

On the landing, Preston grabs both my shoulders and meets me eye-to-eye. "Are you sure?"

"Yes!" I scream, more desperate than excited, and shove him toward the bedroom door. Let's get this over with, and then everything will be fine again.

Preston slams the door and locks it, his face flushed and sweaty, eyes focused on me. He untucks his shirt and pulls it over his head in one easy movement and throws it across the chair. In the next minute, he unbuckles his belt, unzips and lets his jeans puddle on the ground. He stands there in all his gorgeousness, in nothing but boxers.

My eyes instantly rove his abs and not because of their rippled goodness. God knows Preston's hot and cut to shreds. But I'm looking for a tattoo. A tattoo that doesn't belong to him. It belongs to Gage. Oh my God. I'm getting ready to have sex with Preston while I'm thinking about his brother. I sit on the side of his plaid comforter wanting to pluck my brain out through my left ear. Too much thinking. That's what's causing this. I need to just go with it. Let Preston run his fingers over my stomach. Really feel his skin burning against mine. Then it'll be good.

His breath licks across my face in warm bursts, his lips hovering a whisper away from mine. I clamp my eyes shut, waiting. Every muscle in my body shivers with tension, the way you do when preparing for the doctor to give you a shot.

Did I really just compare this to a shot?

His lips crush mine, fierce, hot, and hard. There's no sweet, romantic anything to it. It's straight up hormonal frenzy, and I freaking don't know what I'm doing.

I open my eyes to look at him as he grabs the hem of my dress and tugs it upwards, past my waist, then raises both my arms. In one swipe, it lays crumpled beside me. Preston stops to slowly look me up and down, and all that's crossing my mind is how bad I want to die right now. He sees me in my underwear. Oh my God. Mama's going to flip if she finds out.

"Oh, Rayne..." he mumbles, husky-voiced, wraps his hands around my shoulders and pushes me back onto the bed, the Egyptian cotton comforter like silk to my bare skin. He moves on top of me, one hand cupped behind my head, one hand exploring my breasts while his lips graze my neck. But the warm kisses can't squelch the endless thought-loop in my head that tells me this is wrong. Wrong timing. Wrong place. Wrong person. Gage's face is ever-fixed in my mind, his eyes haunting me. The hunger I saw earlier in the mudroom and the hurt when I came here with Preston. Worse than anything is how I imagine they'll look the first time he hears from Preston what we did.

"Stop," I say quietly at first, and then yell. "Stop!" My hands are against his chest, pushing him off.

He jumps to his feet in one move, eyes wild, mouth open and breathing hard. "What's wrong?"

I hate myself. I sit up, crossing my arms over my chest to cover up as the tears sting my eyelids and drip in crooked rows down my cheeks.

"I'm sorry. I'm so sorry, Preston," I repeat over and over.

"What is it?" He stares down at me, hands planted on his hips.

"I'm... not ready." He exhales loudly and throws his head back. "I thought I was, but..."

He turns away from me and looks out the window. I can't blame him if he hates me, but all I can do is sit here like a criminal waiting on a sentence. He slams his hand on the wall, stomps over and grabs his jeans from the floor, and glares at me while pulling them on then grabs his shirt from the chair. He stands there frozen, the shirt dangling from one hand, the other hand balled into a fist against his mouth. I can't tell if he's trying to choose his words or stop himself from cussing me out. Taking a few deep breaths, he pulls on his shirt, tucks it in and walks to the door, then turns back, his hand on the knob.

"I never pushed this on you. Never. I've been way more patient than ever before, but... pretending you're ready and getting me all riled up and then... I don't know... unbelievable."

I grab my heap of a dress and slide it back on. "Please forgive me, Preston. I really thought I was ready... I really did..."

He smashes his lips together and scratches his head before responding. "Take your time getting dressed. I'm going back down to the party." He unlocks the door and walks out, pulling it shut behind him with a soft click. It sounds final, like he's closing more than a door.

I lean over his dresser, rubbing away the black mascara streaks from my face. What the heck do I do now that I finally realize it isn't me standing in my way? It's something much bigger than me. It's him. It's us. Something I never expected to happen. I stop and stare at myself in the mirror, splotchy skin, tangled hair, and a shiny glint in my eye that wasn't there before. The truth? I'm dating a wonderful guy, but I'm in love with his brother.

It's amazing the rush that takes over, first realizing I'm in love. Like suddenly the world falls away and nothing would feel better than holding or kissing him. Endorphins are funny like that. Suddenly I feel invincible, untouchable, but it's all a lie, because that stuff doesn't matter. Other people matter, and I can't go running around reckless no matter how much I want to.

I sit down on the corner of his bed, finger-combing my

disheveled hair. There's no simple solution. If I tell Gage, he'll have to choose me or his brother. Either way, one relationship goes down. I can't live with causing problems between brothers. I can't live without Gage. If Preston and I break up, Gage's loyalty will automatically fall to his brother. That's one of the unwritten rules, right? There's only one way—keep things as is. If Preston even still wants me after tonight. If I can pull this whole thing off without hurting him.

Too many ifs.

I'm in love with Gage, but I can't have him. Not the way I want. I'll have to settle with being his friend even when it hurts —because losing him would be worse.

I walk back downstairs, stopping on the bottom step to sweep my eyes around the room.

"Hey." Jaycee walks up beside me looking sheepish, twirling her bracelet around her wrist. "I'm sorry about earlier."

"You need to quit drinking," I say flatly, meeting her with a hard stare. "We'll talk when you're sober."

"I... I was wrong. I know there isn't anything going on between y'all."

I fold my arms across my chest and tilt my head. "And how did you finally figure this out?"

"When I found out Gage is into Mallory. He was probably asking you about her, and I took it wrong."

Her words are like a vacuum sucking the air from my lungs. "Mallory... yeah. By the way, where is she now?" I need to find them. Stop this. He can't hook up with Mallory.

"Oh, they left a while ago. You were... upstairs." She nudges my side with her elbow, wiggling her eyebrows up and down.

"Oh." I swallow back the tears. "Where'd they go?"

"I don't know, but Mallory looked happy about it."

I bet she did, and I'll hear about it Monday morning, every excruciating detail.

"Go. Have fun with Barrett." I point to the couch where he's sprawled out, legs resting on the coffee table. In the kitchen, Preston's downing yet another beer and chatting up the "biology babes." I've managed to drive away two good guys tonight because they both want easy, uncomplicated, one-track minded girls. I'm not. For the first time, their family resemblance is clear.

I walk to Preston's room, change back into jeans and chucks, and leave the black dress and heels crumpled in a pile on his comforter. At least if he tries scoring with a "biology babe" that'll put a hitch in his plan.

Sneaking down the stairs and out the back door, I walk home, counting the sidewalk cracks as I go, with only the lonesome howl of an occasional wind gust and the screaming thoughts of my conscience ramming into my brain for company. Mama'd love this—her innocent girl walking home alone in the dark—the stuff of her nightmares.

Just past the library on Main Street, a familiar rumble cuts through muted sounds of background traffic. Over my shoulder two amber orbs approach from my six, and I squint my eyes for a better look. Gage's hands are on the wheel, Mallory's feet are propped on his dash and frizzy tendrils of red hair whip in the breeze from the open passenger window. They pass me without a glance, the air swirling behind them, blasting my face and whipping my hair around in a frenzied cloud. I stand paralyzed, watching his red taillights disappear into the distance.

22

GAGE

*H*er shoes are leaving scuff marks all over my dash. I just polished it, too. All that hard work for nothing. And I'd yell at her to get them down if she'd shut up for two seconds. But she hasn't. Not for the trip through the drivethru to get her extra-large sweet tea, and not even after the straw is stuck in the middle of her lips. She just talks around it.

Unbelievable.

It's not like me to bottle up my angry comments and not go ballistic on her, especially for screwing up my clean Scout. But right now, even as annoying as Mallory is, I'm enjoying the distraction. Anything to not think about what's going on in my brother's bedroom. Or that freaking dagger that plunges deeper with each heartbeat.

As we turn out on Main Street, I roll my window down and motion for her to do the same. She stares at the armrest for a minute like some automatic button will magically appear, and when it doesn't, she finally leans forward and cranks the lever, lowering the glass. The wind rushes in, pricking my arms with chill bumps, and funneling a loud whir of air into the space between us. Perfect. Now I can just pretend to listen.

I lock my grip on the steering wheel, so tight a ripple of pain shoots over my knuckles and burns in my palms. As if the sheer force will stop the images from infiltrating my brain.

It doesn't.

She was ripping at his clothes, fingers twisting in the fabric, hands running all over him. My stomach churns. God, just let this night be over. Please.

Mallory's voice rings out over the wind. "Do you know him?" I glance sideways. She's leaning toward me, hand cupped around her mouth, as she yells.

"Who?"

She rolls her eyes as if I've asked her for some lengthy explanation. Wah. I wasn't paying attention to her boy saga. Sue me.

"The guy I'm meeting. You know him?"

I shake my head, barely remembering the name she originally gave me back at the house. Something like Raymond. Or Drummond. Or... who cares? All I know is this girl needs to chill her jets. Who finds a random guy in a coffeehouse and less than 24 hours later sneaks off to meet him?

A girl who wants to be a Criminal Minds episode, that's who.

I pull into the Piggly Wiggly parking lot, driving slowly up the first row until I see his white truck, pulled catty-cornered across two spaces. He's half-hanging out his window, waving us over, his black hair long and shaggy. I edge beside him, making a mental note of his license plate number, just in case.

Mallory swings the door wide and slides off the seat, her feet slapping the pavement. She bends in front of the side mirror to swipe on lip gloss.

"Hey." I reach over and tap her shoulder. "You sure about this guy? I'll be happy to drop you off at home if not."

She smiles as she slams the door, then leans back in the passenger window. "So you do have a softer side... just like

Rayne said." My mouth drops open, my brain hitting overdrive, as she saunters over and gets inside Shaggy's truck. "Thanks for the ride," she says as he revs the engine and they take off across the lot.

She can't just throw that into the conversation and then ride off into the night. What does it even mean?

The drive home might as well be 200 miles instead of two minutes for the number of times I run Mallory's comment through my head. *A softer side. Just like Rayne said.*

So she's been talking about me? In passing or conversation? She said I was soft. Like "Gage is nowhere near as strong as Preston" or was it more like "Gage is so sweet to me"? There's no way to know exactly what was said or implied. But through all the chaos detonating in my thick skull, one question screams loudest.

Why the hell do I care?

Okay, so I do care. About her. Obviously. And she's sending signals like crazy that she's feeling it for me, too. Ridiculous and borderline torture since it's all a flirting game, some kind of dance around each other because there are obvious lines that can't be crossed. But damn. Rayne doesn't realize how much she affects me. Too much. There are times I have to physically insert distance between us so I won't do what I really want to.

Like kiss her. And touch her. And hold her.

Her invitation would be all the incentive I need, and that's what scares me most.

My stomach turns to fire. It's unacceptable. So what if I think she's possibly the most amazing human I've ever met?

She's dating my brother.

Done deal.

Too bad, Gage.

That's why I told her to stop earlier. It's why after the finger-licking at the French project I basically pushed her back into my brother's arms. Because no matter how many times we push the limits, we absolutely cannot cross that line.

I sigh and turn into the driveway, dodging the cars still littering the pavement while making my way to the garage. The music's bass thumps through the walls, and a sweetly-sour whiff of beer hits me in the face as I sneak in the back door and up the hidden staircase.

My bed is where I want to be, but the only problem is getting there requires passing Preston's. His door is ajar, a long sliver of yellow light cutting across the carpet.

Damn. I don't want to see. I don't want to know.

I trudge forward, scrubbing the side of my body into the wall, my eyes glued to the patterned carpet. But the temptation's magnetic. I have to look. I have to know. Whether I want to or not.

The edge of his bed is barely visible, and on it, Rayne's black dress and heels lay in a crumpled pile. That can only mean...

I stagger backwards, my feet tangling up on themselves. The background music fades to a loud buzz, and the oxygen stalls in my throat. Every nerve ending vibrates with one message: Leave.

The stairs disappear two and three at a time under my feet as I dart back out into the garage and through the double doors to our home gym. The door slams shut, and I reach up to slide the lock in place. The heavy bag hangs solemnly from the ceiling mount, the cotton wrist wraps stacked on the shelves to my right. I grab them, twisting the strips over the bones.

Rayne... she wrecks me every damn time she looks at me, and this infatuation isn't going away. It's growing. And I've lost all control.

Inhale. Draw back. Exhale. Power.

My knuckles connect with the leather, the anger exploding out from the point of contact, the incredible tension in the muscles becoming fluid and active. Repeated with a right, right, left, and each accompanied by a strong declaration, my voice getting louder with each one until it's echoing off the overhead beams.

Bam! She sang to me on karaoke night. To me.

Bam! The way she tilts her head and fingers her curls when we're talking in the hallway.

Bam! Her warm fingertips on my tattoo.

Bam! I can't feel this way.

Bam! This is wrong.

Bam! She's with him.

Bam! I can't have her.

My last swing whizzes by the bag in a total miss, the momentum carrying me head over feet to the floor. I roll over on my back, the sweat trickling down my temples, the saltiness stinging my eyes.

Oh shit.

I'm in love with her.

23

———

RAYNE

I sleep most of Sunday, telling Mama my throat's scratchy from the night air of the changing season. She believes it because who doesn't have seasonal allergies in the South? It's like a birthright. And an excellent fallback excuse for anytime I just want to be left alone. Like today.

Preston calls me six times and texts twice. They all go unanswered, especially after I receive his last text saying we need to talk. Hello Dumpsville to the girl who wouldn't put out after pretending she would. So I sink under the covers, binge-watching Gilmore Girls reruns and drinking loads of sweet tea with lemon, which Mama says will help my throat. I'm hoping it puts me into a deep sugar coma, so I'll sleep through tomorrow and miss all the fabulous details of Mallory's weekend affair.

———

She's sitting in front of the lockers Monday morning, her head mashed up against the grey metal, red ringlets fanning out like flames. Yep, a she-devil. Ainsley, Jaycee, and a few of the other girls circle around her like she's a chief with a war story to share.

"There we were, sitting in his car, when he leaned in really close. I knew he was going to kiss me. And when he did... oh my gosh, y'all, it was so good. I just couldn't stop myself," she gushes on and on while her cronies giggle like morons. No way I'm listening to this. It's like knives in my heart. I throw my jacket in the locker and grab my books, making excuses about some big research I need to do in the library. As I walk around the corner, her voice finally fades but not before I hear, "He's already asked me out again!"

By the time the last bell rings, I've managed to hide out most of the day, even volunteering to help Mrs. Cravitch in the guidance office. She sent a note to Madame excusing me from French class. When the halls are nearly clear, I drop by my locker on the way to cheer practice, praying Mallory's all talked out about the weekend before I see her.

I check my eyeliner in the locker mirror. Why they even call it a mirror is beyond me. The freaking thing's so foggy it's more like Saran-wrap-covered reflective plastic. I grab it from the door, angling it a particular way so I can see a semblance of my reflection. But it's not just mine. He's there, standing way too close behind me.

"Boo," Gage says in my ear as I slam the mirror back on the door. "Where ya been hiding today?" He already has on his uniform, helmet tucked under his right arm. The black padded shirt clings to his midsection and the pants fit like a second skin. Damn him for looking this hot when I want to hate him and choke him and punch him right in the face.

I sweep my hair into a ponytail then fling my backpack over my shoulder. "I'm not hiding." My locker door slams so hard, the flimsy mirror crashes down inside.

"Damn. What'd that locker do to you?" He sounds so jokey, like it's any old day. I guess hooking up with a red-headed junior does that for you.

"Nothing. The locker hasn't pissed me off."

"Have I?"

"Have you what?"

"Have I pissed you off?"

I stare at my shoelaces, avoiding his eyes. "No."

"Liar. You looked down." How can he know me so well, notice all my weird habits, and not see I'm totally in love with him? Maybe he doesn't want to see it. Or maybe he does and is trying to let me down easy.

"I did not."

He stops walking and grabs my shoulder, turning me toward him. "What is it, Rayne?" He pauses but I don't answer. "Please? I can't fix it unless I know."

"I'm fine. Leave me alone."

"Is it because of the laundry room incident Saturday?" *Yes.* "Are you mad at me because I told you to stop?" *Partly.* He breathes hard, tapping his class ring on his helmet making a *tick, tick, tick* sound. "I didn't want someone thinking the wrong thing. You know how people are. Especially that drunk crazy-ass friend of yours."

The wrong thing? Because loving me is wrong on every level, and so he doesn't. He won't. He'll choose Mallory because she's easy, uncomplicated.

"Okay."

"Okay? Fine." He lets go of my shoulder and we start walking again. "You headed to cheer practice?"

I ignore him and pick at the fuzzies on my black skirt. *No, I'm just wearing this polyester spirit suit for the hell of it.* He knows where I'm headed. It's the same every afternoon. He has foot-ball practice on the field opposite of where the squad meets.

Every practice is the same for him—stretching, water break, running, water break, and then O-line drills. He's grasping for conversation, which means he's stalling. And he's fidgeting. So not a good sign.

"Rayne, there's something awkward I wanted to talk about." My stomach somersaults. This is it. He's going to tell me all about his new girlfriend.

"Go ahead." Let's get this over with.

"Homecoming's in two weeks, and I don't have a date. I was wondering if you could fix me up with somebody." He's not looking at me now. Suddenly the design on his football gloves is so freaking interesting. Can he not ask Mallory himself? After making out and arranging another date, it should be easy.

"Can't you ask Mallory yourself?"

"Huh? Mallory?"

"Well after your fun Saturday night, it should be easy to just ask her to homecoming. Do it yourself. Don't involve me."

"What are you talking about?" His brows furrow together like a big hairy caterpillar on his face. Once again, he grabs my shoulders and turns me to face him.

"Did you really think you could hook up with her and the whole school wouldn't find out?" I'm shouting, control slipping, and beating my fists against my thighs with each word. "We all heard it this morning. I hope you enjoyed sucking face!"

Gage grabs my chin and holds it firm. "Wait a minute. You look at me right now, Rayne. I don't care what she said this morning, I did not hook up with that girl in any way, shape or form! If she said that, she's lying!"

But it couldn't be a lie. I saw them together. "How can it be a lie? I saw y'all in the Scout."

"Wait, what? Where did you see us in the Scout?"

"On Main Street when I walked home from the party. Y'all passed me."

"First of all, Mallory asked me to drop her off at the Pig to meet some dude. Some guy she met last week at the coffeehouse. She rode to the party with Jaycee and Barrett, and you know neither of them could drive. I just made sure she got there safely." Relief and embarrassment drop like bricks in my stomach. "Second of all, what the hell were you doing walking home? Last I saw, you went upstairs with my brother." Now he's the one red in the face with the accusatory tone.

I step back from Gage, breaking his grip. "You haven't talked to him?"

"No, he and Trevor left early Sunday to go hiking and didn't come back until late last night. He'd already gone to classes this morning when I left. Why?"

I sink my forehead into my hands. "We kinda had a fight. He got pissed and went back down to the party with those girls from his biology class, so I snuck out the back."

Gage swipes my hands from my face. He's frowning. "He let you walk home all alone at night? Son of a—"

"It's not his fault," I interject. "He didn't know."

"He should've. Have y'all talked?"

"He called yesterday, I guess when he was out with Trevor, but I let it go to voicemail. It might not go well when we do talk."

"What happened? Y'all seemed... happy... when you went upstairs."

"It's complicated. Let's just say I instigated something I couldn't finish."

He sighs. "If he's mad about that, he doesn't deserve you." I smile and snug his arm. He didn't hook up with Mallory. He didn't want her. But he's looking for someone, and the very thought of it makes me sick.

"Thanks, Gage." I glance down at my cell phone. "We're going to be late to practice if we don't hurry." We rush down the hall and walk through the double doors to the fields when he takes up his case one more time.

"So... about the other. Have any friends who might be my date?" He looks at the ground and fingers the mouthpiece on his helmet.

"I don't know. Most of the girls I know wouldn't be a good fit." Why won't he just let this go?

"Geez, thanks. I must be hideous if none of your friends would consider it."

"I didn't say that." I slap his shoulder, rock hard under the silk-weave fabric. "It's just you deserve the best. They're not good enough."

He looks over and smiles at me, a rosy hint dotting the apples of his cheeks. "I love the way you look out for me." Suddenly his smile fades as his eyes fix on something across the field. I turn to stare in the same direction.

Preston.

He's standing on the sidelines, a dozen red roses in hand. When our six eyes lock, Gage takes four steps sideways, leaving a gaping hole between us.

Preston walks out to meet us halfway. His eyes, rimmed with dark shadows, dart back and forth between the two of us. His khaki pants and gray polo look like the cows have chewed them. "I've been trying to call you, Rayne."

"I know. I figured it'd be better to talk in person."

Preston nods, and Gage, uneasily shifting from foot to foot, points his finger at us. "I'm gonna let y'all talk in private." He steps backward, but Preston grabs his arm and stops him.

"No, Gage. Stay. Everyone needs to hear this." He's still holding the roses but drops them to his side. What are they for? Breakup roses? Forgive me roses? "Rayne, I'm an ass." Not what I expect to come from his mouth. His face is calm, almost sheepish.

"I don't understand."

"You were honest with me, but I left you alone because of hurt pride. I'm sorry. Forgive me." He offers a weak smile and extends the roses to me. "These are yours."

Gage looks on, his expressions flat-lined. I accept the roses and his apology, but they're heavy in my hands. Like an anchor. "Thanks," I mumble. It's much easier to be mad when he's pouting, but when he's genuine, Preston can make anyone forgive. It's too bad I can't forget that my feelings for his brother are all too real.

Preston brushes his hand down the side of my face, the same way my nana does when she's commenting on how much I've grown. His fingers linger at my chin a moment, and then he pulls his hand back, shoving them both in his pockets. "So, you two looked like you were having an intense convo. What's up?"

Gage and I glance at each other before he first breaks the silence. "My love life, bro. Begging Rayne to hook me up for homecoming. Only two weeks left to find a date."

"Two weeks?" Preston shifts his gaze to me uneasily, the sudden onslaught of dilated pupils and "oh shit" bottom lip tuck all too familiar. "Uh-oh."

"What uh-oh?" I clench the rose stems in my fingers, the thorns stabbing my skin.

"I'm going with Dad to Charlotte. Company seminar." I click my tongue against the roof of my mouth and look at the turf. Different day, same story. "I'm sorry, but you know I have to focus on this. I can't worry about high school stuff anymore."

His matter-of-fact excuse pisses me off.

"Fine. I'll go to homecoming alone." If I throw these roses at just the right speed, will one of them thorn him right in the eye? I might try...

Suddenly, Preston snaps his fingers in the air then rubs his hands together. "I've got it! It's perfect!"

"What? You'll stay here?"

"I can't, but..." he pauses and flicks his finger between me and Gage, "you can still go with a Howard brother. Why don't you and Gage go together?"

Bad idea. Good idea. My feelings are all over the board in an instant. Maybe bad in a really good way? Gage's wide eyes soften around the corners, his lips twisting up ever-so-slightly.

"No. We can't. People won't understand. Besides, Gage's looking for a date and..." I keep talking without taking a breath, trying to drown out the inner voice that's elated with the possibility.

"I'm game," Gage interrupts, nodding at me. "If Rayne is." My insides become a compass, and Gage is north. Staring at him, the pull intensifies.

Preston steps forward and pulls one long-stemmed rose from the bunch in my hand and holds it out. "Here Gage, ask her properly."

Gage grabs the rose and walks in front of me, positioning himself between me and Preston so I only see him. Our eyes lock, his blue ones reflecting back glints of the afternoon sun. "You've become my best friend. You listen to me. You get me. Go with me to homecoming?"

Every molecule in my body breaks into a happy-dance but I'm careful to keep all traces of it off my face. Except for my eyes, which pinch together, tugging at the hairline above my ears. It's involuntary. "Gimme that rose," I say, yanking it from his grip.

He steps forward and wraps his arms around me, squeezing tight as he leans in to whisper, "You're stuck with me now."

"Gladly," I whisper back. Over Gage's shoulder, Preston stands to the side, grinning and completely unaware of our private conversation or the domino stack he's just flicked over.

Gage's football coach yells at him to join the team run, and he loosens his grip, grabs his helmet from the grass and runs toward his team, his toothy grin big as ever. Preston beams, basking in the brilliance of his plan, as he walks over to plant a kiss on my forehead. "Two birds, one stone. Y'all have fun, and don't worry about what people say. I trust you."

Funny he trusts me when I can't trust myself. "Thanks Preston." There's nothing else I can say without it being a lie. We'll miss you? I wish I were going with you? It won't be fun without you? None of that's exactly true so I shut my mouth rather than add to my mounting list of sinful thoughts.

I loop my arms around his neck. He smells good, like soap and expensive cologne, and I wonder how I'll ever be able to break his heart. His sweet, trusting heart I love only second to his brother's.

When I get home, I carry the bouquet of roses upstairs to my room. But the single red rose—that one I press between the pages of my journal.

———

The desk behind mine sits empty in French class the next day. I slip into my seat and pull out a book, flipping it open, pretending to read.

"Where's your boyfriend?" Jaycee asks, leaning forward.

"Statistical math? I think that's what his first class is today," I reply, not looking up from the page.

"No, not Preston." She glowers at me, hovering over my desk. "Gage. Where is he?"

"How should I know? And what about dropping that whole snarky crap about me and Gage?" I shut my book, holding the place with my finger and glance over at her.

"I did when I thought he was into Mallory. He's not. He's always hanging around you. Speaking of which, what was all that about on the field yesterday?" She taps her pencil on her bottom lip, waiting on me to dish.

"Nothing," I lie. "Preston won't be here for homecoming, so Gage's taking me."

"And I'm sure he didn't mind doing that favor, right?"

"Quit making a big deal of nothing. Preston solved a problem, that's it," I insist.

"Yeah, good ol' Preston. Good ol' clueless Preston."

I hate being late to class and walking in with everyone staring at me. Especially when it's French class.

That's my time—with Rayne.

Sure, we steal moments to chat every day—in the hallway at class change, by the lockers before school, and at lunch—but French is where we can sit, her desk in front and mine behind, for a full, uninterrupted, fifty-five minutes.

I glance at my watch. Down to forty-five today.

The brown, wooden door is already closed. As always. Madame believes in starting class promptly with the bell. Through the skinny sidelight window, I scan the room. Madame's at the Promethean board, arms flapping in and out like a scalded chicken, talking so loudly her words blast through the door and spill out into the hallway. English words.

Madame only speaks English in two instances: she's either giving assignment directions or she's ticked. The way *conjugate*, *re-test* and *disappointed* pepper the rant, and considering she promised test grades back today, I'm fairly sure most of the class tanked.

Madame readjusts, leaning on her other hip. It's enough of

a shift to unblock my line of sight to Rayne, sitting alone in our row at the back of the class. She stares at the open notebook on her desk, chewing her thumbnail, pausing every so often to glance over her shoulder at my empty desk.

Is she looking for me? The thought is enough to shoot a charge through me, like paddles to the heart.

I ease the door open, but it squeaks, and 20 pairs of eyes turn on me. WD-40, anyone? Geez.

"Monsieur Howard!" Madame screeches. "Class started 10 minutes ago!"

"Oui, Madame. I have a parent note." I produce a half-sheet of yellow legal paper and toss it on her desk. A note from Dad, for all intents and purposes. Preston actually wrote it, but Dad approved it, so I guess that counts. Our parents had already left this morning when Preston and I walked out to discover the Mustang's battery completely shot. Neither Mom nor Dad could find it in their schedule to come home immediately and give Preston a ride to school, so it was executively decided that between the two of us, I should be the one who drove him to class, even if that meant being late for my own. Mom insisted Preston deserved priority. He's a college man now, after all, and I'm just the peon high school kid with nothing significant to do.

Funny how high school seemed so much more important last year.

I wind my way through the desks and slide into my seat. Rayne's spicy vanilla perfume hovers like its own weather system around my desk, and I lean forward on my elbows to take in a bigger sniff. She turns around in her desk at the same time, nearly knocking her shoulder into my nose, and holds up her hand. A piece of notebook paper, neatly folded into a square, is between her fingers. I grab it and unfold it on my desk as she faces forward.

That whole thing with Preston was kinda awkward. You'd just asked me to fix you up, and then Preston volunteers you to take me. I want you to know that I totally understand if you want to back out. Really. You should go to Homecoming with someone you really like.

Someone I really like.

I wish it was as simple as liking her, but it's so far beyond that. Maybe I should back out of this whole thing. That'd be safest. Preston has no idea what he's done, forcing us together yet again. But as much as I don't want to hurt him or do anything to compromise our relationship, I can't look at this opportunity with anything but excitement. The thought of spending an entire evening alone with her—going out on a date—has replayed through my mind on a reel. We can't cross any lines, but there's nothing wrong with pretending.

I pull a pencil from the small pouch on my backpack.

Who said I'm not? I'm happy with the way things are.

I fold it along the creases and drop it back over her shoulder. Jaycee clears her throat, and when Rayne glances up at her, she slashes her knife-hand across her neck and mouths "Stop."

Rayne shrugs and opens it. Her laugh is so low, it's barely more than a whisper. She scribbles a reply and, when Madame turns her head, tosses it onto my desk.

Me, too. Want to plan everything during lunch today? First floor, back hallway by the janitor's closet?

The smile's involuntary, despite Jaycee's evil-eye stare, which is now focused solely on me.

An entire lunch period just the two of us, tucked away downstairs where almost no one goes? Yes, please!

I'll be there.

I tap her on the shoulder. When she turns around, I flip the note, pinched between my fingers, toward her. She reaches for it, her skin touching mine and creating a firestorm that spirals like a tornado within.

Heck yeah. I'll be there.

Brrrrrrrrrrrring!

When the bell rings to end fourth period, most of the other kids in the class lean down to zip their backpacks. Not me. Mine's been zipped and on my back, shoved between me and the chair for nearly five minutes now. I squish past all the slow-movers crowding the main hallways and even hurdle over some girl on her knees in front of the stairwell door, scooping up a big pile of dropped papers.

Normally, I'd be nice and help.

Not today.

Today, I'm going to meet Rayne downstairs to plan Homecoming. Truth is, I don't give a crap about the plans. We can do whatever she wants, and it'll be fine. I just want to spend time with her.

Alone.

While I can.

Though I can't touch her or get too close.

Even though I'll want to.

Like I already do.

Geez, I'm a masochistic idiot.

Normally, the trek from the third floor to the first takes a solid five minutes with foot traffic on the stairwell. I make it in about five seconds. There must be something about a 200 lb. offensive lineman barreling down the center of the staircase at 90 mph, taking two steps at a time. People scatter, pushing into each other while navigating to the handrails on either side. My size probably has something to do with it, but the get-out-of-my-way-and-nobody-gets-hurt scowl imprinted on my face seals the deal.

I slam through the door and around the corner. She's not here yet. No one is.

It's completely deserted so I throw my backpack on the floor and sit against the wall in the small niche beside the janitor's closet. It looks as if at one time there might've been a water fountain here, but now it's long gone, leaving only a strange little nook in the wall. Just big enough for two people to sit side by side.

Perfect.

My cell phone pinches into my side so I slide it from my pocket, staring at the screen's wallpaper—a shot of me and Preston from last year's championship game, both of us with matted, wet hair. That was a good night, but now that I stare at the picture, his eyes take on a new life, seeming to connect with mine. Like year-ago Preston knows what Gage-of-today is thinking.

My stomach crumples in on itself, and I click the side button, turning the screen black. That's better.

Footsteps echo on the other end of the hallway, and I lean forward to get a peek. If someone's crashing our spot, I'm going to remove them. At the far edge, Rayne stops by the trash can, talking to someone with animated hand gestures and a few laughs mingled in. As she turns and heads my way, I crane my neck further, catching a quick glimpse of Jaycee maneuvering toward the stairs.

"Sorry," Rayne calls out, her voice marked by a happy lilt. "You know how Jaycee is. She wouldn't shut up."

Yeah, I know exactly how she is. But never mind her. As long as she's gone, who cares anything about Jaycee?

"Anything interesting?" I ask as Rayne tosses her backpack onto mine and squeezes into the cramped space beside me. Her leg slides along the side seam of my jeans, and for once, I'm glad to have this fabric between us. Otherwise...

"She wanted to know why we're meeting down here." She gathers her hair into a ponytail and twists an elastic around it. "I told her we're planning homecoming."

"Wait. You told her we're going together?"

"It's not like it's a big secret. Everyone saw us with Preston on the field yesterday. And I think they'll kinda figure it out when we, you know, show up at Homecoming together."

"Yeah."

"Gage, if it makes you this uncomfortable, we don't have to do this. I can…"

"No. I want to go with you."

"Well, then stop complaining."

I put my fingers to my lips, twisting them as if I'm putting my stupid tongue under lock and key. No way are these insecurities going to mess up this opportunity. So what if people talk. They always do.

Let 'em.

Twenty minutes later, the only things we've decided is I'll pick her up at her house and bring a wrist corsage—no pin-on types because she hates those—and that after the game, we'll make some semblance of an appearance at the school event in the cafeteria and then wing it from there.

"You do know there will be dancing." She says dancing as if it's synonymous with a stomach virus. "It's okay if we bypass that, since you probably can't—"

"Probably can't what? Dance?" I cock my head, wagging my finger in her face. "See? A common misconception. The big, dumb football jock can't possibly have any coordination on the dance floor."

In fact, I can dance. Pretty damn well, if I do say so myself. I learned it by proxy. When we were in middle school, Mom hired a dance instructor to come to our house for weekly instruction. For Preston only. None of that frou-frou stuff, but those elegant ballroom styles you see most of the old people do. Mom said all fine Southern youth learned a specific group of "suitable" dances for cotillions and weddings and social events. Those included the fox trot, the tango, the waltz, the simple box-step and the South Carolina state dance, the Shag.

I was never subjected to these lessons, though I was used as a substitute for Preston when the instructor needed to show him how it should look from the casual observer. After about a few thousand times, I sort of picked it up.

But I'm not telling her all that. Too embarrassing.

"Do you know how many agility drills I do every practice? It's good for form."

She leans forward on her elbows, propping her head in her hand. "Football form?"

"Among other things." A crimson flush invades her cheeks as she drops her gaze to the floor. I tip up her chin and lean in nearly nose to nose, waggling my eyebrows. "I've got moves you won't believe."

She pinches her lips into a slight pucker. Shivers race over every inch of me as I think about how soft they'd be to kiss and if they'd taste like the watermelon lip balm she keeps in her bag. "Prove it."

Challenge accepted.

I jump to my feet and grab her hand, yanking her up beside me so fast she stumbles a bit and reaches out to brace herself against my abs. She lingers there for a minute until I pull both of her hands into mine, one arm extended out and one squared and firm between us, regurgitating the same instructions I'd heard so many times before.

Forward-side-together. Backwards-side-together.

She picks up the rhythm easily, our feet moving around each other in seamless coordination. Her eyes never leave her feet, mouth moving in silent repetition as she remembers each step. I look at nothing but her. The way her eyes pinch up at the corners, the way her nostrils flare just a bit as she makes the step forward.

Beautiful. But more than that, she's real. Natural.

Every fiber in me begs for her, gnawing inside like a pack of wild beasts. I drop her hands and reach around, pulling her into me with one hand on her shoulders and one pressed firmly into the small of her back. Every curve of her connecting with me in pinpricks of fire. Then I bend her backwards into a dip, so low the end of her ponytail drags the floor.

What am I doing?

I can't.

No matter how much I want to.

I pull her back to vertical, and she steps back, open-mouthed. "Where'd you learn to do that?" Her words fall out between heavy pants, her chest bouncing up and down like a pogo stick.

"Long story," I sputter. "Point is I can. And I will."

"You better." Her smile drops, a new seriousness washing over each feature. A weird force brews behind my lips, making them want to pucker toward hers as if they were a life source. She steps closer, and the force intensifies, the whir of rushing blood thundering in my ears. "Sometimes, I feel like I know everything about you." She places her palm against my chest, almost as if she's torn between pulling me in and pushing me away. "Sometimes, I feel like there's so much left to learn."

I swallow hard. "I'm pretty simple, actually. I know how I feel, and I know what I want." My heart beats so loud, I swear it echoes against the concrete walls.

Brrrrrrrrrrrring!

The bubble we've somehow landed in breaks, and she looks down at the floor. I grab our backpacks, handing over hers. "Come on. I'll walk you to class.

25

RAYNE

When the doorbell rings, I'm already seated in the ladder-back chair beside the front door, peeping out the mosaic sidelight window. I've watched him park, get out, and walk up the front porch steps, and now he waits patiently on the other side. Meanwhile, I've blown that "lusting in my heart" thing all to hell. The feelings aren't going away. They're getting stronger, and this "ol' buddy, ol' pal" routine sucks. But it keeps him around, so I do my best.

I throw open the door and say through the screen, "No thanks, little boy. We don't want any."

"Well, if you don't want any..." He shrugs and pretends to head for the steps.

"Oh all right. Get in here and give me your spiel." I push open the screen door with my foot.

He grabs the door and swings it wide. "You're gonna want what I'm selling." Yeah I do. *Gimme Gimme Gimme.* The door's pewter handle bumps him on the padded football pants as it tries to shut. Never has an inanimate object created such jealousy in me.

"You know what they say about the doorknob hitting you in the—"

"I might've heard that one before," he interrupts, nodding, and walks into the foyer. His eyes rove over me, up and down. "Damn girl, that dress..." He runs his hand down my arm and then interlaces his fingers with mine. "It's... you're beautiful." His voice is at least half an octave lower in a rough whisper. It's as if some invisible person is standing between us, slugging me repeatedly with a rubber mallet to the chest. My lungs don't expand right when he touches me like this, like my body is caught somewhere between life and death, floating and rooted all at once.

I'm glad he notices the dress. It'd taken forever to select the perfect one and even more effort in convincing Mama to buy something she deemed "too revealing" and "immodest" because of its scandalous mid-thigh length and v-neckline. And it's red—the devil's color. When she said that in the store, I nearly choked on my gum and died right there. Even the saleslady had to walk away "to assist another customer," but I saw her snickering behind the counter with the other associate. When I pointed out the school's colors were red and black, and that she herself had worn a red dress to her own Hillcrest homecoming nearly thirty years earlier, her argument lost its legs. Now seeing that expression on Gage's face—these are the spoils of victory.

"Thanks. You look good, too." My voice barely registers a whisper. There's something about the way he looks in those football pants that stirs semi-indecent daydreams like Gage tackling me in the turf or bending me in a pretzel like those pre-game loosening stretches. "Is it hot in here?" I pat sweat droplets from my hairline.

He smiles. "Nah, it's just me." Yes. Yes it is. He flips my hand palm-up and places the corsage box there. "For you. Hope you like it."

The black box is knotted crossways with a white silken ribbon, which I untie and place on the foyer table. Inside rests a white orchid wrist corsage with a single fire-and-ice rose in the center. Gage lifts it out gingerly and slides it on my wrist. "It's perfect. This corsage is totally me."

"Not totally. It's a little me, too." He brushes away some baby's breath on the wristband to reveal a small silver medallion with his jersey number, 67, engraved on it. I stroke the sunken numerals. "I hope it's okay. The others are wearing huge numbers on their corsages, but I didn't want you—or Preston—to feel awkward. This'll be our little secret."

Our secret. Quite a few of those hang in the air around us lately. He hid the charm in my flowers and covered it with baby's breath. I hid the fact I'd fallen for him in my heart and covered it with dating his brother. One's much more dangerous than the other.

Before I respond, Mama and Daddy walk in. She picks up my hand and studies the corsage. "Very pretty." She grimaces as if slamming her thumb in the door. I hate that expression. This isn't one of her good days, and she's grappling to keep it together. Daddy walks up behind her, puts his hands on her shoulders and pulls her in tight to his chest. He's walking Prozac to her, the one medicine that religiously calms her anxiety.

"Let's get a picture." Daddy waves his new Nikon DSLR around. "Been looking for an excuse to try this out."

"How about the front porch?" I edge Gage out the screen door and away from Mama's impending meltdown. Daddy sits Mama in the ladder-back chair and walks out behind Gage. I stop to say goodbye.

"Be careful. Drive safely. Watch out. Boys... expect things..." Her voice is quivering and choppy except for the word "boys," which she spits out like soured lemon juice.

"Mama, he's a good guy." I nod toward the porch. "He won't

let anything happen to me. Remember, I'm spending the night at Jaycee's. I'll text you when I get there." I kiss her on the cheek and look back once more. She's staring at me, bottom lip trembling, as I carefully shut the screen door behind me.

The parking lot is full when we get to school, but Gage finds a space on the last row and backs in under the pine trees. He insists on coming around to open my door, and as I wait on him, I run my fingers over the tattered arm rest, the yellow foam peeking through the tan vinyl. Gage had apologized he couldn't bring me "in style" the way Preston could've, but I couldn't care less. I love his old Scout. It's his two-ton metal twin—rough around the edges but dependable.

But the high lift is impossible in a dress, especially when I'm trying to climb down without flashing the whole senior class.

"Grab hold." Gage presses himself into the seat, slides his arms behind my back and under my knees and lifts me out princess-style. His arms fold around me, his biceps bulging under the silky dry-weave shirt.

"Selfie before you put me down!" I hold out my phone, and we squeeze close together in the frame, his freshly-shaved face butter-soft against mine.

Across the parking lot, Jaycee and Barrett stand by the double doors. When she catches me staring, she waves us over.

"Do we have to?" Gage whines through pouted lips.

"Just for a minute." I grab his hand and haul him behind me like a toddler.

Jaycee runs to me, grabs my shoulders and spins me a full 360. "That dress is on fi-ah. You must've drugged your mama to get out of the house in that."

"Nope. She let her walk out—with me." The irritation seeps

through Gage's words. Aggression looks good on him, especially when he almost seems possessive.

"Hi, Gage." Jaycee shakes her head and clicks her tongue in annoyance then plunges her finger between the 6 and 7 on his jersey. "Your old uniform? That's the best you could do?"

"Kinda have to play the homecoming game." He inches backwards and breaks contact.

Jaycee snatches her hand back and plants it on her hip. "Really Einstein? I hope you brought a change of clothes for after. Hopefully your brother lent you a nice suit, like he lent you his girlfriend." She throws Preston casually into the conversation like a grenade, armed and ready to explode. Gage steels his jaw, his molars grinding against each other.

"Bitch much?" I grab hold of her arm and sink my nails in.

She jerks it loose and rubs the five little indentations with her opposite hand, frowning. "Geez. Take a joke."

"You are a joke," Gage mumbles beside me.

Jaycee stares at him, eyes narrowed. "You say something?"

"Not a thing," he says, returning her stare. When she finally looks away, he turns to me. "I gotta get stretching. Wanna come watch?"

Jaycee, now in deep conversation with a small throng of followers, weighs in on some sophomore girl's new butch haircut.

So. Not. Interested.

"Absolutely." I lace my arm through his and we head to the field.

After the game, I walk alone to the gym where we've agreed to meet post-shower. It's dark, the music from the cafeteria pumping through the walls with booming thuds. Staccato high-heel footsteps echo through the shadows as girls make their way to the dance while I wait in silence. I sit down on the wooden bleachers and check the time on my phone then flip through the photos from earlier. The selfie of Gage and me is perfect, smiling and happy. Definitely Facebook-worthy but I don't post it. No point rubbing our good time in Preston's face.

"Look at those hotties," Gage whispers in my left ear. I scream and drop my phone on the hardwood. "My bad. Didn't mean to scare you." He reaches down to grab it.

"You scared me half-to-death!" I gasp, my heart still bouncing around in my stomach. Then I look at him, hair still damp, spiked up a little in the front, and wearing a crisp, black suit fitted to skim his muscular build. The top two buttons of the white shirt are open. No tie. And I thought the football pants were hot. "Wow. Gage... you look..." The right words escape me.

"Hot?" He spins around and huffs on his nails, which he then polishes on the coat sleeve. "I clean up pretty good. I'd do Preston proud."

And then that—the pink elephant in the room. Realizing his mistake, Gage looks up, eyes wide. He reminds me of the little boy next door I've babysat who once had to confess to breaking his mama's china vase. Guilty. Fearful. Anxious. A mix of all three. This evening is about forgetting Preston and focusing on Gage. Tonight may be my one-shot deal to share this closeness with him.

He clears his throat and jingles the car keys in the air. "Wanna blow this whole thing off and go somewhere else?" Yes! Yes! Yes! That's what I want, but we can't—not without a lot of questions.

"Not so fast. You promised me dancing, remember?"

His blue eyes sparkle in the glare of the overhead fluorescents. "I promised you a dance."

"It's like potato chips, Gage. You can't just have one. How about five?"

"Three and then we go do something else."

"Deal." I slide my hand in his and pull him toward the cafeteria.

The music pumps so loud it reverberates in my chest. Strings of Edison light bulbs crisscross the ceiling above our heads and large panels of translucent black fabric drape the walls, backlit by hundreds of mini twinkle lights. We're on our way to the refreshments table when Jaycee grabs my arm from behind.

"Hey!" she scream-talks over the music, eyes darting back and forth between Gage and me. "I'm sorry about earlier. We're at the far table." She points across the room to a round table where several couples have gathered. "Y'all come over."

Gage shrugs his shoulders, giving me leeway in the deci-sion. "All right. For a minute," I scream back. She smiles and claps her hands as we follow her.

Everyone stops mid-action and stares at us like petri dish specimens. Gage wraps his arm around my shoulders, tugging me in closer. Bad idea. No sooner does he touch me than the crowd exchanges I-told-you-so expressions, complete with rolling eyes and duck lips. Jaycee, now beside Barrett at the back of the table, picks up her cell phone.

"Give Facebook a rest for one night, Jaycee," I say. She's addicted, always texting, posting, or updating her blog.

"Not Facebook—Twitter. See?" She holds out the phone, screen toward me. "We're tweeting under #HHSHomecoming. We all have our own, too. I'll make y'all one." She stares at the screen, way too excited about social media.

"We're good," I insist.

"Wait a minute." She holds up her finger without lifting her eyes. "Now look over here and smile." A quick blinding flash and the tap-tap of a few phone buttons before my phone buzzes with a Twitter notification. I tap the icon to find our happy faces bursting on the screen, tagged #RayneGage.

"RayneGage?"

"Isn't that funny? Even your names go together like those famous Hollywood couples. Brangelina. Bennifer. TomKat. RayneGage."

"Except they aren't a couple," Barrett pipes up before holding his fingertip over the opening of his straw and sucking Coke from the opposite end.

"Aren't they?" Jaycee looks up at us with a sneer. "Could've fooled me." Gage's fingers press into my shoulder. She'd lured us over with lies of her sudden attack of conscious. I want to hit her, slap her right across the face and knock her backwards out of her chair. Gage stares at the floor, his cheeks enflamed, the muscle in his jaw going in and out.

"I've had enough of you tonight," I yell through clenched teeth then look at Gage. "Let's dance then get the hell outta here." He grabs my hand and pulls me toward the dance floor, refusing to look at anyone at the table.

I glance back at Jaycee as we walk away. She shrugs her shoulders, palms up. "Chill guys! I'm just kidding. Why so touchy?" Her yowling-cat laugh fades to background noise by the time we reach the center of the dance floor. We stand there a minute, other couples dancing around us.

Gage grabs my shoulders, bending to my eye-level. "Three dances and we split, right?"

"How 'bout two? That'll give us some time before I have to be at her house."

"If I were you, I'd go anywhere except her house." He says her with the venom of a copperhead.

"It's tradition. The cheerleaders always spend the night at Jaycee's house after homecoming." I sigh, defeated before he even makes a case for his argument.

"Break tradition. Do your own thing."

I shake my head. If there's one thing I'm perpetually not, it's a rule-breaker. Mama's raised me believing that coloring outside the lines leads to bad things, dark and sinful. Good girls follow the rules and do what they have to do, not what they want to do. It's very "Southern belle" to give yourself to the good of society, to see the bigger picture instead of being self-ish. I always do what I'm supposed to, even when I don't like it, and that might very well be the reason why I'll never truly get to love Gage, even though he makes me want to throw all the rules right out the window.

"Jaycee's harmless. She's not the sharpest tool in the shed."

He glares at her, still plugging away in the Twitterverse. "That's what worries me. It doesn't take brain power to be destructive."

"Forget her. Dance with me." I skim my hand down his arm and pull him toward me. We barely begin swaying with the bass before the deejay changes it up. A slow song. A hold-you-close song.

With the first notes of a rock ballad, Gage grabs my elbows and tugs me in close as he hums along with the tune. I rest my head on his chest, his arms around my shoulders, mine circling his waist. Chills run laps down my spine as our bodies sway in rhythm, every ounce of strength mobilized to fight the urge to press my lips to his. The wanting scares me. I shouldn't feel this way. If the others knew, I'd forever be labeled a slut, even if my love for Gage is innocent. Not loving Preston is sinful enough.

I close my eyes, flushing the thoughts away. The noise dies as everything beyond us evaporates, swallowed up into some black void. Gage rests his chin on my head, singing in his grav-elly tone that lulls me into sweet oblivion. That's when I forget. I forget to care what the others think about us dancing so closely. I forget to hide. The light from the Edison bulbs washes over us, and my heart flutters.

When the song ends, I peel myself from his arms. "Ready to go?"

He smiles, not saying a word, grabs my hand and leads me out the door.

We change clothes, hit the Chick-Fil-A drive through, and head to Cedar Falls, a cozy park on the Reedy River. I've never been, but other kids at school have. Ainsley once told us that's where a lot of kids go to hook-up, so when Gage confidently tells me I'll love it, I begin wondering how many times he's been there.

And with whom.

But that's really none of my business.

Still...

"You come here a lot?" Sometimes you ask a question hoping the answer won't blow up in your face, changing everything you think you know. Sometimes you nearly pass out from holding your breath waiting on that answer.

"A few times. It's been a while."

I nod and chew the inside of my jaw. Well that's vague.

"You and the guys?" I prod.

"Nah." He strums his fingers on the steering wheel like that's an acceptable answer and turns down the twisted drive through the metal gates and pulls off into the grass on the river bank. The keys dangle in the ignition, the radio still on. He hops out and grabs our food bags and a blanket from the back, then juts his head in my partially rolled-down window.

"Coming?"

I slide out and slam the door, the anger coiling in my belly. Gage isn't my boyfriend, so he can come here with anyone he likes. I just don't want him to. Ever. I hate everyone he's brought here before.

The darkness is thick, cut only by the moonlight reflecting off the water. No outdoor lights. Not another soul. Tonight, it's only us. He unfurls the blanket, spreads it wide and motions me over. I sit down at the fringed edge, afraid to get too close and push the limits of the torture I can feasibly withstand. That, and I'm still standoffish because of his lackluster responses to my questions.

Gage crams a spicy chicken sandwich in his mouth. I open up mine and peel off a couple dill pickles and hold them up between my fingers. "You want these?"

He leans over and bites them from my grip. His lips brush my fingers, causing me to retract my hand and look down at the chicken sandwich lying on the blanket beside me. Eating would be torture. My stomach aches from the idea of him, at some point in the past, sitting on this very spot with another girl. I wonder who she is. Is she smarter? Prettier? I bet she didn't sit around like a lump, flipping out about toeing some sort of imaginary line. No, she would've been free to curl up beside him, put her arms around his neck, pull him in close, and...

Oh God. I'm gonna hurl.

I jump up, run to the edge of the parking area near the trashcans, and squat down beside the split-rail fence. Gage is on my heels. He pulls my hair back.

"You okay?"

"Felt a little sick. It'll pass." I use the wooden post as a crutch to steady myself. It's hard to stand when the Earth's morphed into quicksand. Gage grabs my arm for extra support.

"Dad brought me and Preston down here a few times a couple years ago—that's when I found out about this place." The knots in my stomach untie at his admission. Gage's eyes fix on a spot near the bank. "He was adamant about father/son time and brought us here to fish. We set up right over there." He points to the spot he'd been watching.

"Sounds nice," I say, though I'm surprised. Jackson Howard doesn't strike me as the outdoorsman.

He snorts. "While it lasted. Then he went back to how it was before. Ignoring me."

I don't know what to say but figure we should be sitting down to have a conversation this heavy. "I'm better. Wanna sit?" I nod toward the blanket, and we saunter back.

He lies down, rolls up his letterman jacket and slides it under his head like a pillow. I sit cross-legged beside him and alternate between picking at my uneaten sandwich and leaning over him absentmindedly fingering the small buttons on his plaid shirt. "What do you want to do?"

"Anything but go home," he says. "Mom's the only one there, and she's always riding me about something. I'm sick of arguing with her."

It's understandable. Being trapped in a house alone with Charlotte sounds like pure torture. He picks up a rock from the ground and flips it over and over in his hand. "Mom loves Preston. I'll never live up to him. He's got perfect grades, perfect football record, the perfect girlfriend..."

Wait. Did he just refer to me as the perfect girlfriend?

He throws the rock down. "I'm the black sheep."

I nudge his arm playfully. "One badass black sheep."

He smiles as a brisk breeze kicks up, bristling the hairs on my arms. I rub them up and down.

"Cold?" Gage springs up, unfurls his jacket and drapes it over my shoulders. His fingers linger on the collar then sweep underneath to free a few trapped strands of hair. Our noses hover an inch or so apart. "Better?"

"Much," I whisper, the magnetic attraction stronger than ever. His lips are close, too close. So close I want to—

"Want to dance?" A mischievous glint, highlighted by the moonlight, reflects in his eyes. He stands and pulls me to my feet onto the flat-topped boulder at the river's edge. The water laps the muddy bank, and the music flows soft and mellow. He yanks me to him, the way he did earlier in the cafeteria, but no one's watching us now. I wrap my arms tightly around him, squeezing out any remaining space. A part of me longs to cross that line. No one will ever know, but there's a fight with the good-girl logic that refuses to step out of line. The resistance falters as he weakens all my defenses.

We turn slowly on the rock. Gage's hands massage my back, and I relax my head onto his chest. The muscles in his arms tense as I slip my hands down his back and into the back pockets of his jeans, my hands warm, nestled intimately close to the curve of him. I squeeze my eyes shut, waiting on him to push me away, tell me I should save it for Preston.

He doesn't.

His hands grasp my hips, tugging me in closer. Every muscle, every ripple, every bulge of his body presses into me, the contact points like subdermal flames.

He wants me, too.

His touch isn't friendly. It's hungry. It piques my longing for him even more, a vicious but completely exhilarating cycle. Neither of us speak because as long as we're quiet, reality outside this moment doesn't exist.

We only have tonight, so with hands roaming and hearts pounding, we blur the lines.

"Can I ask you a question?" His breathy voice caresses my ear.

It's hard to get a decent breath when your stomach's relocated to your chest. "Sure."

"Does Preston make you happy?" Direct and to the point. The question. The big one I'm afraid to answer out loud, because the truth brings consequences.

"I... I don't know..." I stammer. "He's great, but..."

"But..."

"I'm here with you, not him." I can't believe what's coming from my own lips.

"Yes. You are." His fingertips glide up my arms to either side of my chin, pulling my face up toward his. The way he looks at me sets me on fire, crackly and consuming, as if someone has lit a handful of sparklers in my body. He moves closer, and his lips part ever-so-slightly, awaiting mine. We are crossing the line, not slightly but full steam ahead, and whatever consequences come tomorrow, it isn't worth worrying about tonight.

I lick my lips and ready myself for him.

A loud buzzing slices through our moment, and my cell phone lights up on the blanket. "Don't answer it," his lips so close they brush against my skin. "Please."

The buzzing is relentless, a nagging voice of reason saying we couldn't live with ourselves for doing this. I pull away from Gage, holding tight to his hand until I can no longer reach his fingers. I never break eye contact.

My heart slams my ribs as a familiar name registers on the caller ID. I glance up and take a deep breath. "Hi Preston."

Gage turns away and stares out over the falls. He runs his hand through his hair, down to his neck, and lets it rest there, keeping his back turned to me, shoulders slumped forward.

"Gage's here. I'll put you on speaker." I press the button and hold the phone out. "Can you hear me?"

"I hear you. How was tonight?" He's cheerful. Happy. Blissfully unaware his call plucked his girlfriend and brother from the point of no return.

I snap my fingers at Gage, who looks back at me over his shoulder, and motion for him to come closer. "Great. Fun."

"How about the game? Y'all win?"

Gage walks closer to the phone and squats down across from me. "Sure did. Tonight woos our night." The way he's looking at me makes it hard to keep control. I want to push the end call button, lunge at him and fall to the ground in a hot, muddied mess.

"Rayne?" Preston calls out.

"Yeah?" I fumble over my thoughts, caught in my fantasy.

"I asked if y'all were still at the dance?"

"Well, actually we—" I start but Gage silences me by holding up his fingers across his lips.

"I'm about to take her to Jaycee's slumber party," he interjects.

"Sounds like fun. See y'all tomorrow when I get home." The phone clicks, and the silence envelopes us. Again, no words. We just stare at each other.

Gage looks at his watch. "We need to get you to Jaycee's." He pulls me up, then wraps his arms around me and kisses the top of my head.

"Gage..." I begin but he squeezes me tighter and gently shakes his head. It's easy to get caught up in each other out here alone, but once the truth rushes in, the fantasy comes crashing down. We can't hurt Preston this way.

GAGE

Oh shit.
What the hell almost happened?
I thought I was stronger than that.
I'm not.

RAYNE

Homecoming barely ends before preparations for senior night, our last Friday home game, go into full swing. The usual hype surpasses previous years because this time, we're celebrating our school's first ever championship in last year's state playoffs. The principal advised us to prepare for a large crowd. Like whole town large. A team doesn't win a championship and then fade into obscurity in the South. They become idols, the stars of supper time discussions and "remember whens" for generations to come—and Preston's their god.

On Monday afternoon, Ainsley cornered me at my locker and begged me to help her coordinate the senior posters to be displayed in the cafeteria because Jaycee left her high and dry, spending all her time on the half-time slideshow for the jumbo-tron. I'd already done my part on the food committee, securing donations from local restaurants, but when Ainsley was finished with her pleas, there I stood with a bag of glitter glue, Sharpies, poster paper, and a handful of manila envelopes.

By Wednesday night, the completed posters lean against my

dresser. Only Gage's folder remains. I haven't opened it yet. Nervous excitement or guilt, possibly both, paralyzes me at the sight of his name on the red tab. I run my finger along the edge, flip it open and hold up the questionnaire into the lamp light. It's filled out with his distinctive small slanted script. Favorite food—macaroni and cheese. Favorite class—gym. My breath catches hard in my chest at the next entry. Best friend(s)— Preston Howard and Rayne Davidson.

My gag reflex clenches tight, my heart thumping at the validity of our relationship, there in black and white. I'm his best friend, and he's mine. It all makes perfect sense. Except for the fact friendship's no longer enough. I want more. But Gage has avoided discussing anything about homecoming. He's acting as if nothing happened, but the intimacy we shared that night changed us. It means something. Something we can't deny. Something we can't act on.

The folder weighs a ton in my hands, and I drop it on the floor. For the first time all season, Preston's coming to a game. Not for me. Not for Gage. For himself. To receive his ring and the praises of his faithful devoted.

Inside the folder are pictures Gage provided for the poster. They slide out with a shake, and I arrange them across the carpet. Gage in his football uniform; Gage and Preston; Gage driving his Scout; Gage and I dressed up for homecoming.

I lie on my bedroom floor and stencil Gage's name across the top of his poster. Homecoming night comes back to me with each pencil stroke. His hands on my hips. Mine in his pockets. The curvature of his butt beneath my palms. Our almost kiss.

I can't keep pretending he's just a friend when all I really want is for him to make a move, reassure me it's okay to break his brother's heart. I want him to love me as much as I love every facet of him.

Decked out in red, white, and black crepe streamers, the school's ready. The mid-November air is crisp, and my heart keeps time with the drum line as I watch Gage warming up in the end zone, his leg stretching up to the sky.

"Get with it. Time to cheer." Ainsley shakes her pompoms in my face and nods to the fifty-yard line and the rest of the cheerleaders.

From the field, everyone in the stands looks small, difficult to tell one from another. Except Preston. I can't see him exactly, but I know where he is—in the middle of that overly eager crowd. In the bleachers near the top of the stadium, my parents huddle together under a blanket, Daddy's arms tight around Mama.

We perform our set and run back to the sidelines. The crowd roars as the guys take the field.

At half-time, the principal opens the ceremony with a long-winded speech. Blah blah blah. His voice fades into that Charlie Brown teacher whine as I sip from my water bottle. One-by-one, each player from last year's team comes forward but when his name—Preston Howard—echoes over the loud speaker, the crowd, in one mass movement, gets to its feet and breaks out in a full chant, stomping so hard the structure groans under the weight. Preston beams from his pedestal and pumps his right fist in the air. After his MVP speech, he's hoisted on shoulders and paraded around the field as Mr. and Mrs. Howard wave and smile to the crowd from their spot in the bleachers.

The ring ceremony takes five minutes more than planned, so the senior night recognition is crammed into a ten-minute clip. When the principal finally shuts up, the stadium lights dim for the senior night slideshow.

"This is it!" Jaycee waves her hands and hops from one foot

to the other as a few notes of music introduce the slideshow's photo montage. Chest puffed up and hands clasped together, she meets my gaze and an instant shiver slides down my spine. She's too eager.

When her voice booms over the jumbotron speakers, my stomach lurches. "What did you do, Jaycee?"

The corner of her lip curls into a sly smile as she points toward the screen.

Her voiceover cameo continues. "By senior year, we think we know it all, but face it—there'll always be lingering questions we hope to clear up by our ten-year reunion. For instance, what exactly do you have in that bookbag Barrett Sanderson? You always carry it, but all your books are in your arms. You don't study—obviously—so what's the deal? You even take it to the bathroom. Creepy." Pictures of Barrett with his bookbag in the hallway, in the lunchroom, at the farmer's market in town, and beside the boys' bathroom flash on the screen. The crowd roars, even Barrett, who holds up his now-infamous bookbag for everyone to see.

"Number two. Amie Lyndon—what's with your hair? Really? We're all cheerleaders, bouncing around, hair all over the place. Yours doesn't move. Like ever. Not normal. Your real hair or helmet in disguise?" Pictures of Amie and her perfect hair cover the screen. Amie in a tumbling series with her gravity-defying hairdo. Amie standing by me during practice, my frizzy hair attacking her silky-smooth locks. Again the crowd laughs as Amie gives a cheer for her awesome hair.

"And, last but not least, perhaps the most intriguing mystery of the senior class. Rayne Davidson and Gage Howard —when are y'all gonna come clean about your secret romance? Seriously guys, it's painful to watch y'all deny it anymore. And it's not fair to poor Preston. He's not used to losing." A barrage of photos, taken while Gage and I were unaware, plaster the big screen: in French class, me wiping crumbs from his lips; taking a selfie in the school parking lot; holding hands in the hallway outside the gym; pressing too close together at the home-coming dance.

My stomach churns with each tick of the electronic score-board timer, the truth parading for all to see. I can't deny it—the proof's in the look on my face in every photo. Hiding in plain sight? More like being stripped naked in front of the entire town.

Stone-cold silence grips the stadium. No laughing, cough-ing, or discernible breathing.

In the stands, Mama's horror-stricken eyes dart nervously between me and the Howards, her hand clasped tightly over her mouth. Preston jumps to his feet and rushes headlong down the steps. I sprint off the sidelines, to the first landing and across the first row of bleachers where we meet face-to-face. I reach for his hand, but it hangs limp in mine, his eyes pleading for a denial.

I don't have one, only a burning sensation that singes my throat like a lit roman candle. "Preston, I... Preston... give me a chance to explain—to do something—anything."

He wrenches his hand from mine and throws it up like a stop sign. "I've been watching this come on for a while. Dammit, I asked Gage, and he swore nothing was going on."

"And it wasn't. I swear it wasn't..." At least not physically. We'd toed the line but never crossed it. The burning races to my eardrums.

The fire in his eyes subsides, allowing for something much worse. Hurt. His parents finally arrive at his side, Mrs. Howard's venom hitting me like a million poisonous darts.

"You little bitch..." She stabs her inch-long red nails in my face before Preston calls her off and pushes himself between the two of us.

"I never meant to hurt you Pres," I say, shooting sideways glances at Mrs. Howard in case she throws a hook. Even I can't believe I say that. It's not you, it's me? But it's true—I don't understand why it happened this way either. Loving Gage isn't what I planned, but it's something I can't ignore. Now thanks to Jaycee, no one can look the other way.

Preston opens his mouth to respond but stops as he focuses on something over my left shoulder. "I can't do this..." He swallows hard and rubs both hands over his face and down his neck, which has turned feverish red, then turns and walks away. Jackson follows, eyes wide and sweat beading on his forehead, but Charlotte shoots me the stink eye, her eyebrows hooked together by deep creases running vertically above her nose before darting into the still-paralyzed crowd.

It's then his hand rests on my shoulder, and I hear his voice in my ear. "Rayne."

I peek around, too ashamed to face him fully. Gage stands there shell-shocked, as if just crawling in from a gruesome battle. I can't look at him. I can't look at the crowd. Their eyes dissect me like a frog in science lab, their whispers and jeers like razor-sharp scalpels. The huge stadium collapses in, sucking air from my lungs, and I can't get a deep breath. On wobbly knees, I rush past Gage, down the steps into the dark void beneath the bleachers.

I'm not in love with Preston, but he doesn't deserve to be humiliated. Jaycee's supposed to be my friend—bitchy, yes, but evil, no. I'm so stupid. I defended her when I should've listened to Gage.

Gage. I left him standing alone in the stands when he's never run away from me. I trust our connection, but what if it's not enough? He can't defend both me and his brother. He'll have to choose, and I'll be the loser.

He enters my hiding place, cutting through the slivers of darkness underneath the bleachers. I can't see him clearly, but an electrical current surges through me, blue-hot and stronger than ever. I push my back against the support beam, willing it to open up and absorb me into the concrete pillar, as his footsteps draw closer. Suddenly he's in front of me, close enough to reach out and touch. Through the darkness, my eyes trace the curvature of his jaw and the angle of his nose. A single beam of light bleeding through the bleachers falls across his eyes and sets them ablaze. I can't tear mine away from his.

"Is it true—any part of it?"

"It's stupid mean girl stuff, Gage. She's an overindulged princess determined to cause misery."

Gage scuffs his football cleats in the dirt. "It's more than that, Rayne." He grasps my chin, holding firm. "Tell me the truth! I don't give a damn about her. I want the truth. From you. Is this my fault?"

"No, you didn't do anything wrong." I fidget with my bracelet. He didn't. I did. I trusted the wrong people, felt the wrong things. Only somehow in this moment, amidst all the drama, it doesn't feel wrong. Gage's breath falling hot across my face, his arm grazing my left shoulder, feels right. He pulls me closer, the smell of sweat on his jersey musky and dense. A single salty bead trickles down his jawline and over the throbbing vein in his neck then disappears into the t-shirt under his shoulder pads.

"Preston's a friend but—nothing more."

"Why'd you pretend?"

"I don't know, Gage, okay?" I interrupt. "Preston's wonderful, handsome, sweet, everything any girl would dream of, but..."

He reaches out and grabs my elbow. "But what?"

"But not me. He's not meant for me, and I'm not meant for him."

"Then who, Rayne? Who do you want?" His eyes slice me like blue daggers, filleting my insides, exposing the truths I've hidden away. He knows—it's silently hanging in the air between us. The connection is chemical, the reaction, palpable.

I turn to hide the teary free-fall, but Gage moves closer and spins me back into his arms, my face pressed into his chest, his aroma intense and masculine. The truth intimidates and excites me simultaneously, but I'm scared he'll have to reject me in defense of his brother. I can't reasonably believe he'd pick me over Preston, so I try inserting physical space between us. He refuses and tugs me closer, the pads from his pants hard against my thighs.

"The truth," he pleads. "No Rayne 'duck and cover' maneuvers. That doesn't work with me. I know you too well."

"The truth is..." I stammer.

"You love me?"

Silence. Why can't I just say it?

"I know you do. Good God, Rayne—look at me." He grabs my shoulders and pulls me face-to-face. "You act like I'm worth a damn. No one else cares about me like you do."

An icy warmth circulates through my body. "I don't know."

"Fine. Let me tell you what I know. Jaycee made you the butt of her joke, offering you up like a sacrificial lamb." He pauses, clasps his hands then rubs them across the top of his head before reaching out to cup my chin. "Preston loves you, Rayne, and to hear that you don't love him is bad enough. To hear it in front of hundreds of people we know—that's worse. To hear you might love his brother—that's torture."

"We can't undo this." I push his hand away and turn my back.

"I lied, Rayne."

"Lied? About what?" I turn around, confused by his words.

"I lied to my brother and told him I didn't love you, but... I do."

The sound in my ears hums loudly like an idling engine. The scene plays in a slo-mo movie montage with Gage standing in front of me confessing his soul's secrets and me wishing—no, praying—the next words I hear are life-changing.

He throws his hands in the air. "I love you, Rayne! Every-thing else be damned!"

My heart pounds in my ears as it sinks in. I love him and he loves me back. My legs turn to jelly.

He quits talking and edges closer, his face millimeters from mine, his fingertips on my arm. Chill bumps blanket my body when he grabs hold of my hand. "Can't you feel it... this thing between us?"

"Gage, I—" Before I can finish, he crushes his lips to mine and moves them softly, yet feverishly. It's better than I dreamed, and I refuse to imagine ever living another day when I don't kiss him. The touch of his lips burns like hot coals that shoot smoldering embers into my fingers and toes.

I pull back just long enough to tell him the truth. "I love you, Gage."

I grab his hair and wrench him back to me then cover his lips, cheeks, and neck with all the pent-up emotions building for so many weeks. My reputation might be shot to hell, but I'm not going to let that ruin the most perfect moment with him.

28

GAGE

Something's off. Not that I expected everyone would come home from the game and quietly tuck themselves into bed, but the fact every light downstairs and upstairs is on, blaring through the windows like some suburban lighthouse, is something Mom would never allow.

It calls too much attention. Makes it look as if something's wrong. Attracts the neighbors' interest in all the unsuitable ways.

Too late.

But considering that shit-storm we just came through, I'm assuming propriety's out the window tonight.

I stop in the driveway. Opening the garage door will only clue them in that I'm home, and I'd rather take my chances sneaking in the back door and wait until tomorrow to deal with the fallout. I slide out of the Scout and press the door softly in place, using a hip nudge to secure it. But as I turn around, putting the keys in my pocket... wham!

In an instant, my body slaps the pavement, the little rocks tearing at my skin. Fire explodes across my eye and a stabbing sensation grinds in my ear. I blink my eyes. Everything wavers between focus and blur as I push myself to standing, using the side of the Scout as a crutch.

Before I can even turn around, Preston's screams rip through my still ringing ear. "Why'd y'all do it? Behind my back! Y'all made me look like a fool in front of everybody!"

The feeling once again registers in the side of my face and down to my jawbone as the tingling eases a bit. Of course Preston's pissed. I'm sure he'd love to rip my arms off and beat me with them.

And I can't blame him.

"Pres, we didn't mean for this to happen. We never intended—"

"All you can give me is cliché bullshit?" He jabs my shoulder, spinning me backwards just enough that I'm facing him. "I asked you! You said it was nothing. Come on, Gage. Cheating doesn't just happen."

He's right. Cheating doesn't just happen. That's the only reason Rayne and I had successfully been able to keep our hands off one another when the tension's been full-throttle for weeks. The desire to slide my hands over her, put my lips on hers, was there every second. But we'd resisted. "We didn't cheat. Ever. We never crossed that line because we cared too much about you!"

"Oh, y'all cared so much, right?"

I slide my hands up the sides of my face and grasp the top of my head. There'll be no reasoning with him tonight. No explaining. "Rayne and I... we fell in love." Preston grimaces as if he'll hurl at any second. "I know you're mad. I know you want to kill me. It's been a long night, and you really don't want to do this right now."

He laughs, something guttural that emanates from deep in his chest. "No, you're wrong. I so want to do this. Now."

"You got your shot in. A damn good one. I deserve it, but can we please cool down and talk about this tomorrow?"

Preston doesn't respond, only narrows his eyes like a predator sizing up his prey. "I'm not going to fight you," I continue, throwing my hands up in surrender, and head toward the house. "I'm going to bed."

"Like hell you are," Preston yells and charges me again from the side.

Except this time, I anticipate it, and I grab his shirt and throw him belly-first onto the Scout's hood, holding him in place. He wiggles under my tight grasp but can't free himself. "Dammit, Preston. I told you I'm not gonna fight with you. We didn't mean for this to happen, but we fell in love. I'm sorry. Rayne's sorry. But... you and I are still brothers. I love you, and we're not doing this."

I push off the car, leaving Preston laying there. His voice echoes against the metal hood. "Y'all betrayed me!"

This. This is the reason he couldn't make it work with Rayne. Preston only looks at things from his perspective. How does it hurt him? How does it benefit him? What about HIM? Ugh. He never stops to consider how everyone else is affected.

A true product of his raising.

"It's not all about you." The acid-laced words snap off my tongue. "Lots of people got hurt tonight. You, me, Rayne, mom and dad, the Davidsons. Even the town has their panties in a wad. Everyone's reeling. Not just you." I blow out a loud breath and walk toward the house, yelling back over my shoulder. "I'm going to my room."

Footsteps slap the ground behind me, and suddenly I'm falling face-first into the dewy grass. Preston lands to the side of me, taking a haphazard swing on the way down. He misses.

I won't.

For the first time, I return fire, jabbing a left in his direction and connecting with his ribs. After regaining my balance, I take another swing, my right hook crashing into his cheek, the contact shooting slivers of pain up each knuckle.

I stumble to my feet, shaking my fingers out to extinguish the pinpricks of fire.

"Get your hands off your brother right now!" Her voice is shrill and rings out through the darkness. Mom and Dad tear through the front door. She's definitely losing it. Never would she create such a scene otherwise.

She beelines for Preston who rolls on the lawn, cradling himself in the fetal position. "He's not my brother," he whimpers. "Brothers don't do that." Mom bends down, running her fingers over his bruised cheek.

Funny, she doesn't give a damn about mine.

She jumps to her feet, hurdling over Preston's body, and snatches the collar of my shirt, pulling it so tight the cotton neckline cuts into the skin. "You are a traitor, and a liar, and an embarrassment since the day you were born. And I can't stand to look at you."

I glance at Dad who stands, head down, shoulders slumped, and hands in pockets. Doing nothing.

"Ditto," I growl, grabbing her fingers and ripping them from my shirt. "I'm outta here." I jerk my keys from my pocket, slide in the front seat of my Scout and fire up the engine. The tires squeal as I peel backwards onto the road.

Clearly it's them against me, and I'm the one leaving while they fume on the front lawn. I throw it into gear and stomp on the accelerator, the engine revving like thunder. The neighbors won't care, though. It won't wake them from their precious beds because none of them are asleep. They're all standing on their front porches, outside lights off, like that somehow shields what they're doing.

Spying. Listening. Eating popcorn as they take it all in.

The Howard Family Implosion—an event to be remembered for generations to come. A delicious piece of gossip to precede the "I told you so" and self-righteous expression.

And just like that, our perfection turns to shit.

A couple minutes later, I pull my cell phone from my pocket and tap out a quick message. The scout idles, lights off, by the stop sign at the corner of Rayne's street.

<Gage> *I'm on your street. Need to see you*

It buzzes in my palm within seconds.

<Rayne> *Where?*

<Gage> *Stop sign at corner*

<Rayne> *K. Be right there*

I get out and lean against the fender. Waiting on her. Intentionally.

Not a chance meeting. Not a "stuck together because Preston bailed" situation. Not even a friendly chat in the hallway. I'm waiting on her—to see her, touch her, kiss her. On purpose. Because now, she's my girl.

The days of pretending are over.

She emerges, a dark silhouette at first, from between the bushes that edge the line between her house and the neighbor's, tiptoeing across the lawn. I'm not surprised. No way would her parents let her parade out the front door to see me tonight. Not after everything that went down. Not after that expression on Mrs. Davidson's face that I can only describe as some mash-up between a horror flick scare and falling off a 10-story building.

"Hey," she whisper-yells through the darkness, her features becoming more clearly defined as she approaches the streetlight, which reflects in her eyes. They sparkle as her mouth pinches into her cheeks, her lips full and slightly parted. My heart flutters against my ribs, and I reach out for her hands, soft and warm as her skin slides over mine. "How did things go—"

I squash her question with a kiss, pressing in so hard I'm afraid I'll hurt her. But she doesn't pull away. Only pushes into me with increasing pressure. I let go of her hands and grab her hips, tugging her in closer, as she runs her fingers up my back, through my hair and down across my face. When she grazes the bruise, I flinch and step back. The tenderness is no joke.

"What's wrong?" She cranes her neck, manipulating my chin in her grip to get a better view in the light. When she spots it, her mouth drops open and she slaps her hand across her mouth. "Oh my God," she says from between her fingers.

It's not pretty. I know because I kept looking at my reflection in the rearview mirror as I drove. Reddish-purple with the eye retracting under the skin's new heft. The last thing I want is her worrying or feeling guilty about any of this.

"He's just blowin' off steam."

Tears glisten on her lower lashes. "Your eye... your cheek... it's horrible." The lumpy mass is hot and hard under her gentle touch.

"His looks worse," I laugh, shoving my hands deep in my pockets.

"Wait a minute." She grabs my arm and yanks my hand to her face. The knuckles are bruised and scarred by erratic lines of dried blood. "Y'all didn't—"

"Fight? It's kinda what guys do."

"Not y'all," she says, dropping my hand, and sits down on the front bumper for no more than a few seconds before she's back on her feet, pacing by the car, head in hands. "This is a mess. And your parents. What did they—"

"Not much, but apparently, I'm a traitor, liar, and an embarrassment since the day I was born. Not sure what the hell that means." My words do nothing to ease her panic-stricken look, and I'll be damned if all this family drama is going to screw us up before we've even gotten started. "Maybe they'll put me up for adoption," I laugh, trying to diffuse her anxiety.

It doesn't work.

She scowls. "Not funny, Gage. Your parents know everyone

in town. They'll make sure our life is hell. Your mom already hates me."

"Don't worry about her. Besides Preston, the list of people she actually likes is pretty slim. I'm pretty sure she hates me and Dad, too." She stops and stares, unaffected by my comedic efforts, and then wraps her arms around herself, shivering. The fall night air is nippy, and she burrows further into her navy hoodie, pulling the sleeves down over her hands so just the ends of her fingers curl around the hem.

"Come 'ere," I say, folding her into my chest. She relaxes her head against me, the natural curves of our bodies melting together. "Forget it. Nothing can tear us apart if we don't let it." I press my lips to the top of her head, inhaling the vanilla undercurrents of her shampoo.

"But you and Preston..."

"Preston and I will be fine." I pull her lips to mine once more, the softness of her skin and the fullness of her tongue sweeping away any lingering concerns, fading them into radio static. "And you and me? We'll be better than fine."

The weeks following what came to be known as Prestongate were hell. Stares and whispers lurked behind us in the hallways and nasty notes about Rayne's supposed promiscuity appeared randomly on lockers, scrawled out in bright pink lipstick—a shade I'd seen Jaycee wear more than once. She basked daily in her newfound popularity, the queen bee who single-handedly outed the two biggest villains in the entire town.

No one directed public attacks at me, probably because word got around that Preston's face looked like pulverized hamburger meat after The Fight. I was ostracized, kicked to the curb by most of my and Preston's mutual friends because, you know... loyalty. And while social media's never been my thing,

Rayne found her friends list dwindling by double digits nearly every day. There'd even been a few pissed off messages about how both of us were going to "rot in Hell" that showed up in her inbox.

It's a running joke that we check the lawn nightly for townspeople wielding their lanterns and pitchforks and red letter As to plaster on our pajamas.

One Tuesday in French class, Madame hands me a note requesting I go to Mr. Hernandez's office. Terrific. A date with the school guidance counselor. It's a real mystery what this could be about. Rayne insists on coming along, and I'm secretly glad she'll be there to navigate this with me.

Mr. Hernandez—Frank, according to his ID—welcomes us with a smile, panning his hand out to the chairs in front of his desk. He clasps his hands under his chin, looking at us over the rim of his glasses.

"You probably know why you're here. It's no secret what you both have been going through. We can do our best to control the harassment here at school, but the internet is a different story. The only thing I can tell you is to please report any cyber incidents to your parents immediately. They're more equipped to handle that."

That's an eye-roll. My parents give two shits about the torment Rayne and I have endured. When he's actually at home, Dad locks himself in his study and hides from the world, but mostly he's out of town on one of the fifty million business trips that suddenly filled his calendar. And Mom rarely speaks to me unless it's to criticize my appearance or gripe about my room.

Yeah, let me just go tell my parents. Bullies helping to prevent bullying. That's classic.

"Is there anything else?" I grab my backpack from the floor and hoist it to my lap. This little talk must be the school's way of covering its ass should anything arise from all this. I imagine the principal, shoulders shrugged, explaining to the six o'clock news that they did everything possible to stop it.

"Actually, there is one other thing. This is by no means a suggestion, just... information. An option." He clears his throat and pulls out a manila folder with my name—Howard, Gage Lucas—written in black marker in the top right corner. Inside is a stack of papers with a snapshot of my school history. Is this the dreaded permanent record everyone used to warn me about as a kid?

Don't get a referral. It'll go on your permanent record. Don't get bad grades. They'll go on your permanent record. Don't even think about stepping outside the lines. It'll for sure go on that freaking permanent record.

I glance up. Mr. Hernandez is staring at me, waiting on me to zone back in. "An option?" I ask.

"With block scheduling and your fulfillment of all English requirements by semester's end, you are eligible for early graduation. I'm talking diploma in hand in a few short weeks." He reclines in his high-back chair, arms folded and looking awfully pleased with himself.

Wow. This must be how prisoners feel when granted parole. Finished with high school and these people by the New Year? Yes, please. Football's over so that's off my plate. The only other reason to stay is Rayne.

But she's one hell of a reason. I shake my head. She needs me, not only to be here with her, but also to be a buffer.

"But... I can't leave Rayne here alone to shoulder this. She—"

She blows out a loud breath and grabs my hand, squeezing so hard my knuckles pop. "I think you should do it." I jerk my head in her direction, starting to protest, but she shushes me with a finger over my lips. "Maybe if they don't see us together every day, they'll ease off. Let this go."

She's wearing rose-colored glasses. No way is anyone letting anything go. Maybe they'll eventually quit talking about it, but the truth will always hover there in the background, waiting for the day one of them can snatch it back to the present dialogue and reopen all the wounds. "No, I won't leave you."

"I can handle it. At the end of the day, I have a place to go where things are at least comfortable." She reaches up and strokes my cheek. "You need to find some peace, too."

"I don't know…"

"Do it."

The decision drops in my lap like a fifty-pound dumbbell. I could get a part-time job, put back some money, and start looking into college options for the fall. Maybe take a few online classes to get ahead.

I swallow hard, nodding. "Okay. Where do I go from here?"

Mr. Hernandez smiles and slides a packet of paperwork across the desk, then hands me a black pen. "This is a good place to start.

29

RAYNE

he doorbell rings. It's the first official time Gage is having sit-down supper with my family. It's only taken six weeks.

Hopefully, this is the first sign of acceptance. We've waited long enough, not hiding our relationship, not flaunting it either, but meeting in the school basement and sitting out in his Scout is getting old. We just want to be normal. Have our chance.

I've been a little stir-crazy keeping a low profile in town, so Mama's friend Sharon at the coffeehouse gave me a job waiting tables. I start next week. Mama's happy since she knows I'll be well supervised, and I'm happy just to get the hell out of this house for a change.

I called Preston a few times, but he refuses to answer his phone or texts. Then there's Charlotte. She and "Legs-a-lot" were rifling through sweaters in the boutique downtown a couple weeks ago when I walked in. I'm glad the store was pretty dead because the looks they shot me would've turned everyone to pillars of salt. At least there was no collateral damage. Except maybe the cash register. They deserted their purchases in a pile on the jewelry counter and huffed out after commenting about the shoddy clientele.

But none of that matters now. Not when Gage is here, walking in my front door looking like a belated Christmas present in his red button-down. I whisper, "You ready for this?"

Before he can answer, Daddy walks in, wearing a silver-speckled paper hat with "Happy New Year" on the brim. At least he's trying. Mama promised to give Gage a chance but she's nowhere to be found. Probably in the kitchen with her head in the oven.

"Gage! Good to see you, son."

Gage shakes Daddy's hand. "Thanks for having me, sir."

Daddy steps between us, one arm thrown around Gage's shoulder, the other around mine, and ushers us toward the dining room. "Come on young'uns, let's eat."

Mama's filling the glasses with sweet tea when we get there, but quickly places the pitcher on the table and stands by her chair. Gage offers her his hand. She takes it without looking at him. "Hello, Gage."

"Hi Mrs. Davidson. Thanks for having me." His eyes dart back and forth between Mama and me.

"Have a seat." Her voice is somber as she motions toward the other side of the table, her gaze still directed at the rug.

We take our places, me across from Mama, Gage across from Daddy, and after the blessing begin heaping our plates from the casserole dishes lined down the middle of the table. Our simple ceramic china and Mason jar glasses are a far cry from the Howard's multi-course feast called in by ringing a bell. If Gage even notices the disparity, he doesn't say so. He helps himself to a scoop of Mama's pork chops with a side of green bean casserole and chats with Daddy about college football playoffs and the Heisman winner. I toss in a comment here and there but maintain focus on Mama, who's chewing her food ever so slowly, grappling with her neck as if she's having to massage it down her throat.

"What are your college plans?" Daddy's question draws me back to their conversation. Gage is using his newfound freedom to work a part-time job at the local auto mechanic shop to put back a little of his own money for college.

Daddy says something about how his work ethic is commendable. Mama keeps on chewing, but on what I'm not sure. Her plate's still full, and the fork never makes it to her lips. Gage swigs his tea and wipes the corners of his mouth with a napkin. "Rayne tells me y'all have lived in Fountain Inn all your lives. Even went to Hillcrest?"

"That's right." Daddy tilts his chair onto the back legs and crosses his arms behind his head. "We started dating as freshmen. Been together ever since." He reaches over and squeezes Mama's hand, then winks at her when she finally looks up. "She can't get rid of me."

Gage sets his fork on the plate. "I bet you remember my parents moving here?"

"I sure do. The whole town was fascinated. They were the first 'outsiders' we'd had—"

Mama's voice surprises everyone. "What do you know about your parents moving here?"

In an awkward moment of silence, everyone's attention turns to Mama, who's wringing her hands, arms drawn in tight to her chest.

Gage crinkles his eyebrows together and clears his throat. "Not a lot. I think I was a baby."

"You were five weeks old." How does she remember that? This from the woman who usually can't remember her shopping list at the Pig. "Why did they move here? Did they ever say?"

"Um..." His voice is hesitant as he twirls his high school ring on his finger. Great. Everything was going fine, and now she's made him nervous. Leave it to Mama to ruin this. "Honestly, no. All I know is they lived in Charlotte back then, but Dad was spending a lot of time in Greenville scouting out opportunities to open up a branch of the firm. I think he fell in love with it."

"Fell in love?" She leans forward as if at any moment she might crawl right up on top of the wooden tabletop.

Gage adjusts backward in his chair, leaning away from the conversation. "With the area. He always said it's a great place to raise kids." He pauses, then laughs. "Plus, I guess Mom was kinda getting tired of being the brunt of jokes."

If Gage's trying to ease the tension, Mama's not biting. "Brunt of jokes?" she repeats.

Gage rows his hand in front of him, the way you do when you're trying to get someone to figure something out. "You know... Charlotte from Charlotte?"

She ignores his smile, oblivious to the joke. I don't like the way her voice is changing, like she's sucking in more air with each syllable. "I see. And do your parents like it here? Do they talk about the area?"

"Not really. They're not sentimental. It's all business."

"Except with you kids, I suspect? You and Preston?"

It's the first time Gage breaks eye contact as he separates a green bean from the rest of the casserole heap on his plate. "Not really. Preston, maybe, since he's helping out with the company. My parents and I have never been close."

"I'm sorry to hear that." Mama's eyes well up with tears. She's not lying or evading for once. She truly looks sorry. Verging on heartbroken, actually. It's weird, even for her, and that's saying a lot.

Suddenly, she scoots back her chair and tosses her napkin on the table beside her still-full plate. The panic slithers into our meal like a snake scoping out its prey. Her voice trembles, breathy and uneven. "I... I'm not feeling so well. Need to lie down." She disappears upstairs, leaving the three of us staring after her.

Her bedroom door is cracked, a thin beam of light edging out onto the hallway carpet. I press my cheek into the molding enough to peek into the room. Mama's in the corner chair, book laid in her lap, solemn. The only light in the room comes from the antique brass lamp on the dresser beside her.

I fling open the door, so hard it bumps against the wall behind it with a loud thwack. "Really, Mama?" My tone is harsh, more so than our normal scuffles, but I don't care. She swore she'd try, but it was a lie. Like always.

"What?" Her innocent stare kicks the rage up a notch.

"You bombard Gage with a slew of weird questions, then spaz out and run up here? You promised you'd..."

"Give him a chance? I did. I was perfectly pleasant down-stairs. I just... don't... feel well..." Very matter-of-fact. Very cold. She pushes her nose back into the book.

I snatch it from her lap, snap it closed, and toss it on the comforter. It's the first time I've done anything this forward, and a piece of me is fully expecting her to slap me. "You're feeling just fine!"

"As an adult, I think I know when I'm under the weather." She plucks a tissue from the box on the table and blows her nose as if that somehow should convince me. It doesn't.

"And as your daughter for almost eighteen years, I think I know when you're lying!" The anger spills out. This time the floodgates are down, and I can't stuff it all back in and pretend nothing's wrong.

Mama pokes her finger in my direction, fire and brimstone ripe on her tongue. "You weren't raised to speak to adults that way. The Bible says..."

"Don't Bible-whip me, Mama." I corner her in the chair, my hands planted firmly on each arm rest and lean in close to her face. "I've spent my life 'honoring my father and mother' and every other God-forsaken old biddy in this town. Groomed to do just what a good little Southern girl's supposed to—sit down, shut up, don't question, don't cross any lines. It almost cost me Gage." I push off with my arms, turning my back to her. "Hell, it's almost cost you your sanity."

Okay, that might've gone a little too far. She sniffles. I turn back. The stubbornness leaves her face, only a residue of shame remaining.

"I'm perfectly sane, despite what you or this town thinks. I worry about you... your choices... your future. Does that make me certifiable?" Her eyes are sharp as laser beams, cutting straight to the heart of our conversation. Is it a rhetorical question? Because if not, I still don't know the honest answer.

I sigh and drop down to sitting on my shins in front of her, the way I used to when she'd brush my hair into pigtails. "I don't know. Does it?"

"I just want you to be careful. Don't make mistakes, have regrets, like me." A warning dances in her eyes, side-by-side with the golden flecks of color that'd lost their shine long ago.

"Is your life really so bad, Mama? You've had Daddy since ninth grade, and y'all still look at each other like it's all-consuming." I grab her hands and fold them into mine. "It's the same way Gage looks at me."

"I know. That's what worries me." Her lips stretch into a thin line. She talks in riddles, in shards of truth-bits that never add up to anything substantial and usually just end up confusing me.

"Why do you hate him?"

"I don't hate him. It's just..." She pauses and blows out a deep breath. "When you're young, you think it's all a fairytale. Life's hard. Love's harder."

No, she's wrong. The feelings come easy. Too easy. It's everything else that gets in the way and makes it hard. "Is it love that's hard, or just people screwing everything up?"

Finally, a genuine smile breaks through her hardened mask. She chuckles. "Well, there ya go. The key to all the world's heartache. To err is human..."

I squeeze her hands, clammy and trembling in mine. "All I'm asking for is a chance, Mama. Please." Her eyes bore into me, smile faded. She looks through me, into my future, as if discerning and absorbing any and all heartaches ahead. She shuts her eyes and nods.

I spring up on my knees and hug her, my arms wrapping around so far my fingers touch the opposite elbows. My God, she's lost weight. Like twenty pounds down. When did that happen? I pull back, and her t-shirt wafts out, baggy at her sides. "Mama? You've lost weight."

She grins and strokes my hair. "Anxiety's a bitch on the human body."

"I know. I'm sorry. Let's change that. New Year, new start, right?"

"That's what we said."

I get up and walk over to the bedroom door. The sound of Gage and Daddy downstairs talking football and yelling at refs floats in. I smile back at her, extending my hand in her direction. "What d'ya say we go make them turn off sports and watch a Lifetime movie?"

30

GAGE

*D*amn, it's cold. I'm not exactly sure when the Arctic Circle relocated to South Carolina, but it's time to head back North. I reach in the backseat and grab my coat, the thick winter one I've used all of four times in the past two years and shrug it on before getting out of the Scout.

This isn't the weather I ordered for our first Valentine's Day together, but then again, maybe someone's throwing me a bone here. Rayne's not a fan of being cold, which means she'll put up little resistance when I pat the bench seat beside me with a wink. Every time I've tried it before, she's rolled her eyes and firmly declined.

Why? Too redneck, she says. Looks like we can't keep our hands off each other for two seconds.

That's when I smile over at her, the truth written across my face. We can't keep our hands off each other. Then she clicks her seatbelt in place, defiance personified, and tells me to shut up.

But not tonight. Tonight's Valentine's, the most romantic time of the year, and I've been planning my little surprise for over a month, down to the last detail. I jog up to the front door and push the bell. The door opens before the tone even fades away. She's wearing the same jeans and blue blouse she did that night. Perfect.

"So, are you gonna tell me what this is about?" she asks, twitching her finger between our two outfits.

"I could, but what fun would that be?"

She steps back and I walk into the foyer. Mrs. Davidson's in the living room, sitting in an armchair by the lamp, studying a stack of papers clutched in her hand. She doesn't look up. Surprising, considering today, of all days, I figured we'd be getting the extra-tough "retaining the virtue" talk. But nope. Nothing. It's as if she doesn't even notice we're leaving.

"Bye, Mama," Rayne calls from the door.

Mrs. Davidson glances up for only a second, her expression flat. "Have fun. Be careful."

The door slams behind us, and I hold out Rayne's coat as she folds herself into it.

"What was that about?" I whisper. Even though we're outside, a small part of me still fears Mrs. Davidson has the place bugged.

Rayne shrugs. "I don't know, but I'm not questioning it. Nice not to have the third degree for a change."

I open the passenger door and she slides in. By the time I jog around and get behind the wheel, she's already rubbing her arms up and down, teeth chattering.

"Does this thing have a heater?"

"It's on. High."

"It's 32 degrees outside and 35 in here!"

"Pretty much. Of course, there are other ways to get warm." I wink at her and pat the bench seat beside me. "They say body heat is the best kind of heat."

She deadpans then shrugs, defeated. "What the hell. It's Valentine's Day." She scoots across the vinyl, straddling the gear shifter and clicks her seatbelt in place. "Happy now?"

"Very."

Twenty minutes and a trip through the Chick-Fil-A drive-through later, I pull into the first parking spot by the river at Cedar Falls Park. The same exact place we spent Homecoming night.

"So this is a re-creation?" Rayne asks, gathering the pile of blankets I stashed in the backseat.

I walk around and open her door, and she jumps to the ground, her breath swirling out in white hazy spirals in the night air.

"More like a re-imagination. Homecoming night—like it was but better. The way it should've been."

I grab a blanket and unfurl it on the grassy patch in front of the Scout then pull her down to sitting beside me. The night is pitch, no artificial lights, no moon. Only a trillion stars, distinct and brighter than ever, thanks to the cold, clear air.

She shivers and scoots closer to me, turning to run her fingers through a few strands of hair that have fallen against my brow. The close proximity is too much. The fires inside rage, and in one quick move, I scoop her into my arms, pulling her into my lap. She straddles me, our faces close, and bodies closer. So close I'm sure she feels my excitement when her kisses accelerate, scattering icy droplets over my skin. Her lips are flames that cut through the bitter cold. My breathing is ragged and uneven, sometimes feeling as if I'm being strangled, sometimes as if there's too much air in my lungs.

Her body responds to mine, arching in as if the elemental core of her being craves mine with the same insatiable appetite. I slip my hand under her blouse, dipping my fingers into the cup of her bra and wishing the damn thing was Velcro that I could easily tear away. Her hand wanders down, down, down and finds me through my jeans, the sensation like rockets blasting off inside. Everything speeds up. Her hands, my hands. Her lips, my lips. Her tongue, my tongue.

She rips her lips from mine, throwing her hands onto my chest and pushing us apart. Her words lope out in uneven breaths. "We need to talk about this. There are things I need to tell you first..."

Talk about cold water. The flames turn to faint embers within seconds. "Should I be worried?"

She bites her lip and looks at the ground. "Preston and I... we never..."

My stomach sours at the mention of his name, and I twist away, the muscle above my jawline flexing in and out. Talking about him is definitely not on tonight's agenda. "I know. He would've told me."

"I just couldn't... I..."

I sigh and turn back. Her eyes are wide, pupils dilated into large black pools. "You weren't ready..."

"No. It was more than that." She palms my cheek, her fingertips pressing gently into my skin. "I couldn't do that with Preston, not when I was thinking of you. And I was always thinking of you."

I swallow hard and shut my eyes, the memories returning to me like knives. "It killed me every single time he took you to his room. Preston has a reputation with girls. You challenged him, but he can be... persuasive."

"He can be, but there's one thing you didn't count on."

"What's that?"

"He's not you, Gage. I was always in love with you. Not him."

A warmth floods over me, and the hard expression on my face naturally softens. I tug her closer, chest-to-chest, arms tangled around each other's bodies. The flames renewed, a moan escapes my lips as I kiss her then pull back, whispering into her hair, "I want you so bad."

Her breath is hot on my neck where her lips touch skin, and suddenly I'm hoping she's changed her mind. That tonight will be the night. The need rips and claws in my body, the same way it did on Homecoming, now a million times stronger.

"I want you, too... so bad... but I can't."

My lips freeze in place, and I pull back and clamp my hands to the blanket. "I'm sorry. I didn't mean to pressure you."

She grabs my cheeks between both hands and pulls me to her face. "You're not. We're feeling the exact same things, but I promised myself a long time ago that I'd wait until I was 18. Sex is an adult decision, and I want to officially be an adult when it happens. I never want to look back and regret breaking that promise to myself."

I slide my fingers along her jaw, stopping at her chin to angle her eyes squarely on mine. "I never want you to regret me."

"I regret trusting Jaycee. I regret hurting Preston. But I will never, ever, regret my feelings for you."

Dear God, I love this girl.

"For you, I'll wait." I grab my phone and thumb down the screen to the calendar app. "What, like six more weeks?"

She laughs, one of those half-breathy, half-snorty ones, and taps her finger to her chin. "Forty days, four hours, 23 minutes. But who's counting?"

Me. I'm counting every second. Because being with her is the stuff of my fantasies. My every wish fulfilled.

"We have one last re-do." I get up and run to the Scout, turning the radio up, then grab a huge plaid blanket and wrap it around my shoulders, each arm out wide. "Join me in a dance?"

I lead her to the rock where I snuggle her into me, the

blanket engulfing us in its warmth. I lean down to her ear and whisper, "Put your hands in my back pockets."

She gasps, red swirls coloring her cheeks. "You remember that?"

How the hell could I forget it?

"Remember how I pulled you in like this?" I squeeze her tighter, my own excitement pressing into her stomach. "And then I tried to kiss you, but..."

"No time like the present to correct that, and—" she starts.

My lips are on hers before she can even finish the sentence. She completely underestimates the magnetism her body has over mine. Loving her is easy. So damn easy. "You sure we can't consider you 18 already? You're so close. We can always round up."

She shoots me a lopsided grin. "The anticipation will make it even better."

I crush my lips to hers, and from the ripples of excitement that course through me, I know she's right. The anticipation that's built since our first time on this rock explodes within me like a gazillion fireworks. Just a few short weeks from now, it will only be better.

31

RAYNE

I float through the door, the spicy scent of his cologne still enveloping me, his soft caresses rippling over my skin. I toss my coat on the couch. The living room's dark, but as I start up the stairs to bed, muffled voices come from the kitchen. I sneak across the den floor and stop short at the kitchen doorway, leaning out just enough to peer around the corner. Mama sits at the kitchen table, elbows propped on the top and her head buried in her hands. Daddy's beside her, his chair scooted up to hers, arms around her shoulders. They're both crying. Why?

"Mama? Daddy?" I creep around the corner. Daddy immediately stands up and Mama swivels in her chair, wiping away the evidence. "What's wrong?" My heart sinks to my toes.

No one speaks. Mama turns to Daddy in silent communication.

"What? What is it? Tell me!" My breath staggers short and fast as I look between them, nightmare scenarios flashing forward in my brain—somebody died, Daddy lost his job, they're forbidding me from seeing Gage.

"Sit at the table with your mama and me." Daddy pulls out a chair directly across from Mama before retaking his place beside her. I crane my neck to catch her eyes, but she evades mine, and that's the scariest thing of all. This is bad.

"Let me, hun," she says to Daddy, placing her hand atop his. He nods a go-ahead as the tears puddle in his eyes. They're in Mama's as well.

"Rayne..." she says, her voice clear and deliberate, "I'm sick." She pauses a moment. Daddy squeezes her hand. "I've felt poorly for a while now, chalking it up to old age and stress. The usual. But you said something to me on New Year's Eve that got me thinking."

I scan the memories in my head, recalling the moment in question. It was in her room when I mentioned her weight loss. "I remember, Mama."

"I figured if you noticed something was off, then I better make a doctor's appointment. I expected he'd prescribe me iron supplements or maybe a new anti-depressant and all'd be well."

"Did he help you?" I nod as if my positive body language will ensure the best possible news, but I know very well it can't be all good or else we wouldn't be having this conversation. And there wouldn't be tears.

"No, baby." Her voice cracks as the tears streak her cheeks.

"What is it?" I lean forward in my seat, trembling. Part of my brain is screaming for her not to tell me. To let me ostrich my head in the sand.

"Cancer." She looks down at the table.

The world stands still. It stops cold in mid-rotation for a few seconds as the word soaks in. It's like one of those carnival tricks where the magician rips the tablecloth from underneath a stack of dishes. Somehow, I've got to keep standing.

"Cancer?" I choke out and inhale deeply. "Okay, we've got this. We'll beat it."

She's not looking at me again. "Pancreatic. Stage four. Unfortunately, this'll beat me. There's no recourse. It's too far gone for anything to be done. Medicines will ease the pain and prolong my time, if we're lucky."

"Your time?" My throat tightens, stopping air flow to my lungs. Dizziness grips me as my cells scream for oxygen.

"Woah!" Daddy jumps up from his chair, grabs my shoulders, bending me forward, head between my knees. "Deep breaths."

"Rayne, honey, are you okay?" Mama asks. She's suffering and all she can ask is if I'm okay?

When the spinning stops, I lean up and shake my head. How can I be okay? Mama's dying, and all I can think is how I never even really got to know her.

"We have to live with the hand we're dealt. I know my cards now," she says matter-of-factly. "I have up to six months."

"Six months?" I squeak out in disbelief. I won't have Mama next fall when I start college. I won't have Mama at Thanksgiving or Christmas. We just started mending fences, coming together as mother and daughter, and now we have an expiration date when it's barely started. "It's not fair. It's not true! There has to be something they can do instead of just letting you... die!" The words sting my tongue the way they sting my mother's heart. She flinches and brings her hand to her mouth. I should've never said that. The d-word. Die. It's too final. "Mama, I'm so sorry." I get up from my seat and circle my arms around her neck.

She pats my hair. "We ain't gonna brood around here like life's ended, because it's not over until it's over." She kisses me on the forehead, then Daddy helps her up and they go upstairs to their room. I stay behind in the kitchen, unable to reconcile how dramatically my life just changed. Life's fickle—happy one minute, sad the next; healthy one minute, dying the next. You can be so sure of your future up until the moment the rug's yanked out from under you. I'm floating and falling simultaneously, but whatever the sensation, the utter loss of control surges through me. I pull my phone from my pocket and dial Gage's number. He answers on the second ring.

"Can't get enough?" He's so happy. So oblivious. I wish I still was.

"Gage..." I choke out the words.

"What is it?" His voice drops an octave.

"It's late, but... can you come over? I need someone... now."

"Be right there." Silence. He's on his way.

I walk through the den to the bottom of the stairs. My parents' room is dark, no lights shining underneath. I grab a fuzzy gray blanket from the basket by the couch and walk onto the front porch, quietly letting the screen door latch.

Gage drives in the yard moments later, runs up the steps, and kneels down in front of me.

"I came as fast as I could." He's breathless, eyes pooled with anxiety. "What's wrong?"

I'm suddenly mute. When the floodgates open, I sob, ugly crying, and melt into his arms. He says nothing, just wraps them around me. When the tears subside, I pull his hands into my lap, holding them as if they're keeping me afloat.

"It's Mama."

Gage's eyes knit together in a frown.

Between ragged breaths, I whisper, "She has cancer. Stage four. There's nothing they can do. She's dying."

His mouth falls open. "Oh my God. I'm so sorry." He pulls me back to him. My tears soak the shoulder of his hoodie. He doesn't know what to say, and I get it. I don't need his words. I just need him.

"Just hold me," I say through the tears.

He moves beside me on the swing and pulls me to his side, nestling my cheek into his chest. He drapes the blanket over me and gently moves the swing back and forth, the tenderness of his hands warm against my skin. We say nothing—we just hold each other.

32

GAGE

The look on Mr. Davidson's face is somewhere between *Son, you've gotta be kidding me* and *She's 18, so what can I say?*

It's been a rough six weeks for their family. Rayne's mama sleeps near-constantly, her energy sapped from the medications prescribed for pain relief. Rayne and her dad are shouldering all the household responsibilities in addition to her home medical care, school and work, and frankly, they're tapped out.

I help as much as I can. People can only take so much before a total collapse, and when I'm there, doing all the mundane stuff, that's when Rayne and her dad can enjoy those quiet times with Mrs. Davidson. The opportunities that'll soon be gone. They need it. Rayne, especially. The emotional toll on the family of cancer patients is something they don't measure in all those blood draws, but how can you measure the fear that, no matter what you do, it'll never be enough?

So I've come to Mr. Davidson with a simple request. Let me take Rayne away from all this, just for a weekend. To celebrate the birthday that quietly passed without much attention last week. On top of everything else, she's been sick the better part of two weeks with a sinus infection and ordered to take two rounds of antibiotics and get lots of rest.

I've yet to see her actually rest.

Rayne's not convinced he'll say yes. "No way Daddy's gonna let me go. He likes you, but come on."

I'm not taking no for an answer, though, so I offer a solution. I'll persuade him with "misdirection."

"You mean lying?" she asks. You say tomato, I say to-mah-to.

And it's not straight-out lying. It's all truth, just vague and misleading. AKA misdirection. I ask him to let me take Rayne on a weekend camping trip to Edisto Beach State Park—two nights in a tent with park rangers, gated access, and cameras galore. Totally legit. The not-so-truthful part comes in when I promise that a group of five is going to the beach. And a group of five is going. It's just that the other three are going to Myrtle Beach, and we're headed 150 miles south.

Mr. Davidson stands in the yard and scratches his head while examining a hangnail on his left hand. "I know it's been stressful around here." He quits scratching and pans his hand toward Rayne. "And she is eighteen now…"

"Please?" Rayne asks, hands folded in front of her. "Less than 48 hours and I'll be back."

He sighs and folds his arms against his chest. "Okay, I trust y'all, and you deserve a break." He glances toward the house. "You'll probably be back before your Mama even knows."

Our bags are loaded before the first slivers of orange sunlight break the blackness on the horizon. Mr. Davidson hugs Rayne then reaches out to shake my hand, tighter than ever before. My knuckles crack under the pressure of his not-so-secret warning to take care of his daughter.

Four hours later, we cruise the marshy two-lane out to the island under a canopy of Spanish moss hanging from hundred-year-old oaks. The rotten egg stench of the marshes, so intense it lands squarely on your taste buds, wafts in through the open windows, and Rayne slaps her hand over her mouth and nose.

"Ah, smell that briny air," I tease, wafting my hand. "Gotta love some swamp gas."

"Love is a strong word," she says from between her fingers.

"Yes, it is, and I love you." For the last 300 miles, I've watched her from the corner of my eye, head relaxed into the seat, brown curls flying around her head in the breeze, eyes closed, and a slight smile creasing her lips. Perfect and peaceful.

She drops her hand and pivots her head on the seat to face me. "I love you, too."

We pull through the double gates of the state park, down the tightly-packed path of gravel, sand, and broken shells, into our shaded lot, secluded on all sides except the oceanfront, which stretches out wide in a blanket of caramel sand and blue-green waves cresting in the distance. I pitch the tent while Rayne inflates the air mattress, my mind wandering to happier places as I watch her stretching the Egyptian cotton sheets over the rubbery surface—imagining their silkiness rubbing against our skin, tangled in our legs, our bodies intertwined.

A bead of sweat rolls down my forehead and drips onto my nose. For the first of April, it sure is hot.

Or is it me?

We finish setting up camp and fill two knapsacks with beach provisions. Out front, our bikes lean on their kickstands. Showing Rayne the island is important to me. From the time I first saw this place as a kid, I told everyone this was where I was going to live someday. I still believe it. Except now, the desire to make her love it as much as I do burns inside.

I help strap on Rayne's backpack then grab mine from the ground just as she throws her leg across the bike, pops the kickstand, and puts one foot on the pedal. "Race ya." A cloud of gravel dust billows behind her, and I jump on my bike, giving a hard shove and closing the gap easily.

At the end of the trail's seven-mile jaunt is a bike rack, stuffed in between a stand of palm trees. My thighs burn and sweat soaks my shirt. We slam our bikes into the rack, the metallic clang of hers just seconds ahead of mine.

She jumps off the bike and commences an awkward, yet what I believe she feels is necessary, victory dance, some hybrid of the 'running man' and the 'dougie.' "Boom! I beat you!"

"You always have to win, don't ya?"

She shrugs, her smile never dissipating. "I like to win."

"You think I don't?" I pout my bottom lip.

"Fine," she concedes, patting my chest. "It's a tie."

She's cute—the way her eyes sparkle while she's gloating. Her freckles shine under the sun and sweat. I step forward, wrapping my arms around her, and she kisses me, her lips gliding over mine like an ocean breeze.

"How about a tiebreaker?" I suggest.

"Sure."

"First one to the ocean." I wink, plop her down behind me and take off running, glancing quickly over my shoulder as she stomps her foot and takes off toward me, her footsteps echoing mine off the wooden boardwalk.

"Cheater!" she yells, but by the time she catches me, she's laughing as she meets me in the waves, the water splashing up around us and spraying our clothes. She leans in to kiss me, and I part my lips, waiting. She pushes away, though, and glances around as if at any moment her mama will pounce from the sea oats.

"Maybe somewhere a little quieter?" she asks, eyeing the crowd of families around us.

I nod and lead her toward a stretch of wide-open beach bordering the marina. We walk the water's edge, the still-chilly water washing in and out over our toes as we go. On a large blanket on the sand, we spend a few hours laughing and talking, but mostly just lying next to each other, skin to skin but in a completely decent public beach way. Although I do admit to letting my hands wander from time to time, rubbing too long in one spot or trailing too low in another.

Damn hands need to mind their own business.

Her breathing quickens and her fingers mash deeper into my skin before she jumps up. "I bet I can find more conch shells than you!"

I throw my head back laughing. "You're cute when you're embarrassed, but okay, I'll take your challenge." For five minutes we scour the sand then meet back at the blanket. She shoots out her hand: a small silvery conch with the spiral top still intact but half the side missing. I pull out four near-perfect specimens. One look and her face drops.

"You win again." She frowns and flops down belly-first on the sand.

I snuggle beside her and prop up on my elbows, leaning in to kiss her cheek. It's salty like the ocean. "I'll make it up to you."

"I'll think how." She blushes as she says it, and I wonder if there's a deeper meaning to her words. Maybe she's thinking all the things I've been—I hope so.

From where we're lying, my attention focuses on a house, situated where the shoreline curves and the sea oats are thick on the dunes. "See that house?" I point to the weathered gray bungalow on the far edge of the Sound. "I've wanted that place since I was a kid. That's where I want to live one day. Raise a family."

Her eyes ping-pong from one gable to the next, growing so wide her eyelids melt under the brow bone. She smiles looking at it, and my heart melts. Eighteen is way too young to be thinking of families, kids, and mortgages, but that house has always been part of my future plans. And now she is, too. It's only proper they meet ahead of time.

"It'd be awesome painted a marine blue with white trim. Oh, and add a white wooden swing on that corner so you could look out over the ocean."

A swing. Her swing.

"I like that." I pull her fingers to my lips. "Gonna come live here with me?"

She stares at me, and it's like a silent conversation is going on between our subconscious minds. Rayne. Me. Together. Long term.

Butterflies. All in my stomach.

"Absolutely. You buy it, and I'll be here."

"One day," I vow and kiss her head. "One day."

33

RAYNE

*B*efore sundown, we head back to camp, take showers, and dress for supper. Gage takes me to his favorite waterfront restaurant because according to him "you haven't eaten shrimp until you've eaten fresh Edisto shrimp." And he's right. The seafood is phenomenal, buttery and tender, but we can't help overhearing a couple local fishermen at the bar talking about a strong cold front pushing through with heavy storms by morning. When the food is gone and the bill paid, Gage and I drive back to the campsite, kick our shoes off inside the tent and walk out to the beach via the palm-laden access from the front of our site.

The heavy clouds are building, their inky blackness creeping over the millions of stars dotting the night sky. We pad through the sand, ending up just shy of the pier, holding hands and not saying much of anything, though my mind is flying ninety miles a minute. I love the way our fingers interlace, the way his skin is tougher than mine but tender at the same time. I love the fact we don't have to talk—we can just be. I love him. I want him. *All of him.*

"Gage..." I say as a huge streak of lightning zigzags across the sky and fat raindrops start falling.

"Run!" he yells, but as I take off, the hem of my maxi-dress catches underfoot and nearly trips me. Gage scoops me up in his arms and sprints toward our campsite, the raindrops falling harder with every step. When we get there, he throws the tent flaps back and sets me down, then zips them tight.

He peels off his saturated t-shirt and tosses it in the corner. His v-lines cut diagonally down his body, and his hair, which spreads out across his chest, filters into a trickle that runs down the center of his abs and beneath the waistband of the black boxer-briefs peeking out from the top of his jeans. I've wanted him for so long, but tonight I know the wait is over.

He balls up a towel, patting the water off his shoulders and arms, when he looks up and catches me watching. I imagine myself looking like a dog whose owner is dangling a bacon treat over its head, eager eyes and tongue lolled out. "Whatcha thinking about?" he asks.

"You. Me. Why you're way over there, when I'm way over here."

"We can fix that." He steps over and presses into me, his front to my back, so close, his tangible desire pushes into my skin. I close my eyes and take a deep breath to regulate my heart rate, which has surged to light speed. He takes the towel and blots the water droplets from my arms, then gathers my hair and pushes it to one side, sliding the towel down the side of my neck. "Hold on," he whispers. "Still have a few in the hard-to-reach places, but don't worry. I'll get those." He brings his lips to my bare skin, flicking his tongue before finishing off with light suction, in a trail down the curve to my collarbone.

"I'm ready," I whisper. When he doesn't respond right away, I look up. He's staring at me, stroking the stubble on his chin. "Did you hear me?"

"I think so. Say it again."

This'll be a first for both of us and for that I'm grateful, because I want to give this part of myself to him, and I want his in return. "I'm ready. I want to be with you, Gage."

"That's what I thought you said." He smiles and spins me toward him, tilting my head up to his. "I love you, Rayne. I want you to know that first. There's no one else for me. Only you."

"I love you. I'm yours, Gage. All of me." The way he hovers in front of me, I think he's going to kiss me, but he doesn't. He sweeps his fingertips down either side of my jaw, and then down my neck to my shoulders, where he slips them under the straps of my dress, nudging them over the edge.

When he takes my arms, which are circled around his waist, and straightens them, the dress slips down and puddles on the ground at my ankles. He grins again, this time letting his eyes skim over my body, pausing at my breasts, and he runs his finger along my bra's lace-and-ribbon edging, into the small void between the two. His hands reach behind my back, fumbling with the clasp, which he unhooks and allows the bra to fall away. I shiver, not sure if it's from his touch or the bareness of my uncovered breasts. He palms both, kneading the flesh, rubbing the skin in circles.

When I think the intensity may kill me, Gage trails one hand down my stomach and fingers the lacey waistline of my panties before sliding his fingers underneath the silken fabric and down. I softly moan his name as my body arches toward him. I may have a heart attack. This might kill me, but I'll die happy.

I could let his hands explore me all night, but I want him to know I want him with every ounce I've got. "My turn." I stand on my tiptoes and whisper in his ear, then nibble the lobe and softly blow on it, a move that makes the hairs on his arm prickle against my skin. He shudders. "And I'm just getting started," I promise with a smile, my lips now pressed to his cheek, grazing ever-so-softly as I form the words.

My breasts flatten against his chest, the skin-to-skin contact hot and wet as the sweat and leftover rain drops squish between us. I want to be bold, to physically show him my desperate need. I rub my hands, palm to skin, over his pecs, tracing the ridges of his ab muscles with my fingertips outward to the inked lettering. Tonight, no rules apply for us.

By the time I get to his jeans, his breathing is slowed, almost non-existent. He's waiting on me, anticipating my next move, and I love the sense of power. We lock eyes, his brimming with smoldering heat, as my fingers find and unfasten the button and slide the zipper down. He leans in and crushes his lips to mine with tender force as he steps out of his jeans. We come to a standstill, taking a moment to look at each other, head to toe. He swallows hard and reaches for his wallet.

"Stop."

Gage turns back quickly, eyes wide. "You're not ready?" He can't hide the disappointment.

"No, I'm absolutely ready. It's just..."

"Just what?"

"We don't need that." I point to his wallet. "I've been on birth control a couple years now... for my complexion and my cycles. The doctor's idea... so, we're covered."

He closes his eyes and opens them, the fire renewed, as he looks at me and tosses the wallet over his shoulder, walks back and slams his lips to mine. They move faster now, furiously searching, his tongue jutting out across mine, stopping only briefly to nibble my lower lip. Suddenly he grabs me, his fingers burning like branding irons, and lifts me up, walking us backwards to the inflatable mattress on the tent floor.

"My God, you're perfect," he whispers. "I love you so much, Rayne, I can't contain it."

"Then quit trying," I whisper back.

His kisses rain over me, and he presses his body into mine, a new level of intimacy that robs my breath, and in between the booming thunder and roaring waves slapping the beach, Gage and I melt into one another, salty lips and sandy skin, hot breath and soft touches, finding perfect satisfaction in our slice of heaven.

I awake the next morning with a smile on my face, but Gage is no longer beside me. Light streams in and the waves roar as if right outside the tent. I push up on one elbow and look around. He's in the doorway, flaps thrown open as he watches the tide go out. The still-wet sand glistens in the morning sun.

I crawl on my hands and knees behind Gage, wrap my arms around his shoulders, and rest my head in the curve of his neck.

"Morning," I whisper in his ear.

"Morning, beautiful." He keeps looking out over the waves.

"I am, aren't I?" I tease, pretending to fluff my unruly hair. Between the ocean air and last night's rolling around, it's about ten times puffier than normal.

"Yes." He turns and puts his hand on the back of my head, pulling me in for a kiss. His blue eyes sparkle with the prismatic effect of the sun. "Last night was... God, I love you. I belong with you."

"Then stay." I climb onto his lap. "Stay with me and don't ever leave."

They say there's a calm before the storm. We're in its sweetness for only a couple more hours before Daddy's call comes in. Mama's worse, and we have to get home. Now.

Endless rows of pine trees swish by in a green blur outside the passenger window, hazy and shapeless, kinda like my head right now, which swirls with the sweet memories of last night wrapped up in the worries about what lies ahead. Daddy didn't say much on the phone, but I heard the cracking in his voice, the long pauses of silence. In the side mirror, Edisto fades further behind us. I hate leaving. I hate being left.

I squeeze Gage's fingers in mine. He's not going anywhere, but Mama is—any day now. Daddy's simple words struck my heart like an arrow. "It's not good, Rayne."

Gage pulls my fingers to his lips. "I got you. Whatever you need."

"Just stay by me, Gage. I can face anything with you."

Daddy's slumped in the front porch rocking chair when we pull up, his eyes fixed on the slatted floor, not even acknowledging the crunch of gravel beneath our tires. Gage squeezes my hand, leans in for a kiss, and pulls back, his eyes roving my face. "Call me."

I nod and slide out, running toward Daddy as the hum of Gage's engine dissolves into background noise.

Daddy unconsciously runs his fingers along the arm of his glasses, something he only does when upset, but musters a small smile when I walk up. "Glad you're home safe." He pushes his glasses back onto the bridge of his nose, and then grabs my hand. "She's asking for you."

I hug him and kiss the top of his head. It reminds me of how he used to tuck me in at night. It's much too early for us to be having this parent-child reversal thing going on, but a part of me realizes how much he needs me to be strong.

The rhythmic beep-beep-beep of monitors surrounding Mama's hospital bed echo in the otherwise silent den. Her head is turned, facing the triple windows. Only a few fringes of natural light filter in across her body.

"Rayne, honey." Her frail voice startles me. I thought she was sleeping. "Open up the windows. Let in a little fresh air." She gasps between the words as if there's not enough air left in her lungs to string them together.

"Yes ma'am." I raise each window halfway, never taking my eyes off her. She looks no more than a corpse already, all skin stretched over bone. It's difficult to look at her, but I do. Because no matter how sick she is, she's here right now, and we can't waste any more time. "Need any water, pillows?" I move close to her bedside and pour water into her cup from a small pitcher on the side table.

"Answer a question," she says, her voice wispy. I have to lean close to hear the words. "Does God forgive all sins?"

I spring back. The woman who's always lectured me on all things holy is asking for my spiritual opinions, and for a split-second I wonder if it's some sort of trick question—her testing me one last time. "If we repent, He forgives."

She winces from pain or my answer, or both. "What if the sin... is too big?" She pushes the words out. "What if other people... get hurt?"

The thought of Mama's involvement in some major, life-altering sin is laughable considering the woman is religious to a fault and has pretty much been paralyzed by her anxiety all these years. Her anxiety. Isn't weakness of spirit some sort of sin? Maybe Mama's apologizing for her "episodes" after all these years.

"Forget all this. Relax." I take a cool washcloth from the bedside table and lay it across her forehead.

"No." She grabs my hand, her eyes wide. "There's something I need to tell you." She gasps loudly and coughs. "Before it's too late."

"Mama?" My voice is high-pitched, almost squeaky. I wring my hands, massaging so hard the bones in my fingers ache from the pressure.

"Sit." She nods toward the chair beside her. I do, but keep her hand tucked in mine. "You know it took us so long to have you... three rounds of in-vitro... so many failures... before you." She gives me a weak smile as the screen door opens and Daddy walks in. He joins us and grabs Mama's other hand before she continues. "That summer was so hot, so dry, but on the day we found out about you..." she pauses and takes a deep breath, "on July 26th, the rains finally came."

"You found out you were pregnant on July 26th?" I laugh and clamp my free hand to my mouth. "How crazy is that? That's Gage's birthday!"

Her chest caves in and she's struggles for breath. "I know." Daddy's hand squeezes into hers tighter. "There's more to that day than I've ever told you... or anyone... except Daddy."

Her words are ice chips in my veins. What could she possibly say that links my conception and Gage's birth? She wouldn't have even known the Howards then because Gage was over a month old when they moved here. Still, my stomach's churning, and I don't know why.

She continues, her voice wavering and broken. "I was driving home from my doctor's appointment downtown when the rain started. So hard," she whimpers. "Impossible to see." Daddy grabs a tissue and blots the corners of her eyes, but she pushes his hand away. "There was something in the road... a horrible noise... the thump against the fender... I'll never forget it." She pauses and looks down. "I just knew I'd hit a dog, but it was too dangerous to stop." She sobs, pulling her hands from mine and Daddy's and collapsing into them. "I had to think of you. My baby..."

"A dog?" I move to the edge of my seat and touch her arm. "I don't understand..."

"It wasn't a dog, Rayne!" She grips her side and grimaces in pain. "It was a person. I killed someone!"

Suddenly I understand Mama's anxiety. Surely I'm in its

clutches now, my heart thumping hard against my ribs, my last meal rising up from my stomach, ready to spew. It's like a million bursts of energy going off simultaneously in me, and I can't keep still. I jump up and pace beside the bed, gripping my throat, trying to ward off the unseen force that's threatening to collapse my airway. "What? I... I don't..."

"That's not all." She takes the cloth from her head and drops it over the side of the bedrail. "The woman was eight months pregnant."

Pregnant. July 26th. Gage's birthday. "Oh my God." I back away from her, my mind in overdrive. She couldn't have hit Charlotte because Charlotte's alive. So how does this all fit together? My gag reflex twitches as my throat spasms again. "The baby?"

"He lived. The woman was single, no husband, no family."

"How do you know all this?"

"A contact in the NICU." She closes her eyes and leans back in the pillow. Daddy leans down and whispers in her ear, but she shakes her head. "Let me finish." She opens her eyes and motions me over. I walk to her and prop myself on the foot of the bed. "A father came forward after a few days, a high-profile businessman, married with a family. It could've been a major scandal, but he was close with the hospital administrator, so things were done hush-hush. Only the family, the administrator, and my nurse friend knew the truth. The media was told it was a private adoption."

My heart slows to an unnatural pace, like minutes lapse between each beat. My head's quiet as if separated from my body. Outside looking in. "So, the businessman is... the baby is..." I sputter.

"Gage is the baby, Jackson Howard the businessman. They moved to town shortly after taking Gage in, so people here wouldn't know the truth." She makes eye contact with me for the first time in a while. "Now you understand... why I am the way I am... why I wanted to keep you away from the Howards..."

I shake my head. No. It can't be. She's mistaken. So many things don't make sense. "The police? If you killed her, why aren't you in jail?"

"There was no evidence at the scene, no witnesses. And I," she drops her eyes again. "I never came forward. I couldn't. Because of you."

Because of me. Mama has lived with this gut-wrenching secret for nearly two decades because of me. But what about Gage? He wouldn't keep this kind of secret from me.

"Gage would've told me if he was adopted. He would've!" I insist, stomping my foot on the hardwood.

"He doesn't know." She says it solemnly. The three of us sit in silence until the screen door slams behind us.

I stand up quickly. "What're you doing here?"

Gage's cheeks are red, face stoic. He swallows hard a couple times. "You left your bag in my car. I was putting it on the swing out front when I heard you talking." He looks at Mama. "I want the truth. All of it."

Mama, so fragile, nods and motions Gage toward the empty chair by her bed, where he sits, leaning forward, elbows on knees and hands clasped together, while she tells him the whole story. When she finishes, when he knows his very existence has been a lie, he buries his head in his hands. He doesn't cry. Doesn't scream. He's still.

Mama pulls her Bible from the side table and leafs through the front few pages before pulling out a yellowed newspaper clipping. She clears her throat. "Gage?" He looks up, and she hands him the article. "I've kept this since the accident." She pauses, the words getting harder and harder, her strength failing. "Every day I pray for forgiveness. I hope you can forgive me, too, Gage... one day."

He stares at the paper, his bottom lip trembling. I peer over his shoulder at the article in his hands. It's a news report of the hit-and-run, the details we've just learned staring back at us in black and white. I wrap my arms around his shoulders, but he stiffens at my touch. He pushes my arms away, gets up, and walks to the door without a word.

I follow him. He twists the screen door handle as I grapple with his shirt sleeve. "Gage? Gage! Please... talk to me."

He turns around, eyes hollow. "It all makes sense now. I feel like a black sheep because I am one." We stare at each other. There are so many things I want to say, so many things I should say, but no words come. He slams his hand into the knob and the door flies open wide. "I gotta go."

Before I can make it out onto the porch, he cranks the Scout and with a hard rev of the engine, peels out of the driveway and doesn't look back.

34

GAGE

When they walk out tomorrow and see two muddy ruts across their manicured zoysia grass, maybe then they'll know I think driveways are overrated. Just like this "happy" family bullshit they've been hiding behind. Jackson and Charlotte Howard with their 1.5 kids and mansion. And this point-five-child is freaking over it.

The quaint boxwood wreath with the monogrammed "H" falls off its hanger and onto the hardwood floors at my boots when I sling open the front door. Stupid wreath. Stupid frou-frou crap Mom—I mean, Charlotte—keeps around to make her feel important. The anger ricochets inside, surging down my body like a roman candle, with a power that explodes when my foot makes contact. I kick the shit out of it, hurtling it across the foyer into the perfect vanilla wall with the perfect display of china vases.

The door to his study is cracked. I slam it open, swinging it back into the bookcases with a loud thud. His chair squeaks as he pushes back from his desk, eyes locked on mine. "How could you?" I growl, but before he gets to the door, Charlotte rushes down the stairs, all dramatic-like in her slipper-heels and loosely-fastened silk robe billowing out behind her.

"What is going on here? I'm upstairs trying to get ready for the Elkins' party, and—" She pauses in the foyer and glares at the damage then stabs her finger at the mess on the floor. "Look what you've done, you little bastard!"

"Damn straight." Everything swells inside me like a tsunami —all the mistreatment, all the chilly interactions, all the animosity. I grew up believing my mom hated me, but my mom doesn't hate me. My mom never got a chance to love me. This is only an imposter bitch who thinks I'm not worthy, and quite frankly, she can kiss my ass. They all can.

"Gage..." Dad stands beside me in the doorway. I jerk my eyes to his, my lungs shriveling in my chest, like all the oxygen's being sucked out. His lips move, but the words don't register in my brain, just a high-pitched buzz ushering in a slew of blackish spots that stream through my vision. I lunge toward him, fisting his polo in both hands, and pin him against the wall.

Dad's eyes are saucers as my knuckles grind deep into his chest, the shirt pulled so tight the threads pop. The room is silent, except for the click-clack of Charlotte's heels as she stomps over, hands on her hips. "Take your hands off your father this instant!"

"Shut up! This is between Dad and me."

"Gage, don't talk to your mother like that." His voice wavers.

"I'm not! My mother's dead." My fists dig in deeper as the recognition filters into his startled gaze, and his body goes almost limp against the wall.

"Jackson! Do something! You promised me! He's trying to ruin my life!" She grabs my shirt, yanking hard against me, nails clawing into my skin through the cotton. I jerk my arm away, trying to shake her off, and she falls to the floor, underwear half-exposed as her bathrobe splays out around her.

The back door slams open and heavy footsteps sound in the hallway. "Oh my God, Mom!" Preston rushes to her side, and she plays it up as usual, gripping her knee. Always the victim. "Why aren't y'all helping her? She's hurt."

He refocuses on her knee as she whimpers, "Gage did it."

Preston stands up, shoving forward into my face. "How dare you attack Mom!"

"She's your mom, not mine. Mine's dead."

He grimaces and blows out a breath. "That's a sick thing to say."

"No. It's the truth." I look over his shoulder to the two of them. "Right, Dad? Charlotte?"

Preston narrows his eyes and whips around toward them.

Dad squeezes his eyes shut, lips flat-lined, as he takes two deep inhales. He opens them, fixating on me. "I take full responsibility for this. There's no need to blame Charlotte."

"Oh, I don't. I blame you, because you knew the truth, and you still let her treat me this way my entire life. You could've stepped in, but you didn't. You let me bear the brunt of her anger all these years, and for what? To save your reputation?"

Dad steps between me and Preston, wrapping an arm around each of our shoulders, his voice calm and even. "Gage, you and I need to talk, and then Preston, I'll explain everything to you."

Behind us, Charlotte's shrill laughter cuts through the moment. "Oh, I'm sure you will. You'll explain it all with a pretty little bow on top. But there's nothing pretty about the fact that you whored around with a little slut from your office while I was at home, alone, with an infant who depended on me for…"

A flame ignites in Dad's stare as he pivots to face her head-on. "Spare me the histrionics! You were never the little wife and mother, alone at home and burdened. You were at society luncheons and getting your nails done while the nanny raised

Preston. You treated me like a business partner, someone to dress your arm for public appearances and provide the lavish living you believe you deserve. I was content to live the life I got myself into, until I found out just how different it could be. Leighton was no slut. She was a warm, beautiful woman who…"

Preston's expression goes blank, his hard breaths rocking his chest up and down. "Enough!" he screams, pulling his keys from his pocket. "To hell with all of this and all of you! I'm outta here."

He throws open the front door and rushes out, Charlotte on his heels, pleading with him not to go. When the Mustang revs and the tires squeal into the road, she closes the door and turns in slow motion, an expression straight from Lucifer himself burned on her face. "I hate you, Gage. I wish you'd never been born."

"Yeah, what's new?" I shoot back, pushing past Dad into his study. He steps in behind me and slams the door, muffling Charlotte's shrieking behind a layer of soundproofing and dark mahogany paneling.

He promises full disclosure—no question off limits—as he pours two glasses of scotch and hands me one, saying a man-to-man discussion of this caliber calls for it. I hope it'll dull the shredding sensation in my stomach, but so far nothing's touching it. Still feels like someone let a rabid cat loose in there.

Ten minutes later, we sit there in a moment of silence as Dad digests everything I heard from Rayne's mom. He hunches over his desk, his fingers steepled to his forehead before he balls them into fists, which he bangs down on the wooden top. The vibration creates little ripples across the surface of our drinks. "Mrs. Davidson? I just can't wrap my mind around it. All these years. She knew and never said a word."

"She was protecting Rayne."

"And now you're both paying for the sins of your parents." He mumbles, circling his glass on the desktop. "In some weird way, I empathize with her. We both have Leighton's blood on our hands."

"What do you mean?"

"I put her in the position of being the other woman. She deserved better than that, but I couldn't let her go. I loved her so much I thought binding her up, keeping her in a cage to wait for me, was best. God, that wasn't fair to her. That wasn't an act of love—it was an act of selfishness! I couldn't bring myself to give her up, so I was willing to take away her freedom. Only..."

"Only what?"

"She was giving me mine. She knew I'd never be able to make a decision between my two sons—hell, my two lives—so she was taking herself out of the picture." He rolls backwards in his chair to the wall safe, dials in the combination and retrieves a yellowed envelope. It trembles between his fingers. He rifles inside and pulls out a bus ticket that he drops on the desk. One way, from Greenville to Charleston. July 26. She was leaving him when she died.

I pick it up, the paper heavy as lead. My mother's fingertips had once been where mine are now. Surreal.

He takes another sip of his scotch, watching me over the rim of the glass, grimacing as if the alcohol is reacting with all the reopened wounds. "She wouldn't have been on that corner, waiting on a bus, had I not driven her away."

Something's not clicking in my head. If he loved my mom, why lie to Charlotte? Why stay? People get divorced all the time and still have relationships with their children. The black-and-white, this-or-that decision is just bullshit. "Why would you have to decide between me and Preston? We're both your sons."

Dad chuckles. Not the happy sort but the son-you're-so-outta-the-loop kind. "You're not 'wired' like the rest of us, Gage. You take that from your mother. Thank God." He takes another swig of his scotch and tells the story of how the company was founded by my great-great grandfather and grown into the empire it is today on the backs of all those who came after. Generations of Howard men, slaves to a life of duty and expectations. A life that makes no sense to me, and now I know why.

Charlotte and dad had been groomed for each other, hand-picked and strongly suggested for "holy matrimony" by their parents, who were lifelong business acquaintances. In their world, that was the only type of friends they had. None of the real kind that know your innermost secrets and dreams. Only those who had a solid lead on your five-year plan, retirement goals, and net worth. She was sharp-minded with a knack for social politics and considered beautiful in the superficial sense, even though that quality was lacking in her personality. He was bound by duty and the traditions of Southern pride to carry on the family name, in business and breeding, with someone of "equal upbringing and social standing."

Though he'd loved Charlotte for a brief moment in time, he'd never been in love with her, and divorce was unacceptable, not only as a breach of etiquette and expectations but also because he'd lose half of his assets and the family-built company to her.

His explanation churned in my gut. It was all a very formal way of saying he was protecting his own ass. "So, it was cheaper to keep her?"

Dad grimaces and bites his lower lip. "Not only that. I was just getting to know Leighton when Charlotte announced she was pregnant. I was torn. Suddenly there was a child whose future depended on the choices I made. But no matter how hard I tried, I couldn't give up Leighton. I loved her. Like I've never loved a woman before. Like I never will again." He pauses and stares at an empty spot on the wall before finally continuing. "Preston was only a couple months old when Leighton got pregnant. We kept it a secret, but when she died, I confessed everything to Charlotte. I couldn't pretend you weren't my son."

"You told her about mom and me?"

He nodded. "She was livid, barking about divorce and law suits, but eventually, when she calmed down a bit, we reached a compromise."

A compromise. In typical Howard style, I'd been used as a bargaining chip in a business deal, and my living in this house didn't come without its fair share of conditions Dad was expected to follow to the letter. "If I adhered to her demands, you and Preston could grow up together as brothers. If I didn't, she promised to have you sent away to boarding school and would systematically turn Preston against the both of us."

"So she never wanted me here?"

"It doesn't matter. You're my son, and so is Preston. If you couldn't grow up with your mother, then you could at least have your brother." The realization sucker punches me in the gut. If mom hadn't died, I likely would've never had a relationship with Preston. We'd either never have known about each other or Charlotte would've nixed that for sure.

And while Dad's sacrifice kept me and Preston together, I'm not sure I can forgive the way he's always held me at arm's-length. "Charlotte's demands—is that why you've always kept your distance?"

"If I paid you too much attention, she would've made good on her threats to send you away. And I needed you here. Not just because you're my son, but because... I'm a selfish bastard." He picks up the yellowed envelope again, flicking apart the open end with two fingers while searching the contents, then reaches in and pulls out several faded photographs. "You remind me of her. That sarcastic sense of humor, the way you twist your ring on your finger when you're agitated, and those blue eyes. Those are all her. Little pieces of her wrapped up in you."

He lays the pictures face-up on the desk, sliding them one by one across the top to me.

Mom in a flowing blue dress, her dark hair piled up in a loose twist, sitting at a river bank picnic.

Dad and mom, squeezed cheek to cheek, one of dad's arms extending out to take the picture, the other wrapped around her shoulder.

Mom in a tight-fitting green shirt, standing sideways with one hand on top and one underneath a large, pregnant belly.

Not the stiff corporate headshot in the obituary, but relaxed snippets of her everyday life. Messy, free, and completely in love. It was written in her smile.

The knot in my throat grows to a boulder. "Do you ever think about her?"

"Every day. And every time I look at you."

I pick up the photo of her and dad together. Happy. "I do have her eyes. And her nose."

"I know. You have her strength of spirit, too."

Good. It's that strength I'm counting on to get me through this.

"Dad... I can't stay here. I have to..."

He nods, fumbling in his sliding desk drawer, and produces a ring with two silver keys. The keys to the firm's corporate apartment downtown. "Take a few days to process this. Anything you need—anything—let me know, and I'll bring it to you."

I take the keys and shove them deep in my pocket as I stand up and head toward the door. My hand is on the knob when he calls my name, and I turn to look at him, eyes red-rimmed and watery, his posture slumped, almost broken, as he walks toward me. "I love you, son, and I'll never let anything come between us again. When you're ready, I'll be here."

I nod, open the door, and walk out of the Howard house.

RAYNE

This is messed up.

Two days and Gage hasn't responded to any texts or calls. He hasn't come by either. Mama's in and out of consciousness. Daddy refuses to leave her side. The people I love the most have ripped my world apart and then disappeared when it's time to pick up the pieces. The loneliness stings. The betrayal's worse.

Maybe I'm being selfish calling it betrayal because they're all going through some heavy shit. I get it. But so am I.

I sit on the swing, letting my toes drag along the porch floor, pushing back the crazy emotional tornado. Mama used to have this self-help book that said getting personal with your emotions brings healing. Right now, I'd rather be numb.

I hear him before I see him, the rumble of the Scout's engine coming up the street, nearing our driveway. By the time I reach the steps, he's there. He slams both hands on the wheel before getting out.

If I didn't know any better, I'd think Mama's erratic tendencies have invaded my brain, the way everything's bouncing around. Thank you, God. He came back. I love him. I'm gonna kill him for leaving me.

"Gage!" I rush down the front steps and throw my arms around him. "Where've you been? I'm so sorry... I just... love you." But as soon as I get it out, a new emotion surfaces, fiery hot. "How could you leave me? I need you. You need me. But you walked out! Why the hell didn't you..." I scream as Gage calmly clasps my hands and pushes them down to my side.

"We'll talk. Later. I need to see your mom first." His eyes are dark, voice flat, almost robotic as he steps around me toward the house. I keep my back turned until the screen door slams, then sink to the dirt, leaning against the front bumper of the Scout and looking at the den windows wondering what's going on. A minute later, Daddy slips out and walks to his garage.

None of this is logical or even believable. I don't know how to process it. I don't know if Gage has confronted his parents. I don't know if there'll be legal ramifications for a woman with only days to live. Is death enough? I don't know. Maybe this'll become my cross to bear, and I can pick up where Mama leaves off, mentally whipping myself and living in exile. I can't do that, though, because I love him, even when he's shutting me out. He has to remember why he loves me, why we're so much bigger than this.

"Rayne." Suddenly he's standing in front of the Scout, shifting from foot to foot and twisting his high school ring on his finger.

I refuse to make eye contact, focusing instead on swirling patterns in the dirt with my finger. "Where've you been?"

"Around." He sighs loudly. "My dad..."

"Is he going to the police?" I interrupt, my stomach tying in knots.

"No. Last thing Charlotte wants is a scandal." He snorts and kicks at the dirt. "Or an extra son."

I swipe my hand across the dirt designs, sending dust flying. "Didn't you get my texts and calls?"

"I got 'em." His words, like a brick wall, shut me down. "I need to do this in person."

"Do what?" It's the first time I bring myself to look at him. His eyes are glassy, jaw locked tight, as he folds his arms in front of him.

"Tell you I'm leaving. Tell you..." he swallows hard and looks out across the yard, "it's over."

Why is he doing this? I'm breaking, physically, mentally, the splinters flying in every direction at once, and I jump to my feet, but my knotted insides double me over. "No!" I sob, no longer holding back. "I love you."

He stands hard as a statue. "You don't even know who I am. Neither do I, and I have to figure it out... alone."

I lunge toward him, grab his arms and press my face to his chest. "Please... don't leave me. I need you. I want to be there for you."

He pushes me away, his hands cold and insensitive, and opens the car door. "Be there for your mama. She needs you."

"You don't?" I scream, slamming my hands on the hood of the Scout. Tremors course through me as if I'm on the verge of implosion.

"I have to do this, Rayne. For me. For you." He slides into the driver seat and slams the door, the clanging metal like a gunshot to my spine.

The engine roars to life, and I can't breathe right. I run to his door and grab the rolled-down window. "You can't throw us away! I won't let you!"

"Do what you have to." He pushes my fingers off and accelerates forward, circling behind me. When he gets to the road, he tosses something out his window into the ditch. I run toward it as he disappears down the street.

His cellphone.

I spend Mama's last hours by her side, curled up in the bed next to her, my head on her chest and arms around her waist. The way I did as a little girl. She mostly sleeps, and I stare at her, memorizing the slant of her nose and the shape of her lips before it's only a memory. I'm not bitter we're just now getting close. I'm grateful that when I look back, when I one day tell my kids about her, there'll be no regret. It might be the one good thing to come from this whole mess.

Her fingers brush across my hair, and I look over at her, eyes open but heavy. Tired. "He forgave me," she whispers.

I rise up on my elbow. "What?"

She pushes out a ragged breath. "He forgave me." Why didn't he tell me? And if it's true, why did he leave? "He's confused. Give him time. Be patient. He needs you."

"I don't know..." I look down at the tubes running in and out of her, like flexible plastic snakes against the soft pink cotton of her gown.

She pats my arm and manages a weak smile. "Why would I lie to you now? Trust me. I see the truth."

I collapse back to her side and wrap my arms around her shoulders. "I love you, Mama. I don't want you to go."

"I have to, baby, but I'll never be far. I'll show up in the details of your day and then you'll know without a doubt, it's me." She kisses my forehead, closes her eyes, and relaxes into the pillow.

A few hours later, Mama takes her last breath—a soft pulse of air—and passes from this life. Daddy and I sit on either side of her, holding her hands. All that remains is the tiniest upturn in her lips. Gage gave her the one thing the rest of us couldn't. Forgiveness.

I kiss my fingers and press them to her lips then walk to the front screen door, looking out across the empty yard. The afternoon sun cuts through the trees, freckling the grass with patches of light and dark. Something about it looks different. Feels different. Final.

The ladder-back chair in the foyer sits empty, and my breath catches when I think about all the nights she sat there, waiting for me to get home. Loving me, protecting me in her own weird way. Never thought I'd miss it, but I will.

Daddy walks behind me, squeezing my shoulder with one hand while handing me a slip of paper with the other. The outside is simply marked "Rayne" in Mama's flowing script. "She left this for you." He kisses my head and walks upstairs.

I sit in the chair and unfold the note, Mama's last words to me.

He asked to take one of my photos of you—the one from homecoming. If he didn't love you, he'd have never asked for that. He's gone now, but he's not alone. This is my favorite saying. Commit its truth to heart: "If you love something, set it free. If it comes back to you, it's yours. If it doesn't, it never was." I'll be there when he returns to you, my girl. I love you, Mama.

Silent tears drip onto the paper. Gage's arms should be around me now. He should be drying my tears and holding my hand, but he's not. He's gone, I'm alone, but I can't even hate him for it. I just love him more.

The radio station's fading. For every five seconds of song, ten seconds of static follows. In and out. Over and over. Like coach used to say, it's "enough to make a preacher cuss." While holding the wheel steady with my left hand, I fumble in the glovebox with my right, until my fingers graze the hard edge of my iPod hiding in a sea of old papers and fast-food napkins. I push in the cord and toss it in the cup holder, completely forgetting the last time I played it Rayne was sitting in the passenger seat, bare feet on my dashboard, curly ponytail flapping in the breeze, and singing along to her playlist going in the background.

So unlike the girl I left behind today, the one whose tears I pretended didn't matter. She was holding on to me, begging me to stay, to love her, and I peeled out in a cloud of dust, watching her disappear in my rearview mirror. Oh God, will she ever know how much that ripped my insides apart? How much I wanted to scoop her up, throw her in the Scout, and drive far away where nobody would find us?

But I couldn't. I can't tie her up until I'm strong enough to be her man. That's a Jackson Howard move, and it won't end well. I'm taking a gamble she'll wait on me. That she'll forgive me for walking away. That she'll still be loving me when I figure out whatever it is I have to figure out to come to terms with this.

With who I am.

With who I'm not.

I won't be her Jackson, and she won't be my Leighton. Love so constraining it becomes toxic, rotting what's left of any real chance we have to make it. So I'll give her the freedom she deserves, instead of locking her away until I'm on some sort of higher plane, because that day may never come.

The first notes of November Rain spill out the speakers like acid on all the open wounds. Hell no. I yank out the cord and toss the damn thing on the floorboard. The thwack against the rubber mat sets off the waterworks, the tears puddling and spilling so fast, the yellow lines on the interstate blur into one long smear. Up ahead, the big green sign above the interchange says, Charleston: Right Lanes Only. I pull in a long breath, glance over my shoulder and merge.

The 4x6 photograph doesn't compare to the real thing. I stand on the sidewalk, shifting my gaze between the two. Same triple porches. Same floor to ceiling windows. Same brick and iron fence with an "H" designed into the front gate.

The Harringtons.

I thought the Howard house was big. This one could kick its ass any day.

My next move should be a no-brainer. Walk up there, push the bell and wait for an answer. But my feet won't comply. The walkway is like an impassible river of quicksand, that even if I muddle through, could land me on the steps of people who might not want to face the truth.

So many lives shifting because of lies.

I sigh and lean back onto the Scout. Life was easier when I didn't give a damn.

Inside, the blue file folder lays on the dash. Yesterday, Dad brought it to me, along with a box of food and a duffle bag of clothes. I reach in the open passenger window and pull it out, pinning the photograph back into the metal clip then flipping through the contents. My family history—at least what Dad's PI found of it—all put together in one easy-to-read report complete with surveillance photos. Copies of the pictures of Mom he kept in the safe as well as one of her bus ticket are attached in a clear plastic sleeve. All the tools he suspected I'd need when introducing myself to Lieutenant Colonel Benjamin Harrington and his wife Margaret Ruth Harrington.

Charleston born. Military bred. Intimidating as hell. AKA my maternal grandparents.

My stomach flips. It's now or never. I push open the front gate and walk through. It clangs shut behind me as I clutch the folder across my chest like a shield. A salty, humid breeze wafts through the magnolias, rippling through two flags—one South Carolina palmetto and crescent, and one Army—that jut out from either side of the porch entrance. Eight steps up to the white carved-wood door.

Ding-dong.

Heavy footsteps echo from the other side, and the curtains rumple sideways as a face appears through the cut-glass side-lights. The door flies open wide, the void filled by a stocky man about my height with a firm jaw and piercing blue eyes. My eyes.

I swallow the lump in my throat. "Um... are you... Benjamin Harrington?"

He narrows his eyes, running them up and down me. "Who wants to know?"

"Um... yes, sir... my name is Gage Howard, and..."

"Well, Gage Howard, did you read the sign?" His steely tone

is apt to melt me into a puddle on the spot as he points to a small wooden plaque mounted beside the front window. NO SOLICITING. "We aren't buying anything, we have a church, and we're not interested in surveys. Have a nice day." Without another word, he slams the door in my face, the wind generated by the force of it urging me to backpedal a few steps.

Retired or not, the military is strong in this one. Still, I came here for a reason, dammit, and he's going to listen. I ring the bell again. Within seconds, he's back, grumbling so loud it seeps through the door.

He swings it wide, this time stepping out on the porch, meeting me chest to chest. "What in Sam Hill didn't you understand about what I said, boy?"

"Sir, please, I'm not selling anything. If I could, I'd—"

"Bennie dear, who's this young man?" The voice is a calming force to his gruff one. Probably in her mid-sixties, her salt and pepper hair cropped short. She saunters up behind him and slides her hand over his arm. It's a move I'm pretty sure she's used a million times to calm him down. When she catches my stare, she pauses, angling her head to the side with narrowed eyes.

"Ma'am, I'm here to tell you that—"

"We don't want some great deal on cable," he interrupts again. "Got plenty of channels. Don't need—"

"Shut up, you ol' fool." She slaps her hand over his mouth, a wide grin spreading her lips. "Can't you see he's trying to tell us he's our grandson?" She walks toward me, palming both sides of my face, maneuvering it side to side for a better inspection. "Let me have a look at you."

I pull back from her touch. "But... how'd you know?"

"A mama never forgets her child's eyes, especially when they're reflected back in a grandchild. And even more so, since I look at them every day in this ol' coot." She thumbs over her shoulder at the crotchety old Colonel, who's slack-jawed as he stares at me. Mute for the first time. "Well, come on in. Let's get you a cool drink and sit down awhile. No grandson of mine is gonna be left standing out on this porch like some common stranger." She loops her arm through mine and pulls me into the house, glancing back over her shoulder. "Bennie, get the door."

The kitchen is at the back of the house, twice as large as ours back home but a million times cozier. Despite the sheer size, it's truly a grandma's kitchen, complete with fresh-baked pie cooling on the shelf in front of the windows. She grabs a glass pitcher of iced tea and pours me a glass, then sits down beside Mr. Harrington. "So, tell me. How is our daughter? I can't imagine she'd be happy knowing you're here."

Oh God. My heart flutters against my ribs. "My mom—your daughter—died almost 19 years ago in a... car accident." I stop talking for a minute as the terrible truth sinks in, their pleasant smiles melting down their faces. There's no need going into specifics. The fact that Mom's dead is traumatic enough. She reaches out and grabs his hand, squeezing it. Her bottom lip trembles, and he stares at the table, chest rising and falling faster than before, as I continue. "I was raised by my father and his wife and only recently found out about my mom. Dad gave me all the information he had. That's how I found you."

Mr. Harrington grits his teeth, jawbone flexing in and out. "Damn that wild spirit of hers. I told her... I tried to warn her..." His words fall out in breathy clods as Mrs. Harrington rises from her chair, nearly lunging across the space between, to wrap her arms around him.

"Oh Bennie, she's gone," she mumbles into his hair as they cling to each other, the muffled sobs squeezing out from between them. A weird burning circulates in my throat and spirals down into my stomach as some innate voice calls out for me to comfort them. Share with them the truth about their runaway daughter.

"I don't know if it makes a difference, but... the day she died, this was found on her." They look over at me as I open the folder, pull out the bus ticket and the picture of Mom pregnant, then slide it across the table. "She was coming home... with me. So yeah, I think she would be happy I'm here now. It's what she wanted."

Mrs. Harrington picks up the photo and clutches it to her chest as more tears fall. She motions me over to them, extending her arm out to pull me into their hug. Reluctantly, I join them, bending down to where they're sitting.

"I'm so sorry, Mr. and Mrs. Harrington—"

"Please, call us Nana and Grandpa. You belong here as much as any one of us."

My mom, according to my grandparents, was not one to follow the crowd... or the rules. Mary Leighton Harrington. She grew up a "citizen of the world," never landing in one place long before moving somewhere else. The life of an Army brat. What Grandpa called a "wild streak," Nana described as "fiercely independent." Something about that sounds vaguely familiar.

Her leaving had been a shock, though not wholly unexpected. They came home one day and found a note pinned to the refrigerator. Her heart told her to roam, and she was answering the call. Alone. The 'don't call me, I'll call you' sort of wandering, and then she disappeared without a trace.

Upstairs, Nana leads me to the second room on the right where I'll be staying. It used to be Mom's room. Out front, cars pass on the street below, and I can't help imagining her here in this very spot by the window, plotting and planning her escape.

What went through her mind as she held the return bus ticket in her hand, very pregnant and alone?

What would life have been like growing up here? To have a mom that doted on me?

Too many unknowns. Too many questions.

A brown wooden frame sits on the dresser with a photograph of two girls, around my age, standing side by side, arms linked.

Nana walks behind me and leans forward, tapping her nail on the glass. "That's Mary Leighton, and that's her younger sister, Ruth Ellen." I look at her, eyes wide. "Your aunt. She's married with twin girls, just a bit younger than you."

Grandparents, aunts, and cousins. My world is growing exponentially at every turn. Nana smiles and side-hugs me. "Would you like to keep that picture?"

"Really?"

"Your Mama'd be real proud for you to have it."

For the first time in days, a smile creeps over my face. "Thanks, Mrs. Harrington." She frowns, and I quickly correct myself. "Nana."

She squeezes me again then rubs her hand up and down my back. "If you need to call anyone..." She nods toward the phone sitting on the bedside table then walks out. The door shuts with a soft click.

I stare at the photograph of my mom and her sister. There's one person on my mind. Someone who's been with me through every twist and turn. Someone who's been more than a brother to me. He's been a hero. I sit on the edge of the comforter, gathering my nerve, and reach for the receiver. It's lead in my hands.

My fingers fumble over the first keys, *67. I don't need anyone tracking me down. This call is already breaking my resolve to maintain distance. With a sigh, I type in the next 10 digits.

He answers on the third ring.

"Pres?" My voice squeaks in response to my stomach somersaulting.

"Gage? Where are you?"

"Doesn't matter. I just had to tell you that no matter what's happened, you're still my brother. My only brother. And I love you."

The silence burns through the lines before he clears his throat and tries again. "Come home. Screw our parents. I need you. Rayne needs you."

"I can't... just... can't..."

"Rayne's mama died. About an hour ago. You know she's a mess right now."

God, I want to wrap her in my arms and kiss away the tears. Assure her she'll never be alone while I'm around. But that'd be a lie. I can't be the strength she needs right now. She deserves better. And that's what I'll give her.

"Be there for her. Since I can't. Take care of her."

"She doesn't want me. She wants you. Come back..."

I press the button, disconnecting the conversation mid-sentence. Preston will step in and take care of Rayne. Be her rock when I can't. He'll do the right thing.

He always does.

RAYNE

Our house is quiet. I've lost more than Mama.

I've kinda lost Daddy, too. His taking a new travel-intensive position in the company is a defensive move. For weeks, he's told everyone who'd listen how much I remind him of Mama. Too much. Too painful. It's a convenient way to avoid me and hide out with his grief.

Other than school and working three nights a week, I sit at home, alone, watching TV and eating way too many leftover casseroles the church ladies stocked in our freezer. I think my body's starting to reject them. I've thrown up twice this week already and by the smell coming from the microwave, this might be number three. It's just another part of the new normal I've learned this past month—no Daddy, no Mama, no Gage. He hasn't contacted me, and the few occasions I've drummed up the courage to drive by the Howard house, his Scout's not there.

I pull the container from the microwave and immediately dump it in the sink when the chicken smells more like day-old skunk. I push the remnants down the garbage disposal with a fork and flip the switch. Still, my gag reflex tickles in my throat and I have to pause and breathe through my mouth to calm the ripples it's sending down my esophagus.

I glance at the digital numbers on the stove. Eight o'clock. Maybe I should go to bed. I trudge upstairs and snuggle under the covers with my journal, scribbling down a few thoughts. As I close the cover, the dated pages catch my eye. I flip back through last month's entries, counting the days repeatedly.

Dammit. How could I miss something so important? I get up, throw on a hoodie with my pajama pants, grab my car keys, and sprint down the steps.

The cell phone alarm dings. Two minutes down. My fingers tremble as I pick it up off the bathroom counter, E.P.T.—Early Pregnancy Test printed in small lettering on the handle part. A plus or minus sign to predict my future with 99% accuracy.

I pull it closer and squint my eyes.

Positive.

Oh shit. I'm pregnant.

The implications should be smacking me in the face—how I'm going to do this alone, how I'm going to find Gage and let him know. But that's going to have to wait because I'm overcome with a manic need to get rid of the evidence. I swipe all the packaging off the counter into the plastic bag and run outside to the large green trashcan by the garage. I can't risk Daddy coming home and finding it. I'm not ready to tell him. I can't look him in the eyes and tell him his daughter is going to be a clueless, teenage mother whose dreams of college and a life just went out the window.

I flip open the lid and stuff the bag into an empty cereal box. Extreme, but in this town you can never be too careful.

Careful. I don't get it. I'm on birth control pills so how in the world...? Oh. My. God. I missed a few doses while I was sick, right before our trip. It hadn't even crossed my mind.

"Dammit. You're an idiot, Rayne!" I yell out loud.

"I wouldn't call you that," he says from behind me, his voice hesitant and low—the wrong Howard brother.

"Preston?" I shove the box in the trash but hold onto the test stick. For some reason, I can't toss it, so I pull my shoulders forward to block his view as I wrap it in my palm. "Why are you...?"

"What are you doing?" He grabs my arm and spins me toward him, nearly causing me to lose balance. When I grab hold of the trashcan to steady myself, the test escapes my grip. His eyes lock on mine until the click-clack of plastic on the driveway tears his gaze away, and he leans down to pick it up. His eyes blare wide. "What the..."

I wrench it from his fingers. "It's none of your business."

His mouth hangs open, hands clamped over his forehead. "You're... pregnant?"

"No shit." I spit out the words, lunging at his face like some crazy prepubescent boy provoking a fist-fight.

He grabs both my shoulders to steady me. Or hold me back. I'm not sure. "Is it Gage's?"

I flash my eyes to meet his. I'm not sure what pisses me off more—the question or the fact he's looking at me like he really doesn't know. "Who else's would it be?"

He ignores me. "Does he know?"

"I found out, like, two seconds ago. And in case you haven't noticed, he's not here." I sweep my arms around.

"Where is he?"

"How am I supposed to know? He ended things. He left me." I'm screaming now, and acutely aware I'm about to lose my shit as all the realities of my screwed-up life descend on me in a lump. Holding it in is impossible. I kick the trashcan hard, sending it over on its side, the contents spilling out on the cement.

"Go." Preston orders, pointing his finger toward the house as he bends down to scoop up the mess. "Front porch. Wait for me."

I whirl on my heels and stomp to the swing like a toddler pissed off at the world. Except I have no reason to be angry with Preston. And I'm not. He's just taking the brunt of all my pent-up frustrations, and the weird thing is, I don't know why. Why is he here? I thought he'd sworn to loathe me forever, and now he's cleaning up my mess and acting all saintly?

I unwrap my fingers from the test stick, the pink plus sign staring back at me. I've thought about this moment before, and it's always looked the same—mid-twenties, married, house, job, husband. I don't think any girl dreams of getting knocked up at eighteen.

Preston walks up the steps and sits down beside me. He glances over at the stick. "You know, there are ways to have prevented this—"

"Yeah Einstein, but only one method's foolproof."

"Damn," he says under his breath and picks at a hangnail. "What are you gonna do?"

"I don't know." I close my eyes. The only thing I know is what I'm not going to do—get rid of it. I'm having this baby, this piece of me and Gage.

"You have time to think about it. Nine months, right?"

I snort a laugh. "More like a couple weeks. The jig is up when the bump shows up." I point at my stomach. "You know how... perceptive... this town is."

"I'm so sorry... I..." he stammers, totally out of character for the cool and calm Preston Howard.

"Look, I'm not gonna beat around the bush so... why are you here, Preston? It didn't end well. We haven't talked in months. Your family hates me..."

"I don't hate you." When I look at him, he's staring back. "And I can't blame you and Gage for something that's my fault, too." He presses his lips together, swallows hard, then continues, "I was an ass. I didn't take time for you. I didn't even take up for you. I took you for granted. He didn't."

Gage always had my back, but when the tables turned, he never gave me the chance to prove myself to him. He left and took it all away. Except my love for him, which at this moment is growing in a very real way in the depths of my body. "I miss him."

Preston reaches over and pats my knee, my pain mirrored on his face. "I miss him, too. I guess that's why I'm here. I thought being near you might help me feel closer to him. I didn't know... he'd ended things..." He exhales and leans his head back against the wooden slats.

"He may have walked away, but he left a piece behind." I rub my belly. "I have to believe that'll lead him back. One day."

Preston leans up and nods. "Until then Rayne, let me be here for you. As a friend. Let me do this for my brother, since I can't apologize to him in person. It's the only way I know to make this right."

How can something feel so wrong and so right all at once? Again, I find myself in a proverbial Howard brothers sandwich, albeit this time not some crazy love triangle. Being with Preston did make me feel closer to Gage. And I need someone to talk to. Someone I can trust. Before he'd shown up today, I had no one, and if he leaves, I'll be alone again. I can't shoulder this by myself. I reach out and grab his hand. "I could really use a friend."

I smash the pillow across my face, tugging the ends over my ears. Every night—for 22 nights now—the cicadas and katydids duke it out in a head-to-head match for "most annoying sound" domination. It's a tie. They both suck.

While they're an obvious scapegoat for my inability to string more than two hours of sleep together in the last month, it's a convenient excuse to keep the grandparents out of it. Not that I want to keep my distance from them. I'm just not ready to rehash the past or the love I walked out on.

The one thing I've learned about Nana already is that she's a "fixer." Even with broken messes that don't want to be fixed.

Or can't be.

It's in the way she looks at me over bacon, eggs, and biscuits every morning. Eyes squinting and roaming, head tilting, teeth chewing her inner cheek. Like I'm her project, and she's searching for that linchpin fix that'll make it all better. Problem is, so much stuff's cracked, there's not enough happy mojo in the world to piece it back together.

Grandpa, on the other hand, embraces my loner-hood in the grief and wallowing department. He is, after all, the original. He doesn't try to fix anything. His motto is "Suck it up, buttercup," and forge ahead.

On the mornings her exuberance gets the better of the conversation and she ends up barraging me with questions about the life I left behind, Grandpa utters a loud *harrumph* into his forkful of scrambled eggs and says, "Mags, let the boy be."

There's comfort in their consistency, and always knowing where I stand in the scheme of things. Never wondering what shit-storm is lurking next. But while the breakfast routine is established, so, unfortunately, is the nighttime self-torment-fest, the minutes ticking by like refrigerated molasses. The darkness is a heavy blanket of memories, and the annoying insect serenade threatens to push me right over the edge of sanity.

I miss Rayne.

God, I love her so much. More than I did before, if that's even possible.

Every night starts the same. I slide beneath the covers, shut my eyes, and pray for sleep. Instead, strings of images flow in sequence. Rayne and I dancing by the river. Our first kiss under the bleachers. Edisto. Sometimes those lull me into uncon-sciousness before the sweet images turn to vivid dreams of Rayne crying, holding on to my shirt, getting smaller in her driveway until she vanishes all together. I come to, in a tangle of sheets and sweat, with absolutely no resolution to the throb-bing hole in my chest.

Tonight's been no different. I lean over the edge of my bed and grab the phone, punching in *67 and the rest of the digits before my rational brain can stop this self-destructive torture. I've only succumbed to the temptation a handful of times, but when her voice comes on the line, it's like being stabbed repeat-edly in the chest. The alarm clock's red numbers say 2:38 AM.

This is stupid. *Stupid, stupid, stupid.*

"Hello?"

Her voice, so soft, shoots chills down my spine. The stifled screams burn in my throat. *It's me, Rayne. It's me, and I love you.* But the voice dies inside me.

"Gage?" She whispers into the phone. "Is that you?"

I slam the receiver down. I'm an asshole, trying to get a quick fix while twisting the knife further into her back. No, this masochistic shit has to stop. There has to be a way to take myself completely out of the picture, and I'm going to find it.

Nana sits at the kitchen table, sipping coffee and reading the Lifestyle section of the newspaper. Two dirty plates and two sets of silverware are stacked beside her while a single unused place setting waits at my usual spot.

I glance at the wall clock above the French door. A few minutes after seven. "Am I late?"

The paper crinkles as she folds it over and tosses it in the chair beside her before smiling up at me. "Grandpa and I were just a little early this morning. Your bedroom door was still closed, so I didn't want to disturb you." Her chair scrapes against the tiled floor as she pushes back from the table. "Here, let me get you—"

"Stay where you are. I'll get my food." I grab my plate off the table and walk to the stove, scooping up a small pile of eggs and a couple strips of bacon. When I sit down, she picks up the carafe and pours coffee in my cup. Wisps of steam curl into my nostrils as I pull it to my lips, relishing the nutty bitterness on my tongue and secretly praising the morning gods for the supply of caffeine to get me through another day.

Nana's eyes cut through me like x-rays, the hairs on my neck bristling under her stare. I pause, fork in mid-air, and look back.

"Are you sleeping well?" She leans forward as she says it, an invitation to tell her all my secrets.

"Sure," I mumble and shove the fork in my mouth.

"It's just that…" she pauses and blows out a loud breath. "I got up around 2:30 to use the restroom and your light was still on, and there was some noise, like you were tossing and turning?"

"I fell asleep while reading, and you probably just overheard me readjusting or something."

"Right." She pinches her lips into a flat line and nods, relaxing back in her chair. "So, I was thinking maybe what you need—"

Heavy footsteps echo on the back staircase. Grandpa steps into the kitchen, two shotguns and two boxes of ammo in hand. "What he needs is for you to leave him be, Mags. Besides, he's got plans—a day with Grandpa, an old Army codger, and some clay pigeons. Finish that bacon, and let's hit the road."

An hour later, we turn out across a low-lying flat of grass toward the swampy banks of a canal, the terrain no match for my Scout, which Grandpa insisted we drive. He said something about his pick-up truck needing air in the tires, but I checked. They're fine. Just another one of his sly tricks to get me behind the wheel and perk me up.

A two-tone green 1950's model Chevy truck is already parked catty-cornered beside a short palm dripping with Spanish moss. A tall man, with skin the color of burnt umber and white hair cut in a military "high and tight," gets out of the cab, shotgun in hand, as we approach. Grandpa's referred to him as "Boomer" for the duration of the trip. Apparently the nickname came from some sort of bomb joke that clearly went over my head.

I shift to neutral and pull the parking brake as Boomer walks over and pats the hood of my Scout, then pulls his free hand into a salute, lips and eyes frozen in the no-expression position. The thought of being around this guy with a gun all day shoots chill bumps down my arms.

Grandpa leans in close. "Don't let him intimidate you. He's an old drill sergeant, ornery and crabby as they come. Smells fear." My breathing quickens, and I swallow a few times as Grandpa cracks a smile. "But don't worry, he won't hurt you." He opens the door and slides off the seat, darting his head back in as I'm undoing my seatbelt. "Oh yeah, almost forgot. Don't call him Boomer to his face. He hates that shit."

I slam the door and walk around to the front of the Scout where Grandpa puts his arm around me, pulling me into their circle. "Gage, this is Talmadge Anderson, retired Sergeant Major, US Army. Anderson, this is my grandson, Gage Howard."

His stark expression cracks, lips parting over two rows of perfectly white teeth. "Gage Howard, nice to meet you." He reaches out and shakes my hand vigorously. "It's about time your Grandpa got some testosterone in that house. You shoot?"

Preston and I'd been hunting a few times before on Barrett's grandparents' land. "A few times."

"That'll do," he nods, chuckling.

As he turns, walking out toward the canal, Grandpa hands me a 12-guage and a handful of shells. "Let's see what you got."

Ping. The first clay spins through the air. The gun weighs a million pounds, and it's like a game of cat and mouse. And I'm the cat, always just a little bit behind. Shit.

Ping. The second clay fires. Where the hell is it?

"You do know the object is to actually fire the gun?" Anderson says as the heat rushes to my cheeks. He slaps my arm then grimaces. "No wonder. You're tighter than a clam's ass at high tide."

"Yeah." I blow out a loud breath. "Not really a great time for me."

"Hogwash. If you wait until the time is perfect, you gonna

wait forever. Harness whatever's eatin' you and make it do work instead." Anderson steps behind me, physically repositioning my arms and legs into the appropriate stance. He then grabs the gun still in my hands and buries the butt of it into my shoulder. "You've gotta get control of it, or it's gonna control you."

Grandpa stomps the pedal. *Ping.* Another clay flies in the air. I line up the shot.

This is my life. I make the rules.

My finger crushes the trigger. *Ka-pow!* A hundred shards fall to the water's surface.

"Feels good, doesn't it?" He slaps me on the back with a smile. I smile back and nod at Grandpa to set off another. Then another. And another.

When my shells are spent, I sit on the Chevy's tailgate, reloading.

"Somebody's found his groove," Anderson says and nudges Grandpa's arm before he walks over to me. "You're a pretty good shot. Maybe you should consider a career in the military? My son's an Army recruiter at the office downtown. Go see him. Find out what the Army can do for you."

Grandpa slaps his hand over his eyes, shaking his head with a laugh. "Don't come lookin' for my help when Mags is on your ass."

"It's in the boy's blood. Look at him. Strong shoulders. Flat stomach. Military jaw." He pats each of my so-called attributes with a firm hand. "And if he's half as pig-headed as you, he'll be perfect."

Grandpa grabs his gun and marches toward the canal, yelling back over his shoulder. "Ignore him. Everybody else does."

Later, after a million glory-filled war stories have been told and the sporting clays have been thoroughly destroyed, Grandpa says good-bye to his friend as I get in the driver's seat and yank the belt around me, stopping long enough to pull the business card out of my back pocket before clicking the buckle into place.

The Army. Where clueless boys become disciplined men.

Yep, this ought to do it.

"You did what?"

Okay, so this isn't the reaction from Nana I was expecting. Congratulations possibly. It's your life, maybe. Not this. Immediately, her fingers prod her collarbone, searching for the strand of pearls. When she finds them and clamps down, I'm sure within seconds they'll be pulverized to dust.

"I thought you'd be happy."

"No, that's him," she says through gritted teeth. "I'm gonna beat your butt."

Grandpa reaches over to pat Nana's shoulder, but she shirks his touch.

"Hot damn, Mags. Give the boy a break. The Army is exactly what he needs." He claps his hands then rubs them together as if preparing to dig into pile of barbecue ribs. "I'm proud as punch! Now, when do you report?"

"The recruiter picks me up here tomorrow morning."

She releases the pearls. They slap into her skin as she jabs her finger in Grandpa's face. "You did this, Benjamin Harrington!"

Damn. That's the first time she's called him by his full name. She whips around, marches to the cabinets and pulls out a long casserole dish. She's grabbing an apron out of the drawer when I intercept. Her shoulders are slumped, head down.

"Nana, what are you doing?"

She turns and looks at me, tears rimming her lower lashes. "Well, if you're leaving tomorrow, we're gonna give you the perfect sendoff tonight." Her voice cracks just a bit, but then she clears her throat and lengthens her spine. "Now go tell that pain-in-the-ass Grandpa of yours to call your cousins. They need to be here by seven."

I'm still stuffed from Nana's supper last night. She made enough for the Army itself, though there were only five of us. Ham, macaroni and cheese, dressing, green beans, and potato salad—it's possible she believes I won't eat again until I graduate from basic training. Hell, I may not need to. And from what Grandpa tells me about the PT requirements, I may not want to.

I toss my duffle bag on the bed and stuff it with toiletries, rolled towels, t-shirts, socks, and underwear. The basics, and once again according to Grandpa, the only personal things that'll remain with me over the nine weeks of Boot Camp hell. That, and the personal-sized Bible Nana insisted I include. It lies on the navy comforter, and I flip open the front cover.

Rayne.

The homecoming picture of the two of us her Mama gave me, the ends now slightly dog-eared from all the nights I've laid in this very room, holding it up to my face, memorizing every detail. Remembering. Reliving. It's shoved between the cover and the dedication page.

She's along for the ride, even if she doesn't know it.

Giggles echo in the hallway outside my door, and I quickly close the cover. My twin cousins, Taryn and Farrah, spent the night. Nana decided it was best since they were home alone anyway and could be here to give me the proper Harrington "see you later" this morning.

My aunt Ruth Ellen and her doctor husband have been traveling abroad in Haiti for the last three weeks, doing mission work in the rural villages. They still have a couple weeks left. I met her briefly before they flew out, and the entire time, the urge to vomit clamored in my belly, the feeling obviously mutual. We moved around each other like orbiting planets, close but never actually touching. Cordial but nothing deeper. Her dark hair and angled jaw proved a dead-ringer for Mom's pictures, and she kept saying how haunting my eyes were. Awkward. I guess a severe lack in communication skills might be another Harrington DNA anomaly.

"There's our cousin!" Farrah laughs, bouncing into the room, and then tousling my hair. "It's so weird to say that. We've never had a cousin on Mom's side before."

"Yeah, so weird." Taryn saunters in, rolling her eyes, the sarcasm pouring off her tongue. "You almost packed?" She asks, turning her attention on me instead of her sister who's pushed between me and the bed and is rifling through my bag.

Identical faces, opposite personalities.

"Think so." I grab Farrah's roving hand, removing it from my bag, which I pick up off the bed, inadvertently knocking The Bible to the floor. It lands with a thump, the photograph slipping out from the edge just enough to be visible.

"What's this?" Farrah scoops up the Bible and plucks the picture out between her nails, holding it up in the sunlight streaming through the window. Her blue eyes sparkle. "Is this your girlfriend?"

Taryn shakes her head in disgust at Farrah's obvious lack of boundaries, though her own eyes linger on it as well. She then snatches the photo and slides it back under the cover's safety. "Some things are private, Farrah."

She glowers at Taryn. "I was just asking! Besides..." she turns to me with a wink, "She's pretty."

"She's a girl I used to know," I mumble, staring at my shoes.

"If you say so," Farrah sing-songs as she turns and struts out the door.

Taryn stashes the Bible inside my duffle and slides the zipper closed. "Sorry about Farrah. She's... special, delightfully ridiculous, a hair insane, and a pinch nosey."

I laugh. Farrah's all that, and maybe a bit more. "It's okay."

Taryn smiles back, pausing at the door. "I get there's stuff in your past you're not ready to talk about. It's really hard to open up sometimes, especially when you've been hurt. Believe me, I know." She swallows hard and continues, "But when the time comes, and you do want to talk, I'll be here."

Beep! Beep!

I press my nose to the glass. On the curb below, an Army van idles, my recruiter standing by the sliding back door. Taryn holds out her hand, wiggling her fingers. I hoist the duffle onto my shoulder and join her.

We say our good-byes on the porch, Grandpa slapping me on the back then forcing a stern expression before walking abruptly inside, complaining about a "damn gnat that flew in his eye." The girls kiss me on the cheek and follow. But Nana refuses to leave. Her arms circle me, fingertips pressing down into my skin.

"I'll be back, Nana. I promise."

She nods, tears streaking her cheeks, and palms both sides of my face, pulling me down to plant a kiss on my forehead.

I walk down the steps, out the gate, and get into the van's backseat.

Behind me, Nana fades from sight. In front of me, my future awaits.

39

RAYNE

I stare down at the informational guide in my hand. *Your Baby and You: 8-12 Weeks Gestation.* The tissue paper covering the examination table crackles underneath me with each move. At least my clothes are back on now while I'm waiting on the doc to wrap up. Nothing's quite as uncomfortable as being naked as a jaybird with your legs in stirrups and your crotch exposed for all to see.

It's been two hours. Poor Preston's probably sick of waiting by now. I picked him up to come with me this morning, and then insisted he sit in the car just in case someone saw us. It'd be kind of hard to explain why he's in an OB-GYN office. Honestly, he seemed relieved. Any time I'm reading one of the pregnancy books and it goes into the medical descriptions, he turns a serious shade of green. I smile thinking about it. He puts up with a lot to be my friend nowadays.

Of course, I put up with a lot, too. Especially when he's hell-bent on making sure I participate in all the teenage rites of passage. Like prom. I pleaded with him to stay home, but he wouldn't have it. Walking into that room was like walking into a lion's den of hungry beasts looking for a juicy steak, and we were the T-bones. Once all the stares and whispers died down, a steady stream of people who'd recently been avoiding me lined up to shoot the breeze with Preston and compliment me on my dress or hair. No one asked the big question, but I did hear it being discussed by some kids in the bathroom, a few chaperones by the punch bowl, even the waiters stocking the food platters. *What's Preston doing here with her?* All the smiles to my face couldn't disguise the venom-laced emphasis on *her*.

When Barrett and Trevor stood up and waved Preston over, my stomach lurched at the thought of getting too close to the table where Jaycee'd sat all night with a shit-eating grin on her face that reeked of pure evil. It's stupid to think she'd figure out my secret just being within five feet of me. Girls like her always sniff out the dirt.

When we got to the table, though, Jaycee turned toward the stage and refused to look in our direction. Ainsley and Mallory both shot me a smile on the sly, eyes darting back and forth between me and Jaycee.

That's when Trevor piped up. "So? You two are back together?"

Preston responded, strong and confident. "We're just friends."

I wanted to crawl under the table when Jaycee snorted out loud, still not looking our way. Preston snapped his head in her direction. "Did you say something, Jaycee? You're usually so full of commentary... or something."

She twisted her neck in our direction, her eyes slashing us like daggers but her cheeks just red enough to let me know he'd gotten one over on her. This new side of him definitely had its perks.

The squeaking door startles me from my thoughts as the doctor rushes in with a few pamphlets on healthy eating for two and a factsheet on the prenatal vitamins he's called in to the pharmacy. I'm in the elevator, riding down to parking, when it hits me. This is really happening. Before today, it was easy to think I'd dreamed it. Other than the test stick and the couple bouts of throw up, there was no concrete, medically-provided evidence. Now there is.

The doctor poked and prodded my veins and a few other more personal places and confirmed it. Gage's baby is growing inside me, and in just a few short weeks, the whole town's going to know.

Preston's reclined, napping in the passenger seat when I open the door and slide behind the wheel. The slamming door rouses him, hair tousled, eyes heavy as he looks around all goony-like before coming back to reality.

"How'd it go?"

"Come home with me awhile? Someone needs to keep me off the ledge."

"Rayne, you need to calm down." Preston sips his sweet tea from a mason jar. "You still have a while to figure things out before you're showing. You just graduated last week. You don't have to see those kids again any time soon."

I'd like to slap him, or hug him, or possibly both. He's being strong and sensible like I need him to be, but sometimes I wish he'd give it up and have a conniption with me. Solidarity, you know?

"But what about work? All kinds of people come in there and..."

"You wear a black t-shirt and jeans. You can cover anything with a t-shirt. At least for a while until you figure out how to tell your dad," he says. "Quit flipping out. You and I are the only ones who know, and we'll be the only ones until you're ready." He stands up and walks toward the kitchen. "More tea?"

I stare down at my jar, still full to the brim. My stomach is also in protest right now. "No thanks."

Preston ducks around the corner as the doorbell rings. I set my drink down on the coffee table, walk to the door and fling it open. The antique wind-up clock on the mantel chimes three o'clock, very cinematic-like, marking the hour disaster came knocking at the Davidson house, a terrible blonde-headed disaster holding out a glittery gift bag in my direction. No way I'm taking anything from her. Whatever's in it is no peace offering.

"What do you want, Jaycee?" I glance at the bag and back up to her face.

She frowns and tilts her head sideways, almost looking hurt, except for the fact she's incapable of feeling. "I wanted to talk to you at prom, but I didn't know what to say... then."

"And now you do?"

"Yeah, something like that. I got you a present. It's kinda perfect, actually." She shakes the bag toward me. "Take it. I hope you like it."

"A present?"

"Don't ruin it. This is a gesture, Rayne. A gift from me to you that says I'm sorry. I'm still here. I'm still interested."

In my peripheral vision, I see Preston walk back into the den. He slinks along the wall and presses himself into the space beside the front door where she can't see him. I reach out and take the bag from her hand and pull out a wad of tissue paper. At the bottom is a round bottle. When I pull it out and look at the label, my heart stops. The silence screams in my ears, and when I look up, her lips are curled in a grin.

Prenatal vitamins. She just gave me prenatal vitamins. Oh my God. How does she know? No way.

"Told you it was perfect," she says, her voice syrupy-smooth. "Doesn't this gift say I'm sorry, I'm here, and I'm interested?" I can't form words. My eyes blare so wide they water. Maybe it's tears. There's no explaining exactly what reaction I'm having right now. "No? Let me explain, silly. I'm sorry you didn't listen to me and ended up knocked up and alone. I'm here to tell you I know the truth, and I'm totally interested in seeing you squirm when the whole town finds out. Make sense now?"

"But... how'd you...?" I stammer. The thoughts zoom through my mind at light speed, but they won't connect. They're all scattered and fragmented, weaving together just enough to let me know I'm totally screwed. I cut my eyes at Preston who's squatted down now, hands clasped over his face.

She laughs and slaps her hand against the screen door she'd been holding open with her hip. "Oh, I guess you haven't heard. I'm working at the pharmacy for the summer until school starts. What luck, right?"

"Jaycee, you can't..."

"Can't what? Tell the whole town I was right? They'll see your true colors and how you probably are a little mental like your Mama. And imagine what they'll say when they find out Gage got you knocked up and left you like the trash he is." She pauses and shakes her head. The venom in her voice thickens. "You had an opportunity with Preston, and you squandered it. Now you're dragging him back into your filth. Does he even know you're pregnant, or are you trying to set him up? I'm gonna make sure the whole town knows the truth about you and Gage. They're gonna find out exactly..."

"Shut up, Jaycee. You don't know a damn thing!" Preston explodes to his feet and pushes in front of me. Jaycee gasps and jumps backward, letting the screen door go. It slams hard between us, a battle line drawn.

Her eyes narrow and she clicks her tongue. "You'll never learn. You come in here..."

"I'm here because I'm the father. The baby is mine."

They're in a stand-off in the doorway, Jaycee open-mouthed and Preston, hands shoved in his pockets, wearing a smug grin.

I do the only thing I can think of. I pull Preston back in the room and slam the door in Jaycee's face. Through the blinds, I watch her walk to her car, stopping once or twice to look back, before getting in and driving off. I collapse backwards into the door, staring at Preston. "We need to talk."

The door is the only thing holding me upright. After everything I've been through, is it still possible to be in shock? I don't know. What I do know is I'd like to slap the smile off Preston's face. "What the hell are you doing?"

"Hear me out..." He rushes to my side and pulls me away from the door, his eyes wide as brown canyons.

I shove him away and massage my temples in deep, circular motions. The disbelief in what I've just witnessed pounds like a drum inside my skull. Preston didn't just open a can of worms. He stuck a freaking piece of dynamite in it and blew it sky high. "No! Do you realize what you've just done?"

"Yeah, I saved your butt." As if I wasn't already reeling. This fool's jacked up if he believes that. He points to the door as if Jaycee's still standing there. "You heard her making up stories about you and Gage. That's not gonna happen."

I sink into the couch cushions and contemplate diving under the blankets still lying there from earlier. "So you tell her the baby's yours? How is that any better?"

"This town's not talking crap about Gage... or you. I never stood up for you before, but I am now." If this is his idea of standing up, he needs to just sit down.

"We can't just lie about it. The truth always comes out. What happens if Gage comes back?"

Preston shoots me a sideways glance, his eye-roll conveying more than words ever could. "What if the truth never has to come out?"

"What?"

He sits down beside me and pulls my hands into his. "I still have feelings for you, Rayne. Real feelings. I know it sounds crazy, but I'll be this baby's father." This has to be a joke. We've discussed this before and he knows—at least he said he knew—that my heart has no intention of abandoning Gage. I made him swear to me this was all friendly, and now he's trying to flip the script. Not trying at this point even. Forcing.

"Oh my God, Preston, that makes it so much worse!" I wrench my hands away, refusing to look at him.

"Worse? How?"

"Because I love Gage. Like forever." I whisper it to myself more than him.

"I love him, too. He's my brother." The weight of his palm wraps around my shoulder. His voice is softer but still firm. He's not letting this go down without a fight.

"Exactly!"

"Yes—exactly. If he loved you—loves you—like I think, he wouldn't want you facing this alone. Maybe he's too messed up to be with you, but I'm here. I want to do this. I'm willing to put it on the line and see where it goes." He gets up and walks around, planting himself in front of me, refusing to be ignored.

"What if he comes back?" God, please let him come back. Except the skepticism in my own voice bleeds through this time, and I'm scared. Scared he won't come back. Scared I'll have to do this alone.

"What if he doesn't?"

No. I refuse to consider it. It's why I keep Mama's note tucked in my pocket within easy reach—to help when the doubt sets in. I read her words about setting love free and rejoicing when it returns but always refusing to consider the last line. What if freed love doesn't return? I'll always believe he'll come back because I won't consider that, "if it doesn't, it never was" part. Because if he doesn't come back, that means this rule-breaking, earth-shaking love I'm clinging to was something only I felt. Something not real. Something imagined.

I sigh and look up at him. He nods his head up and down,

coaxing me into playing this charade. I want Gage. Preston wants me. But it's not just me anymore. It's us, me and my baby, and I have to do what's best. I glance at the mantle clock. "Jaycee's been gone ten minutes. By my calculations, we have maybe five to get to your parent's house before the shit hits the fan."

Preston's quiet. He doesn't give pep talks, only chews the inside of his cheek. Don't you at least get a cigarette and a blindfold before facing the firing squad? Anything'd work at this point.

"I can't do this." Walking into the Howard house with a bombshell announcement like this could only be construed as a suicide attempt. My fingers strum my kneecaps as I bend forward, sucking in deep gulps of air. "Your mom's gonna have a conniption." It's been months since I've stepped foot in the Howard house, mostly because I'm as welcome as a flea infestation. For the most part, Gage and I steered clear of this place, and the last vibrant memory in my head of being with Charlotte in her home was the dreaded family dinner when she insinuated I was trash. Can't wait to tell her I'm pregnant. How lovely.

"Mom's gonna have to deal." Preston takes my hand and pulls me from the car toward the house. I think about planting my feet, digging in real good, with pullback. I once had a dog who mastered the technique for each vet visit. Of course, she always peed in the bushes, too, but that one might get me locked up in the asylum.

Our feet barely hit the porch floor before Charlotte yanks the double doors open. "What the hell is going on?" she spits through gritted teeth. "Get in this house. Now." As we hustle in, she thrusts her head out, scanning up and down the street as if at any moment some small-town paparazzo will jump from the bushes.

The door slams, rattling the petite Chinese vases on the shelves. I try to focus on my chipped nails but it's impossible. Staring at my trembling fingers makes me dizzy. The click-clack of stilettos approach from behind, but I don't turn around. Apparently, the jig is up. She knows, and why we thought it was a good idea to come here, I have no idea because now I'm in her house, at her mercy. And that's something I know she has little of.

I lift my eyes to Preston, who, other than slightly dilated pupils, stands tall, hands casually tucked into his pockets. "Mom, we came to tell you... Rayne is pregnant with my baby." His voice cracks at first but grows harder with each word.

Oh. My. God. We talked about this plan but hearing him say it just sounds so wrong.

His baby. No, this is Gage's baby.

I want to scream it from the rooftops, yell it in her done-up, hoity-toity face. But I stifle it because I'm fairly certain the only reason I'm still standing at this point is because Charlotte thinks her DNA, Preston's DNA, is living inside me.

"No! I refuse to believe this!" Her shrill yell hits me like a shockwave and for the first time, I turn to look at her, search her face for any clues of what unholy hell she's about to unleash. She plasters her bony fingers over her mouth, talking out between the spaces. "A father at your age? Your whole future is fucked!"

I cringe at the word coming from her lips, exposing a crack in her all-too-perfect façade. Even her hair is disheveled, with wild sprigs jutting out from her French twist. Her mascara smears out from the corner of her eye. She snorts in a long breath and expels it from her mouth, and I half expect fire to flame from her tongue.

She thrusts her manicured finger at my stomach. "The

entire town is talking about this… problem." Her eyes bore into me. "How did you manipulate this? Poke holes in condoms or…"

"Mother, enough!" He's never called her "mother" before, and I don't believe it's a compliment. Neither does she. She shrinks back, her bottom lip quivers. "No one planned this. You of all people should know that sometimes the unexpected happens. Then what? You deal with it. What do you always say? Be a man, stand up, take responsibility, and that's what I'm doing. I'm standing up for my family!"

She has no clue how true that last part is. He's standing up for family all right, protecting his brother and his unborn niece or nephew, protecting the Howard name, because he knows the town, though they may question his sanity, will never condemn him for this. Only Preston can bridge the gaps and make this palatable for everyone. Except me. My reservations lurk in the shadows.

The verbal tennis match between Charlotte and Preston fades to background noise. Her insults and his rebuttals bounce back and forth without pause, each one talking about me and this baby like we're not even in the room. To hell with this. No one is telling me how to live my life, especially not a snooty-ass Howard who's never been anything but rude and abusive.

I ball my fists at my ears and clamp my eyelids closed, but nothing stops the crazy whir of emotions boiling up inside, which becomes deafening white noise. "Shut up! Just. Shut. Up." Immediate silence. When I open my eyes, everyone's staring at me. "Dammit. Do I get to say anything?"

"Yes. You do." Jackson walks around the corner.

Charlotte whips her head in his direction, staring blankly a minute before straightening her blouse and licking her lips. She pulls back her shoulders and squares herself in front of Jackson as if preparing to tackle him to the floor. "Surprise,

surprise you show up now. Here to defend yet another bastard child, a blot on the Howard name?"

"First of all, I've been listening to this whole thing from the other room, and second, there are no bastards in the Howard house, love. Only my two sons, and now," he nods toward me, "a grandchild. All equally important to me. I've lived with your callousness toward Gage all these years and somehow tolerated it because you were ever mindful of my sin. But this child? Are you so despicable as to hate your own blood?"

Your own blood. The words slice through me like daggers, and I shift my gaze to Preston. He stares back, and then grins. I can't, because in my head, one of Mama's old sayings is playing on repeat. *What a tangled web we weave...*

Charlotte marches forward, her boobs pressing into his chest when she gets so close. "How dare you insinuate..."

"Enough." Jackson juts his palm in her face as he turns to me. "I believe Rayne deserves to speak her piece."

The way he stares at me puts me at ease until Charlotte's evil eyes burn me from over his shoulder, renewing my anger. "I'm not trying to ruin Preston's future. He deserves only the best."

"Yes, he does. Not this. Not you." Charlotte narrows her eyes. "So, what is it you want? Money? Name value?"

"Mother..." Preston starts but hushes when I grab his forearm.

"Stop. I've got this."

Charlotte snorts and stifles a giggle behind the tips of her fingers. "You've got it, all right. Your mama's crazy? Her melt-downs?" She wobbles her head and blares her eyes as she says it.

"My mama was ill, but you—you're just a bitch, and I'm sick of you." Jackson chuckles and shakes his head, muttering "I'll be damned" under his breath. Charlotte's cheeks redden as she darts her eyes between him and Preston. "To answer your question—no. I don't need your money or your name. Rest assured, I do have this. And just so you know, this baby is not a problem... or a mistake. This baby came from a moment of love, one of the happiest moments of my life." I take a deep breath and look at Preston, who's staring aimlessly into the dining room. He knows I'm talking about Gage, and it's killing him. "I can't— I won't— dictate the future for my child's father, but I do love and respect him. He'll always have a home with me, but I'll never be an obligation. If he's with me, it's because he chooses to be."

Preston steps forward and grabs my hand. "And mother—I choose to be, so get used to it. This is my baby. Love me? Then love it, love Rayne. We'll let you think it over." He nods and places his hand on the small of my back, nudging me toward the door.

Jackson runs out behind us, stopping us short on the porch steps. "Preston?"

"Yeah?"

"I'm proud of you, son. Proud of you for being the man I always wanted to be. Never accept less than your heart's desire or you'll live a life of regret." He looks over his shoulder into the foyer where Charlotte is still standing, head cradled in her hands. "I know I do."

40

GAGE

The earthy, musky smells of freshly-trimmed grass on the parade field encircle Charlie Company as we march shoulder to shoulder. Alpha and Bravo are slightly ahead of us, Delta and Echo slightly behind. By the time we all get to the stands on the opposite side of the field, 240 men and women in mass formation, times five separate companies, will equal 1,200 new United States soldiers to greet the people waiting there for us. The people we came from. The people who love us.

None of the people I knew before the age of 18 will be there. Sometimes it feels as if that part of my life has been erased. Like someone pressed the big delete button in the sky and sucked it all away.

She keeps it real for me, though.

In the memories. In the picture I look at just before bed.

She reminds me.

The closer we get to the stands, the louder the chatter rises like a cloud above them. So loud it overshadows the cadence. Mothers and fathers wave their arms, trying to get their soldier's attention. Girlfriends and boyfriends hold up their cell phones, memorializing the moment. Somewhere in that jumble of people, someone's waiting for me.

Grandpa and Nana made sure of it.

We halt and stand at attention. The Battalion Commander takes the podium to make his opening remarks, general bull-shit about family day, tomorrow's graduation, and the training and values instilled by the Army. Having to keep my eyes straight forward through it all makes for a hell of a challenge trying to find anyone in the stands. I rely on my peripheral vision, the images all hazy and indistinct, but I'm fairly positive they're sitting several rows up on my right.

When the drill and ceremony portion begins and we're put "at ease," I turn my head, craning my neck slightly to see past the tall guy in front of me.

Yep. Grandpa and Nana are zeroed in on me, smiles as wide as their faces. And beside them, Taryn and Farrah wave. Suddenly, Farrah leans over and taps the shoulder of the girl beside her and points in my direction. I can't see her face, only the fact that she has curly brown hair.

Curly brown hair. It's shorter than I remember, but basi-cally the same.

Butterflies flap against my chest and for a minute, I imagine myself being one of those soldiers on America's Funniest Home Videos that passes out and falls down right in the middle of formation. Oh my God. Could that be Rayne? Did Taryn and Farrah use that picture they saw to find her?

The ceremony creeps by, and I still can't see her face. Damn that dude in the baseball hat blocking my view. *Move!*

When the last drill and ceremony presentations are finished and the BC issues his closing remarks, the Company Commander steps in front of our group with the usual safety protocol and instructions to be back by 2100 hours. As soon as he dismisses us, the crowd pours down onto the field in a free-for-all. I barely take two steps before Nana's in front of me, throwing her arms around my neck. Grandpa's behind her, patting my shoulder, and Taryn and Farrah stand to the side, waiting their turn.

There's no one else.

Where'd she go?

"Gage! We're so proud of you. We've missed you so much!" Nana chirps in my ear. I squeeze her tight while eyeing Farrah over her shoulder.

When she releases her grip, I walk over to the girls. "Wasn't there someone else in the stands with y'all?"

"No," Taryn says, eyes narrowed with a laugh. "Are we not enough?"

"Of course. I just... I could've sworn I saw Farrah talking to someone. With curly brown hair?"

"Oh," Farrah says, the recognition filtering into her voice as she nudges my arm. "I can't remember her name. Sarah or Sally or something like that. Her boyfriend is in that group." She points toward Bravo Company. My eyes follow her finger to the midst of a large group where a soldier, just about my age, is picking up his girlfriend, a short girl with curly brown hair, and planting a big one right on her lips.

My stomach drops, and I feel like I might spew everything I've eaten today, as morning chow begs to make an appearance on the field. I swallow it back and slap a fake smile on my face. No sense ruining this moment for everyone else.

After dinner, Nana and the girls head to the Post Exchange for tax-free shopping while Grandpa buys us both a coffee. We sit together in one of the molded plastic benches in the food court, silent at first, me staring at the curlicues of steam rising from my cup and him fidgeting, licking his lips constantly. In the little time I've known him, one thing I've learned is

Grandpa only hem-haws when he has something important to say.

"Gage..." He pauses then coughs, one of those low-in-the-throat attention-getters, and reaches his hand into the front inside pocket of his blazer, pulling out a long white envelope. "Your Nana and I would like you to have this."

I take it from his hand and flip it over, loosening the seal. It's thick and heavy. Important. A single folded paper with lots of numbers and a separate packet of papers, stapled in the top left corner, are inside. Something very legal and over my head. I glance up to Grandpa's eyes locked on mine.

"Am I supposed to know what this is?"

"This," he says, plucking the single paper from my fingers, "details your mother's trust fund. I set it up when she was quite small. A few CDs, a few investments. We wanted her to be financially comfortable to follow her dreams." He snorts and looks down at the table. "We now know that'll never happen, but... it can happen for you."

"I don't... you mean... what?" I stammer.

"That other jumble of papers over there is some legal mumbo-jumbo—signatures and initials and such—the lawyer needs to transfer this," he says, pointing to the bottom-line figure on the single sheet, "to you."

I stare at the figure, counting and recounting the number of digits I'm actually seeing. Surely, there's a misplaced decimal point somewhere.

"Grandpa, it's too much. I can't accept—"

"Yes, you can, and you will. Your mother would've wanted you to have it. Nana and I want you to have it. You've brought so much back to us, this is the least we can do to honor your mother's memory and tell you how proud we are of the man you've become. How happy I am to see you wear that camouflage."

Tears begin to form, but I quickly blink them away. No

soldier wants to be seen crying in uniform. Especially not some wet-behind-the-ears Private. I swallow back the lump in my throat, reaching out to shake his hand.

"It's an honor to follow in your footsteps, sir."

This is surreal. Tomorrow I graduate Basic Training then my grandparents and cousins will take me to the airport and put me on a plane to Fort Eustis, Virginia, where I'll spend 15 weeks in Advanced Individual Training. Nine weeks ago—the first time Drill Sergeant met me on the steps of the bus screaming a line of expletives in my face—this day seemed an impossible destination. But now it's here.

Life moves on.

But tonight, I clean. We all clean, to be more accurate. Wall lockers have to be emptied, barracks sanitized, and floors waxed for the nine millionth time this cycle.

One last all-nighter to end this with a bang.

I roll the last of my personal items and stuff them in my duffel. The only thing left in my locker now is the Bible I brought here. I reach into the pocket of my uniform and pull out the white envelope Grandpa gave me then flip open the Bible's front cover.

My breath catches. I look at this picture every night, but the reaction never changes. She takes my breath away every time. Our smiles, big and nervous, barely conceal what both of us were trying to hide.

We were in love.

God knows the time and distance hasn't diminished that one bit for me.

I still love her.

My lungs constrict in my chest, causing me to fight for a

deep breath. Something to ease the pain. It doesn't help. Nothing ever does.

I slide the envelope behind our picture.

My life is falling into place. Things are moving forward, working out like I never expected. But one question lingers, in the quiet moments before sleep, when everything's dark and lonely. When everything's said and done, will she still love me?

41

RAYNE

The parking lot of the Piggly Wiggly looks a little like molten lava, oozy black with watery ripples quivering up from the surface. The morning show newscasters reported earlier that by midday, it'd be hot enough to fry eggs on the sidewalk. They make the same stupid comment every year about this time like it's some newsworthy event that it's going to be hell-hot in the Deep South in late July. Shocker.

I pull into the space in front of the buggy rack and just as I'm shutting off the engine, the baby kicks. It's been happening for a couple weeks now, but it's still surreal. I'm no longer walking through this alone, and I can't help wondering if the baby's just rolling around happy in there, or if somewhere down deep he or she inherently senses the emotions running through my body.

In a few short weeks, it'll be a year. A year ago, in this very parking lot where this whole screwed up saga started. A year ago, when my Mama was having her crazy spell in aisle three. God, how I miss that woman.

A year ago, Preston first admitted he liked me. Now he hangs in with me through all the hormonal roller-coaster rides and makes late-night Waffle House runs for hash browns, scattered, covered, and smothered. He doesn't realize he's my rock.

A year ago, when I first talked to Gage and my life forever changed. The alert on my cell phone calendar makes me want to throw the phone down and run it over, crushing it into the asphalt.

Reminder: July 26. Gage's Birthday.

I don't know where he is, if he's celebrating or who he's celebrating with. He's completely cut me off. The baby kicks again as if reassuring me. *I'm here, Mama.* My own little piece of Gage no one can take away.

What a different world I live in now; it's sometimes hard to recognize. Daddy's shock about the pregnancy has waned, partly because he believes the new life will be good for our family but also because I'm pretty sure he has a secret affinity for becoming a grandpa. Every business trip over the last month has netted this baby at least two or three souvenir outfits and toys. His support has been awesome, much better than the Howards, who, for all intents and purposes, keep their distance. Charlotte has agreed to accept our relationship for Preston's sake, which means little more than her relegating me to a brief mention in her conversations with Preston and otherwise forgetting me completely.

Whomp. Whomp. Whomp. I jump in my seat and drop my keys to the floorboard, and as I bend to pick them up, Mrs. McAlister smooshes her face against the window.

"Rayne? Are you okay, dear?"

I motion for her to move back so I can get out of the car. She does so and clutches her blue pleather handbag and plastic coupon caddy tight to her chest, eyes wide as they rove over me. "You were just sitting so I..."

"Just going over what I needed in my head." I tap my finger against my temple.

"Anything particular? I might have a coupon..." she says,

following beside me into the store while rifling through her stash.

"Thanks, but it's only a short list. Milk, bread, bananas, and mayonnaise."

"Sounds like you're making banana sandwiches. Is that what you're making?" Just so happens banana sandwiches are my craving du jour, not that it's any of her business. "I tell you, add some peanut butter to that sandwich and it'll be fine as frog's hair. You know they say Elvis loved peanut butter and banana sandwiches, and if it's good enough for him, then it's good enough... hey! I found a coupon for Duke's Mayonnaise. Here, go on, take it," she says shoving the clipping into my hand. "That's the good stuff. Not that ol' store brand junk. I never will forget the day your Mama wasn't feeling well and grabbed the wrong kind." She pauses and shakes her head. I'm almost irritated from her speech, but more impressed at how she crammed all those words into one breath. She rubs my back in circles. "Your poor Mama. God rest her soul."

"Yes, ma'am." I force a smile, grab a basket from the rack by the sliding door and dart in toward produce and away from her. "Thanks again for the coupon."

Before I can get to the crate of bananas, Mrs. McAlister has already linked up with Mrs. Sanders, a white-haired old lady from the church group whose thinning hair looks more like stretched cotton balls glued to her scalp. They are quickly engrossed in conversation, pausing every so often to gaze over in my direction. Wonder who they're talking about?

I grab the milk and bread from the outer perimeter then head to aisle three for the mayonnaise. Dukes of course. After reading the fine print, I lean forward to grab the 30 fl. oz. yellow-lidded jar. No condemnation in that. Dukes Mayonnaise in my basket and coupon directions followed to a T. As I turn to leave, Mrs. McAlister and Mrs. Sanders are standing behind me.

"Rayne, dear, we were wondering—how far along are you now?" Mrs. Sanders leans forward and pats my stomach, a move I loathe. How would she feel if I walked up and stroked her turkey waddle and asked how old she was?

"Seventeen weeks." I head toward the end of the aisle, but Mrs. McAlister holds out her arm to stop me.

"What's the sex?"

"I don't know. I haven't had an ultrasound."

"Are you going to find out? Decorating the nursery and buying clothes is so much easier if you know the sex."

"I don't know. Hadn't thought about it."

"Well, what about Preston?"

"What about him?"

"Does he want to know? The sex, I mean?"

"I don't know. He hasn't said."

"Well, honey, y'all need to discuss these things."

"I guess so."

"Are y'all getting married before or after the baby comes? I mean, I assume you are getting married, right? It's only proper if the mother and father..."

As they go back and forth, lecturing me about what is and isn't proper and grilling me over my non-existent wedding plans, their voices blur into background noise, replaced by a weird, high-pitched hum. I can't breathe or swallow and the shelves creep closer, squishing me in between. The urge to run sends kinetic impulses through my limbs but I'm afraid to move, seeing as how the room's now spinning. My knees buckle beneath me, and just as quickly the ladies are crouched down, waving their circulars in my face.

"I suwanee child. I bet you ain't eating like you should, skinny as you are in your second trimester."

"She ain't got no Mama to cook for her no more, and her Daddy's always gone off on business now. You'd think them Howards would be taking better care of her, but..."

They look at each other with arched eyebrows and knowing looks. What they know, or think they have figured out, I have no idea. All I know is I need to get out of this store and fast.

"I... I need fresh air." I scramble to my feet and sprint toward the doors, leaving my basket on the floor in the middle of the aisle. When I get to the bench under the "I'm Big on the Pig" sign, an employee on a smoke-break quickly squashes the butt and heads back inside. I don't even want to think about how terrible I look right now.

My cell phone buzzes in my pocket and I slide it out. Preston's name is on the screen. "Where are you?" My abrupt answer must scare him.

Panic laces his voice. "I'm heading into town. Why? What's wrong?"

"Nothing. I'm at the Pig. Can you stop by?"

"Be there in a couple."

I lay the phone on the bench beside me. So this is how anxiety feels? Oh, the irony. I just had a panic attack in aisle three while buying mayonnaise. I could cry except I don't. I laugh. I'm more like Mama than I realized—and that's a good thing. If Mama lived with this every day and still managed to keep our home running, then she was the strongest woman I ever knew and probably will know. I always called her weak. I was wrong. That woman was strong, and she did it all for me.

At the far entrance, Preston's Mustang darts in and whips around to the curb in front of me. By the time he makes it to my side, I'm laughing hysterically. His eyebrows scrunch together like he's deciding if I should be committed.

"Preston, I had a panic attack."

"What? That's not funny! Are you okay?"

"Ask me where," I say through the giggles.

"Where?"

"Aisle three! Now ask me what I was buying."

"What were you buying?"

"Mayonnaise!"

He stares at me, stunned for a minute, before erupting. We laugh together, our shoulders shaking in unison. He grabs either side of my face and smirks. "You are your mother's daughter."

I nod. I am, and for the first time in my life, I'm completely okay with it.

GAGE

I step under the shower head and let the hot water run down me, taking the opportunity to close my eyes and soak in the silence.

"Gage!" Rodriguez steps inside the bathroom door and slaps his hand on the tile wall. The loud wham echoes around the space and my heart jumps into my throat. "Hurry up. Overnight pass starting in 30 minutes. You, me, and Porter are getting off this Post tonight."

I turn off the water and grab my towel, wrapping it around me as I try to steady my breath. "And do what?"

"That's a surprise."

So not trusting that. I push past him and walk to my locker. The best thing about passes is getting to wear civilian clothing instead of uniforms for a change. My standard black T-shirt and jeans are folded on the shelf.

I've missed you, old friends.

Rodriguez follows behind and joins Porter who's already standing by my bed. Both are fully dressed and ready to go. I shake my head and laugh. Two guys couldn't be more different, but their friendship is bone-deep. Alex Rodriguez hails from

California, was raised by his grandmother, and loves surfing. He's all of 5'5" but stacked like a brick house. The girls forgive his shorter stature once they get a quick glimpse of those abs.

Then there's Jason Porter from Wisconsin. The product of a dairy farmer, he was raised with six brothers and sisters and several hundred cows. He's 6'5", about 170lbs soaking wet, and wears Army-issued thick-framed glasses—also known as Birth Control Glasses or BCGs—for his near-sightedness.

They're the weirdest, most unlikely friends. And they're two of the greatest battle buddies I have. That's why I always fold when they start yammering about a pass. Who can say no to these two?

I pull the t-shirt over my head. "Ok, I'm going, but first you have to tell me the plans."

"We're taking you out for your birthday," Porter says. "Time to celebrate your last teen year."

"I haven't felt like a teenager in months," I say, fastening my belt.

Rodriguez grabs my chin and gives it a shake. "All the more reason to enjoy tonight. Now come on, our ride's waiting."

They bolt out the door side by side with me following on their heels. "Our ride?"

Rodriguez turns with a wink. "You'll see."

Uh-oh. That wink slides us squarely into the danger zone. It means he's been planning, and Rodriguez's plans are known for going... astray.

Awry.

Okay, getting totally screwed up.

In the blacktop parking area outside the dorms, a tan Suburban with a South Carolina license plate idles in the far space. As we approach, the doors on both sides swing open, and three girls walk around to the back bumper. Two I recognize immediately. One I don't.

"Happy Birthday, Cousin!" Taryn and Farrah shout in

unison, throwing rainbow-colored confetti in the air. It rains down on top of us, leaving little metallic pieces in everyone's hair. They pull me into a group hug then step back to introduce their friend.

Her name is Clara Jean Riley from Mount Pleasant, right outside of Charleston. She smiles a lot, awkwardly like she's not quite sure what to say, and shifts from foot to foot. A strand of her straight brown hair, which she habitually tucks behind her ear, refuses to stay put and two seconds later swings back in her face.

I glance at Rodriguez and Porter, their million-dollar smiles evidence enough of their involvement.

"How'd y'all do this?"

"Just call me the master," Rodriguez says, scrubbing his nails on his button-down. "Now, let's blow this joint."

He stole her email address. That's how he pulled it off. I'm in the middle of scarfing potato skins when I remember Rodriguez looking over my shoulder at an email from Taryn then scribbling something on his notepad a couple weeks ago. Sly dog.

I wipe my mouth with a napkin and lean over to his ear. "I figured it out. You jacked her email address and set this up, right?"

We're the only ones still eating. Everyone else is finishing up a game of pool on the table by the windows. He says nothing, responding only with an exaggerated shrug.

Guilty.

He'd seen several pictures of Farrah on some texts Taryn sent and commented on her "hotness." Looks like this birthday surprise has a few perks for him as well.

"So, this... party... was all for me? Nothing in it for you?"

"Are you doubting my friendship?" He slaps his hand across his chest, slack jawed. "A true friend would see I only wanted you to have a terrific birthday. In the meantime, if I happen to hit it off with your cousin, then a true friend would be happy about that, too."

"I thought as much." I finish chewing and take a swig of my sweet tea. "And did you happen to arrange this other girl coming with them as well?"

"Clara Jean? She's cool, man. You should talk to her."

No. I don't want to talk to her. She's incredibly nice and pretty in a wholesome Americana sort of way. But I'm not ready for all that.

"If I wanted to talk to a girl—any girl—I would." My voice's hard edge catches Rodriguez off guard, and he jumps in his seat. I narrow my eyes. "Taryn approved this set-up business?"

"Taryn said it was a bad idea, okay? But Farrah, Porter, and I think it's great." He exhales and steeples his hands to his chin. "Dude, you're pining over a picture. Every night, you get it out, stare at it for like, five minutes, then put it back up, turn over, and go to sleep." He turns catty-cornered in his chair to face me, shaking his head. "It's not healthy. Not right. We're in the prime of our lives, man, and you're giving it up for what? A picture?"

A picture. If he only knew everything that'd happened. But he doesn't. Because I haven't told anyone. It's something I can't face—the shame bites me every time I see her staring back at me from that flat piece of glossy paper. The knife that fillets my heart every time I realize I left her when all she wanted me to do was stay.

"You... you don't get it."

"Maybe I don't know everything that went down, but I do know one thing. You're my friend, and you almost never smile. Put yourself out there, man. Open up to the possibilities." He glances up and nudges my elbow as Clara Jean saunters back to the table. "Speaking of which..."

Rodriguez jumps up and points to his empty chair. The one 6 inches from me. "You may have my seat, lovely lady. I promised Farrah a one-on-one match."

She greets him with a gleaming white smile and walks beside me. He slides the chair under her.

What a gentleman. I roll my eyes.

"Hi," she says in her honeyed Southern accent. "How's your birthday so far?"

"Good," I mumble, staring at my plate and the half-eaten potato skin covered in bacon.

"Farrah said you were living with your grandparents in Charleston before you joined the Army. You gonna go back there when you're done here?"

"I don't know."

"Well, if you do, I'd be happy to show you around, and we—"

My stomach grips my backbone. "Look, I don't know if this was planned as some sort of set-up, but..."

"You're not interested?" She crosses her arms, sitting back in the chair. "I know that look. Faraway eyes staring at nothing, bottom lip all poked out, shoulders slumped." She sighs. "It's the look of getting over someone."

I laugh and look her in the eyes for the first time. They're an icy blue, and the thought floats through my mind that if I'd met her a year ago, I would've thought her pretty. I might've even been tempted to ask for her number. But now, she's just a face. A face that isn't Rayne's. "Is it that obvious?"

"Kinda. But I know it well. From personal experience."

"Sucks doesn't it?"

She reaches over and grabs my hand. Hers are warm and soft but every muscle in my body turns to steel, and I fight the urge to yank my fingers away.

"Completely. But over time... you'll notice a difference," she says. "And from there, it'll only get better, until one day you'll look around and discover you're okay. Fine. Good as new."

I nod and take a long pull of my tea. I don't want to be good as anything. That implies there's a replacement comparable to the original, and that's impossible. No one can be to me what Rayne was.

Is.

What Rayne is.

Because she's still everything to me.

"*E*arth to Rayne." His voice is soft in my ear, broken only by his fingers snapping in my face. "Where are you?" He's leaned across the counter, next to the doughnut case directly across from where I'm restacking the coffee creamers and straws. It's hard to feel pissed off when his brown eyes sparkle like that. Like he's happy. Excited.

As I should be.

I shift my eyes to the table in the corner and Preston turns to see. Jaycee's holding court, Ainsley and Mallory at her side. Umpteen college pamphlets clutter the table, and snippets of conversation, punctuated by Jaycee's shrill voice, float in the air —frat parties, sororities, football games, and new roommates from different states. I want to shove napkins in my ears so I don't hear, because hearing it makes me jealous. And I never want to be jealous of Jaycee. At least I'm working the counter and don't have to wait on their table. Thank God for small miracles.

"Forget her. She's stupid and will fail-out before Christmas break," says Preston. I smile. I'd regret wishing for anyone else's failure, but Jaycee deserves it. And more. "We've got more important things to do. Are you ready? Get your stuff and let's go."

<hr>

The tissue paper covering the reclining chair crinkles underneath me. Preston swivels a round stool to my side, looking all eager-beaver. I press hard into the headrest, studying the ceiling tiles as if they might unlock the great mysteries of the universe. Anything to take my mind off the fact that as much as I adore Preston, I'd rather have Gage sitting on that stool as we see the first glimpses of our baby. No more wondering about who this little person might be. Now, I'll have an actual picture.

A chubby woman in scrubs plods in the room and to my side, and without a word, pulls down my elasticized pants panel and yanks up my shirt to fully expose the bump. She pushes her fingers into my sides, poking from one side to the next. When I shrink back, she looks up at me. "Just getting your little one good and awake."

She takes a seat beside the ultrasound machine and pulls out a clipboard. "Just need to confirm before we start. Name— Davidson, Rayne?" I nod. "Gestation at twenty-one weeks, three days?" I nod again. "We're checking measurements and functions. Are we finding out gender?"

Preston's grin threatens to swallow his face, but I squelch his excitement. "No. I want to be surprised."

Preston immediately gears up to bombard me with the perks of finding out. "But..."

I turn toward him, stoic and unsmiling. "I said no." His shoulders slump and the corners of his mouth droop, and all I can think is how much harder it would've been if I'd told him the whole truth. I want Gage to be with me when the gender is revealed. I'm saving that for him.

"Very good. Here we go." The technician squirts warm jelly across my stomach and pushes it around with the wand. Through the wispy clouds on the screen, a profile emerges with little ears, a little chin, and a nose, wide across the bridge with just a smidge of an upturn at the tip, that could've come from no one else but Gage.

Preston grips my fingers, squeezing them together to his lips. This should be one of the happiest days of my life, but it's more like a knife to the heart. Sharing this with Preston could easily be any girl's dream, but how can I be okay with it? Especially now with Gage's nose staring me in the face, taunting me from the screen like a ghost from the past. If I can barely handle looking at the grainy 3-D image from a screen, how can I do this every single day of my life? But as much as I hate it, I also love it. Love at first sight meant nothing until now. I'm in love with that nose, with that face, with that little person that's a fifty-fifty split of me and Gage. Our baby. Our love. Alive and well.

"Let's check some functions." She swipes the wand around the side of my abdomen, and the screen lights up in blues and reds with blood flow patterns. The heart, like tiny palpitating butterfly wings, beats in perfect rhythm. "Let's have a listen," she says and with a flip of a switch, a crackle of white noise gives way to another much more incredible sound. Woosh-woosh-woosh-woosh echoes rhythmically in the room.

"Is that...?" A myriad of emotions swells in my throat, forcing its way up like a gigantic pressure behind my eyes.

"A healthy heartbeat coming in at 145 bpm."

"That's good? Normal?"

"It's perfect." She smiles and pats my hand then goes back to clicking away on her keyboard with one hand, the other still roaming over my stretched skin with the wand. When finished, she prints out a long strip of still pictures from the ultrasound as a memento.

That night, I unwrap a silver picture frame engraved with "Baby's First Picture" I'd purchased days before. I comb through the printouts and select my favorite profile shot that outlines the baby's silhouette, tiny bow-lips, and Daddy's nose.

44

GAGE

I lay in bed, not sleeping, but staring at the ceiling's popcorn texture, creating constellations with each of the chalky nuggets. The white cotton sheet is pulled up to my chest, reeking of day-old bleach, incredibly sterile in contrast to the general mustiness of the housing quarters. We clean every inch of this place regularly, but somehow it retains the odor of moth bolls-meets-sweat. I guess that's natural. Eight male soldiers smooshed in a couple hundred square-feet doesn't leave much room for clean air.

Or personal items.

Between my bed and the metal wall locker, I have zilch space for anything non-military. But I don't mind. It's sort of the reason I'm here. To shirk off the past and become who I am.

Not who anyone else tells me I am.

Just Gage.

Earlier the place had been a noisy concoction of man-sounds. Two beds down, Porter was snoring, each release sputtering like a sick horse being run over with a lawn mower. Across the room, Rodriguez was talking in his sleep, something he does every night. It was annoying as hell those first few nights, then over time became oddly comforting.

Reliable and familiar.

But now, in the wee hours of the morning, the quiet sets in. Still.

The military is a funny thing. We spend so much time with our battle buddies, not just in training but in talking, sharing stories of us as kids and all our high school exploits. Laughing about what some idiot did in training that morning. Planning our next weekend pass. They become like brothers in that way —a sounding board for advice on shooting strategies, a shoulder to lean on when shit gets real, and a friendly face that reminds you life does exist outside the crap storm muddling inside.

Funny you can know intimate details about other people, but when the night comes and the endless string of thoughts running through your mind are the only things left to keep you company, the loneliness sets in. And you miss home and the people left behind. Even if everything was, and is, a total wreck.

Rayne. Preston. Dad.

I wonder what they're doing, and if they miss me. Can they forgive me for leaving? It wasn't what I wanted to do. It's what I had to do.

I manage to shove the thoughts of them into a mental lockbox all day, but each night, they rear their heads and my stomach churns, waves of nausea sweeping over me and morphing into chills that run the length of my arms and legs, settling into slight tremors in my fingers and toes.

Tonight's the worst it's been. Maybe that's my subconscious way of knowing it's time.

I sit up against the concrete wall behind my bed and ease open my wall locker to retrieve the notebook and pen on the second shelf. One of the only two windows in the entire room is catty-cornered from my bed, and the beams of moonlight stream in just enough for me to see what I'm writing when I squint.

Okay, Gage. Deep breath, and do this. I press the pen to the first lined row.

Dear Dad,

First and foremost, I'm alive. I'm sure few people would actually care, but I do know that you would be one of them. Secondly, my life is full of things I'm not quite ready to face, so your keeping this letter between us would be best. There's still so much to say—so much to apologize for—to the people who were in my life, but there's no going forward unless I start at the source.

That would be you.

So here goes.

I met my grandparents. It's accurate to say my blue eyes—Mom's eyes—are a direct genetic tie to Grandpa Harrington. He's tough-as-nails military, just like you found out in all those investigative reports, but a softer side lurks beneath. He never likes to show it, but it's there. Especially when he's dealing with Nana, who I think must be the source of Mom's generous heart you mentioned so many times when you were telling me about her.

They welcomed me with open arms, even when it meant coming to terms with their worst nightmare. Hearing that Mom was gone—that I never even knew her—was heartbreaking for them. But seeing me, they said it felt as if a second chance was hand-delivered to their door. They're making the most of it.

I won't go into details, but let's just say I'm well taken care of.

They want to meet you. At least when they're ready. And you're ready. No one expects this meeting to be easy, but I do think it's necessary. Might even bring some healing. They want to get to know the man that raised their grandson. The man that their daughter fell in love with and found special enough to want a life with. She was a wild spirit, but you managed to make her dream of settling down.

There are so many blanks that need to be filled in—for both of you—and this might be a good place to start.

Please consider it.

When I left home, my life was in shambles. The thought of seeing another day without the people I loved most, the sting of betrayal, and the hurt of a loss I never even knew about until that night—it robbed me of all the plans I'd made. In a blink, my dreams were obliterated. I had no direction.

But I have direction now.

There's no easy way to say this, so I'll say it outright. Dad, I joined the military. The Army. I've already completed basic training and am currently in AIT. That's Advanced Individual Training, by the way (the military loves acronyms). I'm learning who I am and what I'm made of.

I'm learning what made me.

Every night since I've been gone, the conversations we had in the aftermath of my finding out the truth replay in my head. I'm coming to terms with everything I learned, and though I'll never understand how you could agree to go along with all the façades and let Charlotte drive a wedge between us, I do believe your intentions were good. You only wanted the best for me. Only wanted to keep me close.

I get that now.

Hopefully one day soon, you and I can sit down man-to-man and have a coffee or a beer (guess that will depend on the time of day) and discuss all this in more detail. There's so much to say that a letter wouldn't do it justice. That, and the things I need to say to you require me looking you in the eye.

Despite everything, the lies, the truths, and every shade of doubt in between, I can now say this without hesitation.

I love you, Dad.

Gage

.   .   .

I slip a stamped envelope from the inside sleeve of the notebook, fold the paper in thirds, and seal it inside. On the front, I simply write Jackson Howard and his office address. No return information. Dad will recognize my handwriting, so there's no point tipping off anyone else who might come across the letter. And selfishly, at this moment in time, I don't want anyone knowing where I am. It's the one tiny piece of control I have left in all this, and I'm keeping it.

I slide it into the front pocket of my uniform. Tomorrow I'll give it to a friend who's graduating AIT and heading home to Oregon. That way the postmark doesn't give it away either.

I have to do this on my terms. Reach out to them as I muster the strength. It'll be my first sign of life.

My first attempt at making it back home.

45

———————

RAYNE

The weeks immediately following the ultrasound bring dramatic growth for the baby, and consequently, me. Apparently, "more substantial weight gain" is actually code for "Willy Wonka blueberry-girl fat."

I lay flat on my bed with Mama's old sewing tape measure stretched long-ways over my bump. Twenty-seven centimeters —perfectly in-sync with my due date and bigger than I imagined for the start of the third trimester. According to the pregnancy books Preston bought me, this'll be the most uncomfortable portion of the process, though the first two-thirds haven't been a cakewalk with my crazy hormonal swings and monstrous cankles. The expanse of naked belly skin streaked with silvery-purple stretchmarks swells my heart with pride, though. Like a tiger that's earned her stripes. I've done this so far, and I'm pushing on.

"I think the baby's grown since yesterday," says Preston and I jump and drop the measuring ribbon to the carpet. He's supposed to be in class, not here in the middle of a bland Friday morning.

"Baby's not the only one." I wave my hand over my body,

swollen outward from belly to fingers and toes. "What are you doing here?" I pull down my shirt and slowly roll myself to sitting.

"Surprising you." As I open my mouth, he touches his finger to my lips. "No excuses. Bag's packed in the car."

We don't talk much on the twisty two-lane heading up to the Smokey Mountains. It's easy to see this morning why the Cherokee named them that. Bright leafy flashes of reds and oranges peek through the dense fog snaking through the mountaintops in gauzy grayness, like the hills are truly on fire. Preston's reserved a cabin for the night. He says I need a 24-hour reprieve from reality, and he's right. There hasn't been a day in this pregnancy I haven't cried about something—missing Mama, wondering about Gage, admiring my new swollen figure, or cursing the fast-food guy who put tomatoes on my burger. Through it all, Preston's been there, listening to my rants, drying my tears, and talking me out of murder. I'm still in love with Gage and I always will be, but there's a growing need inside of me to have a partner. To allow myself to love again.

And then there's the baby. An actual little human will be here in just a few weeks, depending on me, and needing me. I'll be Mama. It's the first time the realization sinks in like this, and pulses of energy sliver through my arms and legs, pushing me into something a bit like the Twilight Zone. Subconsciously, I grapple for a life preserver, and my hand finds one, warm, soft, and steady—Preston's hand.

We have an unspoken agreement. No physical affection because it'd be wrong on so many levels, but here I am, fingers laced through his, and he's not pulling away. In fact, his thumb is rubbing up and down mine. And I hate the warmth it spreads over my skin, because it's like I'm cheating on Gage even though he's not here.

I've tortured myself for weeks about what I could've done—

what I could do—to bring Gage home, but the truth is, he doesn't want to be here. Or he would be. And more and more, I fantasize about moving on, but I don't know if that's the hormones, the resentment, or the truth talking. Maybe a little of all three.

"We're here," Preston says as we turn onto a gravel drive which winds back into a block of trees with a log cabin in the center, small but homey. He shifts the car into park and kills the engine, leaving us in silence except for the birds chirping loudly in the trees and a spastic squirrel hauling ass through the leaves chasing acorns.

"I kinda feel like I've stepped into a Disney movie." I laugh. "Quiet cabin in the forest, woodland animals. Are there dwarves inside? Did you get me dwarves?"

"I knew I forgot something." Preston smiles and shakes his head before turning serious. "Honestly, this trip is about you and baby taking a chill. No drama. No tears."

"You better say that louder. My hormones might not have heard you," I say and tug at my ear.

"Your hormones don't get a say. Consider this my baby shower gift to you. Others will get you diapers and bottles, but me? I give you rest and relaxation. Starting now. So stay put until I come around." He gets out of the car, trots around to my door and holds it open for me.

He hands me the key before he gets the bags out of the trunk. I walk up the wooden steps and look around. Two rocking chairs sit on the narrow front porch, a small table and citronella lantern between them. At the corner, the edge of a rock chimney is barely visible. I unlock the door and walk into an open-concept space with a den and kitchen flowing seamlessly together. The interior doesn't match the exterior. It's equipped with the latest electronics and the shabby-chic décor is anything but shabby. There's a fifty-inch TV on the wall above the gas-log fireplace and two complicated-looking remotes to accompany each. It's a far cry from my first camping experience in Gage's ramshackle tent at the beach. My stomach flinches the moment the memory creeps in.

"Okay, here's the game plan." Preston hauls a duffel and a few grocery bags through the door, plopping them on the kitchen bar. "First, we're gonna go for a walk. Then, we're coming back, and you," he points at me, "are taking a long bath while I cook supper. And then we're getting on that couch and having a baby movie marathon."

"Baby movies?"

"*Look Who's Talking* one and two, *Nine Months*, *Three Men and a Baby*. The classics."

"What? No *Raising Arizona*? That's a classic!"

"Really?" He snorts and glances at me from the corners of his eyes.

I grip either side of my belly in defiant solidarity with the baby. "Any baby movie with a prison break and someone wearing pantyhose on their head is tops in my book."

Preston nods me over and holds out a jacket. "You are a weird and unusual girl."

I slide my arms in the sleeves, but I'm too big to zip it now. I sigh and look up at him smiling. "And I'm having a baby. Watch out!"

"The world may not survive." He shakes his head, takes my hand and hauls me out the door for our walk.

Preston props several throw pillows in the corner of the couch. "Come here." He motions me over then pats the pillows. "Lay back and prop your feet up. They're swollen from the walk."

"When are they not swollen nowadays?" I waddle over and slip off the fuzzy socks I put on after the bath earlier. He's right. They're worse than ever, looking like two sausages about to bust their casings. I plop down on the cushion and wriggle myself into a pillow cocoon then physically lift my legs onto the couch. Seriously, is there anything more humiliating than having to use your hands to prop up your chubby, swollen legs because you can't lift them anymore? They should put those tidbits in the pregnancy books, highlighted in little sidebars with warning labels.

"Comfy?" Preston hovers above me, ready to fix whatever is potentially bugging me.

"I'm good. Sit down. Watch the movie." He flips off the light switch, settles on the cushion next to mine, then pulls my legs across his lap and massages my feet. The deep, circular motions are pure heaven, but I'm terrified he'll be crushed to death under the weight of my legs. I nonchalantly check on him to make sure he's not struggling for breath.

Preston's touch is sweet, not tingly or exhilarating the way Gage's was, but comforting and caring. There's love in his hands. Total devotion to me and this baby. Sometimes I want to beat my head against the wall. Why can't my life just sync up for once? It's like I'm always just a little behind the eight-ball. I meet Preston, but I fall for his brother. Gage and I commit only to have him run away. Mama and I make amends, and she dies. I'm cursed, forever destined to have things either this way or that, but never to have one completely happy ending. Here I am again, my heart torn over whether to hold myself back and wait for my one great love or to plow ahead into a life with a great guy who loves me.

I sigh loudly and sit up straight, my throat on fire from the inevitable heartburn of pregnancy, made worse by my anxiety.

Preston turns to me, eyes narrowed, searching my face. "You okay?" The light from the TV screen reflects in his eyes, dancing across them in glints of metallic brown. There's no doubt he loves me. And he's here, sitting beside me, asking me what he can do to make it all better.

I'm not sure what, but something washes over me in an overwhelming urge to forget Gage. Forget the pain. Scratch out all those old memories and might-have-beens. It's time to purge my body and mind of Gage's face, his touch, his love. The remnants he left behind that gloom over me every day. I know what Preston can do to make it all better. He can kiss me. He can make me forget.

I lunge forward, my lips connecting with his in an instant. He's still at first, but then his lips wash over mine, forceful, as he circles his arms around my back, pulling me closer. But as quickly as it starts, he ends it.

"Stop!" he hollers and pushes me back, both hands now on my shoulders, keeping me at arm's length. "What the hell, Rayne? What was that?" He's breathing hard, the words slung out between pants.

"I love you, Preston," I say, my face crushed down into my palms. He grabs my wrists and yanks them down, forcing me to look him in the eyes. They're steeled, and I can't tell whether he's hurt or mad.

"Don't say things you don't mean." He enunciates each word with a staccato hard edge.

"I do mean it. I love you."

"More than Gage?" His question is a direct strike to my wounded heart. I'll never love anyone the way I love Gage. But Preston's a close second. Doesn't that count for something? Am I for real? What guy in the world wants to hear a girl say she loves him second best?

I drop my eyes to my lap. "Don't you still have feelings for me?" My voice is barely a whisper.

Preston strokes my hair. "My feelings have never been the issue, Rayne." I look up at him, his eyes like muddy puddles. "I know you still love my brother, and I know that wherever he is, he still loves you." He closes his eyes and shakes his head. "Damn, we're a messed-up bunch."

"Ya think?" Why can't it just be simple? Why can't I just get on with things, start living my life again? I grab his fingers in my hands. "Preston, you've been everything to me during this pregnancy. You stirred up all these feelings, and... I don't know what to do with them... because I love him, and I love you... and I don't know..." The words fall apart in the sobs, which is probably a good thing because I don't know what the hell it is I'm even trying to say.

Preston leans over and grabs a tissue from the box on the coffee table and blots the corners of my eyes. "Look at me," he says, and I obey. "When you make a decision, your head and heart need to be clear. No hormones, no fears, no coercion. Let's make a pact to wait until the baby's born to decide anything. Give it time to really make sense in your head."

I nod. He's right. I can't make decisions on fly-by-night emotions and hormonal swings. "Agreed. No decisions until after the baby comes. But Preston," I warn, "be strong for me when I can't. Remind me of this pact when I'm crazy-nuts trying to kiss you or slumped in a corner crying over Gage. Remind me to be strong... and wait... no matter what."

"I promise," he says.

I can't believe it. I blink my eyes and check again.

Nope. Still there in black and white.

I click the link and wait for the page to load, fully expecting some pop-up screen to swing out from the left and tell me I've been punked. The screen fills with 34 beautiful color photos from a variety of angles and an MLS listing with the header—DON'T MISS OUT ON THIS SEASIDE STUNNER!

The Edisto dream house. My house.

Wait... Our house—for sale.

Reasonably Priced and Ready to Move!

I flip through the pictures and land on number twenty-seven, a wide-angle view of the front porch.

She said it needed a swing. A place she can sit and look out over the marina. The way she always likes to sit in that swing at her Mama and Daddy's house, running her toes along the wooden floorboards.

What matters most is she said she'd live here with me one day. And we'd be together. Always.

How easy it was to imagine a life there together. How faraway it seemed. But now, it's as if things are falling into place.

The great cosmos telling me that "One Day" is here. Waiting for me.

Waiting for us.

I slide my cell phone from my pocket and punch in the digits. It rings twice before his gruff voice says, "There's my long-lost soldier grandson! How's the Army treatin' you these days?"

"I'm good, Grandpa. I miss you, but I'm calling because I need your help with something."

"Anything. What is it?"

"I know how I want to invest part of my trust fund, but I'll need someone who can get everything squared away. Someone I trust because this is important." I take a deep breath and lay it on the line. "Grandpa, I want to buy a house."

Buying a house is a total chore. Between the legal paperwork, the home inspections, and the insurance quotes, getting every-thing done while away would've been impossible if not for Grandpa. He and Nana equated buying a house with settling down. And on a barrier island only 30 minutes from them? They were only too eager to smooth the process in my absence.

On my last full day of AIT, the mood in the barracks is light. Rodriguez and Porter have already planned a road trip to Charleston and haven't stopped talking about it. My duffel bag is once again packed and ready, and my uniform hangs on the hook near my bed, ready for tomorrow's graduation ceremony.

My phone buzzes against the steel shelf with a metallic echo as it dances in a circle. I grab it and thumb across the screen. A notification blinks in a thin blue block. A picture message from Grandpa Harrington.

I tap the icon and a picture loads—Grandpa's hand, holding a ring of silver keys. In the background my house sits on its seaside plot, and on the porch is her swing. The one I ordered online a couple weeks ago and Grandpa had installed.

Underneath the picture, the caption says—She's all yours! Welcome home!

Home.

Piece by piece, the entire picture has fallen back together.

And tomorrow, my plane will land in Charleston, I'll pick up my Scout and house keys, and then I'll go home.

The one place I'll always belong.

47

RAYNE

The hangry sweet-tooth beast has crept up inside me, demanding to be fed. Rather than instigate World War Three by trying to ignore it, Preston and I launch a full-scale attack on the kitchen, making brownies, cookies, and Rice Krispie treats. He's sliding a pan of brownies into the oven when the doorbell rings.

"Who in the world could that be?" He looks back over his shoulder.

"Probably the mailman. He delivers late on Saturdays, and I'm expecting a few packages for the nursery." I hoist the mixing bowl under my arm while still stirring the chocolate chip batter. "I'll get it."

I wipe my hand on my apron and yank the door open. With a gasp, I drop the bowl to the hardwood. The spoon flips out, littering the floor with dough, and I slap my hand over my gaping mouth.

It's not the mailman. He stands there in camouflage—not the hunting variety. The official kind. His back's to me, but I know who it is before he even turns around because the chill bumps scatter over every surface and the baby kicks.

"Gage?" I whisper. My breath hitches in my throat causing a bout of lightheadedness that makes me grab the door to brace myself. "You came home?"

He turns, the nameplate on his uniform spells out "HOWARD" in bold letters, his blue eyes the same as always. "Of course I came home." He wipes away a few tears escaping down my cheeks. Maybe it's the hormones due to our child growing deep within me, or an absence-making-the-heart-grow-fonder thing, but instantly, those same old feelings surge through my body. Our hiatus has only amplified them.

We stare at each other before Gage speaks, "Rayne, I... I had to..." But Preston interrupts from behind, and Gage's eyes widen as if he's seeing a ghost.

"Gage? What the hell bro? How ya been?" He squeezes past me and bear hugs him, Gage's eyes ever-fixed on me.

He backs up, looking back and forth between us. "What are you doing here, Pres?"

My stomach drops, and I hope all those tastes of brownie batter don't revisit me.

Preston sighs. "If you'd call or text once in a while you might know..." He walks beside me, unties the apron and lets it fall. "Rayne's pregnant."

My eyes race to meet Gage's. He alternates staring between my belly and my face, never visibly reacting to the news. He's stone. Cold. The pain rips through me like a bullet, ricocheting with force.

"So... you and Preston...?" His voice shakes with the words.

"Preston was there for me when Mama died... when I needed someone." Oh God. Only I can make an explanation slap him in the face. He's too calm as he reaches out and shakes Preston's hand then pulls me into a quick hug. The strength in his arms crushes me, like he's trying to squeeze out the memories of us. And I want to scream at him for so easily believing I've moved on without him. To let him know this is his baby. To plead with him to take me away as fast as he can where no one will find us again. But I say nothing. Do nothing. I choke on the words as his arms circle me with an electric warmth. I drown in him.

He pulls away, not looking at either of us. "Congratulations. A baby changes everything."

"That's what they say," Preston agrees. I'm now mute, terrified I'll have no control over spilling the truth if I open my mouth. I want Gage to know this is his baby. I want it more than I want Preston to not get hurt.

Preston motions Gage in. "I figure you and Rayne should catch up. I'll go finish up the brownies and dinner." He stoops down and clears away the spilled batter. Before returning to the kitchen, he leans in to kiss my temple and whisper in my ear, "Remember. No decisions until after the baby's born."

Gage removes his camouflage cap and tucks it in the cargo pocket on the leg of his uniform as he moves through the foyer into the den—the very place he'd learned the truth that forever changed us. The memory slams into me, forcing me to the couch cushions. He sits beside me. Close. The need to kiss him starts as a shiver on my tongue that races down my neck and circulates deep in my breasts, where each beat of my heart becomes a magnetic pulse.

"So…" he starts, "Y'all are having a baby? I never imagined… I mean, I never… that's great."

"Yeah," I agree. "Life and its curveballs."

"But y'all are doing the right thing." He grimaces like the words are bitter on his tongue. "Raising the baby together is best. And you're strong. Babies need their mama."

"They need their daddy, too," I whisper. God, why can't he just look at me and know? See the truth?

"Preston'll do good. As always." Gage's voice is somber as he stares at his boots. "Boy or girl?" He points at my belly.

I shrug my shoulders. "Waiting to find out."

"On what?" he asks but clarifies himself almost immediately. "What are you waiting for?"

For you, dammit. I'm waiting on you to come back and be with me and the baby. "I... I just... hey! Feel this!" I pull his hand to my bump where our baby is doing acrobatics. The baby squirms and rolls in the womb, and Gage's eyes widen at the sensation of each ripple beneath his palm.

This is so messed up. Here's Gage, hand on my belly, unknowingly feeling his child happy and safe inside me. He looks at me, and I'm fighting the truth as it rises in my throat. "Gage..."

He pulls his hand away and throws it up like a stop sign. "Don't" he interrupts, and I'm reminded of another time he said that to me at the Howard house party. "Everything is as it should be. You've moved on, and so have I. No regrets."

The words sting because for at least one of us, it's not true. I haven't moved on, not even a little. I want him still, but now I can't have him so I do what Gage always said I do best. Duck and cover and change the subject.

We talk about his military career, and he fills me in on the particulars of being a reserve soldier working as an aviation mechanic for attack helicopters. He's been in training for the last twenty-five weeks, and it's changed him. There's no boy left in his voice. He's all man, even tougher and harder than before. Except with me. A softness lingers in his eyes and lips when he looks at me, and it kills me to think he might be sharing that with someone else by now. So I don't ask, because I don't really want to know.

"The uniform suits you." I finger the patch on his sleeve. His smile fades when Preston walks in.

"Dinner's ready," he says. "Who's hungry?"

The silence at the table is heavy and awkward, no one knowing quite what to say. Instead the conversation centers on meaningless tidbits of local news. When we finish, Preston stacks the dirty dishes, the silverware clanging against the plates with each bobble as he heads for the kitchen sink.

Gage clears his throat. "Where's your dad?"

"New Jersey." I wipe the corners of my mouth with a napkin. "He travels more now that Mama's gone. Keeps his mind off things."

He nods and grabs my hand. "How 'bout you? How are you since she's gone?"

"Depends on the day," I sigh. "I miss her, but she's still here in a million little ways." Like now, when Gage has come wandering back into my life the way she said he would.

Preston comes in with a plate of blonde brownies. Gage places one on his napkin but never actually takes a bite, only picks it apart with his fingers and leaves it lying there. After we finish, I stare at the sad, crumbled brownie that once looked so rich and promising and is now only a pile of nothing.

I give Gage the guest room at the top left of the stairs. Preston's been staying there on occasion, but for tonight, he'll camp at the foot of my bed on the blue chaise. Preston bear hugs Gage goodnight then slinks around the corner into my room.

The door clicks shut before we speak, and I pull his hand into mine. "I'm glad you're home. I missed your face," I whisper.

"I missed being here, but it looks as if everything's worked out for all of us." He quits looking at me and stares at his boots again.

"I guess so." I don't mean it. His moving on is destroying me and the future I promised our child. "I'm right next door." I point to the wall our rooms share.

"Okay," he mumbles and holds open the door.

I pause in the doorway and look back at him. He lifts his

head to stare back. "I hope you'll stay awhile?" I ask, my eyes burning with the tears threatening to overflow.

"Don't know. We'll see." Short and unemotional. That's never a good sign from Gage.

I nod then walk into the hallway as he shuts the door behind me. I don't move. I stand there, hands on my belly, comforting my baby over the lost promise of a life with his or her daddy. Every inclination in my body begs me to burst through the door and tell him everything. And not just for the baby's sake. I want him back, too. He's my soulmate, my other half. Life's been empty until he showed up on my doorstep a few hours ago. I long to hold him, the way I did in Edisto when we walked under the stars before making love. The memories are distant, the realization setting in this is truly over.

I panic, my heart butterflying in my chest, as I rush into my room and quickly sit on the bed, sucking in deep breaths to calm my racing pulse. Preston's on the chair, elbows on his knees, hands clasped and held against his forehead. He doesn't look up. "Gage has his own life now, Rayne. It doesn't include you. Can't you see that?"

"I do see that!" I scream at him. I hate him for saying the words out loud.

"Shhh! Keep your voice down. He's right next door." Preston points at the wall.

"So?" I throw my hands up in the air as the tears finally break free. "What the hell does it even matter anymore? My whole life's a lie. Everything's a mess, and this baby won't have a father."

Preston shoots to his feet, fire flashing in his eyes. "That's not fair, Rayne. I've been this baby's father in every sense of the word. You can't see what you do have for grieving what you don't!"

"I used to have it," I sob. "He used to love me, but he doesn't anymore."

Preston grabs my shoulders and shakes gently. "I love you, Rayne, but you won't give me the time of day because you're clinging to a dream that's never going to happen." He bends down, his face close to mine. "Never!"

"Please don't say that," I whimper, pulling away and sinking face-first into my pillow.

"Keep living in this fantasy land." His voice is cold, harsh.

I raise my head from the pillow as he walks to the other side of the room and glares at me over crossed arms. "I'm not living in a fantasy. I'm living in a hell of my own making!"

Suddenly he's mimicking me in a sappy, sing-song voice. "Oh Gage, put your hand on my belly and feel the baby move." He pauses and glowers at me, shaking his head. "Did you think he'd magically realize the truth and sweep you away to a happily ever after?"

"I... I..." I stammer.

The blood rushes to his face, tinting his cheeks pink. "I saw you in the reflection of the breakfast room windows, holding his hands on your belly. How do you think that makes me feel?" He's whisper-yelling, but the anger is fading, replaced with hurt, as his shoulders slump.

"It's killing you, Preston. I know! But I told you from the beginning I couldn't make promises. I love you. I do, but Gage has my heart. I can't give you something he has." There's no plainer way to say it.

He sits beside me on the bed, his breath ragged and uneven in the lull of our fighting. "I'm sorry," he says. "You're right. You warned me, and I wouldn't listen." He looks at the floor and pats my thigh.

"Forgive me, Preston. You deserve so much better than this. I only want you to be happy." I grab his hand and cradle it to my cheek.

"I'm happy when I'm with you," he insists. "And you made me promise to hold you to the pact. No decisions until after the baby's born. I know you're mad at me for reminding you about it, but…"

"I'm not mad. You're right. I know it, and that's why I haven't said anything to him… I won't… not yet…" Looking at him right now is impossible so I stare at the floor. "Maybe when the baby's born, and you're there, my thoughts will change. Maybe my heart will accept what's right in front of me. That's all I can promise. A lot of maybes."

"I'll take maybe over no any day," he says, "because while you believe in your dream, I also believe in mine."

At 4 A.M., the house is silent except for Preston's occasional snoring. I slip out of the bedroom and walk downstairs to the front porch swing, the only place to find clarity nowadays. The early morning air is crisp, and I pull my blanket tighter around my shoulders, swinging lazily back and forth. All the moments that made me fall in love with Gage come rushing back. All the moments that let me know I still love him.

My thoughts scatter at the squeak of the screen door opening.

"Gage? What are you doing?" He jumps, startled by my being there. As he shuts the door and turns to face me, the duffel bag in his hands becomes visible. "Where are you going?" I try hard to keep my voice from cracking.

"I'm leaving, Rayne. Causing problems between you and Preston isn't my intention. If I'd known… about y'all, the baby… I'd have never come back."

"You aren't causing problems. Please don't leave again."

He sighs. "I heard y'all arguing," he says as my eyes widen in embarrassment. "I couldn't hear words, only yelling. I'm smart enough to realize my coming here creates problems for you."

"You're not a problem," I insist, shaking my head.

He bites his lower lip. "I have a life of my own to get back to. It'd be easier for everyone if I just leave."

My lips quiver under the weight of his words. "Don't go. I've missed my best friend." I walk over and wrap my arms around his waist. He belongs here.

He drops his duffel bag on the porch floor, circles his arms around my shoulders, and hugs me tightly. "I'll always be your friend, but Preston deserves to be your best friend now. He loves you. Your baby's one blessed kid."

He breaks my grasp, picks up his bag, walks down the steps, and jumps into the driver's seat. The headlights come on and the door slams, a sound I know will serve as an audio reminder of the exact moment my hope died when I lost him all over again.

The taillights of his Scout fade, blending into the faint glow of streetlights on the horizon. I'm alone again and the emptiness returns, deeper than ever.

Inside the house, I cocoon myself in the blanket on the corner of the couch and look out toward the road, praying he'll reconsider and come back. A couple hours later, Preston stumbles down the stairs, confused.

"Where's Gage?" he asks, rubbing sleep from his eyes.

The road in front of the house is quiet, deserted. "He's gone," I say. "Again."

48

GAGE

The early morning air is chilly, especially in this damp parking garage. I shrug on my jacket, happy at least to have felt the cold on my skin—the rest of me numb. The senses deadened.

After an hour of leaning across the steering wheel, willing it to hold me up when my muscles refuse to do the job, headlights flash across the expanse of gray concrete as his car pulls into the first space. The one with the placard that reads—HOWARD, CEO.

I suck in a deep breath, as if the air will be infused with strength and calm, and get out of the Scout, falling in line behind him with perfectly-synced footsteps. He's far enough ahead that he doesn't notice me there. Close enough that I can catch him before the elevator arrives.

He presses the button then sets his briefcase at his wingtips as he readjusts his tie.

"Dad?"

He jerks around, hand still clenching his perfect Windsor knot. His eyes widen, pupils black as tar. "Gage? When did you—?"

"Last night. I went to see Rayne."

He drops his head and nods as he stares at the cement. The elevator doors open with a shrill ding, but he makes no move. They slide back together.

His brow furrows as he swallows multiple times. "How are you?"

"How do you think?"

His eyes rise to meet mine, and there, for the first time in my life, I'm completely in-tune with my dad. My pain reflects back at me as if he's a human mirror. His own still burns in him. A grim picture of my future.

"Why don't you and I grab a bite for breakfast?" He glances around the abandoned garage as if at any minute, Charlotte will arrive and find us. "There's a quiet diner on the opposite side of town. Few people. Good pancakes. It's where your mother and I used to meet."

Two short stacks sit in front of us, swimming in butter and syrup, mostly untouched. We discuss everything—Grandpa and Nana, my Army training, and the letter I sent. He asks me where I'm living, but I dodge the question, though I do enter my new cell phone number into his contacts.

I want to hear from him.

But only him.

One subject remains absent from the conversation. How can I say out loud to him what's really circulating in my brain? Preston's his son, too, and he shouldn't be stuck in the middle. Especially since he's lived the last 20 years in that exact position.

Instead, I quietly swallow the strong desire to drive back, punch Preston square in the nose, and rip his head off his shoulders. The truth restrains me.

I put all this in play. I asked him to comfort her. Be there for her.

Boy, did he ever.

I stare out the window at a line of passing cars, each one kicking up a few of the colorful leaves lying along the roadside. Beautiful reminders of what had once been alive and will soon be nothing more than brown, dried-up dust.

Familiar.

"Gage... I wish I'd had a chance to prepare you for..."

I raise my hand, stopping his words. "It's not your fault, Dad. I'm the one who left."

"You left because you were hurting."

"I left because I didn't want to be like you, Dad."

The words spit out with no filter. He swallows hard, nostrils flaring as tears rim his lower lashes, and shrinks back in the booth.

"I couldn't risk holding onto Rayne if that meant breaking her heart while she waited on me to get my head together. Crushing her to keep myself from that pain. But now I see..." I drop my fork. It clangs against the cheap diner china. "I hurt her anyways. Maybe more. And now she's with Preston."

Dad leans forward again and grabs my hand. It feels off, almost unnatural. This sort of compassion isn't something I grew up with. I try to pull away, but he grips my fingers harder. "No, Gage. You're better than me. You did what I couldn't do for your mother. You gave Rayne freedom when you couldn't give her yourself. You put her needs ahead of your own, because you loved harder and better than I ever could. You showed courage."

I snort. "Yeah—courage—but now I've lost everything. Forever this time. They're having a baby. Nothing will ever be the same. Never can be." I free my hand and gather my phone and wallet from the table. "A baby needs both its parents. I should know."

"I wish you'd stay a little while longer. If you could only see the things I see. Understand the way I do. Experience brings so much clarity. Don't lose hope, son."

Hope? There is none, and that's why I have to go. I stand up, throw a twenty on the table, and pull on my jacket. "I have to go."

I glance at the passenger seat as the gravel of the driveway crunches beneath my tires. She was supposed to be sitting there.

She was always supposed to be there.

Now she never will.

My stomach somersaults, and I have to scramble from the driver's seat and rush to the cluster of palms near the sidewalk. I drop to all fours as the convenience store coffee I grabbed on the road revisits me repeatedly. I sit back on my knees, wiping the sweat from my forehead.

The house I wanted so much is in front of me, and I can barely look at it because instead of the marine blue siding with white trim we'd once imagined, now I only see the weathered, gray wood, the dilapidated staircase, and the overgrown underbrush.

The future is gone. What could've been is gone. Only reality exists.

I grip the handrail, my duffel thrown over my shoulder, and trudge to the front porch. The sun's last rays warm the surface of the cold, choppy water that rushes to shore in foamy gurgles. The small waves slap the sand and rock jetties, spraying water into the air. As if the ocean is crying along with me.

I reach into my pocket for the keys and turn the corner.

There it is—the swing, swaying on a ghostly breeze, the chains groaning under some invisible weight. My lungs forget how to expand, and I gasp for air, my head spinning from the lack of oxygen. I toss my duffel and keys to the ground and sit on the swing, running my fingers over the wooden slats.

This was for her. This was all for her.

I scream out, so loud and unexpected, that a few seagulls nesting in the dunes take flight. The tears streak my face, and I lie down and pull my knees up to my chest.

I've lost her.

49

RAYNE

I'm tired of seeing Preston clench his jaw.

His 'stressed out' tick is habitual around me. Probably because I'm acting like a sullen brat, moping around the house except for the hours when I'm working at the coffee-house, which are few and far between since Sharon cut my shifts because she's worried about my swollen ankles that are muffin-topping out of my socks. Consequently, I spend lots of time on the couch, lying under piles of blankets and drowning my sorrows in infinite amounts of sweet tea.

The weeks since Gage left have been gloomy, gray as the blanket of clouds and drizzle that refuses to let up. If you ask me, my grief has permanently shifted the atmosphere into some sort of global depression, especially when every day's the same with me standing still and everyone else moving forward with life. Wake, shower, eat, watch TV, work, eat, sleep, and repeat, sometimes but not always in that exact order.

"What do you want to do today?" Preston's sitting in the corner chair looking out the window. He only had one class, and it was cancelled so he dropped everything and came here. There's no lamp on and only minimal light filtering through the glass, but from my angle, his jaw's moving. *Clench. Clench. Clench.*

I groan, repositioning my ever-expanding body on the cushions, and yank the covers to my chin. "Don't know." The words come out breathy and uneven. Who knew adding twenty-seven pounds would make you feel like a dump truck?

From across the room, his eyes connect with mine. "Don't do this, Rayne."

I already know what he's going to say, and I already know he's right. But I don't care. I'm pregnant and I don't want to face reality right now, so come hell or high-water I'm going to lay my ass on this couch and sulk about Gage even if it kills me. "Do what?"

Preston gets up, walks across the room, and kneels on the floor. "Don't lock yourself up in this house and quit living. For the last month and a half, you've barely budged. Your eyes are swollen. Your hair's a wreck."

"If you're trying to make me feel better, you suck."

Preston's eyes dart back and forth over mine. "I'm not insulting you. I'm trying to wake you up! I get it. You love him. He left again, but I'm here."

He is, and I love him for it. Just not as much as I love Gage —who broke my heart again and again. Gage, who so easily lost faith in what we had. "Why did he leave again, Preston?" My voice quivers with each syllable. "Why couldn't he do the math and figure out..."

"He's the father?" Preston arches his eyebrows. "You told him I 'comforted' you when your Mama died. That was only a few days after y'all..." He pauses and swallows hard. "Besides, we'd all found out our parents weren't who they pretended to be. It's not hard to see how Gage might be a little screwed up in the whole 'love' area." He snorts. "We might all be."

He's right. We're all broken. Our families, our lives, ourselves, and no matter how hard we try, it's possible the pieces won't ever fit back into place. "Has he called you? Texted?"

"No." Preston shakes his head and runs his hand down the side of my face, stopping to cup my cheek in his palm. "I know we're all messed up, but it'll get better. I promise." He reaches down and tucks the blanket around me. "Take a nap. I'm gonna work on putting the crib together, and when you wake up, we're getting outta here for a while."

I force a smile and a nod, mostly to get some time to myself so I can think about Gage. The thought of him tucked away somewhere, pining for me is both heartbreaking and comforting. In that daydream, he's still mine. It's the other one that kills me—the thought of him in the arms of another. The vision creeps into the cracks of my happier daydreams, with the nagging thoughts that this must be the case. It's the only reason he hasn't called, hasn't tried to win me back.

I clamp my eyes together and pray for sleep to come, pray for the pain to subside, and when the edges of darkness filter through, I welcome them.

Something's buzzing. I flutter my eyes and lift my head to better see the mantle clock. A little after noon, which means I've been asleep for an hour and a half. Again the buzzing starts, and I glance around for the culprit. Preston left his phone on the side table.

I push myself up off the couch and walk over to grab it. If there's something he's needed for at work, Charlotte will be pissed if he doesn't respond right away, but as I pick it up, it's not Charlotte's name on the screen. It's Ashlyn's.

What does she want? Call it hormones, call it a Southern woman's right to know, but no way in hell am I not reading that text.

<Ashlyn> *Looking for you. Call me when you're not with HER.*

How dare she call me "HER." But that's not the most disturbing part. As I thumb through the listing, multiple texts from Ashlyn, dating back to the week Gage left again, fill the screen. I click open a few, the fire coursing through my veins with each word.

<Ashlyn> *You never struck me as a guy who liked sloppy seconds.*

Skank. With her, it'd be more like sloppy double digits.

<Ashlyn> *Per our earlier discussion, I like it hot and sweaty. It really gets my body going.*

Why were they talking about her body dripping with sweat?

<Ashlyn> *Why are U with her if baby's not yours? WTF?*

Oh dear God. She knows the truth. He had to tell her. How could he do this to me?

My heart thumps loud in my ears, like tribal drums calling for Preston's head to roll. I run to the end of the stairs and yell up at him. "Preston! Get down here now!"

Within seconds he runs down the stairs so fast he nearly plows into me at the bottom. One look at my face and he steels up, jerking to a stop. "Is it the baby? Are you..."

"What the hell is this?" I throw his phone at him, plugging him in the chest. "How dare you talk to her about me! How dare you tell her our secret? I hate you, Preston! I really hate you!"

He reaches down and grabs the phone from where it's fallen to the carpet and looks at the screen. A part of me wants him to deny it, to pretend it's all some giant hoax, but when he looks back up at me, eyes wide, skin pale, the truth is evident. "This is all a mistake..."

"Hell yeah, it's a mistake. My mistake! I trusted you, and now you're talking to her? About me? About the baby? Is this your plan? Some sort of revenge?"

"No! It's nothing like that. It's—"

"Oh really? Sloppy seconds? She's hot and sweaty? The baby isn't yours? How would she know that if you didn't tell her?"

"Okay. I did tell her. I freaked out when Gage showed up and you got all depressed. But it's nothing... she and I... we've been friends forever..."

"She's no friend of mine! You had no right! Go be with her. Make your mom happy!"

"I don't want her. Look at the phone." He shoves it in my face. The repetition of her name in the sender line makes me want to puke. "Look. How many did I respond to?" I set my jaw and turn my head away from him. "None. Not one reply."

"Uh, 'per our discussion' sounds a lot like replying." The stink eye from over my shoulder riles him up.

He clenches his fists and slams them into his thighs. "That was from work. We signed a new client—a yoga studio downtown. They gave us free passes to different classes, and she wanted the hot yoga. That text was just her fooling around."

"That's right. My bad." I whirl around and slap my hand across my heart. "Ashlyn is so innocent. She'd never be a psychotic bitch on purpose. She'll do anything she can to get you." The rage whips within me, slamming into my insides like it might blow me apart. A searing pain shoots through my abdomen causing me to grit my teeth for a second to withstand the pain. Preston takes my shoulders and walks me to the armchair. I sit down and breathe through it.

"I'm not encouraging her. She's just jealous and petty, but she doesn't mean..."

"Stop it. You may not be encouraging it, but you sure aren't discouraging it either. I'm done with this. I let Gage leave without telling him about the baby because of our agreement, and then you carry on with her?"

Preston jumps to his feet. "You're right. I'm putting an end to this. Right now." He slips his phone from his pocket and calls her number. Before she answers, he puts it on speakerphone.

Her honeyed voice spills through the line. "Hey Pres. Finally you call."

"Ashlyn, I'm sick of these texts. I have to deal with you at work, but that's it. Do not text me. Do not talk about Rayne. Do not make advances at me. And, most of all, don't you dare even breathe a word of Rayne's baby to anyone or I'll tell my dad and you'll never work at the company again. Leave us alone."

"She's sitting there, isn't she?" Her voice is silky-smooth, unscathed by his words. "Say whatever you need to make her happy and keep her from having one of those psychotic melt-downs like her dead Mama. You and I will be together, Preston. You know it. I know it. That fat, pregnant, gold-digger better know it. I won't let her stand in our way."

Before he responds the line goes dead, and with it, my hopes this situation will be over.

50

GAGE

"Some housewarming party this is," Taryn leans over and says, wiggling her fingers in air quotes. She sits beside me, arms folded, eyes shifting around the room and stops only to lean back and flick apart the blinds on the picture window behind us, as if she's expecting the cops to show at any minute.

In her defense, the rap music is pretty loud, vibrating the newly-hung picture frames on Farrah and Clara Jean's apartment walls. Still, it's a moot point to worry over the neighbors calling the cops when all the neighbors are busy dancing and shooting tequila in your living room.

She sighs loudly, like her twin powers will have some cosmic effect on Farrah. I smile. Taryn looks the part of an 18-year-old, and dresses the part, too, though her style ranges more on the conservative end of the spectrum as opposed to Farrah's over-the-top, so-revealing-she-might-as-well-be-wearing-a-bikini wardrobe. She doesn't act her age, though. Uber mature, thoughtful, and intelligent, she's a stark contrast to her sister's party-girl attitude.

That's probably why Taryn and I have bonded as cousins

ten times more than Farrah and I have. Every time I speak, Taryn stares at me as if I'm a jigsaw puzzle in pants, some experiment she can pick apart and dissect like the fetal pigs from her medical classes, then bandage up again in like-new condition.

She leans forward and picks up a bowl of fried mozzarella sticks and crinkles her nose, tossing it back on the table. If this were Taryn's party, there'd be petit fours and finger sandwiches and punch. Traditional Southern stuff. Not the wings, dips, fried cheese, beer-and-liquor-fest this is.

Clara Jean weaves through the crowd and sits on the coffee table across from me and Taryn. She hands us each a shot glass of tequila and a wedge of lime. "Shoot 'em!" she laughs, and I throw mine back then bite the lime, its sour fingers wrapping around my tongue.

Taryn stares at hers, holding them both mid-air. "Go ahead," I say, leaning over to her ear. "It can only make this party better or make you not care. Win-win."

She smiles and chucks it back, lapsing into some sort of full body shiver as she swallows. Clara Jean reaches for the shot glasses but pulls back when her phone buzzes. She squeezes it out of her skin-tight leather pants and glances at the screen, eyes narrowed.

Taryn leans forward and grabs her arm. "Is it him again?"

She nods, and I can't help noticing the bright redness that creeps into her cheeks. "Same old thing. I miss you. I love you. I want to get back together."

"Yeah, you've only heard that one about nine hundred times."

"Yep, and that's 899 times too many. I'm done with it." Clara Jean says it with authority, but her voice trembles on the back end like she's putting on a front. She's nowhere near as strong as she says she is.

She scoops up the glasses and heads to the kitchen, where

once again she pauses by the sink to check her texts. Damn, this guy is persistent, and not in a good way.

"He cheated on her," Taryn whispers. "More times than I can count. Talked down to her, telling her no other guy would want her. Did a crazy number on her self-esteem."

"Her?" I shake my head. No way. "But Clara Jean's a beautiful girl. She's smart and funny. Why does she listen to that?"

Taryn shrugs. "If someone tells you that you suck long enough, you eventually start to believe them." She stops and stares at Clara Jean and bites her lower lip. "She keeps going back because he's her first love. First love's a bitch, and it's rarely love at all. More like a walk down Hell's highway."

The edge in her tone hints that she speaks from experience. And then I realize these two wonderful girls are reeling because of dipshit guys, and my mind immediately goes to Rayne. Is this the way she feels about our relationship? Is that why she's with Preston now? Because I'm the dipshit guy who messed her up?

But no matter what happened between me and Rayne, what we had was real love. I know because I still feel it, even more if that's possible.

Three hard knocks sound at the door and Taryn immediately stiffens, as if the police are about to charge in and throw everyone in handcuffs. She does a quick count, noting each guest with a head tick. "Who could that be? Everyone's already here."

Clara Jean ducks out of the kitchen and walks to the door, pausing to smooth her shirt and hair before opening it. She takes a deep breath and blows it out slowly. She obviously knows who's waiting on the other side.

The door swings partway in when a blond guy in a gray sweatshirt with Greek letters grabs it, throwing it the rest of the way open. Behind me Taryn groans, confirming my suspicions. He grips Clara Jean's elbow and directs her into the hallway leading to the bedrooms, but she resists, pushing back against him.

"I told you it wasn't happening again, Jeremy. I'm over it."

He jerks her closer to him, leaning down to look her almost eye-to-eye. "You know you always come back to me."

"Not anymore. Never again." Clara Jean shakes her head profusely, tears welling in her eyes as she wrings her hands. "Now I want you to leave."

"I'm not going anywhere until you talk to me," he growls.

Something snaps inside me. The way he's hovering over her. The way she's shrinking under his glare. I push through the crowd and grab her shoulders, pulling her backwards beside me. "I think she's made it clear she's done. So get outta here."

His attention is now fully directed at me. "Says who?"

"Says me."

"And who's me?"

"You're looking at him. Leave Clara Jean alone. She's with me now."

The crowd gasps, people exchanging open-mouthed glances. Taryn pushes through the bodies, coming into the little circle that's formed around our showdown.

"Is this true?" Jeremy laughs, panning his hand up and down in front of me.

The apartment is silent, the music on pause, everyone's eyes glued to the scene. Clara Jean flits her eyes between me and Jeremy, then wordlessly reaches out and twines her fingers with mine.

The laughing halts, and his face hardens like stone, jaw clenched. He shakes his head and turns to go, then whirls around with a balled fist and lands a punch square on my chin. I trip backwards against the wall, knocking the back of my head into the sheetrock. Farrah screams, so loud it adds to the ringing in my head, and sweet, conservative Taryn runs by the door and says, "Hey Jeremy!"

When he turns around, she kicks him square in the man-biscuits and he drops to his knees on the welcome mat where she slams the door in his face and slides the lock in place.

My head spins and I'm not sure if it's from the hit or watching Taryn level some justice on a dipshit guy. Maybe both.

Clara Jean sobs into her palms and runs to her bedroom, locking the door behind her.

A couple hours later, I'm on my way to the bathroom when I pass Clara Jean's room. The door's cracked open now, the only light coming from the outside courtyard lamppost. A series of grunts catches my attention, and I push the door open wider, glass clinking as it meets the wooden door. My boot kicks one of the objects and it rolls into a sliver of light. A vodka mini bottle. She's just behind it, crumpled on the floor, head and arms slung over her trashcan.

Terrific. She's drunk.

"Clara Jean?" I ask, squatting down beside her. She lifts her head slightly and darts her eyes up at me. Even in the dark, mascara is visible in rivers down her face.

All because of some dipshit.

"I'll be right back," I say, slipping out of her room and into the bathroom where I grab a cool washcloth. I creep back to her room, kneel down, and press it to her forehead. We sit in silence for several minutes, and I'm unsure whether she's just quiet or passed out, but then she speaks, slowly in slurred words.

"Your ex? Was she mean like that?"

"No. never."

"Did she cheat on you?"

"No."

"Did she appreciate you?"

"Always."

"Did she make promises and flake out?"

"Nope."

"Can I ask you a question, Gage?"

"Sure."

"If she was so great, then why is she your ex?"

"Because I made a stupid decision. Took a gamble that she'd wait for me, but... she didn't. She moved on."

I half-expect another question, but I check, and her eyes are closed, mouth slightly open. I get to my feet and scoop her in my arms, carry her to the bed, and lay her down. I take off her shoes and toss them in the corner, then grab a blanket from her desk chair and cover her.

I tiptoe to the door and ease it open, trying not to wake her. "Your ex is the one who made a mistake. Moving on from you? She's an idiot. You deserve better." When I turn around, her eyes are still closed, but she's talking to me just the same.

51

RAYNE

"I won't let her stand in our way." Ashlyn's threat makes loops in my head as I clean tables on my Friday morning shift. Preston says it's nothing to worry about, but her tone suggested otherwise. Plus, Preston doesn't know we've already waged war in round one last year at the Howard house party. She's out for blood.

I sweep all the crumbs into a pile and off into my palm, then wipe my hands over the trash bin. The crowd's much thinner now than when I worked morning shifts this summer. The late November temperatures have finally dipped into the 40s and the constant drizzle makes it pretty darn miserable. Plus, all the kids I know who used to come in here are in the throes of fall semester. And I'm still here in the coffeehouse—going nowhere.

"I think you got that table just about clean enough, hun." Sharon walks behind me, rubs my shoulders then takes the dishrag from my hand. "Your Mama'd die if she saw you mopin' around here like this."

"Little late for that one." In my side-eye glare, Sharon tilts her head and frowns in that I'm-gonna-whip-your-butt-if-you-don't-straighten-up way all Southern Mamas have perfected. In some ways, she's sort of a surrogate Mama, always doling out advice and suggestions without my asking. The way she huffs out a huge breath, I know I'm in for another lecture.

"Youngin' you know what I mean. All your Mama ever wanted was for you to be happy. Now she ain't here no more, but I am. The town is. We're gonna see you through because that's what Southern folks do."

I snort-laugh and shake my head. "Really? Cause I thought they only gossiped about you behind your back."

She grabs my chin and pulls me to facing her. She licks her lips the way she always does when a big lecture's coming on, but I can't imagine anything she says changing my mind. I'm pretty darn sure small-town politics suck. "Now you look me in the eye. Living in a small town is a double-edged sword, baby. Yeah, they all up in your business, and yeah, they love to share the dirt when they got it. But I'mma tell you something, and don't you forget it. We ain't all perfect, and we run our mouths when we just need to shut the hell up, but when one of us is in trouble, you best bet we all gonna band together and figure it out."

"That all sounds... quaint... but I must be the exception. Since the great casserole apocalypse after Mama died, I haven't seen much of this town making any efforts with me."

The smug grin on her face hints that she knows something I don't. "But that's a two-way street, now ain't it?"

Why should I have to be the bigger person here? They're the ones that gawked at Mama's Piggly Wiggly scene and called me names for the whole Preston debacle. Of course, maybe we did kind of bring some of that on ourselves, but still...

I drop my head and stare at my shoes. "Maybe you'll feel different after you see this." Sharon walks behind the counter and pulls out a giant basket brimming with diapers, wipes, bottles, and onesies, all tied up in cellophane with a big yellow bow. "Mrs. McAlister and her ladies' league put this together for you and dropped it off last night." I'll be damned. A few tears wet the corners of my eyelashes. Stupid hormones. "People might surprise ya, if you give 'em the chance."

"That's good advice." Her voice surprises me and simultaneously sends chills up my backbone. I turn around. Charlotte, in a sapphire blue pantsuit, manages a soft smile, a look I haven't seen on her before. I'd like to take it at face value, but I know her too well. She doesn't make courtesy calls. Her visits are really missions, usually having to do with some unpleasant sort of business. Every muscle clenches, and the baby kicks in response.

"Charlotte? Why are you here?"

"I wonder if we might chat a moment?"

Sharon strokes my forearm. "You're due a ten-minute break. Those ankles need it." She points to the table I just finished cleaning. "Y'all take the window seat, and I'll bring you both a coffee. Decaf for you, missy."

"Mine to-go, please," Charlotte calls after her as she struts to the table and sits down, crossing her legs. She pats the table across from her with an invitation to join. I sit, careful to slide my chair back a few inches. I never trust being too close to her. "You know I don't mince words, so I'll get to the point. I'd like to speak with you about Preston and this situation with Ashlyn."

Of course she does. The old kick-me-when-I'm-down maneuver. I brace myself for the spiel about how Preston and Ashlyn are made for each other, and I'm a stumbling block on their path to happily ever after. "Look, I've already heard about how I'm a—"

"No dear, you misunderstand me. I've come to tell you first-hand that I've counseled her and warned her to keep a distance."

Huh? There's no freaking way she just said that, but she's calmly looking at me as if her words make perfect sense.

Preston must've given her an ultimatum. There's no way she'd endorse me over Ashlyn. "Because Preston wants her to or you want her to?"

She purses her lips and snaps her head back as if incensed I question her motives. "Preston's happiness and well-being is of utmost importance to me. That being said, there are certain... expectations... in Southern society that one dates and makes a life with someone of... compatible breeding. My son, however, displays a penchant for the less refined, uncultivated life. Preston has an affinity for it, much like his father."

I don't get her. Is she trying to be a bitch? Or is she trying to be nice and just screwing it up? "Should I take this as an insult?"

"No. I simply mean you have not been accustomed to the demands of an upper-class upbringing, but Preston sees something in you, something worth committing to. My son is an upstanding young man, doing all of us a great favor. He's protecting you and your child, but he's also protecting our family name, our firm. You see, for years after Jackson's indiscretion, I worked relentlessly in damage control, so the Howard name wouldn't be marred by rumors and gossip. Now Preston is picking up that flag, and we owe it to him to be a united front of support."

"I agree. Preston is concerned about—"

"Very well." With a wave of her hand, she shushes me before I finish. "To reiterate, Ashlyn is no threat, lots of talk but harmless, and also Preston needs our support. He's under a terrific amount of stress. Do what you can to ease his suffering. I know I'll do anything for my son."

"Of course, Charlotte," I nod as Sharon's words bounce around in my head. Maybe I have no reason to question Charlotte's motives. I'm 99.9-percent sure she loathes me, but maybe she's really offering me an olive branch for Preston's sake—a pleasant surprise, like Sharon suggested—as long as I'm open to it.

"I've enjoyed our chat, but I must get back to the office." We both stand up, Charlotte side-hugs me and heads for the door, turning back briefly. "It almost slipped my mind. In light of the tension between you and Ashlyn, and the fact that her family is traditionally a guest at our Thanksgiving meal, I told Preston to consider spending the day with you and your father. A low-key affair might do him some good. Bye now." She wiggles her fingers and glides out the door.

Sharon steps behind me, and we watch Charlotte slide behind the wheel of her BMW and peel out of the parking space. "Ya see? What'd I tell ya?"

I force a smile, but inside my stomach churns. This new alliance may very well be the product of Preston's coercion or a goodwill gesture on Charlotte's part to please him, but it's evident she still thinks I'm not worthy. And if she can't hide it from me, how in the world could she convince Ashlyn to leave it alone? The questions drop on my shoulders like a heavy blanket.

I'm still thinking about it two weeks later as I step on the elevator at the doctor's office. Now more than ever, the gravity of what's at stake if Ashlyn makes good on her threat haunts me. The ultrasound photo in my hand makes it all the more real, the legs and arms squished so tightly in the womb like a blob of flesh. One month left, and our baby will be here. The last stop before 'D-day.'

I think about Preston. How he's been there for every milestone and all the little bits in between. Just last week, he spent Thanksgiving with me and Daddy, suffering through my first attempt at cornbread dressing and candied yams, edible, but nowhere near the caliber of Mama's. He'll be there when the big day comes, too, and as grateful as I am, I'll be wishing it was Gage. I can't help it.

The elevator dings and the doors open to the parking garage. I'm in the second row to the left. I walk quickly to the car. Something about the parking garage freaks me out. As I open the rear door to toss in my purse, I lose grip on the ultra-sound print-out and it goes flying, down, and under the back fender. Terrific. Nothing like being eight months pregnant on all fours, scrounging around on a concrete floor.

I stretch my arm under, my fingers flicking around before they make contact with the smooth paper. I'm pulling it out when someone yells my name.

I look up as a sudden, searing pain explodes across my forehead.

<hr>

The world comes back to me in flashes.

Someone tells me to hang on, but my eyes are heavy, almost weighted.

Blackness.

The high-pitched beeps of medical equipment.

Blackness.

Preston's voice, a higher octave than usual.

Blackness.

The frail whimper of a baby.

Blackness.

The sounds of a television playing somewhere in the background. Only this time, the images are registering, kicking out the nothingness.

I flutter my eyes. A sitcom is playing on a TV suspended in the corner of the room, which is very white—too white. It smells like bleach and the sweet chemical scent of latex gloves.

A rhythmic beep undercuts the TV dialogue, and over my left shoulder, a small machine prints out up-and-down patterns of a heart rate on a long strip of paper. It's only when the machine makes a whirring sound I realize it's connected to me. The cuff on my arm tightens, stops, then releases slowly.

It's like putting together a jigsaw puzzle, but not understanding what picture will emerge. I'm in a hospital. But why? Why can't I remember? Recalling facts is futile, like my brain's ramming headfirst into a concrete wall. The last thing I recall is looking at the sonogram picture. The sonogram. My baby.

My arms are heavy and largely immobile, but with concentration I'm able to slide my fingers over my belly. Instead of baby legs swirling below the skin, I feel nothing but soft, swollen skin through the thin cotton gown. I slide my hand down and find a tender spot just below where my jeans would sit, as if someone's wrapped a rubber band around my waist. My baby's gone. What happened to my baby?

"Ga—Gage," I whisper. In my head I'm screaming, but my voice doesn't match up. It's weak. "Gage, are you there?"

In a flash, Preston is by my side, leaning over, touching my face. "It's me. Preston. I'm here, Rayne." He looks away, yelling over his shoulder, "She's awake!" then reaches down, pulling my fingers away from the cut.

"Where's my baby? What happened to my baby?" I'm clawing at his hand with all the strength I can muster. I'm empty. There's a void where our baby used to be. It's gone. And I don't know where. *Please God, don't let him tell me my baby's gone.*

"Shhh..." He pulls both my hands into one of his and strokes my forehead with the other. "The baby's here. He's going to be fine."

"He?" I can barely muster the words. My baby's not gone. He's here. He's okay. Gage and I have a son. But somehow I've missed the whole thing. My baby came into this world without my knowing and without his daddy here to see it. Oh God, we've let down this little life so much already by playing stupid games and letting circumstances become bigger than this. This was supposed to be ours.

"You have a son. He's in the NICU because his lungs needed a little help from arriving early. But the doctors say he's tough like his mama," Preston says as my daddy rushes into the room.

"Doctor's on his way," he says out of breath. "Glad to see you awake, baby girl."

I squeeze my eyes closed—it's the only way I can forcefully step back from the storm raging in my head and try to make sense of what's going on—but no matter how hard I try, nothing adds up. "Why am I here? Why can't I remember?" Someone must know something.

"The doctor said this was a possibility," says Daddy, an ominous note undercutting his tone.

"What? What's a possibility?" Tears finally slip down my cheeks, which, in some odd way, is a relief. Before, my body seemed slower and non-responsive. It's finally catching up.

"Calm down." Preston pads his fingertips below my lashes to whisk away the tears. "You need to heal—for yourself and the baby. I'll tell you everything."

He sits down on the bed covers, still holding my hands. "You were attacked this morning in the parking garage at the doctor's office. Someone hit you on the head, and it knocked you out. You were only there a few minutes before someone found you and called EMS. You have a concussion, which caused you to lose consciousness for a while. The trauma caused the baby's heart rate to spike, so they performed an emergency C-section. He's early, but at 35 weeks, he should only have to be in the incubator for a couple days."

The pounding in my head gets louder, like a drumline at the Christmas parade. Unbearable. "Why can't I remember any of this?"

"The doctors warned you may have some memory loss, especially around the incident. It could be permanent or only temporary. They don't know." As he finishes, the doctor and two nurses rush in, sweeping everyone away from the bed and converging on me like vultures on a dead opossum, shining lights in my eyes and asking me to focus on their moving fingers. Up and down, back and forth, one corner to the other, and suddenly everything's blurry and the room spins.

The snare drum in my head intensifies with the dizziness, and I have to close my eyes and escape into the darkness to keep from hurling. The beeping monitor runs triple time. The cinched line across my lower belly radiates a deep ache throughout my abdomen, and I don't realize I'm tense and holding myself up until the doctor takes my shoulders and lowers me back onto the pillows.

"You need to relax. After a head injury and major surgery, your body needs to heal," says the doctor. "Stress is only going to set you back." He turns to Preston and Daddy. "There'll be time later to get more details about the attack. Right now, she needs to rest. Recuperate." He pats my hand and slides the chart back into the plastic holder on the door and follows the two nurses out.

Daddy walks over and kisses me, saying he's going to the cafeteria for a cup of coffee and will be back later. After the door closes behind him, Preston once again sits on the edge of my bed. "You need to sleep so you can get stronger. So you can see the baby. But, maybe this will bring you sweet dreams." He leans forward, holding his phone out toward me. There on the screen is a baby, so small, so perfect. I know he's mine, because the first thing I see is Gage's nose. I'm crying again and not just because I haven't held him yet. It's because I miss him. I miss Gage, and seeing his baby, his flesh and blood, every day without being able to share that with him is going to kill me.

"Sleep now." Preston brushes my hair to the sides and kisses my forehead. "I'll be here when you wake up." And with his words, I let go and fade into blackness, my escape from reality.

An hour or so later, the new nurse comes in at shift change, writing her name and contact information on the whiteboard by the door. It's not quite nighttime yet, probably around four o'clock because faint remnants of sunlight are still streaming through the big double windows overlooking the parking lot. I take it all in through one slitted eye, not letting anyone know I'm awake. It's easier than having to talk about everything.

She carries in a large brown bag and hands it to Preston. "These are her personal effects. Clothes, shoes. Her jewelry and anything in her pockets was put into the plastic bag on top," she says.

"Thank you, ma'am." He takes the bag and places it on the rolling bedside table as the nurse walks out. He glances in, then rifles through and pulls out a tattered note I've carried with me religiously for the past eight months. I can't bear watching him with Mama's last words to me, her reassurances that Gage's and my love was real. True. Lasting. Preston's reading it, knowing it'd been on me when I was at the sonogram, will destroy him. He doesn't deserve that. He deserves someone who can give him her whole heart, because he's wonderful. Now he knows for sure that's not me, because I'm still living in a dream world where Gage loves, wants, and needs me.

He turns the paper over and something falls to the linoleum with a metallic tinkle. "What's this?" he mumbles as he bends down and retrieves the small, pewter "67" charm, flipping it over and over in his fingers before looking at me. He sighs loudly and pries up a corner of the tape, which held the charm, and secures it once again to the note. Sliding his cell phone from the pocket of his jeans, he slips out the door into the hallway.

*O*ne thing I've discovered in my time with the Harrington family is that Grandpa and Nana are all about traditions. Holidays, family dinners, even football tailgating. One such event—the annual post-Thanksgiving barbecue held the weekend after the turkey extravaganza—is a sort of farewell to Fall and Grandpa's whole-hog smoker that'll lie dormant for Charleston's standard six weeks of mild winter.

I drove in last night, as did Taryn from her dorm at USC, to spend the night with them and help get everything organized. A large group is coming, an eclectic mix of Nana's gardening club members and Grandpa's old Army buddies. Taryn and I'd spent much of last night working side by side, polishing Nana's silver, which she insisted on using for barbecue, and rubbing the water spots off the iced tea goblets. Only Nana can make a backyard barbecue the stuff of social elegance.

Taryn broached the subject of Rayne several times, but I always diverted the topic to something about her semester finals or when she'd hear back on her medical school applications. But she's not the type to give in.

It's evident this morning I'm in for round two when Farrah

walks in, making a beeline to the table where Taryn and I are tasked with emptying potato chips into an assortment of crystal bowls. Farrah, giddy as always, can't wait to tell me that Clara Jean is coming this afternoon, and "Oh yeah, she's kinda in love with you."

Taryn shoots Farrah a look that could melt glaciers, but Farrah shrugs and continues. Apparently, I'm all Clara Jean can talk about and she thinks we'd be great together. She rattles off the rest of her gossip then saunters off to find Nana, completely unaware of the swing she just took at my messed-up heart or the fact that Taryn may now be plotting to kill her or sew her lips shut.

Taryn's eyes burn into me, and I glance over at her, biting her lip, ready to plunge in again for the umpteenth time. "Gage, I think we should talk about—"

"Nope. Not interested. Thanks." I crumple up the chip bag and toss it in the garbage, then head into the house away from Taryn and all her uncomfortable questions.

———

My empty plate sits on the picnic table, faint smears of leftover sauce around the edges. I lean back in my chair and take a pull on my beer. Farrah skips up to the table, Taryn hot on her heels.

"Oh, Ga-age," she sing-songs. "Clara Jean is looking for you."

"He doesn't care about Clara Jean like that!" Taryn fumes and jerks Farrah around by the arm. "Drop it!"

I snort. How can either of them know what I want or need? Hell, I don't even know. What I do know is I'm sick of everybody in my life always making decisions that affect me without me being a part of it.

"How do you know how I feel about anyone or anything?"

My words shoot out like a spear, and from the way Taryn pivots in my direction, it's obviously a direct hit. She's got a story as well. A secret heartbreak that's still eating at her.

"If you'd ever sit down and talk to me about it, then maybe you'd realize I totally get it. I've been in your shoes!"

"You have no idea what you're talking about."

"Oh really, Gage? You're still not over your ex. I know this. You know this." She takes a wide stance, her fingers gripping her hips. "Clara Jean is our friend, and she likes you. But you can't lead her on. That's not fair to either of you. You barely talk to me, only give me cryptic tidbits here and there. You won't let me in, and I'm smart enough to know what that means. You're still in love with her, that girl from the picture. Slow down and give it time."

What the hell is time going to do? Make me want her more? Drive me a little crazier every day? "Time? You have no idea about the time I've spent hoping and praying we'd find our way back, and for what? To find out she's moved on."

"You said yourself you knew that was a possibility when you left."

I stand up and slam my bottle down on the wooden table and stomp toward the porch where no one's standing and can overhear our argument. How dare she insinuate Rayne's moving on should be laid at my doorstep. Heap the blame on me like everyone else in my life always has. She has no idea the things that've happened. "Fine. Blame me. It's all my fault."

Taryn grabs my arm, but I shirk her touch. The fire in her eyes dwindles, replaced with sadness. Pity. "I'm not blaming anyone, Gage. I see the pain in your eyes. I just want you to talk, get it all out."

"I don't want to talk. I want to forget. Move on. Like she did."

She stomps her foot on the concrete pad. "Dammit! Why aren't you listening when I—"

"Take all your opinions and go to hell, Taryn. You don't even know me." The words sour on my tongue before they even make it into the air. I've always heard to be careful what you say. Once words are said, they can never be unsaid. And as much as I hate hurting Taryn, I just need everyone to butt out. Leave me alone.

Her bottom lip trembles, the tears flowing in buckets, as she rips away from Farrah and runs into the house. Through the window, I watch her dart up to her room. Farrah's behind her.

Damn.

A voice behind me makes me jump. "What was that about?"

Clara Jean walks up on the porch beside me, her brown hair pulled back into a ponytail, exposing the slope of her long neck as it runs into the black silk blouse.

I sigh and shove my hands in my pockets, leaning back onto the porch rail. "Taryn thinking she's the god of everything."

"Okay?" She beckons me to continue with a wave of her fingers.

"She says I'm not ready to move on yet. That I'm still not over my ex. But I say I'm ready to try." The words—the lies—fall out of my mouth with such ease. How do you move on from your soulmate? How exactly does that work? Rayne did it. Hell, she's having a baby with him, and here I am having to force myself to talk to a girl who's looking at me like her own personal bowl of chocolate. But I'm so not interested.

Maybe I can make myself interested. Maybe if I just get it over with, then whatever damn wall is around my heart will break.

"I think you'd know best, right?" She giggles and brushes my hair from my forehead. "Taryn's super protective of everyone in her life. She means well, but—"

"But what?"

"If you're ready to move on, you should." She takes a step closer to me, my back pinned to the porch post, the peaks and valleys of her body bumping into mine, her face mere inches away. "I know one person who'd be happy about it."

"Who?" I know who. It's pretty damn obvious she's coming on to me, but panic sets in. My stomach clenches.

"Don't act like you don't know I've been crushing on you since we came to Virginia. But it was at our party—when you stood up for me—that won me over." She pushes up on her tip-toes, whispering in my ear. "I think you're ready to explore."

"Exploring's good?"

"I think so." Her lips graze my cheek as she speaks.

"Me, too."

She slams her lips to mine, her hands running up my neck. Her fingers curl into my hair. I squeeze my eyes closed and kiss her back but keep my hands shoved firmly in my pockets.

It's nice. Pleasant.

But it's not Rayne. It doesn't have her fire, her heat. Our love.

Then again, I have to start somewhere, and this is as good a place as any.

Clara Jean leans back, her breathing heavy. "Let's go somewhere private. I'll meet you upstairs in your bedroom. The one beside Taryn's, right?"

I nod, the words refusing to come out. Probably a good thing, because if I open my mouth right now, I'll probably vomit on her shoes. Private? Bedroom? Oh God, no. The kiss was hard enough. I can't put my hands on her. It's impossible.

I dart in through the backdoor and head up the stairs, swearing to myself I'll let this girl down easy. Broken hearts suck, and I don't need more grief under my belt. I'm halfway up when an image pops in my mind, and my heart plummets to my toes.

Rayne kissing Preston. Her hands on him. His hands on her.

How could it be so easy for her? And why am I letting the

memory of us stop me when she's tossed it aside like yesterday's garbage?

No. Hell no.

I grip the brass knob like it's a life preserver. The door squeaks open. Clara Jean stands by the window, her hair loosened and falling over her shoulders, her blouse unbuttoned down the front just enough to reveal the rounded tops of her breasts.

I swallow hard and shut the door. As soon as it clicks in place, she charges toward me, grabs my shoulders and wrenches me down with her on the foot of the bed.

I want to give in to it. I want to let go and feel again. But there's nothing. Her kisses feel warm, soft, and wet, like all kisses do. Rayne's had always felt like flames that melted down to my core and stoked my own fires. I clamp my eyes shut harder and try to focus. To enjoy something. Anything.

She grabs my wrist, directing my hand toward her chest, but the muscles in my arm stiffen, and no matter how hard she pulls it toward her, it won't budge. Like two magnets with the similar poles together, a bubble of resistance sits staunchly between us.

I rip my lips from hers and jump up, straightening my shirt. She gasps and stares up at me with wide, watery eyes.

Damn.

"I'm... I'm sorry," I mumble. "I can't..." Before she can speak, I run out, slamming the door behind me and sprint down the stairs, stopping on the bottom step to catch my breath. My arms and legs tremble.

A beautiful, smart girl is interested in me, and I run. Sure, she's not Rayne, but no one else is either. No one ever will be. At some point, I have to quit running and give someone else a chance. Break the pattern before I keep repeating it.

I glance behind me. I should go back and apologize. Explain my hang-ups, why I can't give away my whole heart. It hasn't been whole in a while. Things can only get better if I'm honest, right?

I turn around and go back up. On the landing, my phone rings and I pull it from my pocket.

Preston's number. I answer it on the third ring.

"Hello?"

"Gage, it's Preston. I got your number from Dad. Don't get mad." Everything rambles out in one long run-on sentence. I'm fairly sure he didn't even pause to take a breath. His voice is shaking and lacks its normal confidence, and he's whispering like he doesn't want someone to hear he's on the phone. "Something's happened and you need to come home."

Something's happened is one of those phrases you never want to hear uttered over the phone. It usually means death, sickness, or accidents. My heart accelerates, thumping in my chest, as a million different horror scenes unfold in my imagination. "What is it?"

"It's Rayne." Oh dear God. No. "She was attacked—we don't know all the details right now—but she's in the hospital. They had to take the baby."

The barbecue and beer I had earlier churn in my stomach. "How are they? How is... she?" My words stumble out, barely able to keep time with the racing thoughts. Attacked. By whom? Why? Is she... alive?

"The baby's in the NICU. He's tough. Rayne's in and out of consciousness right now, but stable."

Thank God they're both alive. And one word sticks out from his report—a pronoun that makes it all the more real. "He?"

"Yeah, Rayne has a son. And she needs us—all of us—to pull through this. Please, Gage, come home."

"I'll be there." I swallow hard and end the call, shoving my phone into my pocket.

I lean into the bannister, willing my knees to remain strong. Knowing she's hurt, lying in a hospital bed, claws at my insides.

If I could, I would trade places with her. Take away all of her pain.

Sitting at her bedside is where I have to be—to see her through, hold her hand, look into her eyes, and when she's well, do the impossible and give that hand to Preston, smile and wish them well. Watch him hug, kiss, and love her.

The way I did.

The way I'd planned to forever.

But our forever didn't come, and now I'll pretend I'm happy for them.

For her sake and mine.

But I can't do this alone. I need someone to stand beside me, hold my hand, be my strength. Give me hope when everything else has died. And now more than ever, I truly believe she can help me.

If I haven't alienated her completely.

I steady my breathing and open the bedroom door. She sits on the edge of the bed playing with a strand of her brown hair, eyes still red-rimmed from earlier.

"I'm sorry," I mumble, the words straining through my broken voice. "Please forgive me for what happened. There's been an emergency with my family and I have to go home right away, but I could use someone to talk to."

She stands up, walks toward me, and grabs my hand, rubbing it between both of hers. "Talk to me, then, because I'm coming with you."

Gage is on his way. I know because I heard Preston tell him to drive safely. He'd walked away for a while but is now sitting in the blue chair outside my door, staring off into space holding the note. When he finally gets up and opens the door to my room, I stir under the covers, moving my feet around, twitching my hands in a semi-stretch, as if just waking up.

"Hey, sleeping beauty," he whispers, taking his normal place at my bedside and handing me the note. "I found this. Thought you might want it back." Straight to the point. Even after all these moments of knowing he's read it, I still have no idea what to say.

"Preston, I…"

"It's okay, Rayne. I'm fine," he nods, then continues. "I checked in on the baby. He's doing great, wiggling, eating, and complaining he needs a name." He stops and laughs. "Just kidding about that last one, but the doctor did say he can visit his mama tomorrow."

I take a deep breath for what feels like the first time all day.

So deep the incision pulls, and a twinge of pain travels up my side. "Tomorrow? Our baby's really gonna be okay."

"He's not my baby, Rayne." His tone is subdued. I raise my head, expecting to see a look of disappointment, but I don't. It's matter-of-fact. "Don't get me wrong, the kid's got me wrapped already, but Gage is his daddy. One look at his face, and I knew it."

"But Preston, you've been..." I pause, thinking back over the last few months. Preston's been everything to us—singer of stupid songs to my belly, fetcher of food cravings, shield against town gossip. All I've given him is more heartache.

"I called him." He smiles at me and grabs my hand, squeezing tight. "I called Gage, and he's on his way. Y'all need him. He needs y'all."

The emotions today are like a roller coaster, surging hard one way before going 90 mph in the other direction. "I don't know what to say." I spread my arms wide, pulling Preston in to hug him tighter than ever before. It'd be so easy to pick him, but I can't, and he gets that. He forgives me before I even ask. And I do love him.

"Don't say anything. Just... love each other." His tears wet the back of my shoulder as his voice cracks. When he pulls away, a fire replaces the tears. "And while y'all are doing that, I'm going to find the jerk that did this to you."

My foggy brain, spinning from injury and raging hormones, can barely keep things straight. Someone attacked me. It's hard to believe even when I know it's true. Sure, I'm not everyone's cup of tea, but who wants me dead? "Any leads from the police?"

"Not much. Hundreds of people go in and out of that parking garage every day. No one suspicious on any of the surveillance videos, no eyewitnesses, nothing. But they don't think it's random. You weren't robbed, nothing was taken. It was a wallop to your head, just a little closer to your temple and we wouldn't be having this conversation."

The words suck the air out of my lungs like a vacuum. The thought of never seeing my baby, never seeing Gage again, scares me more than death. "What if they come back? What if they try to finish what they started?"

"That's not going to happen." He gets up and shoves his hands deep into his pockets. "No one's getting through that door without my approval. Only family is allowed in here to see you. You and the baby are safe, I promise."

I nod and force a weak smile. Promises, promises. So many promises in my life splintered and destroyed, but surely not this one. My baby needs me. I have to live. I'm going to live.

Preston walks back and kisses my forehead, his lips warm and trembling. "Rest now. Gage will be here soon."

A million noises rouse me from sleep, and each time it's a disappointment. A candy striper with a meal tray, then a nurse checking my vitals. After that, it's an alarm going off somewhere in the hall, Preston sneezing, or the TV. Each time, a surge of adrenaline shoots me straight up off the pillows so fast my stitches scream, and a surge of pain plows through me. My heart thumps until I realize it's not him. It's dark now, the pitch black snuggling up to the window outside, bringing along with it doubt that he's actually going to show.

It's 8:30 when his voice rouses me. He's talking to someone in the hall, but as the door handle turns, my heart pounds against my ribs.

He came. He's only feet away, and as if it senses him, my body goes on full alert, tingly tension running over every surface. A little painful. A lot euphoric. My baby's father, the love of my life, is here.

Gage walks in, but he's not alone. She's with him. I don't know her, but I hate her, Miss straight brown hair and jeans and... I glance down at her shoes... Chucks. If I'd met her anywhere else, we might've become friends. Not now.

He stares at me, but I can't force my eyes to meet his. In fact, it's kind of hard to breathe right now. Especially when she's touching him like that, rubbing his shoulders, reaching for both of his hands and patting them between hers. As if she's genuinely concerned.

Yeah right.

The vomit rises, burning my throat and sucking my stomach in like a vacuum. It's the same feeling I had on home-coming night when I kept picturing him hooking up with other girls at Cedar Falls. That'd been all imaginary, but this... this is real. They lock eyes, conversations flowing between them without a word. She squeezes his hand, her palm wrapped tight around his fingers. He squeezes back and pulls her hands up to his chest.

Oh God. Please God. No. How can he touch her like that? Lean on her? Share things with her he's supposed to be sharing with me?

I'm an idiot for not preparing myself for this. I laugh under my breath, and everyone's looking at me like I'm two steps from the psych ward. I deserve this for pushing him away, lying and telling him I'm having Preston's baby. Our baby. He's never going to know his daddy now. Because Daddy has a new family. He's moved on because I made him. Now he's standing here with someone else, loving her, holding her, and I can't help wondering what they're like behind closed doors, kissing, lying together, sharing themselves...

"Preston," I say through gags. "Trashcan!" He grabs it, and I lean my head in, dry heaving over the rim. She and Gage exchange glances. Poor pitiful Rayne. Poor stupid girl.

While Preston wipes my forehead with a cool washcloth,

Gage walks closer and grabs my hand. The mere touch of his skin sends chills down my body, and I want him so bad. Like we've never been apart. Like this has all been a dream. Like she's not standing there, watching. For a minute, I consider pulling him down to me, kissing him, and secretly flipping her off behind his back. How dare she come in here? In this place where our love is being tested yet again, where our son was just born hours earlier. But I don't do anything because she didn't force her way in here. He chose her, and he brought her here. He's the one that made her family, and if I can't have him or touch him, then he needs to go. Like, now.

"Don't touch me," I snap, leaning away and right into the opposite bedrail and nurse call button.

Her much-too-bright-and-cheerful voice fills the room. "Yes, Ms. Davidson? Anything you need, honey?"

A machete. A loaded gun. A hit man and an alibi. "Tylenol. Just Tylenol."

Gage steps back, eyes wide and lower lashes glistening with tears he's holding back. Good. I hope he feels as bad as I do. I've cried lots of tears—so many over these past months, waiting and wondering where he was, alone and pregnant. But every time I was tempted to give up, I held onto our love, so sure he'd wait on me. But now he's here, and he didn't wait. He's moved on, and all that's left of us is that precious boy in the NICU who's losing his family and doesn't even know it.

Gage and I have always been dealers in the shattered pieces, putting together our future plans from the broken shards of other long-lost dreams. Now he's trading it all in on shiny, new love, leaving me alone with the remnants of us—the 'what-used-to-be' and, even worse, the 'what-could-have-been'.

Preston moves to Gage, placing both hands on his shoulders and coming in close, face-to-face. "Give her time. She just had a baby. Her hormones are all over the place." Gage peeks at me over Preston's shoulder, but I turn my head away. It hurts too much.

God, I hate myself right now. I'm pushing him away when all I really want is to hold him. Tell him I love him and need him. My body sets off all sorts of reactions when he's this close. Reactions I'm no longer entitled to because he has her.

She grabs his hand, ushering him toward the door, away from me and our life and our dreams. She pulls him to her.

"Leave!" I yell, choking back all the words I want to say, which build up like a boulder in my throat.

Gage closes his eyes, his breathing ragged, as if he's been running. "I'll come back later," he whispers more toward Preston than me. I hear it anyway, and the hurt-fueled verbal vomit spews out again. I can't stop it.

Hurt is an awful thing. It makes you vengeful, spiteful. "Don't bother," I grumble not-so-quietly from the bed. "Who needs you? Why the hell'd you even come?"

Gage lashes back. It's probably passive-aggressive on my part to bait him this way, but between my pounding head and the fact that I'm losing him, I don't give a damn.

"How can you even ask that?" He steps toward me, but Preston grabs his arm, holding him back.

"Gage, don't. She's been through hell today. Let her rest," he reasons, but Gage isn't having it.

"No. Rayne asked me a question, and I'm answering it, dammit." His eyes never leave mine. They're fiery and dark. I've never seen him this upset. "Preston called and said you'd been attacked, and they took the baby. Of course I'm coming, Rayne. You know I'll show up. At least you used to know that!"

Trying to shut myself up when I'm mad and cut to the core is like trying to wrestle a rattlesnake. Someone's getting hurt. "Yeah, well picking up and leaving everything behind can kinda ruin that trust. I don't know anything about you anymore. I used to, but not now, so go do what you do best—leave!" I regret the words as soon as they exit my mouth. I don't mean them. I know he still loves me to some degree. He just loves her more, and I can't deal.

The words punch him in the jaw, and he steps back into the doorway, where she grabs his hand and pulls him out in the hall. Preston closes the door, but I still see them through the sidelight window. They stand close, talking, as she pats his hand, then pulls him close, wrapping her arms around him as he buries his face in her shoulder.

"Close the blinds," I hiss at Preston, whose tortoise-like response isn't acceptable. "Close the damn blinds!" This time I'm yelling.

Gage hears the commotion and raises his head, meeting my eyes through the slim window. I stare back until Preston yanks the cord, the louvers clanging against the glass as they fall, blocking him out.

Twenty minutes pass before Preston dares to speak. He's been sitting quietly, reading a magazine in the corner arm chair, glancing at me from time to time. He's checking to make sure I'm still here and not off stealing scalpels and plotting murder.

"I'm an idiot," I finally say. "I'm sorry." The tears have disappeared again, so I sit emotionless and hard. Preston lays the magazine down and moves to where I pat the covers beside me, stroking my hair the way Mama used to when I'd fall off my bike. Except this isn't a bike accident, and Preston's best intentions can't heal this wound.

"This is all my fault," he begins. "I'm sorry. I had no idea he'd show up here with..."

I stop him before he can say her name. Saying it out loud means she's real and this isn't an awful screwed-up dream. "With his girlfriend," I spit out, as if her name is synonymous with Brussels sprouts.

Preston shakes his head. "He still loves you, Rayne." He

looks at his hands instead of me. "Didn't you see the look in his eyes?"

"Of pity? Yeah, I saw that look. Of admiration for her? Saw that one, too. Don't need a recap. And quit saying he loves me. He's moved on."

"We made him think you moved on, too. But you haven't." Hearing Preston admit that out loud catches me off-guard, and I look up quickly. He's smiling. "You two are so stubborn. I know you've tried to love me like that, but you can't. Because it's him. You need to tell him. Maybe if you told him about the baby, then—"

"No. I'm not telling him anything, and neither are you. If he wanted me, he'd fight for me. He hasn't. If he loves her, let him have her." Brave words to mask my destroyed heart. This feeling—so hollow, so unloved—this same feeling is why he left that morning. Feeling sorry for myself had been easy, but I'd never considered his struggle. He couldn't see me with Preston any more than I can see him with her now. But she's not the bitch. I am. She's picking up the pieces of my mess. She's the good one, and now he's with her.

"Who the hell actually buys this?" Taryn holds up a white straw cowboy hat decorated with blue bears, plastic rattles, and a banner reading *It's a Boy!* in one hand and points to it with the other, eyebrows tented into her forehead. She tosses it back on the metal shelf. "Such a waste of money."

"I don't know," I grumble. "Isn't it tradition to buy hokey shit and put it on your door after you have a baby?"

"Tradition, maybe. Stupid, definitely." She fingers through a collection of baby photo frames, side-eyeing me the entire time, like I'm going to break at any moment, hit the tile floor like a lump.

I might.

It's worse than I thought. Rayne hates me. The flames in her eyes. The way she ripped her hand from mine. The ruthless barbs about my leaving and destroying her trust in me. With the words she spit at me, she ought to have just had a knife. It's all the same sort of carnage.

Taryn walks over and rubs my arm, gazing up at me. The

one thing I love most about my cousin is that she only looks at me with concern, never pity.

"She's emotional," Taryn says. "The hormone levels go spastic in post-natal women. Preston was right. Give her time."

I snort. "That wasn't hormones. That was animosity. Hate."

"Not necessarily," Taryn says then folds her arms and clears her throat, her usual stance that means I'm in for a scholarly lecture on a subject she's studied in her medical classes. "My psychology professor says anger is merely a symptom of a much larger problem. One generally rooted in fear or hurt." She deadpans waiting on a response, but I don't give one. "My guess here would be hurt."

"Thank you for that analysis, Dr. Taryn."

"I'm just saying, I know the story now. Any idiot can see there's a boatload of hurt feelings between the two of you. Mostly because you're both dumbasses because you refuse to confess how you really feel for fear of hurting some other person's damn feelings." I glare in her direction, but she only shrugs. "There, I said it."

Truth is, Taryn only knows a Swiss-cheese version of the story. There's no point taking her back through the beginning when Preston and Rayne were together. That was messed up enough, and I don't think any of us want to relive that. No, on the drive up, I told her our story starting at good-bye, the day I found out the truth. Everything else was just summed up as we were in love.

"That's because there are more people to consider here, Taryn."

"Since when is love between more than the two people in it?" The question marks practically float around her. Valid ones, too. "For two people self-described as out to break the rules, you two sure do fall right in line with what the world tells you. And you're losing each other because of it."

Her words cut to the quick. "It's not that simple."

"Love never is, Gage." Her eyes land on an assortment of monitors and camera devices along the back wall. She pushes past me and stands in front of the shelves, marveling at the selection. "Now these are sensible baby items. I say get something from this section."

I walk beside her and scan the merchandise. A brown teddy bear Nanny Cam, whose eyes are a miniature camera and nose is a microphone, catches my attention. And it makes sense. Someone attacked Rayne and the cops don't know who. It never hurts to be cautious.

The saleslady smiles as we approach the counter. She scans the box and then my debit card and asks if I want a complimentary gift bag and bow. While she measures out the ribbon, Taryn and I take a seat on the park-style iron bench in the hospital atrium.

"I knew it was going to be hard," I whisper, having to force the words out that want to stick on my tongue. Taryn grabs my hand and squeezes it. "I didn't realize... I mean, how can you prepare..." I close my eyes and lean my head back against the mirrored glass wall tiles behind us. "If only..." I lower my head. No, it's too late for that now.

"Not if, when. 'If' implies looking back, and you need to look forward. When. As in when you both get things off your chests, let it all out, then you can move on."

"I'll never be able to move on with Rayne. A baby changes everything."

She sighs. "They're trying to do the responsible thing. No one intends to get pregnant as a teenager. It happens, and you deal with it. You're right when you say a baby changes everything. Rayne's entire life got flipped upside-down today, and you remind her of everything she's had to give up, whether she wanted to or not. She's broken inside."

She's not the only one.

The gray-haired lady brings out the bag, blue tissue paper

and ribbons fluffing out in every direction. I muster a grin and head to the row of shiny elevators. Something about having the gift in my hand gives me a greater resolve, like I have a legitimate reason to actually go up to her room now.

We get off on the fifth floor and check in at the nurses' station with a black-haired woman in purple scrubs. When I tell her we're headed to Rayne Davidson's room, she frowns and purses her lips. "I'm sorry, but Miss Davidson and Mr. Howard have specifically requested no visitors tonight." She rises up in her chair and looks over at the gift bag. "You can leave that at the desk if you'd like, and we'll deliver it for you."

I crane my neck to look down the aisle. Her door is shut, blinds still closed tight, and I can't help imagining them in there together. My stomach sinks.

Taryn side hugs me. "It's probably best. Give her tonight and come back in the morning. I'll stay at the hotel so you can go alone. Maybe somehow, you two can find peace."

I drop the bag on the nurse's desk and we turn back to the elevator. It slides open and Taryn reaches forward to press "L," for lobby. I hope she's right. Maybe tomorrow we can find a way to have closure.

Then again, maybe not.

55
─────────
RAYNE

The sunlight streams in the double windows, the muted whir of rush-hour traffic in the background. It's easy to forget where I am and what's happened in the first moments of waking, but one glance around this sterile rooms brings it all back. I'm alone.

It's the first time no one's hovered over me in the last 24 hours, making this the perfect time to think, though I don't know whether that's a good or bad thing. Yesterday was about unexpected endings. Today is about moving on, but I have no idea how.

I miss my baby. For weeks, waking up was my favorite part of the day because the munchkin was active, kicking and rolling. I'd pull up my shirt and watch the waves ripple under my skin as he moved deep inside. The last time I felt it, I had no idea it would be the last time.

My baby isn't part of me anymore. He's down the hall, in an incubator, and I haven't even held him yet. I haven't named him, either. People keep asking. I keep stalling because there's only been one boy name on the table since the beginning. Gage

Lucas Howard, Jr. But how can I use it now when things didn't work out like I'd hoped?

That's an understatement. The whole situation's screwed. Preston released me yesterday, gave me permission to break his heart and go get my family. I was too late. When she walked in with Gage, the months of hoping we'd find our way died. I was lonely before. Now I'm hopeless, and the only thing keeping me hanging on is that sweet boy. My last piece of our love that even she can't take away.

I glance around the empty room. Better get used to this. I no sooner think it than Preston opens the door with his elbow, finagles his foot in the crack, and swings it open with a hip thrust while carrying two Styrofoam coffee cups and a ginormous blue bag overflowing with tissue paper.

"Darn. I was hoping to make it back before you woke up." He hands me one of the cups. "I snuck you a coffee. Don't tell the doc."

"Lifesaver." I inhale the nutty aroma. "What's in the bag?"

"A present dropped off at the front desk for you." He pulls out clods of tissue paper and tosses them in the trash, then reaches in and pulls out a large box decorated in primary colors with all sorts of "pediatrician approved" stickers. "It's a teddy bear 'motion-activated A/V monitor with flashing lights and soothing heartbeat rhythms to lull baby into safe, lasting sleep,'" he reads from the side of the box.

"You sound like an advertisement. Who's it from?" I ask, sipping my coffee. Who would leave a gift at the desk instead of bringing it to me?

"Hold on." Preston pulls a card from the bag, opens it and reads, "Congratulations on a sweet baby boy. Love, Gage and—"

"Stop!" No way he's finishing that sentence. "I don't wanna know. Put it over on the counter." Unbelievable. Gage stomps on my heart then drops off a peace-offering. Print me a freakin' t-shirt. Gage tossed our family to the wind, and all I got is this lousy teddy bear.

Preston pulls the electrical plug from its butt and sticks it in the socket. "This is actually pretty cool," he says, waving his hand in front of it.

"Yeah, yeah, yeah. On the counter."

He rolls his eyes and pushes the bear away, turning to pack up his laptop and notebooks for a morning class. Beady eyes stare at me from the counter, taunting me, like the freaking thing has a life of its own. The more I glare at it, the more it looks like her, fake and squinchy-eyed. Flipping off a stuffed bear is juvenile but called for. I've earned the right.

My finger's barely down before Preston turns around, packed up to leave for his morning class. "Your dad has a few conference calls this morning, but he's coming in later. You need to rest. Sleep. Watch TV. Read." He pounds one fist into the other palm as he ticks off the list as I roll my eyes and stare out the window. "Tonight, you get to hold your son." Zinger. The cherry on top of my well-behaved, sedate day.

Fine, I'll behave as long as that doesn't include not joshing Preston. "Sure you have to go? What if my attacker barrels in here and tries to hatchet me to death?" I pause and blare my eyes, pulling my covers up to my nose. "What then? Read with him? Take a nap?"

He scowls and pulls the shoulder strap from the laptop bag off his shoulder. "Not funny, Rayne. I'm just gonna stay here and skip—"

I push the covers away from my face. "No way, kill-joy. I'm joking. I'm safe in here. I know you've sweet talked all the staff, worked your charms, batted your eyelashes..."

"Too bad that kind of thing never works on you."

"I'm impervious to your charms, a real solid wall."

He nods, smiling, and kisses my cheek. "You and little man hold it down today. I'll be back in a bit." As the door clicks shut behind him, I turn on the TV and flip through a couple stations. News, sports recaps, educational cartoons, infomercials, and a black-and-white '60s sitcom—any of them great for background noise but not much else. I reach under my pillow and pull out the note from Mama. It's been under there since Preston gave it back to me. Funny how it's always the first thing I go to when I'm feeling this way. Hopeless, helpless, and useless.

Something about it is soured now. If you love something, set it free. If it comes back to you, it's yours. If it doesn't, it never was. What if it comes back to you but brings along a friend? What then? Is it yours or not? Even this note, my comfort for so many months, is making my non-stop headache worse.

When the door opens, I quickly turn my back, shoving the note under my pillow before Daddy can see it. Mama's handwriting always brings tears to his eyes, and there's been enough of those lately. "You're here earlier than I expected. Preston said it would be—" The click-clack of stilettos approach me and unless Daddy's taken to wearing heels, it isn't him.

She's wearing black peep-toes and a red suit, the pencil skirt hugging her in all the right places and the peplum jacket tailored to her frame. Her pearl necklace skims her collarbone, the signature look of money. "Good morning, Rayne."

"Morning, Charlotte. I wasn't expecting you."

She smirks and reaches down to fluff my pillow, not that it needs it. "Now, now dear. It doesn't sound like you're too happy to see me."

Sure, I'm happy to see her. Like I'm happy to see a boil or a stomach virus. She's that enjoyable. "Of course I am. It's just... Preston's not here. He had class..." Surely she's not here to see me. I can't imagine her having some sudden attack of conscience and giving two shits.

She cocks her head in my direction, one eyebrow arched. "I know Preston's in class. He gave me his schedule and told me your father would be delayed today, so I thought I could help out. Keep you company and visit that sweet grandbaby. Just look at this picture I took a minute ago of him in the nursery." She clicks a button on her phone and shoves the screen in my face. My baby, my beautiful boy, in the incubator down the hall and a timestamp that tells me she was there just five minutes earlier. "He's absolutely a doll, it'd be a shame if anything ever happened to him. He is my grandchild... for all intents and purposes, that is."

She looks at me, expressionless, as she sits on the edge of my bed. My heart picks up tempo, thumping hard against my ribs. "Why would you say something like that?"

"Oh Rayne." She clicks her tongue, "Did you really think Ashlyn wouldn't tell me everything? But don't worry. The baby will be just fine... as long as you do what I say." Her voice changes on the last part, low and sinister. It sends a shiver through me.

Oh my God. She knows the truth, and she's only going to use it for evil. "I don't understand?" I'm thinking I don't want to.

She rolls her eyes and laughs. "Preston obviously didn't pick you for your intelligence, did he? Let me spell this out for you. Get lost or you and the baby are going to die. And this time, I won't miss my mark."

It starts as a burning in my throat that spreads out into icy ripples. The scary reality. Something that never even crossed my radar. "It was you? You attacked me?"

"You act like you didn't have it coming!" She crosses her arms and looks at me as if she's shocked by my audacity to question her actions. "You single-handedly ruined my family. My son never needed to know about his father's infidelity. I had taken care of all that years ago, but no, your crazy Mama's little deathbed confession dredged it all back up. You cheated on Preston with that bastard brother of his and humiliated him in front of the whole town. Now you have him roped into all this.

You deserve every bit of it. You should have died." Every time she says "you," she jabs her finger in my direction.

I give it right back, as much as possible from this hospital bed. "You're insane! How did you think you'd actually pull it off?"

"Please. I run this town," she laughs again and shakes her head. "I did it before with no problems. Some desperate, mentally ill woman even took the blame for it. When it broke you and Gage up, that was the cherry on top of my sundae."

"I... I don't..."

"Try to keep up, Rayne. It's not that hard. I killed Gage's mother. That slut ruined the life I'd worked so hard for. She seduced my husband and got pregnant while I was at home with an infant. My marriage to Jackson had been planned for years, and I refused to let some common trash ruin it. A quick blow to the temple, and she fell without a fight into the street. I must say, though, my aim has grown fairly shoddy over the years. I'm sure you're thankful for that, right dear? How is that wound feeling? Sore?" She reaches out to touch the bruise, but I shrink, batting her hand away with mine.

Her words scramble in my brain like eggs, rolling around in some squishy, formless mass I don't quite understand. The images of Mama lying in bed, crying, confessing her sin, and all the memories of her anxiety spells throughout my childhood flash back. Mama suffered and died because of this monster who tore her life apart and is now trying to do the same to mine. The fear runs out of me like water down a drain, and the fury rolls in.

"My mama died thinking she'd killed Gage's mother. She blamed herself all those years because—"

"Seriously, blah blah blah. I'd quit worrying about your mother, Rayne. She's dead. You and that baby are going to join her if you don't get the hell out of this town and never return. Never call Preston again. Don't leave a note. Don't leave a forwarding address. Don't leave a number. Just get out of our lives. For good."

"Preston will never let you treat me this way. He will—"

"Preston is loyal... to me. I've been his mother for 21 years. I've taken care of him and protected him. He knows Mommy loves him, and he'll take my side. Don't try me, little bitch, or your son will be the first to go. Remember," she holds up her phone with the picture of him in the nursery still on the screen, "grandmothers can visit any time they wish. Preston put me on the list, and I'll be more than happy to spend some quality time..." She bends over my bed, her nose so close to mine her breath blows across my face as she talks.

When the door opens unexpectedly, Charlotte leans back, standing straight as an arrow, a fake smile plastered across her face.

Gage. Thank God. He walks in, shifting his eyes between me and Charlotte. "What's going on?" His steps are slow but deliberate as he inserts himself in front of me like a first line of defense against her. "What're you doing here?"

"I might ask you the same thing, son. Or do I even need to? You've always wanted what Preston had."

"Rayne, are you okay?" He looks at me but never turns his back on her.

"Of course, she's okay. There's nothing wrong with me visiting my grandson and his mother, right?"

"I wasn't talking to you," he snaps. "Rayne?"

"She did it, Gage. She's the one who attacked me!" My voice gets louder with each word, the realization pouring in that she's about to make good on her promises.

Instead, she laughs. "Nonsense! Obviously, she's on too many medications or the bump on her head has caused some brain damage. Quite possibly she's going crazy like her mama."

"You bitch!" I scream, slamming myself forward, my abdominal muscles screaming. A surge of blood oozes, hot and sticky, down my inner thighs and seeps through the white cotton sheets. Searing pain shoots through me like a bullet. "Ow!" I extend my arms, trying to cover the bleeding with my hands but it escapes through my fingertips.

Immediately Gage focuses on me, but unless he's developed super-human healing powers, it's futile. "Get her. Don't let her leave," I mumble through the deep gasps I'm forced to take with each stabbing pain. "She said she'd kill the baby. She tried to kill me. She's the one who killed your mother. Get her!"

In two seconds, he's across the room where Charlotte is slipping into the hallway. He grabs her arm and pushes her into the wall. "You aren't going anywhere." Gage leans through the open door and yells for security and nurses.

I turn my eyes from the blood rapidly discoloring my sheets because the lightheadedness kicks in, threatening to make me throw up or faint. The room spins and all I can focus on are those two beady eyes. Oh my God, those eyes. The monitor. That horrible, awful, beautiful, wonderful A/V monitor.

The nurse runs in first, bee-lining to my bed when she sees the blood, the doctor hot on her heels. They talk in medical jargon and give me a shot of something so fast-acting my vision blackens from the outside in. I can barely turn my head, but in the corner, Gage and the security officer have Charlotte sitting in a blue arm chair. She's smug, assured she has nothing to worry about. With my last strength, I call to him. "Gage." He turns, his eyes clouded with both fear and anger. God, I love him. "Check the monitor. It's on the cabinet." His eyes immediately go to the stuffed bear, and he smiles.

Blackness.

56

GAGE

harlotte sits in a plastic chair in the hospital conference room, one wrist handcuffed to the table leg, the other hand clacking her nails across the top. We've been sequestered to opposite sides of the room, each being questioned by an officer who's taking our statements.

"This is preposterous! Do you know who I am? How important I am?" Her shrill voice bounces around the room as the officer beside her scratches his head, looking down at his notepad. "How dare you treat me like a common criminal! What's your badge number? I'll have your job when this ordeal is over. I'll sue the police department!"

I lean in close to my officer. "I take it he drew the short straw?"

She snorts and adjusts the walkie-talkie on her side. "He has more patience than I do."

I'm signing the form with my written statement when the brown wooden door swings open and Dad and Preston rush in, eyes wide and mouths open.

"What's going on here?" Dad demands, panning his hand around the room. His eyes land on me, and he darts to my side, gathering me into a hug. "Gage. Thank God you're here. What happened?"

I take a deep breath and recount everything from my statement. Everything I saw. Everything Rayne told me.

Preston shakes his head. "There has to be some mistake."

The empathy for my brother tears into me. Not so long ago, I learned horrible truths about who I was and where I came from. It sucks when the rug's jerked out from underneath you in a heartbeat, but the truth needs to be told. "No. There's no mistake."

Preston slaps his hand over his mouth as the color drains from his face, and Dad sinks into the chair, one hand gripping his forehead, the other arm wrapped around his stomach. He mumbles into space. "Oh my God. Leighton. I'm so sorry, baby. I'm so sorry she did this to you."

The door squeaks open again and another officer walks in, carrying a laptop. The Howard family lawyer trails close behind and rushes to Charlotte's side, whispering frantically in her ear. She rolls her eyes and flounces back in her chair.

The officer places the laptop on the table and grabs the bear off the counter, pulling out its hidden USB cable, and plugs it in. A few taps of the keys and the video uploads and begins playback, the first scene showing Preston and Rayne in the room then Rayne flipping off the bear with a nasty grimace.

I smile to myself despite the chaos surrounding me. In one video frame—there's my girl.

"She's obviously mentally ill!" Charlotte stabs her finger at the screen. "It runs in her family."

"Shhh!" Her attorney squeezes her arm and shakes her head with force. Good luck trying to get that evil witch to not incriminate herself.

The footage continues to roll, with audible gasps circulating in the room each time Charlotte spills another one of her nasty secrets.

Get lost or you and the baby are going to die.

You act like you didn't have it coming.

You should have died.

I killed Gage's mother.

The fury hits me like a tsunami, and all I can imagine is hurdling the table and ripping her head off. Doing to her what she did to my mother. What she tried to do to Rayne. Red and black spots form in my vision, my heart relocating to my throat. I jump to my feet, ready to unload when I stop short. I don't have to say anything, because Preston and Dad erupt in unison, screaming in her face, reaming her. Destroying her.

If nothing else, one small victory can be claimed in the midst of all this tragedy.

Dad and Preston are finally free.

I reach for the doorknob. There's no reason to be here anymore. I've seen enough.

"Hey!" Preston jogs up, his voice interrupted by short, jagged breaths. He grabs my arm before I can escape. "You okay?"

"Maybe I should be asking you that." I glance past him to Charlotte who sits stone-faced as Dad yells, stabbing accusatory fingers in her direction. "But yeah, I'm good."

"Do me a favor. Go talk to Rayne. Y'all have things to discuss." He dips low, catching my gaze. "You need this. Trust me."

Preston turns and re-joins the interrogation as the wooden door clicks shut between me and them, stifling the voices inside. I walk down the hall to her room, my footsteps echoing in the narrow hallway. The blinds in the sidelight window are cracked open enough so I can peek in. She's lying in the hospital bed, covered in white blankets, arms stretched out across the top. Each have several tubes and monitors attached.

I ease open the door and step into the room, but she doesn't move, and her eyes remain closed. Probably still sleeping after the dose of medicine. Behind the bed, a teal reclining chair sits catty-cornered, and I pull it closer to her side, settle in, and wait for her to wake up.

She's so small, so helpless, lying there. Lost and almost child-like, her brown curls flattened by the pillow and swirling around her face in a frizzy crown. Beautiful. As always.

The same questions keep filtering through my brain. How did we get here? And how do I go on without her? God, equip me with the strength to look at her and smile, give her my congratulations on her new life and walk away... again. An impossible journey, and I fear either my feet or my mouth will betray me and simply refuse to do what I have to do.

Once more, I want to enjoy the warmth of her skin. Experience the way her hand curves neatly in mine. I lean forward, folding my fingers around hers when a piece of paper, shoved under her arm, scrapes my skin. It's folded into a neat square, but its edges are dog-eared and yellowed as if it's been handled frequently. A twinge of guilt creeps in, saying I shouldn't be nosing into Rayne's private business, but the one part of the handwriting that's visible piques my interest.

"...when he returns to you, my girl. I love you, Mama."

I unfold it despite my hesitations and read the words with tears in my eyes. Mrs. Davidson knew all along I loved her daughter. She told Rayne I'd return for her. But now, if after all this time she's with Preston, then why is this here?

A nurse knocks on the door and sticks her head in to see if we need anything. I say no, but then think better of it.

"Uh, ma'am?"

She steps inside the door with a smile. "Yes?"

"This note... it was under her arm?" I hold it up in the air so she can see for herself.

Recognition filters into her expression. "Oh yes. Miss Davidson had it under her pillow, and it dropped to the floor in all the excitement earlier. It was originally found on her person when she was brought in after the attack. We figured it must be something special and didn't want her to lose it. Can you make sure she gets it when she comes to?"

I swallow hard and stare at the words and, below that, the silver medallion. The one from her homecoming corsage.

"Yes, ma'am. I'll see she gets this."

She clasps her hands in front of her chest. "Wonderful. In the meantime, if you need anything," she says pointing at the control panel on the bed. "I'm just a buzz away."

She disappears out the door, and I refocus on the letter. This must be what Preston was talking about. Here he's got a life with Rayne and their baby, but she's still carting around memorabilia from our relationship. My heart flutters at the thought of her, reading and rereading this every night, waiting on our lives to resume from the ashes. She still loves me. At least a little. The euphoria crashes over me then rushes out just as fast, replaced by a gnawing in my gut. If she loves me, and I love her, then how are we ever going to manage good-bye?

57

RAYNE

When I wake up, everyone's gone. Except one.

Gage is sitting by my bed. He's pulled up the teal arm chair and is leaning forward, elbows on knees, and head in his hands. I want to hate him, but I can't. It goes against every cellular-level craving in my body. He's mine and no one else's, and while he's sitting here alone, it's easy to pretend he always will be. There are things we need to discuss. I'm not stupid, but I need this moment to last just a little longer because I'm not ready to look in his blue eyes and know we don't have a tomorrow. I love him. For me, there's no one else.

He lifts his head, staring back at me. His eyes hollow, haunted. "Hey you."

I love you, I love you, I love you. Please don't leave me. The pleadings crowd my head, but I squelch them. "Hey yourself. What happened?"

"Charlotte was arrested. The entire confession was on the bear's memory drive. You're safe."

I'm safe because of him. Here he is, involved with someone else and still saving me. We're meant to be together, and I'm sure of it now more than ever. But how do you tell someone you love them, that they're the one, when they're with someone else? When does it quit being about them and start being about you? Is it right to tell the truth or is it selfish? He's given me everything, including my son, and I can't take away his chance at happiness.

As always, I rely on smartass responses to hide the pain. "Yeah? Well, thank God for that bear then."

"Didn't look too thankful in the first part of the video. I recall something like you flipping it off?" He bites his lower lip and arches his eyebrows.

Caught in the act. No one was ever supposed to see that. "I can neither confirm nor deny." Gage narrows his eyes and stifles a laugh. "Fine, I did. Blame it on hormones."

"Nah, you were like that way before the hormones," he jokes but quickly turns serious, resting his hand on my stomach. "Doc patched you up. Gave you something to stop the hemorrhaging you caused when you tried to whip Charlotte's ass. Still wishing I could've seen you do it."

We're dancing around the subject so much I'm dizzy. If I'm coming out of this alive, it's time to get moving. "Why are you here Gage?"

He swallows hard and sits back in the chair. "Preston thought we should talk."

So this isn't of his own accord. Preston forced this. "You're here for Preston?"

"Is that easier for you to believe? No. I'm here for you. I read this..." He pulls my note from his pocket and lays it on the bed. It's folded inside out with the words "when he comes back to you" in black script against the white blanket. "Should we talk about it?"

I shrug my shoulders because speaking at this moment means crying, and I'm holding on to the promise I made myself that I'm staying strong for my baby. I can't crumble.

"There's so much I want to tell you, Rayne, like the places I went, the people I met." One person in particular I'm sure. Hearing his love-at-first-sight epic romance isn't topping my entertainment list. Thankfully, he's not talking about her right now. "I found my grandparents, aunt, even cousins."

He has family. Real roots, real people. Over the next 10 minutes, he tells me about his mother, Mary-Leighton Harrington, her childhood, her well-to-do family of strong military lineage and deep Southern traditions, and newfound aunt and several cousins close to his own age. For the first time, my black sheep has found his niche.

"You've met one of my cousins already," he adds. "Taryn? She came with me yesterday."

I'm not expecting it. Surely, I'm delusional. Maybe it's a dream, and I'm about to wake up. But when I look, he's still sitting there, nodding, as if he didn't just drop a bomb. The feeling is somewhere between the rush of riding a roller coaster and having all five numbers on the Powerball ticket. "Taryn's your cousin?" I say, laughing so hard I hardly choke it out.

He stares at me, eyes scrunched together in confusion. I'm stupid and embarrassed about being so hateful to this girl, refusing to call her by name, shooting her ugly glances. She's probably told him to run for the hills by now, away from my crazy ass. His eyes are far-off as he puts it all together. Any minute now he's going to laugh along with me. Only he doesn't. He's serious, which doesn't happen often, as the pieces fall into place.

He moves to the bed, sitting so close now, his thigh grazes my side as he pulls my hand into his. "Rayne, did you think...?" He pauses, eyes searching mine, breath labored. "Did you believe...?" The tears well up in my eyes. Dammit. I don't want to cry. "Baby... no. Never." I'm short of breath now too, and the only thing running through my mind is that he called me "baby."

He continues, "Dammit. I swore I wasn't going to do this."

"Do what?" I whisper, not taking my eyes off him.

He bites his upper lip between his teeth, pausing to consider his words. "Interfere. Say things I shouldn't. But I can't look you in the eye, I can't be this close to you, and not be honest. I can't keep hiding from you." He cups my chin in one hand and slides the other up my arm, the tingles taking over, running up and down, round and round inside like a tornado. "Rayne, there'll never be anyone else for me except you. Maybe I shouldn't tell you that since you're with Preston but..."

A burning circulates deep in my lungs, like fingers of fire weaving through my chest. My breathing adopts the rhythm of a drum beat, each thud reverberating in a wave. I blurt out the truth before my brain interferes, the words pouring out with lightning speed and no pauses in between. "I'm not with Preston. We lied. It was all pretend for the baby."

Gage sits up, running his fingers through his hair, and then leans back in, grabbing my shoulders. "You and Preston aren't together?"

"No. I can't be with him when I still love you." I reach up, grabbing his cheeks, and pull him nose to nose. "I can't live without you anymore. I love you. Only you. Do you still love me?"

"Always." He plunges his lips into mine, so hard it knocks me back into the pillows, but I don't mind. I pull him closer, needing more, not wanting to let go. His mouth is hungry, eager, and mine, just as much so, crushes back into his. I want him bad, which is slightly ridiculous since I just had a head trauma followed by major abdominal surgery.

The doctor, and my general health, would frown on the things I want to do right now. But just wait. In six to eight weeks, this boy better get ready for the months I've held this all back. It's like he's unleashed a fire inside I didn't even know was there anymore, and all I can imagine is us together again. Like we were in Edisto. Like I've replayed a million times since.

He tilts my head to the side, softly planting rows of kisses down my neck to the tender spot that always sends shivers coursing through me. He stops, holding his mouth against the curve of my neck, smiling.

"I've missed you. I haven't stopped thinking of..." he begins.

A nurse interrupts us, opening the door wide and rolling in a bassinet. Gage quickly sits up, and I grab his hand, interlacing our fingers and squeezing. My baby. Our baby. I can already see a tuft of dark hair and a small fist extending up into the air. With the first coo, my heart skips, and I extend my arms out to take him. The nurse nestles him to me, soft and new-smelling, with my eyes and Gage's nose. I'm not prepared for the surge of emotion that hits me. It's a rush to finally hold the life you created. It's mind-blowing seeing both of your features reflected back in harmony. It legitimizes your connection. I look up at Gage and find that holding our child instantly changes my feelings for him. They're stronger, deeper, and hotter than ever before.

The nurse tells me Preston came in earlier to dress him for the occasion, and when I see the white smocked outfit I know why. In blue embroidery on the chest, it says "Daddy's Boy." This is Preston's blessing, his green light to our family, but Gage can't understand, because I haven't told him the best part.

He blanches, his face ghostly white and he swallows hard, backing away from me. "I can't do this, no matter how much I love you. Work it out with Preston. Y'all have a baby who needs his father..." Gage says, pushing himself off the bed. I grab his hand. It trembles in mine.

"Yes, he does need his father," I say, our baby warm against my chest. "I need his father, too. Don't leave us, Gage, because you're his daddy."

'm the daddy.

Hell yeah.

She doesn't love Preston. She never did.

It was always me.

Always.

The baby's ours.

She's mine, and I'm hers.

Like I've always been.

And always will be.

This is only the beginning.

I slide my phone from my pocket and call Dad. He answers on the first ring. "Dad, there's something I need to do, and I'd love it if you came with me."

---

age Lucas Howard, Jr.—AKA Luke, Lukey, or Luke-man depending on who's holding him at the time. It's hard to believe he's two months old, so wiggly and handsome. I sit on Daddy's couch, holding him and watching Gage pack up the Scout. Today's the day we officially start our life together. Today's the day we go home to Edisto.

It's impossible to believe the things that've happened over these months, but I've lived them, so I know them to be the gospel truth. After I revealed everything to Gage and after he had to sit down a minute to absorb my words, I knew we'd be okay when he rushed headlong from the chair and smashed his lips into mine once again, taking time out only to kiss Luke on the head. We're both thankful for forgiveness and love that kicks your ass and puts you back together even when you screw it all up.

Charlotte's in prison, where she belongs, and she'll be there for a long time if the lawyers have anything to say about it, which pleases Jackson who, for the first time in his life, is happy and carefree. It's never so evident as when he's playing with Luke.

Daddy's still working hard, traveling often, but must be trying for "Grandpa of the Year" because he never comes home from a business trip without some kind of souvenir for the baby. Preston's started spring semester but is going on to Clemson in the fall. It's done my heart good to see him and Gage repairing their relationship, back to the way it used to be.

Four-and-a-half hours later, the sand and gravel crunches under our tires as we pull in the drive, our home's exterior completely redone in marine blue and white, a total departure from its original worn gray. The pictures Gage had shown me from his phone didn't do the place justice.

"Wow." I scoot close to the dashboard and look up at it.

"There's still a lot to be done, but we'll get there." He jumps out and comes around to my door, helping me out, then reaches in the back and retrieves a sleeping Luke from his car seat. "Come on," he nods toward the stairs and I follow behind. The hand rails have been sanded smooth and painted a crisp white and there are, like, twenty steps to take us to the main living level. The stairs open into a wraparound porch. There's a swing at the end, overlooking the Atlantic.

"You know I like this," I laugh, sitting down and giving a little push with my legs.

"It's the very first thing I did. For you. It's where I slept that first night back here after I found out about you and Preston." He rubs the wooden swing arm, a grimace on his face as he remembers. "Rough night."

I stand up, grab his chin and pull him down to me. "Let's never be that stupid again," I say and then kiss him hard.

"I won't if you won't," he whispers. "Let's get Luke down, and I'll show you the place."

"Get him down? We don't even have his bed set up yet."

"You doubt me, woman?" Gage laughs and leads me through the front door. We walk room to room, each spacious and beachy, though dated. The house needs serious TLC, except for two rooms in the back that look professionally renovated.

"Luke's gift from his Nana Harrington." He smiles and sweeps his hand around the room. It's beautifully decorated in pale blues and neutrals with matching furniture and fully equipped with wipes and diapers and a large oak rocker in the corner. In the center of the room is a hand-carved wooden bassinet with ivory bedding. Gage runs his hand along the edge. "This one's a family heirloom. My mom slept here." He lowers Luke onto the tiny mattress. The baby sputters a little, readjusts his fingers, but never opens his eyes.

Gage walks back to me and squats down to eye-level. "Now I can show you our gift." He leads me down the hall to the next door, a master bedroom done up in white and neutrals with a large iron bed. A trickle of sun shines through the window sheers, bathing the room in golden light.

"It's amazing," I gasp, breathless.

"You don't know the half of it." He pulls me to him, hands grasping the back of my head as he tugs me in for a kiss, moving fast over my lips and tongue. He breaks away and holds his arm up to my face, tapping his watch. "We have at least an hour before the others get here, and baby's asleep. You've been cleared by the doctor, and it's been a long almost eleven months. How 'bout we break it in?" He nods toward the bed and slides his fingers down the front of my shirt, unfastening the first few buttons and baring my breasts.

There are no words as I tangle my fingers in his hair, pulling him down into me. "This has been a long time coming," I say, sliding the belt from his jeans.

"And well worth the wait," he agrees and pulls me onto the bed.

Later, he's still tangled in the sheets, dozing off and on, when I get up, slip on my clothes and check on Luke, who's still sleeping peacefully. I walk out to the porch and sit on my swing. The waves slap the shoreline in an uneven rhythm, and the sky is gray except for a sliver of sunlight dancing far off on the water's surface.

I love those two so much, but how are we going to do this? We're not much more than kids ourselves, and now we have one of our own. Neither of us even have mothers to offer advice, to tell us we're not irrevocably screwing up our kid as we navigate this parenting thing. How will I know what to do when he gets his first fever or his first tooth or his first heartbreak? I'm almost nineteen and Gage twenty, but talk about jumping in with both feet. No, it's not the way I planned my life, but now I know, I wouldn't change a thing.

Because we have love. We didn't come all this way for nothing. Our love is more than most people get in a lifetime, and so no matter our age, we owe it to ourselves, and little Luke, to grab hold and enjoy every up and down along the way. Maybe it'll be messy. Maybe there'll be surprises, but we'll make it through. It's what we do.

Footsteps echo on the stairs, snapping my thoughts back to the present. It's Preston, Jackson, and Daddy to deliver my car and more of our stuff. I'm happy they'll all be spending our first night here with us.

"We come bearing gifts," says Jackson and shakes a few grocery bags in his arms. "The men are cooking my famous Lowcountry boil."

Preston walks past him on the steps and bends down to kiss my cheek. "Hope you're hungry. He makes a ton." He pauses and looks around. "Where's the big dope?"

"Napping," I say but Gage suddenly walks through the door, now fully clothed but disheveled, with a hungry Luke in his arms.

"I'm up and so is Luke-man," he says. "And someone's got a growling belly."

"Give me that boy," Daddy says, dropping his bags on the wicker chair and taking Luke in his arms. "Papa's gonna make you a ba-ba," he says in baby talk. Everyone laughs.

Gage walks over to me and whispers in my ear, "Let's take a walk while we have babysitters."

I nod and take his hand. We walk down the steps and across the boardwalk over the dunes to the hardened sand, lying just out of reach of the cold wintertime ocean. The temperatures are moderate in the 50s, but a brisk chilly breeze has me tugging the sleeves of my sweater down over my fingers. "I've missed this place." The realization is stronger standing on the shore, a million memories flooding back. This was always meant to be our home.

"I have an idea." A sly smile inches up the corner of Gage's lips. "Remember when we were here before, and I found all those conch shells and you found squat?"

I narrow my eyes, sticking out my tongue. "Your point?"

"Rematch? If you can handle it, that is."

"Name the rules." We're in a stare-down with me doing that tough-guy tooth-sucking thing.

"Two minutes. Best shell wins. Winner gets a kiss and bragging rights."

"Let's do this," I say as he sets the stopwatch on his phone.

I take off, scouring the sand where the ocean's just pulling out. Down the beach, Gage is hot dogging, talking smack like always, but when I find a tiny but perfect conch, I know I'm golden. It's no bigger than my thumb but fully intact, a creamy tan color with veins of blue and pink running throughout.

When the alarm sounds, I skip over to Gage. "Take that!" I flash the conch in his face. He's hiding his behind his back in one hand, but uses the other to inspect my find, scrunching his eyes as he looks it up and down.

"Pretty damn good," he says, and I smile before he finishes. "Not good enough."

"Whatever. I'd like to see you top this." I hold it up like a trophy.

"Sure you can handle it? Mine's good." He wiggles his eyebrows.

"Baby, I know you're good, but what's your shell like?" I tease and roll my eyes.

"You tell me." He extends his hand toward me and unfurls his fingers. He's right. His is much better, and I drop my puny, insignificant conch to the sand.

It's a ring. A diamond engagement ring.

I raise my eyes to his. He's smiling, not in that smartass way but in the same way he looked at me about an hour ago in our room. My legs tremble as he drops to one knee in front of me. "I love how we challenge each other, Rayne. It's been our thing from the get-go. I thought my biggest challenge in life would be winning your heart, but it turns out my biggest challenge—the one I can't win—is not being with you. Yes, we're young. But we're a family. I need you. I need us. Cuddling on the swing, camping out under the stars, or even baking a little cherry pie now and then. Will you marry me?"

I look at him and remember the broken pieces, the shards of old dreams and old loves that all fell together perfectly to create ours. We cry when we're broken, but the truth is maybe we're all meant to be broken. Because that's how we grow, and real beauty comes from taking those pieces and melting them together into something real and lasting—a mosaic of the life we've created, the life still to come.

"I accept the challenge of being your wife. Yes, Gage, I'll marry you," I say, without tears, only smiles because I know without a shadow of doubt this is meant to be. I drop down in front of him and he lunges forward, smothering me in kisses, and stopping only once to slip the ring on my finger.

When we make our way back to the house from the board-walk, everyone's on our porch, clapping and hollering. I bury my head in Gage's arm as he hams the whole thing up, bowing before them and saying, "thank you, thank you." Everyone shakes Gage's hand and hugs me, including Preston, who offers his sincere congratulations.

Daddy is the last to wrap his arm around me, long and tight, with Luke on his other side. "I wish Mama could be here to see this," I say.

"She's here. I think she knows, and she's proud of you," he whispers. "I bet she's watching over this little man, too. He would've been the apple of her eye." As he speaks, a breeze touches my cheek, and the wind chimes on the porch tinkle out a melody.

Mama shows up. I feel her.

I take Luke from Daddy and hold him against me. Gage walks up, wraps his arms around us and leans in to kiss my forehead. For the first time in a long time, everything in my world is perfect.

ACKNOWLEDGMENTS

My name may be on the cover, but this was more than a one-person show. So many people rooted for this book in their heart and dedicated umpteen hours to the pages you now hold in your hand. If not for their labor, love, and confidence in this Southern romance, my dream might never have been more than a saved document on my laptop.

Now it's real, and I'm grateful to every person whose hands have lovingly grabbed this novel and tugged it along this journey.

To God: You put the desire in my heart to pursue writing. You instilled in me the patience to wait on Your plan (I know that in itself was no easy task!) even when I couldn't always understand the reasons why things happened like they did. Now, looking back, I know why. You had the foresight, and now, I have the hindsight. Thank You.

To Carla and Jena: My girls. When I found you two, I found more than critique partners. I found friends. I found family. I found sisters. They say you should never become friends with your critique partners because you need the distance in order to feel completely at ease with issuing all the "tough love" your job entails. I love that we've found a way around this. Whether we're calling, emailing, texting or chatting online to simply check in or tell the other one that their MC is acting like a total —ahem—in the latest chapter, it all seems to flow together seamlessly. Your honesty, support and friendship mean more to me than you will ever know, and I'm proud to call you "my girls."

To Nick: The one critique partner I've actually gotten to meet face to face. It was such a pleasure to visit with you and your wonderful family. You were "lucky" (LOL) enough to read a super-early draft of this manuscript and somehow make it out alive. The advice you gave me was always on point, but, even better, was the encouragement and support. Your positive attitude was a ray of sunlight on all the dark days of self-doubt.

To RJ, Christina, and Chelsea: Y'all never hesitated to step up and read or give me some great advice along the way. Your thoughts and support helped shaped MtbB in significant ways, and for that, I'll always be grateful.

To the rest of my "Writing Bootcamp Buds" and the afore-mentioned CPs: Who would've thought one online course could link us all together? Best. Investment. Ever. You guys have been there for YEARS now, ready with support, consolation, advice, and encouragement. It's a pleasure to ride this crazy writer life with you. Y'all are truly My Tribe.

To all the people who've invited me into their lives, be it family, friends, coworkers, clients, and beta readers: Thanks for your time and energy. Each of you has left your mark on me in some form or fashion. We travel through the years, often never realizing how the simple act of just being in someone's life can affect them. Be aware. Be kind. Be you, always.

To my children—Maddox, Hayden, and Colton: Never let anyone tell you a dream is not worth chasing. That inkling in your heart will lead you. Y'all make me proud—every single day. You're the reason I fought for this dream, desperate to show you that you're capable of achieving all of your desires through hard work and determination. I love you.

To my husband, Gene: Words fail. Nothing I can pen here could ever demonstrate just how big your role is in all of this. From brainstorming sessions to patiently listening to me read (and re-read) chapters to cooking supper when my nose was buried in the laptop, you made this possible. Thank you for believing in my dream, but most of all, thank you for believing in me. I love you.

To my readers: My greatest wish is that you would take Rayne and Gage into your heart and care about them as much as I do. If you laugh, curse, cry and maybe even fall in love along with them, then my goal is fulfilled. Thank you for letting me share my story with you.

ABOUT THE AUTHOR

Brandy Woods Snow is an author and journalist born, raised, and currently living in beautiful Upstate South Carolina. She earned a BA in English/Writing from Clemson University and worked in corporate communications and the media for nearly two decades before pursuing her true passion of writing novels brimming with Southern culture, twisted family dynamics, young love, and deep-diving emotions.

When Brandy's not writing, reading, spending time with her husband or driving carpool for her three kids, she enjoys kayaking, family hikes, yelling "Go Tigers!" as loud as she can, playing the piano and taking "naked" Jeep Wrangler cruises on country roads.

www.BrandyWSnow.com

Romantic at heart, Southern to the core.